LEE PIPER

EVERNIGHT PUBLISHING ®

www.evernightpublishing.com

Copyright© 2017

Lee Piper

Editor: Stephanie Balistreri

Cover Artist: Jay Aheer

ISBN: 978-1-77339-342-1

ALL RIGHTS RESERVED

LEE PIPER

PRAISE FOR LEE PIPER

I loved this story. I couldn't put it down! –Rabid Readers Book Blog on Rock My World

This book is full of wit, sarcasm, and it's a smart and fun romance. –Uncaged Book Reviews on Rock My World

I have a feeling that Lee Piper will now be another rock star romance author favorite of mine –Lisa M. Mandina

This book captured me from the very first page. –The Book Addict's Reviews on Rock My World

Lee Piper showed us the strength it takes to love someone who is broken and the mental struggle a person battles to just let it all go and live again. Not an easy task, as a real person or as an author writing about imaginary people. To have a reader actually feel a character's emotions, feel their pain as your own is a challenging feat BUT Lee conquered this task. –Kameron Brook on Rock My World

Lee Piper showed a talented writing style that instantly had me and I couldn't turn the pages quickly enough. I don't want to forget to add that the cover is HOT! I'm super excited about this new series, so I cannot wait for the next one to come out. HIGHLY HIGHLY HIGHLY RECOMMEND! –The Power of Three Readers on Rock My World

Oh my gosh, this book was so good! I loved everything about it. I'll definitely be reading more Lee Piper books in the future. –Brandy Paige Roberts on Rock My World

Holy crap! The banter between these two is hysterical at times. –LHamp on Rock My World

This was a well written rocker romance and the sex scenes are HOT! –Margaret Lander on Rock My World

A great debut and I will be keeping an eye out for upcoming books from this author. –B2B Kelly on Rock My World

This is the first book I read by Lee Piper and I thoroughly enjoyed it. The banter between these two characters will keep you in stitches. –Delish, Devine and All Mine on Rock My World

Very well written. The author takes you straight into the story and keeps you interested and wondering how this may end. –Smut Lovers Wonderland on Rock My World

DEDICATION

To Chantal, who never doubted. Not once. This one's for you.

ACKNOWLEDGEMENTS

If I had a dollar for every time I asked my husband to listen to the latest section of Rock My Body, I'd be a gazillionaire. So thank you, Mister, for being my sounding board, cheer squad and spider killing ninja. I'd be lost without you.

Chantal, I would have given up long ago if it wasn't for your phone calls, messages and continued belief in me. You're the best cousin a girl could ask for— thank you.

To my beta readers, Tarina (holy shit, this book would have been a total mess without you!), Rosie (I still have no idea how you squeeze in the time to read my work but I am forever grateful), Lesley (one of the most beautiful people I know), and Mum (I can't believe you liked this one), thank you for reading my manuscript and for offering super helpful feedback. There's a swagger in my step with you by my side.

Thank you to Stacey and the team at Evernight Publishing for taking a gamble on me. You guys are beyond awesome and I love working with you. Let's do it again sometime.

Jay Aheer, your book covers blow me away. Every. Damn. Time. Thank you for bringing my vision to life in such a kickass way.

To my editor, Stephanie, one day I'll know the difference between 'which' and 'that'. Not sure when but I'm hopeful it'll be soon. You are a goddess among women, thank you.

A huge shout out to the team at Enticing Journey Book Promotions and all of the bloggers who jumped on board to help spread the world about this firecracker. You rock my world.

Readers, I am so flipping humbled by your support. Thank you, thank you, thank you for joining me on this rollercoaster.

And finally, to those of you living with mental illness, to those who feel broken, imperfect, and alone. I want you to listen to me carefully because shit's about to get real. Ready? You're not broken, you're not imperfect, and you're definitely not alone. I see you, I am you and do you know what? We're motherfucking beautiful.

Author's Note

Rock My Body Is Book Two in the Mondez series. The storyline runs parallel with *Rock My World* and it is therefore advised that each book be read in chronological order to avoid any spoilers.

Much love,
Lee x

ROCK MY BODY

A Mondez Novel, 2

Lee Piper

Copyright © 2017

Chapter One

Was it something that I...?
Or was it...?
There's something in the way you move.
—MONDEZ, "Stranger"

My running shoes pounded the hard sand as I kept my eyes locked on the horizon. On a day like today, any rational person would pause and slowly breathe in the cool ocean spray of Geographe Bay, Western Australia— spring in these parts was especially beautiful after all. They would then probably marvel at the white, sandy beach as it stretched uninterrupted for miles in front of them, before casting their eyes toward the sparkling aquamarine water which mirrored the endless blue sky above.

I wasn't that person.

Hell, in that moment I was the physical embodiment of internal pandemonium. And I tried so hard to remember everything my psychologist, Doctor Powell, taught me about working through my anxiety-induced panic attacks—they had become more and more prevalent in the past few months—only nothing came to mind except the bleeding obvious.

Breathe, Riley, just breathe.

Way to be helpful, Doctor Powell.

So instead, I ran. Yeah, Doctor Powell was not going to be impressed. She always told me that rather than fixing the problem, avoidance exacerbated it because sooner or later I would have to deal with the issue I was trying to evade anyway. She was right, of course; the memory of my horrendous morning at work refused to dissipate. I shut my eyes for a split second as the recollection of my patient's beseeching voice sent a sharp lancing pain through my stomach. "Nurse, what's wrong with my baby? Why is he so quiet? Answer me, *please*."

I stumbled, righted myself and then forced my legs faster. Stupid stomach.

The salty sea breeze whipped my straight blonde hair into my eyes and I agitatedly brushed it aside, for once not caring if I was channeling my inner Angora rabbit.

Her cries were unrelenting. "Nurse, please. Help. *Help*."

Only I couldn't.

It was hopeless.

And if she was being honest with herself, my patient knew it too. After all, it was obvious from the twelve-week scan that the eventual outcome was never going to be good.

Why didn't she listen?

Her obstetrician and I continuously spoke to her, counseled her, even bluntly told her the likelihood of her son surviving delivery was slim-to-none. But she persisted anyway. Faith, she called it. I snorted. More like delusion.

Tears stung my eyes. I hated feeling helpless, and that's exactly what happened in the labor ward today. As much as I tried, I couldn't force the little heart to beat, I couldn't take away his mother's agonizing grief. Hours later, I couldn't even block out her hysterical sobs.

I couldn't do a goddamn thing.

So, rather than find a quiet spot to sit with the tormenting emotions and analyze each of them in turn like a scientist with OCD, I escaped to the beach for a run. There was no doubt about it, avoidance was definitely my coping mechanism of choice. However, in my defense, it turned out to be one heck of a workout. Surely, that was something, right?

Right?

I shook my head.

If someone happened to be strolling along the coastal promenade at that very moment and glanced down at me on the shoreline, it would have looked like I was being chased by an imaginary rabid dog which had just been burned with a branding iron. And then stung by a bee. Honestly, the speed I maintained was ridiculous, even by my standards.

I'd never pushed my body so hard. Even in my darkest days I always kept a little in reserve, but not in that moment. Heck no. Instead, I forced my legs faster again, ignoring the lactic acid as it slowly burned its way up my calves. My lungs were almost bursting and my vision blurred dangerously but still I didn't stop.

At breakneck speed, I blindly rounded the rocky outcrop. It jutted toward the ocean like an old woman accusingly pointing her crooked finger up at the sun.

And then wished I hadn't.

Oomph.

I hit a cement pillar. Well, one which swore like a drunken sailor. Even my best friend and housemate, Grace—arguably the most foul-mouthed woman in the history of the universe—would have been impressed. I flew through the air and landed flat on my back, sprawled out on the damp sand. I couldn't breathe. Literally. Rolling over until I was crouching on all fours, I gasped, choked and quite possibly retched, pleading with my lungs to filter through some much-needed oxygen.

"You all right?"

I was too busy heaving to reply to the deep, male voice. Probably for the best; his gravelly tone sounded like sin-wrapped temptation. Instead, I dropped my head onto the sand, begging my breathing to return to normal. Unfortunately, when it finally did, embarrassment set in along with my ever unhelpful inner monologue.

Oh, my God, I fell over in front of a total stranger, who does that? Maybe he was looking the other way and didn't see? Who am I kidding, he totally did. Probably filmed it and everything. Knowing my luck, by this time tomorrow I'll be an internet sensation, there'll be memes and everything. Sweet Lord in heaven, I actually want to crawl into a hole and die.

"You okay to sit up?" His low, husky voice cut through my internal meltdown.

"No," I mumbled into the sand, ignoring the fact that my thighs instinctively clenched together at the sound.

Is he kidding me? There's no way I can face him. Not only will he think I'm the most uncoordinated woman alive, but his voice is sexy enough to feature in a Kendrick Lamar song, for God's sake. I'm not strong enough to deal with that shit.

"You ever gonna sit up?"

"Nope."

He snickered again. "So, you're gonna stay like this until the tide takes you out?"

"That's the plan."

I could almost hear the man smile and felt heat rushing to my cheeks, though didn't for one second forget my weakness for badass musicians—real or imagined—and my consequent decision to steer clear of them at all costs.

"Look, if you sit up I'll promise not to say a word about the epic fall you just had. Okay?"

I swore under my breath. Mortified, that's what I felt. Completely. Fucking. Mortified.

"Come on." His large hands gently gripped my shoulders, shifting me to sitting position. I inhaled sharply as the contact of his fingers against my bare skin sent a shiver of pleasure down my spine.

Please don't moan, please don't moan, please—

And then he laughed.

Fuck.

It was deep, throaty and by far the most panty-obliterating sound I had ever heard. I squirmed in the sand. Nope. The movement did absolutely nothing to ease the sudden tension between my legs.

"Open your eyes, angel."

"Do I have to?"

"At some point, yeah."

I sighed, peeked out the corner of one eye and then forgot to breathe. Again. My other eye instinctively popped open and I'm pretty sure my mouth did too.

Holy shit.

Two bright blue eyes gazed laughingly down at me. His straight nose, full lips, and chiseled jawline led to what was in all seriousness, the most stunning male physique I'd ever had the pleasure to ogle.

Wow. I mean… Just wow.

I swallowed.

A grey t-shirt slick with sweat stretched across the most unbelievably ripped upper body in the history of pecs and abs. This guy was strong. Not bodybuilder strong, more like I'm-gonna-push-you-up-against-the-wall-and-have-my-wicked-way-with-you strong. In other words, everything I'd ever dreamed about strong.

My stomach almost folded in on itself.

Through the soaked fabric of his t-shirt, I could see broad shoulders, strong biceps, washboard abdominals. and—I almost groaned out loud—my most favorite of all body parts, the distinctly molded V leading directly down to…

I licked suddenly parched lips.

Beautiful.

He laughed again.

Slapping a hand over my mouth, I gasped. "I actually said that out loud, didn't I?"

"Yep."

"Oh, God."

If there was ever an ideal moment for a king tide, it was now.

Thankfully, the beautiful stranger ignored my mammoth foot in mouth and held out a hand for me to grasp, his pupils dilating when our fingers touched. Dazed, I wasn't at all prepared for the quick jerk of his arm and ended up face first in his muscular chest.

Oomph.

Again.

Seriously, can this day get any worse?

A short while later, we were slowly making our way back along the foreshore. I refused to look at the man strolling next to me, doing so would only end in further embarrassment and I'd had enough for one day. Sadly, the guy in question would not let me walk back to my car alone—I had smacked into him pretty hard—and if I wasn't so concerned about doing or saying something stupid, I probably would have thanked him for his kindness.

I sighed. If only I was one of those girls who

could easily make sparkling conversation wherever they went. Don't get me wrong, Mum did everything she could to improve my awkwardness. She dealt with it like a long-term disease, one which needed continual treatment. I was systematically signed up for dress and deportment classes, hair and beauty lessons, public speaking programs, the works. Being the daughter of a world-renowned cardiologist and a bored housewife meant that from childhood I'd had to endure more glittering charity galas than I cared to remember. But despite everyone's best efforts, I still didn't know what to do with myself when surrounded by anyone other than close friends.

It sucked.

I shook my head and stared down at the imprints my shoes made in the sand. There was no way a deportment class could have prepared me for colliding with the hottest man ever to grace running shorts. And there sure as hell was no guidebook outlining what to do after openly gawking at said man and blurting out how beautiful his cock was. I bit my lip to stop an anguished groan.

"You're blushing."

I glanced up before quickly looking away again.

He nudged me teasingly. "Why are you blushing?"

I kept quiet.

"Forget it, I already know why anyway. You're not the first woman to lose her shit over my—"

I stopped and glared up at him. "Enough, okay? This has already been the day from hell and you're only making it worse."

His mocking smile slipped. "Hey, I'm just joking around."

"Yeah, at my expense."

Shrugging one shoulder, he replied, "You kinda make it easy. All I have to do is look at you and your skin flushes pink or you say something fuckin' hilarious."

I blushed again.

Damn it.

He grinned. "See?"

I made a frustrated noise in the back of my throat and stalked off in the direction of my car. I needed to get as far away from the guy as possible, his earthy scent was messing with my equilibrium and the way his lips quirked up in the corners made me want to bite something. Hard.

So I unzipped my pocket and hastily fished out some keys, only heavy footsteps chased me.

"Wait up."

Internally, I groaned; however, not wanting to appear rude, I took a deep, steadying breath and slowly turned around.

In my peripheral vision, I spied a group of bikini-clad women openly admiring the mouth-watering man candy as he winked and leisurely jogged past them. "Ladies."

Great, a live audience. This is going to be beyond awkward.

He rounded the top step and held out a large hand while I warily stared down at it. "My name's Dominic, by the way."

After a moment's pause, I reached out and clasped his fingers, biting my lip at the heated contact of his skin and the power it could wield over me if given half a chance.

"Riley, Riley Sears. It's a pleasure to meet you," I mumbled.

Thanks, Mum.

"Trust me, Riley Sears, the pleasure's all mine."

His lopsided grin had me dumbly gaping at him for a while.

This guy can't be for real. I mean, he's way too attractive for his own good. He knows it too, oh yes, he knows exactly what he's doing. He'd probably take me right here in this car park if I let him. Would I let him? Focus, Riley.

I scanned Dominic up and down. Yep, the man had *player* written all over him, from the tips of his unruly light brown hair, all the way down to... I had to stop staring at his junk.

I shook my head. Well, I wasn't going to be distracted, and I certainly wasn't going to become the latest notch in his bedpost. Besides, Doctor Powell explained months ago how unhealthy relationships were a trigger for my anxiety and she was right of course, now that I think back. So there was no way this conversation was heading anywhere good, even if it was with someone as obscenely gorgeous as Dominic.

Sigh.

"What? Why are you looking at me like I just ran over your puppy?"

I ignored him. "Thanks for walking me to my car but I've gotta go, I've got stuff to do."

Like removing sand out of every orifice and with any luck, the memory of his fingers touching my skin.

Fun times ahead.

"Wait, you're leaving? Just like that?"

I heard fits of giggles and frantic whispers in the background.

"Uh, yeah."

"So that's all the thanks I get?" His gaze turned incredulous.

I stared at him.

He stepped in close, his voice dropping to a husky

17

murmur. "I'd like to get to know you better, Riley."

I consciously ignored the heat that pooled in my stomach and instead narrowed my eyes at him. "Really? And are you talking intellectually, emotionally, or physically?"

"Definitely physically."

I bit back a laugh. Damn he was forward, wish I didn't like it so much. But, shaking my head, I murmured, "Not gonna happen, Dominic. I'm not that kind of girl."

He stepped closer again, his eyes trained on my mouth. "You sure about that?"

Once again I forgot to breathe. This was going to become a real issue if I didn't get it under control ASAP. So, taking a deep breath I squared my shoulders. "Look, unless you've planned a romantic dinner for two, got some scented candles handy, and quite possibly an engagement ring…"

The man actually blanched. "Fuck no."

I laughed. "Exactly. But I'm sure one of your admirers over there," I gestured to the bikini brigade, "will be more than willing to, ah, help you out."

He glanced over at the twittering women before scrunching up his nose in distaste. "I never go back for seconds."

"I'm sorry?"

He turned back to me, his stare unwavering. "I never sleep with the same woman twice."

"Please tell me you're kidding."

"Nope." He looked over at them again. "The redhead was last weekend, the brunette two days before that, and the sisters…" He whistled. "Let's just say I had my hands full on Monday night."

I stared heavenward, desperately trying to rid the image of Dominic naked and in the throes of passion out of my head.

He chuckled and my stupid knees turned weak. "I'm joking, Riley." I glared at him. "Kind of. Look, I'm not gonna lie to you, I love women." He paused for a moment. "And it really was a fuckin' awesome Monday night."

Right, then. That's my cue to leave.

Turning to my car, I opened the driver door before settling myself inside. "Goodbye, Dominic."

"You're missing out on the best sex of your life."

Be still my beating heart.

Shaking my head, I shut the door before lowering the automated windows. "See you around."

"When?" He bent forward, his arms resting on the side panel. Once again I was hit with a wave of his masculine scent mixed with ... mint? I closed my eyes, desperately trying not to breathe him in.

This man is definitely trying to kill me. Doesn't he know mint is my favorite scent in the whole world? I'm in serious trouble here.

When I opened them again, his face was only inches away from mine and those full, kissable lips hovered so temptingly close. My breathing turned erratic as I tried to ignore the pulse which jumped at the base of his throat.

Dominic's smile turned wicked, plain and simple. "Same time tomorrow?"

"Okay," I whispered.

Hang on, what? That was not what I meant to say. Dominic was the type of guy to steer clear of, not agree to see again. *What the heck am I doing?*

I shook my head. There was no way I wanted to become yet another random name in his little black book. The blasted thing was probably full.

His eyes promised everything I told myself I

didn't want, but so help me, I couldn't look away. Grinning, he slowly stood and thumped the canvas roof of my convertible before stepping back. "Looking forward to it."

I drove home in a haze.

"No. Do it again."

I sighed, before staring down at the endless row of shining silver cutlery in front of me. We were dining at the fanciest restaurant Geographe Bay had to offer but I just wanted to hide under the table, not sit at the head of it while Mum kept telling me off for stuff I didn't know.

I tentatively reached for the largest fork.

"No, no, and no." Mum rapped my knuckles with a spoon.

I wanted to yank it out of her hand and hit her over the head with it, though my life wouldn't be worth living if I did.

"How many times do I have to tell you, Riley Jayne?" I flinched, hating it when she called me by my first and middle name. "Always start from the outside.*"*

She groaned dramatically. "How are we ever going to get through tomorrow night's dinner if you don't even remember which fork to choose first?"

I wanted to remind her that I was only twelve. I wanted to remind her that I didn't even want the stupid dinner or the table full of people who cared about what type of silverware I ate with. I wanted to remind her that this was an awful way to spend my birthday and I wasn't enjoying myself at all. But as usual, I kept quiet. As usual, I did my best to please her. And as usual, I failed spectacularly.

****

"You gonna eat that?"

I blinked. "Huh? Oh, yeah, of course."

Grace eyed me from across the kitchen

countertop. We were seated on two bar stools, eating dinner in our shared apartment, and normally the conversation flowed seamlessly. I mean, she was my best friend and we'd known each other most of our lives so there was always plenty to chat about. However, tonight I couldn't stop thinking about my parents. For some reason my birthday always coincided with an unhealthy side-helping of despondency, probably because 'dysfunctional' didn't even begin to cover the breadth or width of our relationship. Anyway, I wasn't exactly Ms. Conversationalist and Grace being who she was, picked up on my silence straight away.

"Where'd you go just then?"

I sighed. "Nowhere good."

"Your mum?"

"Yeah."

"You know she'll want to see you for your birthday, right?"

I sighed again. "I know, I'll head over there tomorrow night for a bit."

Grace nodded. "You're a brave woman." Then changing the subject, she asked, "So, what do you think?"

I stared at her, confused.

"Of your birthday dinner," she said slowly. "You know, the one I've been slaving over for hours."

"It's a salad."

"It's not just any salad, it's a falafel salad." She looked down at her plate grumbling, "Didn't even know what a fucking falafel was until this afternoon."

My eyes softened. "It's an awesome dinner, G, really." I took another bite, pausing thoughtfully. "The dressing is, um, interesting."

Grace's eyes turned mischievous. "My own special recipe."

I rolled the food around in my mouth before

swallowing. "Can't put my finger on it exactly but—" I stopped, staring at her. "You didn't."

She grinned.

"Oh, for God's sake. You put *whiskey* in a salad dressing?"

"It adds a little something, don't you think?"

I groaned, dropping my head onto the top. "You're seriously unhinged, you know that?"

"Come on, Riley, I haven't had a single drop all day. And do you wanna know why?"

"Not particularly."

"Because I drove halfway across the fucking country to a health food store run by a guy named Rainbow freakin' Storm Cloud, buying you goddamn organic chickpeas and scallions which, I might add, you're not even eating."

I raised my head and dutifully took another mouthful. After a slight pause, I grudgingly muttered, "It actually tastes really good."

"I know, right?"

"Thank you."

"Save the groveling for after dessert."

My eyes lit up. "G, don't mess with me now. You know my poor heart can't take it."

"How much do you love me?"

I jumped up and ran to the fridge, squealing in delight when my eyes found heaven ... in mud cake form. "No way, it's—"

"Triple chocolate, just like you not-so-subtly asked."

I ran back to the table and threw my arms around her. "G, you're amazing. That thing is *huge*."

"Happy birthday."

Best. Friend. Ever.

Not long afterward, Grace and I migrated to the

lounge room where we sat cross-legged on the couch while stuffing our faces with a cake so sweet it actually gave me a headache. Win. On the whole, I was actually pretty healthy. I ate cleanly, exercised regularly, and even meditated when the time called for it. But chocolate anything was my Achilles' heel—along with smokin' hot bad boys going by the name of Dominic, it would seem.

I shook my head.

Grace licked her spoon, eyeing me. "Okay, who is he?"

"Who?"

"The guy you're thinking about right now. Who is he?"

"Don't know what you're talking about."

She snorted. "Cut the bullshit, Riley. How long have we known each other?"

After a quick mental calculation, I mumbled, "Seventeen years."

"Exactly. You were a terrible liar when you were five and you're a horrible one now." She smiled. "Your ears turn pink."

Of course they do. Is there any body part that doesn't?

I swore under my breath and Grace smirked. "My smart mouth is rubbing off on you." But then she sobered. "Come on, out with it."

"In all honesty, I don't really know."

She raised a questioning eyebrow but said nothing, waiting for me to elaborate. After a moment's pause, I took a deep breath and then told her about my disastrous day at the hospital that culminated in a desperate need to escape to the beach for a run and then literally running into Dominic's ridiculously ripped pecs.

She was silent for a moment before asking, "Are you going to meet him tomorrow?"

"I'm not sure."

Grace's emerald green eyes softened. My best friend was beautiful, there was no doubt about it. She was a petite, raven-haired bombshell with gorgeous curves, a heart-shaped face and a sprinkling of freckles to boot. When Grace lowered her defenses and opened up to those around her—like she was doing right now—some might even call her breathtaking. However, Grace refused to open herself up to anyone except me. Needless to say, to pretty much everyone else in existence she was a … bitch. I hate to admit it but it was true. Let's just say she sported one very tough exterior—she had a short fuse, was blunt to the point of rudeness, and often selfish. There were many reasons for this of course, but recently she'd been dealing with the unexpected death of her beloved father and the betrayal of an ex-boyfriend. Grace was presently struggling with a deep sense of bitterness, and I'm talking uncharted-chasm-in-the-ocean deep. She never took it out on me though, oh no; my best friend had only ever been loyal, kind-hearted and loving… In her own way.

"Be careful, Riley. You have a way of letting guys get so far under your skin you can't differentiate where they end and you begin."

I looked down.

Ain't that the truth.

She grabbed my hand and squeezed. "Just be careful, okay? Don't give your heart away to someone who's just going to fuck you over, it's happened way too many times already."

"You're right."

"You deserve the world, love, don't settle for anything less."

I stared at the gooey remains of my chocolate cake. There was no way I regretted eating so much as a bite of it, it was too damn delicious. But Dominic on the other hand? Well. A dark part of me knew I would definitely regret meeting him.

Chapter Two

I can't find the reason,
Looking through confusion,
Can't divide illusion.
—MONDEZ, "Distance"

"Riley, this cake is so good I'd actually consider sacrificing my firstborn for another slice."

"No, you wouldn't." I smiled at Mae. "Annabelle is too adorable."

"True. But I'd seriously think about it for a good ten seconds before saying no." She thought for a moment. "Does that make me a horrible mother?"

"No, just a hungry one."

We were both sitting in the cramped office behind the nurse's station of the maternity ward. It had been a busy morning in our part of Castillo Hospital. Both our patients delivered healthy babies within half an hour of each other, so we'd left the respective families to acquaint themselves with their new arrivals and took a well-deserved break.

As much as Grace and I tried to finish off what was in all seriousness the best thing I'd had in my mouth in a *very* long time, we'd hardly made a dent in the cake. So I decided to bring it to work to share with everyone. Sharing was caring, after all.

After swallowing another mouthful, Mae spun around on her office chair, moaning in delight. That woman enjoyed chocolate almost as much as I did. Suddenly, her eyes popped open. "Hey, Riley."

"Yeah?"

"Remember how we were talking about health and fitness plans the other day?"

I glanced down at my cake, refusing to feel guilty. "Yep."

"Could you write one up for me?"

I squealed. "*Of course*. Now, do you want to focus on general toning, muscle development, aerobic endurance, anaerobic stamina…" My voice trailed away when I noticed her shocked expression.

"Whoa. You just got way too excited about inflicting physical pain on someone. You might wanna get that checked out."

"You asked."

Mae took another bite of her cake. "That I did. Reckon it's time to get moving again, shake what my mamma gave me and all that." She wiggled her hips and I laughed because sitting down, she looked like a constipated penguin.

"How about I put together an introductory program for you? We could even meet up and I'll walk you through it?"

"There'll be walking involved?" Mae's dark eyes were hopeful.

"Hell no. There'll be running, jumping, squatting, pushing—"

"Shouldn't have opened my big mouth," she muttered.

"Someone told me there was cake?"

Both Mae and I looked to the open doorway. Robin peeked his head through and after spying the dessert, moved deeper into the room.

"Help yourself." I smiled. "There's plenty to go around."

"Love your work, Riley." Robin started cutting himself a healthy slice while Mae mouthed, *He's so hot,*

27

behind his back. I stifled a laugh.

She was right, of course. Robin was hot. At thirty-one, he was tall, lean, blond-haired and had the most expressive hazel eyes I'd ever seen. He was an obstetrician who ran his own private practice across the road and because of that, chose to send his patients to Castillo Hospital, much to everyone's delight. I didn't know how he managed it, but even after pulling an all-nighter and delivering God knows how many babies since yesterday, he still looked fresh. And I mean, just-stepped-out-of-the-ocean-and-onto-the-sand fresh.

On closer inspection, however, there was no mistaking the expensive designer labels or the fact that his unkempt hairstyle would have cost a month's rent. He never flaunted his wealth, though, and was remarkably good-natured, so I'd warmed to him instantly. Funnily enough, so had every other woman in the hospital. Patients included.

Robin took a mouthful, groaned, and I grinned as Mae started fanning herself.

"What are you girls up to after your shift?"

"I'm picking Annabelle up from child care and then we're hitting the park. She's gonna lose her mind when I tell her where we're headed."

As a single mum, Mae had done amazingly well for herself. She got pregnant at a young age and despite being thrown out of home and no longer having any contact with her daughter's father, somehow managed to score top marks at university. From there, she earned the position of midwife at Castillo and has been going from strength to strength ever since. She was positive, driven, and had a wicked sense of humor. In other words, she was an awesome woman.

"Sounds fun." Robin turned to me. "What about you?"

"Oh, um…" I could feel my cheeks heat and noticed Mae's suspiciously narrowed eyes.

That girl doesn't miss *a thing*.

"I'm just heading to the beach for a run and then have dinner with my parents afterward." I sighed.

Robin's eyes gleamed. "How are Daniella and Stuart?"

I was momentarily taken aback before remembering that of course Robin knew my family. Despite the nine-year age gap, he'd grown up in the same privileged neighborhood as I had. He'd attended the same prestigious schools and even accepted invitations to the same charity fundraisers. Poor guy.

So I tried to keep my face neutral as I replied, "They're still the same."

He laughed, it was a nice sound, not deep and throaty like another one I'd recently heard—

Stop it, Riley.

I sighed again.

"Well, tell them I said hi." He wiped his hands on a napkin before throwing it in the trash. "And thanks for the cake." Robin winked at me as he strode out the office.

I think I mumbled something like, *You're welcome*, but couldn't be sure because I was too busy trying to come up with a reason to extricate myself from Mae's imminent questioning.

It was no use. As soon as he left she rounded on me, demanding, "Okay, who are you meeting at the beach?"

"Wow, would you look at the time." I glanced at my wrist. "Better go and see how little Thomas is settling in." Not the most original excuse, but a true one nonetheless.

As I hastily exited the room, I could hear Mae call out behind me, "Damn it, Riley. You're not even wearing a watch."

To be honest, I didn't want to open up to Mae. Not because I didn't value her friendship or anything—she was a great girl and I trusted her judgment completely—but I was still undecided about seeing Dominic again. I had been in this situation many times before and for some reason always ended up six pounds lighter, completely surrounded by cleaning products and one egg short of a carton. It wasn't pretty. However, a small part of me—the sadist part—wanted to believe Dominic was different from what he first appeared. God only knew why, but I wanted to believe he was willing to form a lasting relationship with the right girl despite what he said about never sleeping with the same woman twice—I mean seriously, who did that? And if I really thought about it, a dark part of me wanted to be the one to inspire this change.

Ah, Doctor Powell, we have so much work to do.

Anyway, I soon found myself pulling into a vacant parking space at the beach, so I guess my subconscious made the decision for me. I was going to see Dominic.

And surprise, surprise, he wasn't there.

Shit.

As I got out my car and walked down the steps, I wasn't sure whether to feel relieved or disappointed he hadn't shown. It didn't matter regardless because embarrassment soon raised its ugly head and gloated over the other emotions anyway.

Needless to say, when my feet hit the sand I took off at a run. However, after ten minutes of being surrounded by nothing but the coast, sea and sky, I slowly began to relax. My thoughts even turned positive after the image of Dominic's contorted face faded when I imaginarily kneed him in the balls. It took a while, but once again I felt comfortable in my own skin.

You see, there was something about running on the beach I truly loved. The gentle lapping of waves rolling toward the shore and then retreating again centered me. The rhythmic beat of my shoes pounding the sand cleared my head, and my metrical breathing channeled otherwise nervous energy toward a tangible primary focus—the horizon. Exercising like this helped keep the demons away. It gave me freedom, space, purpose.

Happiness.

As I rounded the rocky outcrop—more cautiously this time—I felt someone's eyes trained on my back and my heart rate spiked in response.

So, you've finally decided to show up, have you?

Willing my knees to stay strong, I lengthened my stride, secretly smirking as I shifted to a faster pace. A low growl rumbled behind me, sounding like a seriously pissed grizzly bear and I was surprised to find him keeping up. I was also surprised that an irritated man-eater could be such a turn-on. Anyway, undaunted by the challenge I then took a deep breath, steadied myself and shot forward—cheetah style—putting everything I had into a final sprint.

Suck on that one, Dominic.

The remainder of the small, deserted cove flashed past me. Wind stung my eyes as my heightened pulse thrummed through my ears. I felt alive, carefree, boundless.

Untouchable.

It was awesome.

All too soon, however, I had to slow down and stop unless I wanted yet another near-death experience, only this time with a cliff face. So, easing back to a walk, I strode in small measured circles with hands on my hips.

Eventually, Dominic reached me, wavered, and then collapsed onto the sand.

"Fuck, woman. You almost killed me," he rasped, lying on his back. One arm was thrown across his eyes while that muscular chest rose and fell in time with labored breaths. And my insanely erratic heartbeat. It actually felt like the mad organ was trying to launch itself out my body—I seriously worried for my ribcage.

Tearing my gaze away, I stared at the blue water, trying to calm suddenly convoluted thoughts.

What the hell is he doing? Why isn't he wearing a t-shirt? That man has no right parading around the beach like a half-naked cologne model, none at all. Goddamn it, is he trying to kill me?

"Where'd you learn to run like that?"

I glanced over my shoulder at him and soon wished I hadn't.

Yep, he definitely wants me dead.

So, facing the ocean again, I willed the balled tension at the base of my stomach to calm the heck down. "I was on the running team in high school."

"And won every race, am I right?"

I shrugged, feigning nonchalance. He was right though, I cleaned up at every track meet, not that it mattered, of course. After all, Dad was too busy working at the hospital or lecturing overseas to take an interest and Mum refused to watch my races because she considered running an unladylike pursuit. In her world, anything involving me, physical exertion, and sweat were frowned upon. She preferred I take up a classical instrument like the harp or violin. So I did.

Sadly.

Brea grimaced as she stormed into my bedroom and I stopped what I was doing to look at her.

"What the hell is that noise? It sounds like a

slaughterhouse in here."

I sighed and threw my violin down onto the white settee. "Mum wants me to have this piece down by tonight."

"Why?"

"So when Doctor Rubensteel mentions his love for Beethoven, I'm prepared."

Her mouth gaped open. "What the fuck? Your mum wants you to play for that fossilized relic in front of all those people?" She shook her head. "You're not a zoo exhibit, Riley."

I slumped down onto the floor, resting my back against the French windows. After dropping my head in my hands, I wailed, "What am I going to do, Brea? I hate the violin, and believe me when I tell you, it hates me back."

She sat down next to me, her brown eyes kind. "Don't do it."

"What?"

"Don't do it."

I shook my head. "You don't understand, I can't—"

"Yes, you can. You're not a kid anymore, just tell your mum no."

"God, I wish I could." I paused, imagining the unbridled joy of refusing Mum's demand. But then images of her making my life an absolute misery flashed before my eyes—the brooding silences, angry glares, pointed reminders... I shuddered before changing the subject. "Uh, why are you here again?"

Brea laughed. "I'm helping out with the preparations. Nan needs an extra set of hands so I'm getting the bedrooms ready. It's gonna be a big weekend, what with the fundraiser and all of those out of town guests staying here and everything."

"A long weekend, you mean."

She pulled out a turquoise iPod from her jeans pocket and gave me one of her headphones. "Here, try listening to this. It always helps when I'm having a fucker of a day."

She pressed play and I relaxed my head back against the glass, shutting my eyes. I couldn't help the shit-eating grin from creeping across my face as the song progressed. Mum would hate this music, it was heavy, brutal, brash. It was everything the violin wasn't.

It was fucking awesome.

"You okay?"

I turned back toward the deep voice. Dominic had all but recovered and was sitting up, his arms casually resting on bent knees with a curious look on his face. He looked open, honest, beautiful.

I swallowed. "Yeah, why?"

"You don't seem yourself."

"How would you know? You don't know me."

Something akin to hurt flashed across his face before he schooled his features and looked away.

Damn it Riley, the guy just chased you down the beach and asked if you were okay at the end of it. Quit with the defensiveness already.

I sighed. "Look, I'm sorry. I shouldn't have said that, and I definitely shouldn't have run away from you before."

He smiled. "It's all good, I could chase your sweet ass for miles."

Blush in three ... two ... one... There it is, right on cue.

After several attempts at clearing my throat, I finally gave up on verbalizing anything remotely intelligent so resigned myself to staring at him instead.

He's so fucking hot.

Dominic looked at me, his eyes growing incrementally darker the longer we remained gazing at each other. I swear, the space between us sparked and charged with burgeoning energy. It felt like the air was suddenly filled with manic, rock-music-loving particles body-slamming into each other. The overall effect forced me to shut my eyes and take a deep, calming breath.

"You sure you don't wanna fuck?"

My eyes snapped open and his gravelly chuckle almost made me swoon—southern belle style. "How did the conversation turn from me apologizing to you wanting sex?"

"Come on, Riley, it's not rocket science. I see how you react to me." He shifted slightly. "Man, if your cheeks turn pink from a few innocent words, imagine what'll happen when I—"

"How about we try being friends?" I blurted.

Where did that come from?

"Friends?"

The guy seemed seriously dumbfounded and to be honest, so was I. I mean, why would I want to be friends with someone like Dominic? He was a crass alpha male who only took an interest in a woman if he wanted to sleep with her. How could we possibly coexist in a healthy, platonic relationship? It was nonsensical. Not only that, but how the heck could I possibly talk myself into not wanting more? This whole situation was bad. Bad, bad, bad.

Calling Doctor Powell...

But I stepped closer, eyeing him carefully. To my surprise, Dominic glanced away, uncomfortable. There was something about him I couldn't figure out, there was more to him than he was letting on, I was sure of it. And I wanted to know what it was.

All of a sudden it hit me. "You don't have any

female friends, do you?"

"Riley, the last thing I need is a woman hanging off my arm or cock-blocking me."

Interesting.

"What if I promise to do neither?"

"Then you'd be lying."

Only a little.

"I don't lie." Dominic stared at me, unconvinced. "Okay, let me rephrase that. I might purposefully avoid saying something, but I never lie outright. Ever."

"Yeah?"

"Yeah."

He nodded. "Good. Fuckin' hate chicks that lie, pisses me off."

Huh.

"All right then," he continued. "I'll back off trying to get you naked and we'll give the whole friends thing a go. But I'm telling you now, it's a wasted effort because sooner or later I'm gonna be inside you and when I am…" He whistled. "It'll be fuckin' awesome for both of us."

I considered him for a moment, disregarding the molten lava which not-so-subtly pooled between my thighs. "If what you're saying is true, it would only be awesome for one night."

"So?"

"So?" I repeated, stepping closer. God, his eyes were incredible. "You don't get it, do you? I won't be your one-night stand, Dominic, I want to mean more to someone than that. Hell, after the shit I've been through these past few years, I deserve more than that."

We were both silent, me embarrassed by my brutal honesty and Dominic contemplative. Just before I gave up on the rising awkwardness and ran back to my car in shame, he stood, brushed sand off his shorts and declared, "Right. You almost finished me off with that sprint, now it's my turn to repay the favor."

"How?" I asked warily.

"Push-ups."

I swore under my breath.

Now don't get me wrong, I enjoy working out as much as the next fitness enthusiast, but push-ups of any kind were my least favorite exercise. Ever. A training session focused on my legs? No problem, I'd power through it. Stomach and abs? I could deal. But arms and chest? Yuck.

"On your knees, woman." Dominic's grin was wicked.

I bit my lip—at the thought of the set, not at the way his smile turned my stomach to mush—and lay down on the sand. "If I'm doing this, I'm doing it right. No knees."

"Show me what you've got."

I pushed myself into starting position and then slowly lowered down. My arms shook slightly, but I gritted my teeth, refusing to stop. Exhaling on my way back up, I finished the first repetition, proud of my efforts. Not too shabby.

One down, fourteen to go.

Fuck my life.

After finishing, I not-so-gracefully collapsed to the ground and gasped, "Your turn."

Dominic chuckled, before quickly starting his set.

Oh. My. Sweet. Chocolate. Cake.

I kid you not, the way his shoulder muscles rippled and glistened with each movement was ridiculous. Beads of sweat trickled down the undulating valleys on his back and the heady combination of grace and power left me lightheaded. No, worse than that, it left me wanting to climb on board to explore every inch of him … with my tongue.

I swallowed.

It was insane how strong Dominic was. I mean, I could see muscles swelling that I couldn't even identify and my knowledge of anatomy was pretty damn good. I shut my eyes. If he didn't stop soon all hell would break loose, I swear to God, it would be anarchy of the worst kind.

"You want more?"

Yes. Yes, I do. I mean, *no,* of course not.

My eyes popped open. "More?"

His self-indulgent grin left me simultaneously breathless and annoyed. "Are you ready for two more sets?"

"Oh, right. Yeah, sure."

Jesus, woman, show some class.

But I couldn't concentrate. His body had done some crazy voodoo on me. I was no longer in control of my limbs. They refused to work harmoniously together and I found myself halfway through the last set with a spine that rivaled a banana. If I didn't get my shit together soon, I'd be in serious trouble—back injuries were the worst.

After noticing my evident struggle, Dominic's hand flew out and pressed against my stomach, supporting me. Energy crackled and flashed where we connected, the sizzling heat from his palm instinctively answering the searing warmth of my tingling skin.

"Tighten your core," he murmured. "Don't want you losing form and hurting yourself."

No, I definitely didn't want to get hurt, and if I wasn't careful, this man was going to do just that. Only, not in the way he envisaged.

I somehow fumbled my way through the remainder of the set and quickly sat up, hugging my knees to my chest once done. I watched as Dominic's eyes flicked briefly to his palm, a closed look on his face.

"Why won't you sleep with the same woman twice?" Despite my quiet voice, I grimaced at its pleading tone.

He stared at me, his blue eyes flat. "Because I can't offer any more than that."

My heart tore a little. *For* him, not because of him. Honest.

Dominic's last set was markedly faster than the first three, so I looked away, biting my lip and pondering his reply.

When he stopped, his eyes found mine again. "Why won't you have a one-night stand?"

"Because I need more than that."

Our gazes crashed, defiant to the last. And there it was, the instinctive pull that drew us closer, the crackle of air that spiked between us and the resounding tempo of our hearts somehow beating in perfect synchronicity.

Neither of us moved.

Blessedly, we both chose to ignore the neon warning sign flashing above our heads declaring this a disaster waiting to happen. Dominic blinked, gave a wry smile and stood, while I took a deep breath, exhaled, and rose as well. The movement forced me to grimace. My hamstrings had tightened from sitting down for too long so I leaned forward at the waist and touched my toes, stretching out the tight muscles.

There was a strangled groan beside me and Dominic's voice was hoarse. "Christ woman, you can't do shit like that if you wanna be friends. Fucking hell."

When my eyes found his I noticed he was staring directly at my ass, so I straightened up, indignant. "I needed to stretch."

"And now I need a cold shower." He adjusted

himself and I gasped.

Oh, my freaking God, he's huge.

I tore my gaze away and took three wobbly steps back, staring anywhere but at the man next to me. Space. That's what I needed. Lots and lots of space. A whole beach full of space.

"This isn't going to work, Dominic," I told the sapphire ocean.

Silence.

After a minute, I braved a peek and found Dominic gazing at me, his face gentle. He moved until he was standing directly in front of me and I couldn't help it, I breathed him in.

Mmm, earthy Dominic manliness. *Delicious.*

Slowly, deliberately, Dominic skimmed calloused hands down my arms. A stream of goose bumps appeared in their wake and I bit my bottom lip, determined to remain silent despite the overwhelming urge to moan out loud. Dominic looked on, seemingly mesmerized by the way my skin flushed scarlet in response to his light touch. He murmured something under his breath but it was so quiet I couldn't catch it, and when his fingers at last reached mine, they entwined—all of their own accord, I swear.

I shut my eyes.

Breathe, Riley.

"We'll figure it out, angel." His low voice made my toes curl. I opened my eyes again and our gazes locked. "I've got a feeling you're worth my blue balls." His lips quirked up in the corners and it took everything I had to stay upright. "Just don't shove your sweet ass in my face again, okay?"

I nodded.

He looked at me a moment longer, shook his head and then stepped back, releasing my fingers. It suddenly felt like the slightest breeze could topple me over.

"Come on, *friend*." Playful Dominic was back, he was easier to deal with than whoever the heck that other Dominic was, that was for sure. "I'll race you back."

And he took off down the beach at a sprint, taking a part of me with him.

Chapter Three

Do you feel something here?
I can feel something there,
But I'm not gonna change.
—MONDEZ, "Direction"

I stormed through the front door, slammed it shut and threw my handbag down on the kitchen counter. Grace lowered the novel she was reading and raised an eyebrow. "I see dinner with your parents went well."

Growling, I stalked over to where she sat on the couch and collapsed down next to her. "Don't know why I bother."

It was true. I seriously had no idea why I continuously went back to that house. It wasn't as though I could change the past. Believe me, if I could, I would have. Over and over again.

Even Doctor Powell suggested I limit my exposure to Daniella and Stuart. Apparently, they were triggers for me, parental triggers of the gargantuan persuasion, and now I was left feeling empty, unsettled and bloody annoyed at myself. Never a good combination.

Grace picked up a full glass of whiskey from the coffee table before taking a sip. "Me neither. Woman's a bitch."

I didn't try to defend my mother because Grace was right, she was the most horrible person on the entire west coast. Honestly, if I Google searched the word *troll* her Facebook profile would come up.

She hadn't always been like that. Years ago, she'd been kind, loving—heck, she even used to laugh. But not any more. Oh no. Now she was the embodiment of coldness wrapped in spite—a toxic mixture, let me tell you. I had no idea why Dad stayed married to her but guessed with the long hours he put in at work, he hardly saw her anyway. It was useless either of us trying to please the woman because, in all seriousness, nothing did. Well, except his bank balance and my outright misery, which therefore meant every time I left their house after yet another disastrous meal, I kicked myself for going in the first place.

She was impossible.

He was hopeless.

And I was deluded.

I turned to Grace. "Whenever I go there, I'm like this time it will be different. This time she's got nothing to criticize me for." I shook my head. "But she always finds something. Every. Fucking. Time."

"What was it tonight?"

I sighed. "My job."

Grace snorted.

"According to Mum, bringing new life into the world is a crap career choice. Apparently, I was raised for better."

"Well, you do have to get your hands dirty and you know her opinion on personal hygiene."

"That's not what I meant, G, and you know it."

She squeezed my hand gently, her emerald eyes sympathetic.

I could feel my own eyes well up with tears. "It's never going to change, is it? I'm never going to be good enough for her."

"Wanna know the definition of insanity?"

"Huh?"

"Insanity."

"What the hell are you talking about?"

"Insanity is doing the same thing over and over

again yet expecting a different result each time." I stared at her, clueless, while she calmly took another sip of whiskey. "Think about it, Riley. Every time you go over there you assume this Hallmark moment in your head is going to become a reality, only it never does because your mum annihilates it completely by calling you a fucking disappointment."

I took in a sharp breath.

"Total bullshit, by the way. She's a bitter, soulless old cow who should have been euthanized during the Foot and Mouth epidemic." She took another drink, then mused, "Maybe I should become a psychologist? Think Doctor Powell would take me on?"

I was silent for a moment, trying to process it all. What Grace said made sense—well, except for her references to euthanasia and a possible career change—I always naively hoped Mum would see how I'd changed, that she'd mention how proud she was of the person I'd become. But she never did. Not once.

So, after a while, I murmured, "Oh, my God, you're right."

"Wouldn't be the first time."

"I need a drink."

"That's my girl."

"Give me that bottle." I grabbed it off the coffee table and took a swig, grimacing as it burned its way down my throat.

Grace stared at me in surprise, shrugged her shoulders and then clinked her glass against the beverage in my hand. Just before downing the remainder of her whiskey, she toasted, "To the asylum."

"Daddy?" I pushed his office door open and craned my neck through the small gap.

He was sitting behind his desk, the deep mahogany surface polished and shining under the lamplight. Daddy's desktop computer flashed an artificial glare in the otherwise dim room, emphasizing the long, hollow panes underneath his angular cheekbones and sunken eyes.

It had been months since he'd eaten properly.

He stared blankly past the computer screen to the family portrait sitting just to the right of it. It was housed in a glossy silver frame and I remember how heavy it felt when I presented it to him last summer as a birthday gift. It had taken ages to get a good shot of us, ages and ages.

But, there was something in his features—a desperate sadness—which made me question whether interrupting him was a good idea after all. I sighed. However, our latest cook had been firm, if he didn't come down to the dining room soon his meal would be cold.

"Daddy?" I repeated.

He started and quickly made himself appear busy by picking up and rifling through random piles of paper.

"Are you hungry?"

Daddy gave a quick shake of his head, mumbling, "Not tonight. I'm not hungry tonight."

With an agitated flick of his wrist, he dismissed me, so I turned and trudged out the room, closing the door behind me with a soft click.

He still couldn't look me in the eyes.

****

"You did well in there today, Riley."

I swallowed a mouthful of peppermint tea and gingerly leaned back in my chair. According to the barista, it had hydrating and calming properties. However, judging by my pounding headache and shaking fingers—the nasty side effects from dinner with my parents and drinking way too much afterward—I needed to ingest at least a truckload of the stuff for it to work.

Note to self—*whiskey is evil.*

Second note to self—*Mother is more evil.*

I took another sip of tea before replying. "Thanks, I'm so glad you were with me, it might have ended very differently otherwise." I shook my head. It hurt. "I hate when stuff like that happens."

I was referring to the difficult delivery Robin and I had just assisted with. The baby's shoulders became lodged and the umbilical cord was wrapped around its neck, so it had been touch and go for a while there. It also served as a strong reminder about why I needed a clear head at work.

I shuddered.

Robin's touch was warm. "You kept your cool and the mother drew strength from that. It's a crucial skill for a midwife."

I looked down at his hand on mine and flushed. Robin's palm was large, smooth and gentle. I was surprised to find my body relaxing under his touch.

Surely it's just the tea kicking in?

"I mean it, Riley. You were amazing."

After smiling shyly at him, I glanced around the small coffee shop, trying to distract myself from the intensity in his gaze and the fact that he still hadn't let go of my fingers.

The coffee shop itself was just off the main foyer of the hospital and frequented by staff, patients, their family and friends. We were seated on white wooden chairs with a narrow bench between us. Even though the décor was bright and cheerful with sporadic splashes of orange and yellow, for some reason the ambiance always remained subdued. People must have felt guilty enjoying themselves here. I knew I felt ... odd.

Robin and I had been working together for over a year and he'd never made a pass at me before. So to be honest, it was difficult to tell if he was working his magic on me now or not. You see, he was one of those genuinely kind people, the ones who didn't bat an eyelash at some casual hand-holding or arm rubbing. Which left my current predicament all the more confusing because I couldn't figure out if I was misinterpreting the heat in his gaze or not. Now, if he'd stared at me with mischievous blue eyes while saying something completely inappropriate about my ass, however...

Thankfully, my foggy head didn't get a chance to muddle its way through that conundrum because my phone started dancing its way across the table.

"Mae's just gone on her break, do you mind if she joins us?"

"No, of course not." Robin smiled and my belly did a little flip. He had a nice mouth, though I bet teeth like that cost a fortune. As he slowly removed his hand and sat back, my eyes furtively drifted over his taut chest—I couldn't help it.

Not bad.

"How'd dinner go last night?" I grimaced before I could stop myself and he laughed. "That good, huh?"

"It was ... okay."

"You don't get along with your parents?" His gaze was thoughtful. "I always got the impression you guys were close."

"Guess that's the problem with impressions, they never tell the whole truth."

"Swear to God, the shit's gonna hit the fan if I don't get a triple shot espresso in the next thirty seconds." I could have kissed Mae for her timely interruption. "Oh, hey Robin."

"Hey."

"You'd better go order then." I grinned.

"No need, I called ahead."

"Smart move."

"So, have you done it yet?"

Both Robin and I stared at each other and then at her—my face felt like an egg could fry on it. Surely, she wasn't referring to…

"The fitness program, Riley. You know, the one you're writing for me? What did you think I was talking about?" She sat down opposite me, her agitated fingers tapping the tabletop and her dark eyes pointedly glaring at the barista.

Man, she's on edge. Better not make any sudden movements.

"You write fitness programs?"

I smiled sheepishly at Robin. "It's a hobby of mine. I like keeping fit and encouraging other people to as well."

"Ignore her, Robin. The real answer is she gets off on inflicting grievous bodily harm on unsuspecting innocents. She's sadistic."

"I am not."

"Are too."

"So mature, Mae."

"So mature, Mae," she mimicked. I laughed, that woman spent way too much time with her daughter.

"You girls are crazy."

"Only when caffeine deprived. Oh, thank fuck." Mae gratefully took her espresso from the waitress, blew on it to cool it down and took a deep drink.

I waited until her loud moan of appreciation subsided before commenting, "And yes, your program's finished." She clapped her hands, delighted, completely contradicting her earlier comment about my malicious tendencies. "Wanna meet up tomorrow afternoon and go through it together?"

"Sure. Annabelle will be with me, that okay with you?"

"Absolutely."

"Love your work, Riley."

"Hey, that's my line," Robin interjected, grinning at me.

Mae's eyes shifted from Robin's, to mine and back again, a secret smile playing on her lips.

For once she remained silent.

****

I was pleasantly surprised to see Dominic already at the beach when I pulled up later that afternoon. We hadn't made concrete plans to meet again after being relegated to just friends, so I smiled as I walked down the steps toward him. He was the highlight of my day.

No. Scrap that. He was the highlight of my week. And quite possibly month.

Dominic's black shorts hung so low I refused to look at the waistband in fear I'd misstep and break my neck. Only, today he paired them with…

So fucking hot.

A white wife-beater

No words.

Brain splat.

Now, don't ask me why, but for some reason a tank like that on a man like him did wild things to me. My common sense immediately shut down and the wailing sirens of an emergency evacuation alarm sounded in my head. Well, that along with a mass exodus of logic, reason, and intellect out my ear holes.

Whoosh.

Gone.

Thankfully, my legs still worked… Just.

As I approached, Dominic turned around. His eyes widened momentarily and I quickly did a mental check of my outfit, worried I'd picked something horrible. My bright running shorts contrasted well with my favorite cropped black sports top. It had a shallow V-neck at the front and criss-crossed straps at the back. I thought I looked okay before leaving the apartment but the dark expression on Dominic's face suddenly made me second-guess myself.

"Hey," I said.

"Hey."

We were both silent for a minute. I refused to breathe on account of how good he smelled and Dominic stood motionless, glaring out at the translucent ocean. It reflected the endless sky above which was sporadically interspersed with white clouds. The water looked tranquil and the waves gently lapped the shoreline while gulls waded through the shallows. On the whole, the beach appeared atmospherically calm. However, I had the distinct impression the man standing beside me was anything but.

"You okay?"

"Fine."

"Really?"

"Yep."

"You sure?"

"For fuck's sake, Riley. I'm fine."

Right, then.

He stared past me. "Ready?"

"Uh, all right."

We both took off in the direction of the secluded cove behind the rocky outcrop. As we ran along the foreshore, the breeze swept straight hair into my eyes. I pushed it away, just like my thoughts of taciturn Dominic and whatever the heck had crawled up his ass and died. Sadly, it proved ridiculously difficult since I could literally feel the brooding waves of displeasure roll off his body and wash into me like an unstoppable tsunami. He'd never been like this before, granted, we hadn't exactly known each other long, but it still seemed completely out of character.

What the heck have I done?

Half an hour later, we reached the end of the secluded cove. I walked toward the bronzed cliff face that rose high above me and leaned against it, stretching. If Dominic wanted to act like a jerk that was his problem, I wasn't going to let it ruin my runner's high.

While resting my palm against the smooth rock and extending my Achilles, I heard a low whisper over my left shoulder. "Sorry about before."

"It's okay."

"No, it's not." He paused. "Look at me, Riley."

Do I have to? Whatever happened to ignoring the elephant in the room? I'm totally cool with that.

But sighing, I turned to face him.

There was a sincerity in his gaze that made me crave the caged expression he wore earlier.

Whoa.

It wreaked havoc on my panties; the poor scrap of material was now a sodden abomination.

"I was an asshole and you didn't deserve it. I'm sorry."

My chest tightened in response to his words so I focused on breathing instead. And emotionally distancing myself. Definitely that too.

Girl, forget it. He's not the man for you.

Clearing my throat, I changed the subject. "How 'bout we do sit-ups today?"

Dominic scowled, muttering something under his breath as he sat down. His personality replacement was seriously annoying. I mean, what the hell was his problem? He'd never hidden the filth that came out his mouth before and I liked him for that. It was honest. He was honest. In a world filled with people pretending to be someone they weren't, it was a refreshing change, so what could have caused this drastic alteration?

Completely fed up with his attitude, I put clenched hands on hips and towered over him. "Okay, where's Dominic?" Not gonna lie, I loved seeing his breath catch. "What have you done with him?"

"Don't stand with your legs open, I can see up your shorts."

I squealed and gracelessly flopped to the ground like an inebriated flamingo. Dominic threw his head back and deep laughter reverberated off the solid rock behind me, echoing pleasurably through my limbs. Thrilling me. For some reason, I didn't mind him laughing at my expense today, I just wanted to see him smile again.

When the last of his chuckles faded I steeled myself and, ignoring the way my heart began to pound like the percussion section of an orchestra, asked quietly, "What's up with you?"

He looked down, systematically pouring grains of sand through long fingers, refusing to answer. Never had procrastination looked so damn sexy.

"Well?"

When Dominic's eyes met mine, they flashed the brightest blue I'd ever seen. I bit my lip. "I didn't think it'd be this hard. I can't—" But he stopped.

My stomach clenched and I hated myself for it. Just like I hated the way my voice wavered when I asked, "You can't what?"

He paused for a moment, shook his head and then faced me squarely. "Let's workshop a scenario so I can show you."

I gaped at him. As good-looking as he was, the guy was making next to no sense.

Must have left his sanity back in the car park.

"Stand up."

But there was a determination in his voice I hadn't heard before, so warily, I rose to my feet.

Dominic stared at me for a long while, his gaze impenetrable. I just stood there, focused solely on trying to get enough oxygen—it was becoming a regular thing.

After a loud exhale, he shook his head. "Now, pretend you're me, right?"

"Ah—"

"And you haven't blown your load for a few days."

I covered my face with my hands, hating the blush which appeared. "Oh, God."

Gently, he pulled my hands away and gave a devilish smile. My wrists tingled where he touched me. "You're waiting for your friend to show up so you can go for a run. You *really* need this run."

He let go and strode away before turning around to face me, a few yards off. His voice lowered to a seductive murmur, though my clit and I heard him perfectly. "You don't know her that well, but there's something about this girl—" He paused, during which time I came to the conclusion that breathing was overrated.

I watched his Adam's apple bob up and down when he swallowed while staring at me. "She arrives and makes her way down the beach toward you." He deliberately took long, measured steps toward where my feet were anchored in the sand.

My heart thumped.

He's so fucking beautiful.

His eyes darkened. "She's so fucking gorgeous. You know you should look away, but you can't."

He moved closer and liquid heat pooled between my thighs. Again.

He turns me on just by breathing.

He grimaced, adjusting his shorts. "Your cock gets hard just watching her."

With each step, my clit pulsed and throbbed.

This isn't right. I need to stop. Like, now.

Dominic's voice sounded pained. "But friends don't look at each other like that, do they?" He stopped directly in front of me and the fire in his gaze was scorching.

"How fucked up is that?" he murmured. "Wanting to bury yourself so deep inside her, she screams your name. Wanting to own her every breath, every movement, every sound. Wanting her."

I gasped.

Dominic slowly leaned forward and pressed his forehead against mine. His warm breath caressed my skin as I grappled for something to hold onto, his tank would have to do.

Mint, sweat, and Dominic. With God as my witness, there was no better combination.

He shook his head, whispering, "So what do I do, Riley? Because right now, I haven't a damn clue how to be a friend to her."

I closed my eyes and tried to get my shit together. I also tried to stop myself from climbing the man like a jungle gym … and kissing him senseless. Heck, I even attempted to remember what Doctor Powell said about the direct link between previous dysfunctional relationships and my current sense of unworthiness.

Fucking useless.

You see, I couldn't think. At all. My skin burned where he touched me and the heat of our bodies ricocheted and collided until I was certain we were going to detonate then explode.

I have to get out of this. If I don't, my tongue will be in his mouth and my hand will be down his shorts within the next five seconds. Followed closely by mayhem … with havoc right behind. Extricate yourself, Riley.

Now.

After several false starts, I eventually opened my eyes. He was still staring at me and raw hunger pulsed unchecked in his gaze.

So it's true, people really can spontaneously combust. Hope I won't splatter all over his white tank, he looks good in that.

Focus, Riley.

I internally shook, slapped, and then doused myself with a bucket of ice water. After taking a steadying breath, I murmured, "This can't happen, Dominic. It just … it can't."

He was silent for a long time. Finally, he exhaled, nodding slowly. After gently extricating my fingers, Dominic moved away, raking tense hands through tousled hair. He kept his back to me for what felt like ages while I stood there, staring dumbly at him. I would have given everything I possessed to have seen his face in that moment, however, when he at last turned, his expression was blank, empty.

My stomach plummeted. Six stories at least.

What the fuck have I done?

The remainder of our workout and jog back along the beach was done in relative silence. I kept trying to tell myself I'd done the right thing by asking Dominic to ignore our lust for one another. After all, that's what it was, wasn't it? Lust. And what purpose did the emotion serve except to royally fuck up the lives of everyone involved?

I didn't want a bit of it.

No siree.

It just sucked that instead of feeling empowered, I

felt like crap.

Anyway, as we rounded the stairs to the car park, it took an unexpected sight to snap me out of my reticence—the car park was empty except for my convertible. "Where's your car?"

"It's not finished yet."

I stared at him, confused.

"She's at the garage. I'm waiting on the last part to be delivered next week."

I chose to ignore the fact that he referred to his ride as female, the irony was not lost on me. "So, you're a car person." It wasn't a question.

"Among other things." Dominic's smile was dangerous. "Why? What kind of person did you take me for?"

"Trouble."

He laughed. "You're not wrong there."

But then I put my head to one side, scrutinizing him carefully. Yep, there was no denying it, he was the hottest guy I'd ever laid eyes on. I shook my head. "It's strange, I never took you for a car kind of guy. You look more like a…" My eyes raked him up and down.

Delicious.

I cleared my throat. "A musician." Dominic smirked. "I mean, if you swapped those shorts for some black jeans and that," I gestured emphatically to his wife-beater, "for a dark t-shirt, then I'd totally think you were in a band. A badass one."

"Is that so?" Dominic channeled his inner Cheshire cat and the overall effect left me so disoriented I had to look down at my fingers to gather my errant thoughts.

Shit, I'd over-shared.

"For some reason, I say whatever pops into my head around you. Feel free to ignore me."

"Fuck no."

My eyes flicked back to him. His jaw was working hard, and he took a deliberate step toward me. That thing between us sparked again, it was beyond exhausting. And the worst part was, if I didn't distract myself soon we would be tonsils deep before he took his next breath.

I cleared my throat. "How'd you get here, then?"

"My brother, Levi, drove me."

"You mean, there's *two* of you?" Yeah, I may have screeched that last part.

Lord have mercy.

Dominic raised an eyebrow, amused. "Don't even think about it, Riley. Trust me, you're not his type."

Huffing, I crossed my arms in front of my chest. It did very little to intimidate but enhanced my cleavage beautifully. "And what's that supposed to mean?"

His eyes dropped to my breasts as he stepped even closer, lowering his voice until it was nothing more than a seductive murmur. "He likes his women to have … fire."

I shivered, before looking away and mumbling, "I've got fire."

Dominic cupped my face in his strong hands, drawing my gaze back to his and I tried to ignore the way his pulse jumped at the base of his throat before our eyes locked.

"You've got many things, angel, but fire isn't one of them." His hungry gaze roved my face, from my eyes, to my nose, and finally, my parted lips.

I'd forgotten how to breathe—I know, right?—so there was every chance they were blue.

"Riley—"

But he didn't finish because we were interrupted by the arrival of a beat-up old Ford that sounded like the engine was actually scraping against the bitumen beneath it. Dominic stepped away from me and thrust long fingers through his hair. If I hadn't been so busy eyeing the death trap in front of us, I might have wondered why.

"C'mon, asswipe, let's go. We've got sound check in an hour and I can smell you from here."

I stared at the man in the driver's seat. I kid you not, he looked like Dominic's incredibly sexy doppelgänger.

So, this is Levi. Wow.

Levi was smokin' hot, there was no doubt about it. He had the same tousled brown hair, piercing blue eyes and full, kissable mouth as Dominic. While openly ogling him for way longer than politeness dictated, I also noticed he was taller and leaner too. Now don't get me wrong, if I'd met him first, I'd have thought he was ripped but since I'd seen the alternative in all its sweaty, bare-chested glory… I dunno. Dominic struck a fire in my belly, Levi barely lit a spark.

Strange.

"Sound check?"

"He didn't tell you about our gig tonight, did he?" I just stared vacantly at Levi, surprised he couldn't hear the roar of the ocean whistling through my ears.

Dominic and his gorgeous twin brother are in a band. Of course they're in a fucking band. Bet it's a heavy, badass band too.

Sweet. Baby. Jesus.

"Fucking hell, Dom." Levi rubbed frustrated fingers across his brow while the other hand gripped the steering wheel until the whites of his knuckles appeared. I had a feeling this was a common physical response when dealing with his brother.

"I wasn't going to invite her."

I spun on my heel to face Dominic. "Why not?"

But he ignored me. Instead, he glared at his brother who completely disregarded the pointed stare and turned to me. "We're playing a show at The Hole tonight. It'll be the last one we have for a while and you're more than welcome. A word of warning though, if you've got any single friends, keep 'em away from dipshit here."

"Fuck off."

Like Levi, I also ignored Dominic. "Don't worry, Grace would tear him a new one if he tried anything."

"Not likely," Dominic muttered.

"Yeah?" Levi seemed interested.

"Yeah," I replied, disregarding the obscene rumblings on my right. "She doesn't take shit from anyone."

He nodded his head, thoughtful. "Is this friend of yours hot?"

"Stunning."

"I'd like to meet her."

I looked Levi up and down. He was genuine, I could tell. There was a steadiness of character I registered immediately and if he was anything like his brother, he was honest and trustworthy. Well, maybe not with certain female parts but I knew Grace, and that woman could hold her own. What I really liked about him though, was the mocking humor in his eyes that had been lost to my best friend for well over a year. The cogs in my brain began to whirl as a slow smile spread across my face.

"I'd like to introduce her to you."

Chapter Four

Our emotions colliding,
The ocean's too wide,
Keep my head above water,
Breathe for me, love.
—MONDEZ, "Awake"

It only took thirty minutes of outright begging to talk Grace into seeing Dominic's band, Mondez. Apparently, all the guys were related and shared the same last name so they just went with it as a band title. Anyway, I was pretty confident my puppy dog eyes finally sealed the deal. Grace could never say no to my entreating expression or the lingering threat of my academy award-winning sulking skills.

I could mope for days.

Easily.

It was a gift.

But I only brought out the big guns when desperation called for it and this was one of those times.

I tried telling myself we were going to watch them play because I wanted to do right by my best friend. I wanted to get her off the couch, out the house and into the arms of a good man. Like me, she was a homebody who preferred spending time in solitude rather than being surrounded by a sea of faceless people. I could even count on one hand the number of times she'd left our apartment to socialize in the last twelve months. It wasn't healthy. Bottling up that much bitterness and resentment over a broken heart was a recipe for disaster.

At least, that's what I kept telling myself.

As I showered, I tried to ignore the anticipation bubbling up inside me at the thought of seeing Dominic again … and watching him play an instrument like the sex god he was. I shook my head. That guy was the whole package. Okay, except for his gutter-mouth and womanizing ways but I decided to ignore those minor details because it was no business of mine what he said or who he hooked up with.

Truly.

To be honest, a part of me—the rational bit—didn't even know why I wanted to go to The Hole in the first place because he clearly didn't want me there. I wasn't going to let that stop me though, my stubborn streak tended to override logic at times. I guess I just wanted to prove to him that even though we were never going to be anything more than friends, at least I was a friend worth having. After all, who wouldn't want me? I was intelligent, trustworthy, sincere, compassionate—I was best friend material, damn it.

Why doesn't he want me to go?

With that nagging thought in my head, I shimmied into a light blue sleeveless dress. It was one of my favorites, being both comfortable and flattering. The clingy fabric hinted at a modest cleavage without being too revealing, it hugged my ass and hips and was short enough to emphasize toned legs without exposing the lady downstairs. Perfect.

Maybe I said something to offend him?

I slipped on my black ankle boots and carefully thought back over everything which came out my mouth during our run earlier but couldn't remember anything he would have been pissed at. Well, except reminding him to stop thinking with his penis, though that seemed to be the standard topic of conversation where we were concerned.

Maybe he's given up on us being friends?

I wrapped a black plaited leather bracelet around

my wrist and began applying some light makeup, hoping fervently that wasn't the case. I'd come to enjoy spending time with Dominic; he accepted me for who I was and seemed to genuinely like my company. Except when sporadically going all weird on me, of course.

Maybe he thinks I'm boring?

I stopped and my mascara dropped to the tiled bathroom floor, instantly forgotten. That was it. He thought I would be a dead weight so didn't invite me. I gripped the basin, angry. I had been living with this doubt my whole life—plain, boring old Riley. As a teenager, I was the one who sat in the corner at parties, the one who watched other people having the time of their lives because I was so crap at putting myself out there. Turned out, after years of practice, I melded so well into the background, people forgot to invite me at all.

I gritted my teeth. Just because I grew up in a conservative family, didn't drink often, smoke, take illicit drugs or sleep around, didn't mean I couldn't party. Much.

I hung my head.

Fucking hell.

****

Grace hated The Hole. From the moment we walked through the front door, I could tell by her face she wanted to be anywhere else.

Too bad, G. This is for your own good.

Maybe if I said it often enough, I'd start to believe it.

The first thing I noticed about the place was the music. It was loud. Like, residual ear-ringing loud. The pounding drumbeat and edgy guitar riffs pulsed through me like the reverberations of a shockwave.

I loved it.

The second thing I noticed was the clientele.

Wherever I looked, darkly clad, intricately tattooed and heavily pierced band-goers were drinking, yelling, laughing—I craned my neck to see them surrounding a small, raised stage in the corner—thrashing, jumping and moshing.

So this was where the enigmatically beautiful people hid.

My mouth watered.

Thirdly, I noticed Grace's blatant displeasure. Sadly, she hadn't experienced the same overwhelming sense of belonging upon first entering the live music venue as I had, so after looking at her closely and carefully weighing up the pros and cons, I came to a decision. "You need a drink."

I only hoped I wouldn't regret it.

That afternoon, I'd sent a text to Brea informing her that we were going to see Mondez play. She worked part-time at The Hole and her shift finished after their set so we were going to hang out later. I couldn't wait. Well, provided Grace behaved herself and we didn't get kicked out beforehand. Apart from G, Brea was one of my oldest friends. Sadly, between her hours spent studying art design or working and mine spent at the hospital or exercising, we hardly got a chance to catch up anymore. But when we did, it was awesome. That girl was a pocket-rocket, she had energy to burn.

"Riley, you made it."

I gazed down at the pint-sized brunette working behind the bar. With a red and white headscarf tied into a knot at the top of her head, dramatic black eyeliner and a colorful sleeve tattoo, she totally owned the rockabilly style.

"Wouldn't miss this one for the world, Brea." I smiled and gave her a wink. Okay, so I may have mentioned something about Dominic too.

Grace shook her head, that girl could read me like a book. "Now I know this is all a ruse. You dragged me out tonight because you're interested in a guy."

Nope.

No one was offering what I wanted just now and I wasn't about to settle for second best. Heck, I'd even refused the offer of a casual fuck with a man who could win a panty decimating competition through smoldering look alone. Doctor Powell would be proud of me even if my own pussy was presently giving me the cold shoulder. Anyway, there was no rush. I'd meet my soul mate, eventually. If nothing else, being single for the last few months taught me to be unswerving and patient.

What Grace didn't realize, however, was I'd found the perfect man for her—Levi. I knew it as soon as I met him. So, wanting to talk up his many positive attributes I gushed, "He's not just some guy."

Grace actually took a step back, a look of pure disbelief plastered all over her gorgeous face.

Has the woman no faith in me at all?

"Really?" she countered. "How is this one any different to all the rest, Riley? Does he have a chocolate flavored dick or something?"

Now was not the time for crass rhetorical questions, I had to press my advantage while she was still sober. "He's amazing, G. He's talented and funny and clever and—"

"Sexy as hell, or so I've been told."

I spun around, relieved that it was Levi standing behind me and not his brother. It took me a couple of breaths to get my blush back under control and a few more to drum up the courage to say something, after which time I simply threw my arms around him, exclaiming, "*Levi.*"

There was no denying it, being wrapped in Levi's

embrace felt good. Really good. He was tall, solid, strong. His body surrounded mine in a way which made my five-foot-nine frame feel petite and delicate—a refreshing change, let me tell you. But I couldn't ignore that there were no electromagnetic forces drawing me closer, setting me alight, burning—

Cool it, Riley.

I pulled away, only to have Grace mutter in my ear, "Why don't you just shove your tongue down his throat and get it over with?"

What the hell?

I stared at her, confused. But then I figured this biting remark meant she was experiencing emotions she hadn't felt in a gazillion years so I didn't take it personally. What was she feeling then? An attraction toward Levi, perhaps? Perfect. Hoping that was the case, rather than sending her a withering look, I stuck my tongue out at her instead.

Once we'd both recovered from our childish spat, I drew on twenty-two years worth of cultivated politeness and began the introductions. "Levi, this is Grace. Grace, Levi."

But Grace rudely interrupted with, "Drink," before spinning around and leaning against the bar.

There was a moment of awkward silence during which time Levi raised an eyebrow at me. I just shrugged one shoulder. "Never said it was going to be easy. She's worth the trouble though."

He stared at Grace's back for a long while, a contemplative expression on his face. "I believe you," he murmured.

I patted him on the shoulder. "Buy her a whiskey and then hold on to your hat, cowboy, you're in for one hell of a ride." I gave him a wry smile and went to find us all a booth.

After slipping across the cracked leather seat of the last remaining booth, I allowed my gaze to roam The Hole. I'd like to say I was people watching but knew deep down that wasn't the case, like, at all.

I was looking for Dominic.

And after a few minutes of searching, I found him … locked at the lips with a platinum blonde.

Wow. The man has moves.

One of his hands was buried in her hair while the other pressed possessively against the small of her back, arching her into his unyielding frame. Her arms were wrapped around his neck and I was pretty sure she was holding on for dear life. Poor woman, it looked like she was being eaten alive. Not that she was complaining though, I could hear her moans of appreciation from where I sat in the secluded alcove.

When he finally let her breathe again, Dominic whispered something in her ear, took her by the hand and led her into what I guessed was the green room just left of the stage.

Well, then.

Even though he warned me, I still couldn't help the disappointment that washed over me as I observed their retreating forms. I looked down at my hands, they were tightly clasped together in my lap.

No one could say I hadn't been forewarned. Heck, even Levi cautioned me about Dominic's promiscuity. I guess I needed to accept the fact that this was who he chose to be, a connoisseur of women, a player, a lover of pussy. I shook my head.

Why am I finding this so difficult?

As I delved further beneath the layers of disappointment, I felt something else. There it was… Hurt. Dominic's actions hurt me. Granted, he had done it inadvertently, but it still didn't change the way my stomach was churning like a meat grinder. Not five hours ago, he'd called me fucking gorgeous. Not five hours ago, he'd cradled my head in his hands and looked at me as though I was someone worth knowing. And yet here he was, screwing a Barbie impersonator in the dingy green room of a seedy pub.

This sucks balls.

Honestly, what did I expect? A declaration of monogamy because he thought I was attractive? A sparkling diamond because I blush on cue? Never gonna happen. He wasn't that kind of guy, he sure as hell wasn't going to change and it was wrong of me to expect him to.

I took a deep breath.

In lieu of working through these tumultuous emotions rationally, I decided to try something new, and it involved alcohol. Lots and lots of alcohol. Grace was gonna love it.

At that very moment, the woman in question stormed toward the table before plonking herself next to me in a huff. I raised my eyebrows.

"Don't even start," she snapped.

I guess Operation Wingman wasn't going as well as planned.

However, when Levi strolled over not long afterward, the indulgent smile on his face declared otherwise.

Good, there's hope for them yet.

"Here you are, ladies." He handed me a beer—for which I was eternally grateful—and then murmured something to Grace while passing her a whiskey. I didn't catch what it was, I was too busy drinking. In fact, I was too busy begging the alcohol to get me through the night without either bawling my eyes out or having a full-blown panic attack.

When I finally put the empty bottle back on the

table, proving I really could party with the best of them, Levi turned to me. "So, are you looking forward to seeing Mondez play?"

"Absolutely." I smiled. "I've been listening to your music online and really like your sound. I've been talking you guys up to Grace all afternoon and she's really pumped to hear you play too." I turned to her, but she was staring down at her lap. "Isn't that right, Grace?"

She looked up. "Mmm-hmm." The woman hadn't heard a word I said.

Sadly, Levi thought this was hilarious and decided to poke the bear for a bit of fun. Not a good idea. Doing so was like playing Russian roulette, you never knew when Grace was going to explode and when she did… Yikes.

The two faced off in an increasingly heated exchange. I nudged Grace under the table, trying to stop her rant before she got so fired up she blew a fuse. I even tried interrupting their perverted verbal foreplay but neither of them listened to me, they were too wrapped up in each other to take any notice. And it wasn't until Grace yelled at Levi, calling him an egotistical narcissist that I gave up on ever setting my best friend up with anyone ever again.

I dropped my head into my hands.

Can tonight get any worse?

Grace stopped what she was doing, rubbed my back and was halfway through a heartfelt apology when I discovered that yes, it could.

"C'mon, dickwad, we're on in five."

My head snapped up in the direction of that deep voice and I didn't even bother suppressing the gasp that escaped me.

Dominic.

Despite being slightly mussed up, he still looked

like he'd just won the bachelor of the year award. And I could not believe he wore exactly what I said would turn him into a badass rock star—ripped black jeans and a dark t-shirt stretched so tightly over his biceps that the stitching needed reinforcement. For real.

Dominic's eyes flicked from Levi's to mine, widening slightly as recognition hit. But he didn't say anything.

Not a word.

"No worries, Dom." Levi stared pointedly at Grace. "Think I'm done here anyway." He finished his beer, smiled at me and then stood next to his brother. They both turned and walked toward the stage.

Never once looking back.

It reminded me of when I was a teenager.

Grace and I were lying on the plush carpet of my bedroom, listening to heavy music. I stared up at the ceiling, it was covered in posters of famous rock stars, most without their shirts on. I only ever put them up when Mum was away because she would have killed me otherwise. Thankfully, she'd gone to one of those exclusive health spa resorts for the week, apparently she needed to de-stress. I snorted. From what exactly, I had no idea. I mean, it wasn't as though she did anything except host extravagant parties and complain about my shortcomings.

Anyway, Mum once lectured me about how the adhesives used to stick the posters to the roof were unsightly, peeled the paint off, et cetera, et cetera. Long story short, I wasn't allowed to put them up. A load of crap if you ask me. All it did was force me into a life of duplicity because when she was home, I played dutiful daughter and when she went away, I didn't.

"So, what did he say?"

I turned to look at Grace. "Nothing."

"Seriously?"

"Seriously."

"That fucker. When I see him at school on Monday, he's a dead man." We were both quiet for a moment. *"Are you okay?"*

My gaze returned to my favorite poster. It was of a lead guitarist whose face was in deep concentration as he rocked back on his heels, his fingers deftly playing the nickel plated steel strings as though he was born to do it.

"Well, with all the practice I've had with Dad, you'd think I'd be used to feeling invisible by now." My voice lowered. *"But it still hurts. I mean, I know we were only dating for four months but now it's over..."* I paused. *"I dunno, he acts like I don't even exist."*

"Asshole."

"I guess it all meant nothing to him... I meant nothing."

Grace's arm reached out and her hand found mine. "You mean the world to me, Riley."

Through my tears, I smiled.

I was shocked out of my reverie by a loud *boom*. Grabbing Grace's hand, I dragged her toward the stage. There was no way I could even begin to explain how mind-blowing Mondez's set was. Simply put, their music was *insane*. The Hole wasn't a large venue by any means, but the entire place suddenly went crazy as soon as the opening bars of their first song began and an ocean of writhing bodies instantly appeared in front of the stage.

I think it was the constant contradictory melodies which did it. The music those guys belted out was obscure yet distinct, gentle yet brutal, melodic yet raucous. Honestly, I couldn't keep up so I didn't even try. I just mutely stood next to Grace, at a safe distance from the mosh pit, letting it all wash over me.

Holy. Shit.

And of course, my eyes instinctively moved to Dominic. How could they not? The guy went above and beyond every teenage rock star fantasy I'd ever had.

Damn it.

I didn't want to admire the way his skillful fingers dexterously slid up and down the fret board of his electric guitar. I didn't want to ogle the way he ruthlessly shredded the strings or seemed so lost in the epicurean sounds that his eyes looked past the frenzied crowd and stared into the darkness beyond. But I couldn't help it, I was lost. So much so that my mouth actually popped open in shock.

He's so fucking talented.

It didn't excuse his rudeness toward me earlier though.

I shifted my gaze to Levi—man, he could really sing. His vocals deviated between softly crooning and outright screaming. I snuck a quick look at Grace, she was pinned to the spot with an equally shocked expression on her face.

Awesome. Operation Wingman has successfully passed phase one.

Smiling, my eyes moved back to the drummer. He rhythmically pummeled the skins with flailing wooden sticks, his powerful, inked arms whirling so fast they became a blur. And then there was the bass player, a muscular guy with so many piercings I was surprised he hadn't sprung a leak. Don't get me wrong, they really suited him. The guy looked as sexy as all hell and the way he plucked the strings of his cobalt instrument should have been illegal.

Why aren't these guys signed to a major label? What the heck are they doing in a small bar in Dunsborough when they could easily fill stadiums across the country with their live sound?

It made no sense.

After almost an hour, the final bars of their last song faded and the audience went crazy. Completely, utterly, batshit crazy. Entranced, I watched as Dominic carefully stored his guitar away, gave Levi a congratulatory thump on the back, grinned at the other two band members and then jumped off the stage.

Into a swarm of women.

My eyes narrowed as manicured nails raked his sweat-soaked t-shirt, grasping hands slid up his arms, cosmetically enhanced breasts pressed against his pecs, and pouting lips murmured… I didn't even want to know what.

The thought alone made me sick.

"Weren't they amazing?" Brea suddenly materialized beside me. "They make me wild every damn time. What did you think, Riley?"

I tried to say something, really I did, but no sound was forthcoming so I shook my head instead.

"They're gonna be huge one of these days and then watch out everyone, they'll take over."

She wasn't wrong there.

Thankfully, my mind finally kicked back into gear and I was about to ask Grace what she thought of Mondez when the words died on my tongue. The girl looked like she'd seen a ghost. Her skin was pale, her eyes were wide—this wasn't the G I knew. However, before I could question what was wrong, she blurted, "Riley, you'll be all right with Brea if I go grab some air outside, won't you?"

Brea threw an arm around my waist declaring that she would look out for me and a split second later, Grace disappeared. Rather than answer my questioning gaze though, Brea shepherded me toward the bar with a mischievous glint in her eyes.

I had no idea what the deal with Grace was, but knew for certain she wasn't getting some air. As Brea and I leaned against the bar waiting to be served, I asked, "Do you think Grace is okay? Maybe I should go find her?"

"Riley, I'm sure she's fine. She's a big girl and can look after herself. Besides, no one would mess with her, she'd dismember them if they tried."

I nodded absently.

"Now, let's celebrate finally being able to hang out with…" she drew out the word until it sounded like a verbal drum roll, "tequila shots."

"Oh, God."

Three disgusting, battery acid-tasting shots later, I started swaying so violently Brea went in search for a booth so I could sit down. Ironically, I was in charge of getting another round of drinks to take back with me. Never one to question another's logic, especially while drunk, I made my way through the throng of people with two overflowing shot glasses in my hands. As I stumbled and staggered through the crowd, I came to the conclusion that my present physical state was midway between happy drunk and downright messy.

For once, I didn't care.

While maneuvering my way past endless groups of rowdy drinkers, I scanned the room searching for Brea. Sadly, I didn't see her. I did, however, see Dominic … kissing yet another blonde, though this time directly in front of me. Cursing under my breath, I made to detour around them, only tripped on my own lagging feet and accidentally spilled one of the tequila shots all over the miniskirt of *blonde number two*.

She broke away from Dominic, angry. "Hey, watch it."

I mumbled something vaguely comparable to, *sorry* before turning on my heel and stumbling back to the bar for a refill.

After being given a replacement, I was about to begin yet another search for Brea when a strong hand clasped my wrist, stopping me. "How many drinks have you had?"

I glared up at Dominic. "Do I know you?"

"Riley, you need water, not another fuckin' tequila shot."

"Oh, so we're talking now, are we?" I slopped the drinks back on the bar and turned to face him. "Good, because I've got something to say to you."

Wow, Drunk Riley has lady balls.

I poked him in the chest with my index finger, I swear, the man was made from marble. "You, Dominic Mondez," I leaned in close, "are mean." Despite my inebriation, I didn't miss the way his piercing blue eyes softened at my bold accusation. Or the way he still smelled of mint and ... sex. Straightening up again, I stuck my chin out and declared, "I don't associate with mean people." With that, I flipped my long hair over one shoulder, grabbed the shot glasses and pushed past him.

Smooth exit, Riley.

A few steps later, I was once again no closer to finding Brea.

That woman needs a flare gun.

Frustrated, I stood on my tiptoes, wobbling horrendously. I craned my neck, searching left and right only to be almost knocked to the ground by the unexpected thrashing arms of the guy standing next to me—I think he was air drumming. Two strong hands gripped my hips, steadying me before I unceremoniously landed on my ass.

"I've got you," Dominic murmured in my ear.

Yes. Yes, he did.

A searing warmth radiated from where he stood

behind me and I fought the instinctual urge to relax back into him. It would be so easy, it would feel so—

Don't do it, Riley.

I shook my head and the room swam, but even in my present state I wasn't going to become *blonde number three*. However, politeness dictated some kind of recognition for his magical hands so I mumbled to the empty space in front of me, "Thanks."

"You're welcome." I could hear him smile. Jerk.

"I'm still angry with you."

"I know."

"And you're still holding me."

"I know."

We were both silent. I took the opportunity to get the rampaging conga line dancing its way down my spine back under control, while Dominic... Well. Who the fuck knew?

Anyway, it wasn't long before the alcohol I consumed declared censorship of my internal monologue a crap idea. "Why'd you do it?"

He paused. "Do what?"

"Ignore me."

Dominic sighed and took a step forward so our bodies touched, no, *aligned*. We fit together perfectly and the realization made my tear ducts go gangbusters. I blinked—many, many times—and even though his heart thundered against my shoulder, Dominic's voice was hard. "I'm an asshole, Riley. The sooner you realize that, the better."

"No, you're not." I looked down.

Funny, I could have sworn I only had two legs an hour ago.

His hands slid from my hips to splay across my stomach, pushing my ass flush against him. My head automatically fell back onto his chest and I fought the urge to moan.

"I fucked a woman before the set whose name I can't even remember." His voice was harsh in my ear. "And I was about to get my dick wet again before you interrupted me." Somehow his bitter laugh wreaked havoc on my knees, I really didn't want to analyze why. "Still wanna be friends, angel?"

"Yes."

He stilled.

"Then you're a fool."

I shook my head.

Despite Dominic's many faults, I knew he was a good man. There was an integrity I connected with when we first met and, even though there was no explaining how damaged it was or how far beneath the other complexities it lay, I knew it was there.

Waiting.

I honestly had no idea what caused Dominic to hide this part of himself from the world. I didn't understand why he preferred a string of meaningless flings to a serious relationship. He was putting up a false front—to protect either himself or me, I wasn't yet certain. But what I could be sure of was the need to remind this complicated man of his own self-worth. Luckily, I was just the woman to do it. Hormones be damned.

"I'm not a fool, Dominic. I see you."

Dominic lowered his mouth until it skimmed over my exposed shoulder, sending shockwaves across my skin. "You *see* me, do you?" He chuckled. "Do you see me hurting you, Riley? Do you see me fucking with the heart of the purest woman I've ever had the misfortune to meet?" His lips caressed my neck. "'Cause I will. Whether I mean to or not, I'll ruin you." Dominic buried his face in my hair, breathing deeply and I swear to God,

I almost orgasmed on the spot. "You deserve better than a fuckup like me."

"You're not a fuckup."

His hands tightened against my stomach. "Never heard you swear before. Not gonna lie, it's making me hard."

"You're not a fuckup, Dominic," I repeated, vainly ignoring his growing bulge as it pressed against the small of my back. "You're a better man than you give yourself credit for. For some reason you can't see it but I can, I can see what you are. I can see you."

He stopped and was silent for a long time. Each of his soft breaths cooled my flushed skin. Then, the briefest burn of his lips branded my collarbone and I shivered.

"Thanks."

"You're welcome. Now, can you please help me find Brea? I really need to sit down."

Chapter Five

I can still feel it ... us,
Not looking but it's all I ever find.
—MONDEZ, "Stranger"

I didn't remember much after that. Vague, foggy memories came and went like wisps of white smoke amidst impenetrable blackness. At some point, I could have sworn Brea, Dominic and I laughed at some random thing on my phone, though at what exactly, I couldn't say. Then I remembered Levi's wet t-shirt, but my thoughts were too murky to turn that tenuous concept into a logical conclusion. However, just before I passed out, I distinctly experienced an overwhelming sense of completeness. I just wish I knew what it was from because I'd never felt anything like it and would have chased that sensation to the ends of the earth if given half the chance.

Doctor Powell was going to crucify me. Escapism is never the answer, she had said. No matter how much I tried to distract myself, sooner or later I'd have to do it. I'd have to face my demons, deconstruct them until their scary parts became nothing more than boring segments and then move the heck on.

Hmm.

Maybe tomorrow.

"Are you fucking blind as well as deaf?"

Grace was awake.

Her raised voice sent a stabbing pain through my head which prompted a throbbing fanfare to spring to life behind my eyes. Grimacing, I rolled onto my side and then gratefully swallowed some aspirin and water she must have left for me. Judging by the muffled sounds coming from the kitchen, she had a visitor and an unwanted one if her previous exclamation was anything to go by.

Gingerly, I sat up. The room swam so my hands gripped the cool Egyptian cotton sheets, steadying me as I waited for it to slow down enough so I could stand without falling over. I needed to get out there. God only knew what was going to happen to our poor guest otherwise.

After slipping on a cream silk robe, I wandered into the kitchen but then stopped short. "Levi, hey. I thought I heard voices."

Surely, my head was playing tricks on me. I could have sworn Grace and Levi were holding hands a second ago. Shaking my head and instantly regretting it, I tried to smile through the pounding pain. "In fact, I could have sworn I heard *raised* voices." Grace ignored my pointed look. "So figured G had a visitor who needed rescuing."

Levi grinned back. In a red body-hugging t-shirt and faded blue jeans, he was one very attractive guy.

Sigh.

How can he possibly look this good after a massive night? I'm pretty certain I'm sporting raccoon eyes and an eighties perm here.

I ran fingers through my knotted hair.

"Hey, Riley. Thanks, but Grace here is nothing I can't handle." He then turned and winked at G, I would have laughed out loud at his audacity if given the assurance it wouldn't split my head open.

What happened next was... strange.

I mean, it was obvious there was a strong connection between Grace and Levi. In fact, Grace was trying so hard to assume an air of nonchalance it only served to make her feelings for the man more noticeable. She might as well have held up a banner declaring, *Levi,*

79

take me now. However, something was holding her back, and for the life of me I couldn't figure out what it was. Sadly, it was also obvious I was playing the awkward role of third wheel.

Long story short, Grace was going to make Levi a coffee—in our stifling hot apartment—so I offered him a nourishing smoothie instead. God only knew I needed the vitamins, though wasn't looking forward to the racket of the machine or my subsequent agony that would undoubtedly ensue. Anyway, Levi refused, Grace went all weird and then death-marched herself back to her bedroom.

I know, right?

So that left Levi and me once again gawking at each other, I think it was going to become a regular thing.

"What was that all about?"

"She wants me," Levi replied. "But is fighting it. Fuckin' doing my head in."

"Grace seems to have that effect on a lot of people." I thought for a moment, the aspirin must have kicked in because it didn't hurt at all. "Want me to put in a good word for you?"

"Could you?" His eyes were so wide and hopeful I laughed.

"Sure."

"We'll name our first born after you."

I held up placating hands. "Whoa, you might want to chill the heck out, Levi. You only met the girl last night."

He stood up straight, his blue eyes bright. Reckon he must have been a good two inches taller than Dominic. "I can't describe it, Riley. There's this thing between us, you know? It's like..." he paused. "It's like I've been asleep my whole life and I'm only just starting to wake up." He shrugged. "Now my eyes are open, all I can see is her."

I stared back at him, stunned.

Wow.

He nodded and was silent for a moment before changing the subject. "I'd better go. I've got a paper to finish and my teacher placement to prepare for."

My eyes widened. "You're studying teaching?"

"Yep."

"You know Grace is a high school teacher, right?"

"Sure do."

Shaking my head, I murmured, "Small world."

Levi smiled. "I left your phone on the coffee table in the lounge room."

"Uh, thanks? Didn't even know I lost it."

"I'm not surprised." He winked and right on cue, I blushed. "Dom found it, you must have left it in the booth last night. I wanted an excuse to see Grace again, so he gave it to me to return to you."

"Oh, that was, ah, nice of him." I tried not to let my disappointment show. As awesome as it was seeing Levi, I would have much preferred waking up to Dominic instead. Not that I was going to delve into the reasons why, ignorance was bliss and all that.

After Levi left, and I talked a surly Grace into giving him a chance, I flopped on the couch, absentmindedly scrolling through my phone. Suddenly, I stopped. Sitting bolt upright, I exclaimed to no one in particular, "What the hell?" Blinking, I stared closer at the screen and because curiosity always got the better of me, pressed *Dial.*

After a couple of rings, a familiar voice rumbled, "I was wondering when you were gonna call, angel."

My toes curled. "Bootycall? You put your phone number under the name Bootycall?"

His chuckle made my breath catch. "Well, the

offer's there if you ever want to take me up on it." His voice deepened. "Do you get horny when you're hung over? I know I do."

Clenching my thighs together, I countered, "That hardly counts, Dominic. You're horny all the time."

He laughed again. "You're not wrong there."

Internally, I moaned because all this innuendo was doing my head in. I really needed an orgasm, like, pronto. Just not from Dominic, oh no, I wanted some release from a nice, steady guy who only slept with one woman per night—me. Was that really too much to ask?

Apparently so.

I shook my head and, not wanting Dominic to notice how much his vocal cords were affecting my nether regions, snapped, "By the way, this isn't a conversation friends usually have."

"How 'bout we make our own rules about what constitutes friends, huh?"

Damn it, the man had a point. Though I would not give him the satisfaction of saying it out loud; a girl had her pride after all.

"I'll take your silence as a yes." He paused. "You up for a run later? If we're not gonna fuck, I need a run."

Taking a steadying breath, I considered my plans for the rest of the day. "I'm meeting a friend in a little while but can catch up with you afterward. I mean, if you want?" Yeah, that question came out a billion times needier than I intended.

"I want."

Ignoring the way those two words made my belly flip and somersault, we agreed on a time and I hung up. The less I heard his teasing voice in my ear, the better. In fact, it reminded me of an earlier time when another playful voice turned my world upside down, only not in a good way.

"So, how was your day?" I was lazing outside my parents' house by the pool, exam revision notes long forgotten. After all, studying midwifery was a lot more confronting than I expected and there were only so many images of vaginal prolapses I could take. One foot dangled languidly in the cool water as I twirled a strand of hair around my index finger.

"Frickin' awesome. That's why I called."

I smiled. Paul was always so excitable and in the eight months we had been together, he'd started phone conversations by impersonating an overexcited chimp no less than twenty-five times. It was usually because he had discovered a new university course he wanted to study or a new instrument he wanted to play. The guy was a perpetual drifter, he never settled on anything for long and even though it was frustrating at times, it also meant our time together was never boring.

"Yeah?" I asked. "What is it?"

"I'm moving to Canada."

"What?" I sat bolt upright and then had to steady myself on the sandstone brick edging so as not to fall in the pool.

"I know, right?" He laughed, and for once it didn't warm my stomach. Instead, it made my insides churn. Painfully.

"I can't believe it either. But then I thought to myself, life's too short, you know? Fuck, I could be dead tomorrow, Riley."

I shook my head. It felt like my feet were snagged on riverbed reeds and instead of releasing myself from their clutches, I was becoming so entangled they dragged me underneath the water.

"How long are you going for?" My voice was so hollow I was surprised it didn't echo back at me.

"Not sure. Six months, maybe a year. Was

thinking of heading over to Europe afterward."

"But Paul," my voice was quiet, "what about us?"

"What do you mean?"

Ouch.

"Well, what about our relationship?"

He paused and the silence on his end of the line was deafening. Finally, he muttered, "I knew you'd be like this. I knew you wouldn't be happy for me."

"Paul, I am happy. I just—"

"Look, it's something I've always wanted to do, all right? This negativity of yours is draining my positive energy, it's bringing me down."

"But, I'm not. I—"

"You know what, Riley? Now that I think about it, you're not the girl I thought you were." He took a deep breath and then slowly exhaled. "I think we should cool it for a bit."

"What?"

"Yeah." He sighed. "I'll see you around." And he hung up.

I stared down at the phone in my hand, trying to make sense of the last five minutes of my life.

Forty minutes later, I still hadn't figured it out. I was still perched on the edge of the pool, gazing confusedly at my phone while wishing the intermittent Low Battery notification held the answer. Over and over again, a single question circled my muddled brain.

What the fuck just happened?

* * * *

"Oh, my God, you're killing me, Riley. I'm actually dying here."

"You're not dying, Mae." I rolled my eyes. "If you've got energy to complain, then I'm not working you hard enough. One more set and we're done."

"I hate you," she said in between pants while struggling through her final round of burpees.

"You'll thank me when you can get through this program without breaking a sweat."

She mumbled something obscene under her breath which I tactfully chose to ignore and a couple of minutes later, we were both sitting in the sand. Mae had a sports towel draped over her shoulders and was guzzling from her water bottle; the poor woman looked completely exhausted. After glancing across at Annabelle, she commented, "Don't know how I'm gonna pry that dinosaur off her when we get to the car."

"She can take it with her." I smiled. "And next week, she can bring it back to swap for something else." My gaze took in the mountain of toys to our right. "There's plenty to choose from."

"Using the kid as a bargaining tool, I see." I smirked. "Clever tactic." Mae stood, albeit gingerly. "Here, let me help you carry this stuff. When we get home, Annabelle's gonna watch cartoons while my bath and I have some alone time."

We packed up the sunshade, toys and training equipment before lugging them to my black convertible. After quickly filling the trunk, we then shoved the rest of my things into the back seat. Once done, we moved to Mae's car and set about wrangling a squirming Annabelle into her booster seat. With a satisfied sigh, Mae finally shut the door, turned around, and then gave a low whistle. "Hot damn, sex on legs at stud o'clock."

"Huh?" I glanced in the direction her gaze was fixed and stilled. Dominic stepped out of Levi's car and looked… Yeah. Fucking amazing didn't even begin to cover it. Levi maneuvered his beaten-up Ford out of the parking bay and waved to me as he sped past. I self-consciously waved back.

Mae turned to me, her dark eyes incredulous. "You know them?"

"A little." I tried to ignore the way my heart skipped a beat as Dominic sauntered toward us. His sandy-brown hair was just the right side of tousled, his eyes that perfect shade of blue. He wore a white t-shirt that did nothing to hide the rippling muscles beneath and black shorts that hung oh so deliciously low. But it was the animalistic, predatory way he moved that had me grasping for something to hold onto and preferably before I fell over. I blinked. The car door handle would have to do.

Nothing to see here, people, I'm just casually gripping the door of Mae's car like my life depends on it.

He stopped in front of me, a dangerous grin forming when he took in my expression—dazed, aroused, confused? I honestly couldn't be sure.

"Hey."

"Dominic, um, hey."

Wow, that didn't sound shrill at all.

I swallowed. "This, ah, is my friend, Mae and this," I indicated to the little girl who was in the process of squishing her new stuffed dinosaur against the window, "is Annabelle."

Mae stepped forward. "Why hello there, handsome."

Dominic's smile widened.

"Sadly, they were just leaving."

"We were?" Mae looked so disappointed, I almost laughed.

"You were. Unless you and Annabelle would like to join us for a run?"

Mae screwed up her nose in disgust. "Hell no." Smiling appreciatively up at Dominic she murmured, "It was very nice meeting you." I gazed heavenward but Mae just moved past and gingerly lowered herself into the drivers' seat. Once settled, she turned to me. "We'll talk tomorrow." Her pointed you're-gonna-tell-me-every-last-juicy-detail-about-whatever-the-heck-is-going-on-between-that-hot-guy-and-you look made me groan.

"Looking forward to it."

Once Mae had driven off, Dominic's gaze shifted to my black convertible. The tan canvas roof was on but bulged in the strangest of places. It looked like a slater bug with boils.

"What the fuck's all that?"

"I'm helping Mae improve her fitness but she can't focus on the program I've drawn up for her if she's too busy chasing after Annabelle the whole time." I shrugged one shoulder. "So, I decided to buy a few things to keep the girl occupied."

"You bought an entire toy store."

My smile was sheepish. "I might have got a bit carried away, yes."

"You think?"

I threw up my hands. "So I wanted to be prepared, sue me. How am I to know what a three-year-old likes? I'm no expert."

Dominic swallowed with effort and the blood drained from his face. "That kid was three?"

"Yeah." I stepped forward, placing a hand on his bicep. "Hey, are you all right?" Something was off. Way off. Like, a-bucket-of-prawns-left-in-the-sun-all-day off.

He stood as though frozen, his eyes staring unseeingly over the top of my head. When at last he spoke, his voice was hard. "Wanna do sprints today?"

I dropped my hand and stepped back, confused. "Sure." But then smiled. "If you think you can catch me."

His gaze returned to mine and gradually thawed as it raked my body from head to toe. A lazy smile appeared as he drawled, "Reckon I'm up for the challenge."

He did not just incinerate my panties. Honest.

Forty-five minutes later, Dominic and I both collapsed onto the sand, breathless.

"Fuck, I needed that." He panted, looking over to where I lay next to him. "Still couldn't keep up with you though."

I grinned back, too puffed to say anything as I basked in his sweaty glory.

"Wasn't sure you'd be up for a run today after all that tequila you drank last night."

Groaning, I threw one arm over my eyes. "Don't remind me."

"What were you trying to prove, anyway?"

I froze.

"Well?"

When I finally took my arm away and looked at him, Dominic had moved into sitting position and was staring down at me expectantly. But he was too still, his eyes too intent, and to be perfectly frank, it kinda freaked me out.

Struggling upright, I brushed the sand off my back and shoulders, refusing to meet his gaze.

"You gonna answer me?"

"Not if I can help it," I muttered, drawing knees to my chest and staring down at the space in front of me. I really didn't want to go through this with him. Not now. Not ever.

Dominic repositioned himself so his legs were either side of the human-sized ball I was impersonating. Meaning, I couldn't keep my gaze trained where it was previously because then I would be eyeballing his... I flushed and peeked up at him from beneath my lashes.

And then my breath caught.

Whoa.

His face was so close.

And I mean, really, really close.

Kissing distance, close.

How can one man be so attractive? It's really not fair to the rest of humanity.

"As a friend, I wanna know."

I rolled my eyes, thankful for the reminder. "So now you're playing the friend card."

He shrugged, smiling. "When it suits me, yeah." Nudging my leg with his knee, he ordered, "Quit with the stalling and tell me why you wanted alcohol poisoning so bad."

"I don't know," I mumbled, looking away.

Dominic's fingers clasped my chin, forcing me to look at him. "Tell me." The heady combination of his touch on my skin and low voice in my ear made me groan—in exasperation, mind you, nothing else.

It was useless.

Like Doctor Powell, he was not going to let me avoid an awkward conversation, I had to pull up my big girl panties and plow right on through. Self-preservation be damned.

"Fine," I declared, batting his hand away. "But don't you dare judge me."

The corners of his mouth twitched while I attempted to collect my thoughts. Only I couldn't because with each passing second I grew more and more nervous. My hands turned clammy, my stomach cramped. In all seriousness, it felt like someone was squeezing my rib cage in the hopes my head would pop off like a champagne cork.

Breathe, Riley.

I took a moment, braced myself and then blurted, "The whole night was a complete disaster. You acted like an ass, Grace disappeared and Brea kept shoving shots down my throat. I wanted to forget everything for a while, hell, I even wanted to escape myself. Sometimes I get so sick of being plain and boring old Riley, you know? For the first time in my life I wanted to be spontaneous and fun, I wanted to … party."

Dropping my head to my knees, I moaned, "God, even to my own ears it sounds lame. This is so embarrassing."

Dominic paused for a moment while I seriously considered burying myself alive in the sand. "Let me see if I've got this right, you were having a shit night so you decided to get completely wasted?"

"Pretty much, yeah."

"How'd that work out for you?"

"It sucked."

Dominic chuckled.

"I don't even remember half of what happened and woke up this morning feeling like my head was about to implode."

"Look at me."

"Can't."

"Riley."

I shook my head.

His fingers gently lifted my chin. Our eyes connected and there it was, that pulsing energy radiating between us, drawing me closer.

If I leaned in just a little more…

"What am I going to do with you, angel?" His voice was soft and I couldn't stop staring at his lips. "There's no fuckin' way you're plain or boring. No. Fucking. Way. Man, just looking at you makes my cock twitch." I gasped, and he swallowed. "Ease off on the drinking, okay?"

"Okay."

If he keeps looking at me like that, I'll agree to anything. Not good.

I blinked and broke away. "I'd better go."

Dominic stood and held out his hand to me just like the first time we met. And I took it, like I did that day, though this time was prepared for the sharp tug as he pulled me upward. I didn't land face first in his chest, but was pretty close.

Not that I minded.

Tentatively, I gazed up at him. "You're not going to tease me for what I said or for the way I acted?"

He looked past me. "Why would I? We've all done stupid stuff we're not proud of." His eyes found mine again. "But you need to behave yourself from now on."

My voice turned bitter. "Shouldn't I be saying that to you? I might not remember much from last night, but I definitely recall you hooking up with not one but *two* women."

He dropped his hands, shoving them deep into the pockets of his shorts. "Save your breath, Riley, that shit's wasted on me."

Before I could think better of it, I reached out and skimmed my fingers down both sides of his face, cradling his strong jaw between my hands. The bristles of his stubble tickled my palms as I gazed at him steadily. "Be good, Dominic."

A flurry of emotions far too quick to identify flashed across his features. After a low growl, Dominic wrapped me in his arms and I snaked my arms around his neck, breathing in the sweaty, intoxicating scent of him like some mad woman. I never wanted him to let me go, I wanted to stay protected in his embrace until the world stopped spinning and life made a heck of a lot more sense.

But it didn't, and he did.

Chapter Six

Everything shifts,
I'm not satisfied.
I wear this mask,
My perfect disguise,
You won't know the truth,
It's my moment.
—MONDEZ, "Rules"

"So, you guys meet up in the afternoons, get all hot and sweaty but don't screw each other's brains out?"

I stared down at my peppermint tea. "We're just friends, Mae."

She guffawed. "Riley, Dominic's a poster boy for triple orgasms." She leaned across the table. "And he looks at you like you're his last meal."

I rubbed my tired eyes. In truth, I had been up most of the night trying to figure out what to do about Dominic. Since meeting him, I'd ridden a roller coaster of emotions. All of them exhausting. I mean, we both knew there was a strong attraction between us, but neither could give the other what they wanted. And even though we were slowly navigating our way through the uncharted territory of friends without benefits, that pesky magnetic pull kept forcing us to push the boundaries a bit further each time. If I wasn't careful, I was going to lose my heart to the guy and that was bad, really bad.

"Nothing's gonna happen between us, Mae. It just … can't."

"Why not? You're single, he's single, you've got a vagina, he's got a penis. I really can't see the issue here."

After taking a sip of tea, I put it back down and

squared my shoulders. "He never goes back for seconds."

"What?"

"You heard me, he never goes back for seconds."

The bitch threw her head back and laughed.

"I'm serious, Mae. Dominic never sleeps with the same woman twice, he told me so the first day we met." I played with my cup. "And I'm not gonna start something that's already got an expiration date. I mean, what's the point? It'll only mess with my head." I tapped my temple with an index finger.

Mae sobered and then sighed. "Oh, honey. You still seeing Doctor Powell?"

I nodded.

"When's your next appointment?"

"Sometime next week. Can't remember when exactly but it's saved in my phone."

"Okay then." She paused. "What does Grace think about Dominic?"

Refusing to meet her eyes, I mumbled, "She, um, doesn't know much about him."

After a solid minute of silence, I braved a peek at Mae. Yeah, she didn't look impressed. "You've been hiding this from her?"

"I wouldn't say hiding exactly, that's a pretty strong word." I searched the room, hoping to find an answer for my reticence toward Grace somewhere in the gaudy orange floral prints that hung haphazardly on the white walls of the hospital cafe. Nothing.

My gaze shifted back to Mae. "I told her about first running into him on the beach but after that…"

"You know why you haven't told her, don't you?"

"Because I'm a horrible best friend?"

"No, because Grace would tell you to get your head out of your ass and face reality. If you can't have casual sex and be done with it, then Dominic isn't the guy for you. And why the hell would you hang around him as a friend? That shit's just cruel."

I put my head in my hands. "I know."

"So, what are you going to do?"

Inhaling a deep breath, I placed my palms flat on the table and stared at them. "I'm going to take a step back."

"Good girl."

"I'll put some distance between Dominic and me, ease out of this mess before I get in too deep."

She nodded in agreement but then suddenly paused, her eyes lighting up. "That's *it*. I'm a fucking genius."

I didn't trust the look on her face, not one bit, it always led to trouble.

"You're going to date."

"I, um, what?"

"You're going to date. Think about it, Riley, distraction is key here, and what better way to divert some attention away from your kryptonite than with another man? Preferably one between your legs."

"Oh, no. Mae, I—"

"That way, when you eventually see Dominic again, he won't have such a hold over you. Do you know why?"

I shook my head, my mind reeling.

"Because you'll be with a guy who's not a complete clusterfuck, you'll be with a guy who is boyfriend material."

Mae tapped her pursed lips with a finger, musing, "Now, who can I set you up with?"

I stood abruptly and stared at her. "Look, I know you're just trying to help but trust me, this isn't the way to do it. You're only adding to my problems."

But she continued musing as though I hadn't

spoken. "Hmm, Neil from ER? I'm pretty sure he's straight—"

"Mae."

"Peter's always had a thing for you—"

"*Mae.*"

The mischief in her eyes was unmistakable. "Bingo."

I leaned forward, glaring at her. "No. No set-ups. No awkward first dates. No forced conversations. Nothing."

"Hi, Robin." Her singsong voice rang out over the coffee shop. Gripping the back of my chair, I hung my head with a barely suppressed groan. Footsteps approached, but I refused to look up.

Maybe if I stare at the table long enough it'll swallow me whole?

"Hey, girls."

Any minute now, table.

"Thank God you're here, Robin." I looked up and narrowed my eyes at Mae but she ignored me. Vixen. "We've got a situation and you're just the man to help."

"I am?" He looked between both of us, confused.

"You are."

I swore under my breath.

"You see," Mae folded her hands on the table top, like she was chairing a goddamn charity meeting or something. "Riley was telling me about this hot new dessert bar opening up on Geographe Bay Road, only I can't go with her this Friday like we'd planned because something's come up."

"Okay." Robin's gaze shifted between Mae's scheming expression and my apologetic one.

"Is there any chance you could take Riley?"

Robin looked at me.

C'mon portal to another dimension, open up,

open up. Damn it, where are you when I need you?

"I was going to ask her out to dinner at Salt, but if she'd prefer dessert at Cacao, then that's fine with me." He smiled.

"You were?" I croaked.

Mae clapped her hands in excitement and a dimple appeared on Robin's left cheek. I'd never noticed it before; it was cute. "I was."

"Oh."

I'm pretty sure my face is the color of a stop sign here.

"Would you like to go to Cacao with me on Friday night, Riley?"

My stomach did that little flip thing and I couldn't help the smile which teased the corners of my mouth. "Yeah, I'd like that. Thanks."

He took one of my hands, his thumb skimming over my knuckles. "How about I pick you up at eight?"

"Great."

"I'll get your details later in the week, okay?"

I nodded. "Okay."

He looked at me for a moment longer, his hazel eyes searching. I wondered what he saw, amazement? Confusion? Gratitude? Thankfully, whatever was there seemed to please him because he gave me a lopsided grin, squeezed my fingers and murmured, "I'd better let you get back to work."

Nodding wordlessly, I retrieved my hand and turned to walk toward the elevators as though in a dream. It was only when I stepped inside and pressed the button for the second floor that I realized Mae had already left.

Her next workout was going to make prison camp feel like a school dance.

****

Sadly, my natural high from the combination of

scoring a date with Robin and the successful launch of Operation Dominic Detox was short lived. As soon as I ended my shift, stepped outside and lifted my face to the afternoon sun, my phone rang.

Shit.

It was Mum.

Sighing, I answered it, though not even ten minutes later, sorely wished I hadn't. "Mum, hi. What's up?"

"Riley, you need to come home straight away." That woman was a theater director's dream, even Moliere himself would have tipped his debonair hat at her melodramatic skills.

I sighed, steeling myself for the character role of evil villain to her innocent martyr.

"I think I'm dying."

Rolling my eyes, I asked, "Again? What are your symptoms this time?" I wasn't in the least bit concerned because Daniella Sears foresaw her own mortal downfall at least twice a year—mostly during the cold and flu season.

"You're the nurse. Why don't you use that university education your father and I paid for and formulate your own diagnosis?"

I didn't even bother mentioning that she never once contributed financially to the family, or that I was in the process of paying Dad back every last penny of my university fees. To be honest, I just wanted to sever all ties and be rid of them both. But no, guilt always dragged me back. Every damn time.

I hated it.

"Where's Dad?"

"Oh, forget about him. He's lecturing at the Université Sorbonne, again." For all her faults, Mum could really rock a French accent.

"Okay then, what about Matilda? Where's she?" I was referring to Mum's live-in cook/housekeeper/slave, take your pick. The poor woman was the only member of staff who managed to put up with my mother's ridiculous demands without dousing her in kerosene and lighting a match.

Mum sniffed with disdain. "She's taken personal leave. I don't know why and quite frankly, I don't care. The whole affair is a cruel inconvenience if you ask me."

I took a deep, steadying breath. Mum's flippancy toward the health and well-being of anyone other than herself really pissed me off. How dare she treat her staff with so little respect? How dare she ignore the physical and emotional challenges of the people who did everything in their power to please her?

My grip on the phone tightened.

"Pack your bags, Riley Jayne. You're coming home."

No, I'm not.

"Riley."

No.

"NOW."

Fuckety fuck fuck fuck.

Two and a half hours later, I once again braced myself before opening the door to the master suite. Earlier, I'd self-diagnosed Mum with a virus so there was nothing to be done about her temperature or muscle aches except rest, hydration and aspirin.

Just before leaving home I messaged Dominic, letting him know it was unlikely I would meet him for a run that week. What a depressing thought. It was for the best though, I needed to put some distance between us before I lost all sense of reason … and self-control. Definitely that too.

The worst part, however, was that I wouldn't be

able to exercise. With my days spent at work and nights spent looking after Mum, the only way I'd get an increased heart rate would be by letting my simmering frustration bubble to the surface. Not good. Without my daily run, suppressing the urge to smother my mother in her sleep was going to be practically impossible.

I peeked my head through the crack and Mum's grey gaze scorched mine.

"It's hot."

I tread across the plush carpet. The room was a mirror image of mine directly down the hall. There was a king-sized bed on the west wall, flanked by two white bedside tables. At the foot of it stood a cream chaise with a cashmere throw rug casually draped across it. The cream colored walls, gold accents from the traditional artworks, hanging chandelier and the chiffon silk coverlet lent an air of renaissance-inspired opulence to the space. There were three floor-to-ceiling French doors which graced the north wall leading to a private balcony and each was boarded with heavy curtains. Like my own room, the small glass panels inside each window reminded me of prison bars.

I suppressed a shiver before swinging one of the doors open, wide open. "Better?"

Silence.

Turning around, I stared at my mother. She was lying in bed, her lavender silk nightie contrasting against the white Egyptian cotton sheets. Her head rested on several plump goose down pillows as she gazed indolently out the French doors.

It was easy to see why people often commented on our physical resemblances. Like me, Mum's naturally blonde hair was straight, though only just reached the top of her shoulders, whereas mine hung midway down my back. Despite being bedridden, it was so well-styled she looked as though she had just stepped out of a salon. Our round, expressive eyes were often likened to those of a doe; however, where mine were a clear, sky blue, hers were an olive green which eloquently hinted at the stormy temper beneath. Our wide cheekbones and small, straight noses were identical, though and as far as I was concerned, that was where the similarities ended.

Where I was tall, Mum was short. Where I was athletic, she was delicate. Where I felt too much, she felt too little. Where I had a heart, she had none.

This is gonna be a long week.

Thus, Doctor Powell.

Not that Mum knew anything about me seeing a psychologist, of course. I mean, I only started seeing Doctor Powell after moving away from home, and there was no way I would ever bring up the reason behind my decision in her presence. Doing so would be like handing the woman a firearm with an endless supply of ammunition—bloodbath anyone?

I shook my head.

"Riley, I feel faint. I need something to eat."

"You didn't like the sandwich I made you earlier?"

Her arm carelessly gestured to the uneaten snack on the bedside table. "It's stale." I raised my eyebrows. "Matilda always covers my food with a cloche. You didn't."

I bit my lip to stop a scathing retort.

She's such a bitch. Why am I even here? Oh, that's right, because I'm waiting for a fucking miracle, for her to grow a heart.

"I need something restorative, like a broth."

Have we suddenly been transported to Edwardian England? Who the hell eats broth anymore?

"A broth?"

Mum's gaze snapped back to me. "Yes, Riley. A broth. How many times do I have to repeat myself?" But I think feeling annoyed took too much effort because she switched to melancholia instead and, staring out at the sky which had turned a dusky purple, bemoaned, "With your father off gallivanting around the globe and Matilda abandoning me, I'm all alone in this house."

I took a step forward. "You'll feel better in a few days, Mum. Besides, I'm here, aren't I? You're not alone."

She stared at me, her eyes flat.

Silence.

Deep breaths, Riley. Deep breaths.

And so began the longest week of my life.

****

How I ever survived that week is a complete mystery. As the days passed, I grew more and more agitated. The long hours spent at the hospital and even longer ones spent with Mum afterward, contributed to my systematic emotional erosion. I had no time for myself, no time to breathe, and definitely no time to run. I thought about it though. Every. Single. Day.

You see, at work I had to put up with women screaming obscenities at me when their birth plans went to shit, while at "home" I endured Mum's continued dissatisfaction and heavily laden silence. So I constantly found myself dreaming of chucking it all in, flipping everyone the bird and heading to the beach—but I never did. Needless to say, by the time Friday finally decided to show its sweet self, I was bordering on psychotic.

Tomorrow. I'm going home tomorrow. I don't care if she dies in her sleep tonight, nothing is going to stop me from leaving this godforsaken place. *Not a single. Fucking Thing.*

Yeah, my headspace was not great.

In fact, that afternoon I found myself perched on the edge of my old bed with shaking hands, shallow breaths, and a heart that felt like it was about to free-fall out my chest. I swear, the butterflies in my stomach were raging an all-out war and the ants on my skin were enjoying the butchery because every nerve ending felt fried, raw.

Let's just say, I was minutes away from a code blue.

Suddenly, my phone's notification screen lit up. It took me a few tries to pick it up from where it lay on the bed beside me and a little while longer to discern the words typed, but eventually I read…

Bootycall: **What's ur address?**

I could only hope my trembling fingers formulated a cohesive reply because I honestly had no idea which buttons I pushed.

Half an hour later, I found myself sitting in exactly the same spot, staring at exactly the same light switch, with exactly the same chaos running through my body. Well, until I heard the low rumble of a car engine outside.

I moved into the hallway, sleep-walked past Mum's bedroom, down the staircase and out through the front door. As I blinked away the late afternoon glare, in front of me materialized the most beautiful car I had ever seen. It was a perfectly restored red and white 1959 Ford Thunderbird.

Wow.

And out of said car stepped the most gorgeous man I had ever seen.

Double wow.

"Dominic," I whispered.

He shut the door and leaned back against the hood, arms crossed in front of his huge chest and biceps practically bursting. As his eyes roamed the two-story Spanish-style mansion behind me, he said, "So this is where you've been hiding."

I didn't say anything. I was too busy committing to memory every inch of him in case this was all some trick of the light and I was actually staring into empty space. Dominic's grey t-shirt clung to his monstrous frame like a second skin and it was randomly tucked into one small section of his dark, ripped jeans. The black studded belt peeking through looked old and worn, similar to the scuffed combat boots on his feet. But I didn't care. I didn't care about the holes, the scratches, the carelessness, any of it. Oh, no, I only cared about his eyes. You see, as soon as our gazes locked, those piercing blue eyes of his sent a lightning bolt straight through my body and the oppressive, suffocating fog that had been shrouding me all week suddenly obliterated.

"Wanna get out of here?"

I nodded.

A slow sexy-as-sin smile appeared. "Get in, then."

Once I settled myself in the passenger seat and took in the immaculate interior with an astonished shake of my head, Dominic leaned in close, whispering in my ear. "Where to, angel?"

I shivered as his warm breath tickled my skin. Turning to him—so close our noses almost touched—I replied, "Don't care."

My reflection shone in his gaze and it was as though a stranger stared back at me. Gone was the crippling tension, gone was the torment and the shadows. I was seizing this moment with two hands and running with it … and I wanted to run the fuck away.

The car growled to life once more and we sped off down the road. When we hit the highway, Dominic turned right and headed north along the coast. I wound down the window and rested my head on my arms as cool gusts of wind blew my hair back and the sun kissed my skin. I gazed out at the Pacific Ocean and for the first time in over one hundred and twenty hours, and smiled.

An hour later, Dominic pulled into an empty parking space at a coastal lookout. I didn't even wait for him to kill the engine before hopping out of the car and striding toward a lone wooden seat perched high on a rocky outcrop. The bench overlooked the ocean and as I took in the view, gazing both left and right, I saw endless miles of open space. In all honesty, there was nothing as far as the eye could see except water, sand, rock, and sky.

Heaven.

Sitting down, I let the crash of waves, the flurry of the wind, and the cries of gulls overhead buffet through me, soothe me. When I leaned back, resting heavily against the weathered wood, the tension that had been coiled inside finally began to seep out my body.

And that's when the tears started.

Bloody hell.

I guess my angst had to filter its way out somehow, it just so happened to always leak out my eyeballs osmosis-style. Unbidden tears streamed unchecked down my cheeks and a small part of me warned I should really try to stop them because I was not an attractive crier. Like, at all. My eyes turned bloodshot, my nose grew red, and I sniffed constantly. Trust me, it wasn't pretty. However, in that moment, need overpowered want, so I didn't give a shit. I was too exhausted. Which was also why, when two strong arms encircled me, I didn't push them away either. Instead, I turned and buried my head in the broad chest, grasping the soft t-shirt as if it were the only thing keeping me from falling apart.

After quite possibly a bucketful of tears later, my

sobs abated and my sniffs ceased. From deep within that massive chest, a deep voice rumbled, "Tough week, huh?"

"You could say that."

"What happened?"

I shook my head. "It'll just make me cry again. I've wet your shirt, sorry."

Dominic held me tighter, his chin resting on the top of my head. "Forget about it."

We stayed like that for a long time and despite no words being said, I felt more reassured than I had in my whole life. His steady heartbeat quieted my fitful thoughts, his firm body strengthened my tired limbs, and his acceptance of my present fragility fortified me immeasurably. Well, until a different type of tension showed its lustful head.

Turned out, the longer we remained enfolded in each other's arms, the more I noticed my skin tingle like crazy from his hands clasping my shoulder and hip—not good. His earthy scent made my vision swim and the feel of his muscular chest against my forehead did something different entirely. Let's just say parts of me—the dormant parts—suddenly ached for him. Yes, ached.

Crap.

Dominic must have felt it too because as the air between us thickened, his fingers began sensually tracing soft circles on the exposed skin between my tank top and shorts. Goose bumps appeared on my flesh and I had to bite back a moan. Literally. Like, I actually bit down on the fabric of his t-shirt. His breath caught.

Operation Dominic Detox sucks balls.

And yet, I didn't move away. In fact, I moved closer—if it was at all possible. Dominic's heartbeat spiked, it pounded out the same rhythmic torture as mine and the heat between us intensified tenfold. He shifted in his seat.

Desperately trying to find a way to break the mood that was going to have me attacking his neck with my teeth if I wasn't careful, I removed his t-shirt from my mouth and asked, "How was your week?"

Nice save, Riley.

He moved back slightly, allowing a sliver of space between us.

Phew.

"It was all right." He swallowed. "Finally finished my baby, that was a fuckin' long time coming."

I glanced over his shoulder at the lovingly restored classic vehicle, it was all shiny paint and polished chrome. "She's beautiful."

"Sure is."

Something in Dominic's voice made my eyes dart back to his. He wasn't looking at the car. He knew it, and I knew it. In fact, one of his fingers deliberately slid under the elastic band of my shorts, making me suck in a sharp breath. I blushed. Furiously.

Focus Riley. C'mon, you can do this. You *have* to do this.

"You've done an amazing job, you must be really proud of yourself."

Meh. Could have been worse.

The heat in his eyes cooled, before a satirical half-smile appeared. "Not really, I'm just glad I don't have to ride in Levi's piece of shit anymore."

My hand still grasping his t-shirt instinctively clutched it tighter. "Don't sell yourself short." I gestured with my free arm. "Look at what you've done, Dominic, look at what you've created. You did that, no one else, and it's something to be proud of, truly."

He stared at me for a minute, his expression unreadable. Then, shaking his head, he murmured, "I'm good with my hands, that's all."

"Don't I know it."

His smile was sex, pure and simple. And the way it made me crave those hands all over my body, doing sweet, dirty things for hours on end had me all hot and flustered. Big time.

"I meant, you know … with the car and … guitar … not…" I ducked my head. "Fuck."

Dominic threw back his head and laughed. The sound warmed my insides, but that didn't stop me from smacking him with my open palm.

"Ouch." Stupid muscular pecs. They were ridiculous—far too chiseled for their own good. Sadly, my pathetic attempt at physical intimidation only made him laugh harder.

"You're fuckin' hilarious, you know that?"

I crossed my arms in front of my chest, grumbling, "You did that thing with your mouth. I can't concentrate when you do, it's unfair."

His eyes darkened and I squirmed. Heat pooled directly between my thighs. "Angel, I can do more things with my mouth than you've ever dreamed. Just say the word and it's yours." He leaned forward, I was hit with a waft of mint as his fingers delved deeper into my shorts and his nose skimmed along my jaw. "All yours."

I couldn't breathe.

"Riley?"

Nothing.

"You okay?" He moved back to look at me and the genuine concern written all over his gorgeous face would have been laughable if I wasn't in the middle of a life and death situation.

Dazed, I half-nodded, half-shook my head.

No, I'm not okay. I want your mouth, I want it all over me. I want your tongue licking the salt off my skin and your teeth biting my sensitive flesh. I want to feel you so deep inside me the pleasure becomes unbearable and I climax around you, obliterating us both.

But that can never happen, can it? Afterward, you'd move on, you'd find someone else to taste, to bite and we would never share perfect moments like this ever again.

So. Friends it is.

I looked down, murmuring, "We should be heading back. It's getting late."

After a pause, Dominic sighed, disentangled himself and slowly stood. He still held out his hand for me though, and I still took it.

A dark part of me knew I always would.

Chapter Seven

I don't know why,
Too much confusion,
Just tell me why,
To break illusion.
—MONDEZ, "Distance"

The evening spent with Robin was … really good, actually. Hours after Dominic dropped me back at my parents' place, Robin and I were seated outside Cacao, talking easily and enjoying the unseasonably balmy weather. On raised metal stools, our small round table sat adjacent the main promenade overlooking the ocean. The occasional couple walked past, interrupting our otherwise unobscured view of the inky black water, but other than that, the night was perfect.

Go figure.

"Have I told you how stunning you look tonight, Riley?"

I blushed because Robin had, several times. He told me how good I looked when I opened the front door, when I slipped into his sleek silver Mercedes and when we ordered our shared plate of dessert. Don't get me wrong, I wasn't complaining. In fact, I kinda liked the way it rolled off his tongue so easily.

I glanced down at my black heels, fitted blue jeans and shimmery halter top. The ensemble—combined with my smoky eye makeup and straightened hair—left me feeling confident for the first time in ages, which probably accounted for my teasing reply. "You haven't said anything about it for thirty-five minutes. Your chivalry is slipping."

Robin smiled wide and once again that cute

dimple appeared. Dressed in camel colored pants and a loose white shirt with sleeves rolled mid-way up his forearms, he looked almost as good as the chocolate self-saucing pudding we were sharing.

Hmm, tasty.

Sadly, Robin must have read my deviant thoughts because he raised a playful eyebrow, causing pretty much all of the blood in my body to rush to my cheeks. Thank God it was too dark to notice, I hoped. In order to escape that disconcerting thought, I took another mouthful of gooey sweetness, shut my eyes and moaned. "Unbelievable."

"You really like chocolate, don't you?"

I stared at him. "Robin, nothing on this earth is better than chocolate. Nothing." As soon as I saw his expression change from amused to downright illicit, however, I quickly steered the subject in a different direction. "I didn't see you at work much this week, is everything okay?"

"Yeah, I was across the road for most of it," he replied, referring to his private practice opposite the hospital. "We were booked out with consults and scans, so it was lucky I bumped into you when I did. Not sure how I would have gotten your number otherwise." Robin looked at me, his gaze shrewd. "You seemed a bit distracted though."

I tried to laugh it off. "Well, being surrounded by birthing mothers will do that to you." There was no way I was going to rehash my week from hell, it was almost over anyway and for that I was eternally thankful. I was going to spend one more night at my parents' house and then head home for the weekend.

Thank. The. Lord.

There was a short pause. "I still can't believe you run your own practice, and at such a young age." Robin's answering smile made me momentarily lose my train of thought—I shook my head. "Did you always want to be an obstetrician?"

He shrugged one shoulder. "Not really, my father is a doctor and so was my grandfather before him. Just followed in their footsteps, I suppose."

For some reason his reply disappointed me.

"I always wanted to branch out on my own, though. Have something to put my name to."

I nodded. "I'd love to run my own business." But I stopped short because I'd never voiced that secret longing out loud before.

However, before I could retract my last statement, Robin reached out and covered my hand with his. "Why don't you?" I looked at him, unconvinced. "Riley, you're a smart, hardworking woman, you could study outside of work hours and make it happen. What's stopping you from starting a private practice of your own?" His fingers were smooth as they flitted over my skin. "I'd be happy to help, all you have to do is ask."

My gaze dropped to his hand caressing mine. "Thanks." Sadly, I wasn't comforted. In fact, I was a little disheartened because I was actually referring to a business enterprise completely unrelated to the medical industry. You see, for years I'd wanted to…

Never mind.

Robin removed his hand and took a spoonful of dessert. "You're right," he mumbled around a mouthful of chocolate pudding. "This does taste good."

I looked up at him, shook off my despondency and grinned. He was a good man, Robin. He was kind, encouraging, complimentary, funny—definitely boyfriend material. In fact, these musings probably accounted for why I gently wiped away the remaining crumbs from the corner of his mouth before licking them off my fingers. "Don't want any to go to waste," I murmured.

Robin's hazel eyes darkened to a burnt toffee color as he leaned forward, gently pressing his lips to mine. They were so warm, soft and sweet that I melted into him with a sigh. All too soon, however, he pulled away, though not before whispering, "I'd like to take you out again."

Smiling, I nodded in agreement and shifted back on my stool. Robin stood, winked, and walked inside to pay the bill.

It was when I was sitting in the dim light, basking in the afterglow of the kiss that I felt it—the hairs on the back of my neck bristled in warning. Everything was going to change. My entire world was about to be completely upended because of a simple, innocent kiss. Don't get me wrong, the kiss itself was fine, enjoyable even, but did it warrant a total life upheaval? Guess I was about to find out.

My stomach clenched as I slowly turned to the right.

Oh, no.

And my insides plummeted to their grizzly death.

No, no, no.

He was standing there, stock still, glaring at me.

Please, you don't understand.

His body stood rigid while his hands were clenched into fists at his sides.

You don't—

But that wasn't what caused the panic. Heck, that didn't even trigger my jagged, painful breaths. It was the look in his eyes. With him, it was always the eyes, and they sucker-punched me with their brutality. Even when I opened my mouth and called out his name, Dominic didn't assuage his silent fury. Instead, he spun on his heel and stormed away.

Into the darkness.

I dropped my head, thinking back to an earlier time when I felt equally powerless.

"What brings you here today, Riley?"

I stared down at the tissues clutched tightly in my hands. I had brought them with me, figuring I was probably going to burst into a fit of hysterical sobs at some point—it was best to come prepared for that shit. After all, I sure as hell did not want mascara dripping down my face while walking back to the car—never a good look.

So, shrugging one shoulder, I feigned a nonchalance I really didn't feel. "A friend suggested I see someone."

It was true. As soon as I walked out of the bedroom in my favorite summer dress, Grace took one look at how it hung off my diminished frame and demanded I book an appointment with a psychologist. She even threatened to do it herself if I didn't.

So I did, I was here. And I hated it.

Doctor Powell nodded. "Why is that?"

I sighed, it was long and low. "I, ah, haven't been eating properly, I guess."

She took out a notebook, her pen rapidly scribbling across the page. "I see, and what do you mean by, not eating properly?"

Shrugging again, I stared down at the tissues in my hand. After systematically folding and refolding them several times, I took a deep breath. "It's not that I don't eat, I do, I just..." My eyes landed on the bookshelf to my left, it was jam-packed with titles like, I Am Enough: A Perfectionist's Guide to Imperfection, CBT: The Power of Processing, and even, The Art of Mindfulness: Finding Calm Amidst Everyday Turmoil. I looked down at my lap again. "Whenever I try to eat something, it's like I've got no room, you know?"

Doctor Powell gazed at me, her eyes thoughtful.

"Like, my stomach is already full," I explained.

"With what?"

"Lots of stuff, butterflies, barbed wire, sailor's knots—you name it. It's like a junkyard in there." I barked out a laugh, but it sounded so beyond forced I immediately gave up and fell silent.

"I see." She rifled through her notebook, took out a sheet of paper and handed it to me. "I'd like you to fill this in."

In front of me was a double-sided questionnaire. It wanted me to scale the severity of my symptoms when faced with specified situations. The first question asked how often I felt nervous for no good reason.

All the time. Duh.

Once done, I passed it back and waited while Doctor Powell calculated my score. After a conclusive nod of her head, she wrote some more information in her notebook, though this time with several words emphatically underlined.

I chose to ignore that part.

At last she looked at me, her eyes empathetic yet steady. "Tell me, Riley, what do you know about anxiety?"

I swallowed, with effort.

****

"So, are you going to tell me?" Mae panted.

"Tell you what?"

She rolled her eyes. "About the economic impact of soil erosion in Mozambique, what else?"

I blinked. "Huh?"

"For the love of God, Riley. *The date*. How did it go?"

115

"Oh." I looked down at the stopwatch in my hand. We were midway through our second training session, and up until that moment, Mae had been doing really well. She was quiet, focused, driven. And now I knew why; the woman tried to wait me out.

I knew it was pointless trying to keep any details from her and to be honest, I had a really good time with Robin—for the most part—so I didn't mind talking about that section of the evening. I just didn't want to go into Dominic's random appearance—what shitty timing—and my subsequent reaction afterward. I mean, once he disappeared like a goddamn ghost through an impenetrable black wall, the evening grew … strange.

I bit back a groan.

The remainder of it was spent trying to appear upbeat and carefree without quite pulling it off. Robin looked at me strangely a few times, probably because my laughter was too high-pitched, my gestures too grand and my smile too wide, but he didn't say anything. Anyway, I couldn't keep up the pretense for long and gave up entirely during the car ride back. I fell into a fitful silence instead, inwardly sorting through my conflicting feelings of remorse, defiance, and anger without ever coming to a resolution.

Reckon I'll leave that part out.

So, glancing back at Mae, I bargained, "After another set, I'll tell you."

"You're evil, you know that?"

I grinned.

"Fine." Once Mae completed her set of alternate lunges and I stopped the timer, she collapsed on the sand. "Okay, I want details." She paused, collecting her breath. "What car does he drive?"

"Ah, why does it matter?"

Mae looked at me, exasperated. "It matters, Riley.

The type of car and the way it's driven tells a woman what her date is like in bed."

My eyebrows shot up. "It does?"

She nodded. "It does. So?"

"Oh, um…" I thought back. "Robin owns a silver Mercedes." Mae nodded. "Last year's model, I think." She hummed. "And he drives…" I shrugged my shoulders. "I dunno, smoothly?"

She grinned wickedly. "I bet he does."

I rolled my eyes and readied the stopwatch. "Next set."

Mae groaned but got to work. As she did, I reminisced about Dominic's car and the way *he* drove. If Robin was smooth, then Dominic was unrestrained, wild even. I shook my head and internally stamped on any butterflies that dared flutter their excitable wings in my stomach. Not that it mattered, after the way last night ended between us, I'd never see him or his Ford Thunderbird again—butterflies or no butterflies. I gritted my teeth. It wasn't as though I did anything wrong by going on a date with Robin. What the heck was Dominic's problem? He knew we could never be anything more than friends, so why did he act like such an ass?

And why did I feel so guilty?

"Done," Mae gasped. She bent over, her hands gripping her bent knees for a moment. After straightening up again, she demanded, "More details."

My eyes lit up. "Well, the food was amazing, we ordered this awesome—"

But she held up one hand, stopping me. "Jesus, Riley, I don't give two shits about what you ate, I wanna know what happened between you and Robin."

"But the chocolate," I whined.

Mae placed fisted hands on her hips. "Would you

117

forget about chocolate for one second, please? Now, give me some dirt before you punish me with more lunges."

I threw up my hands. "Fine. What do you want to know?"

"Did you talk?"

"Yes."

"What about?"

"Work."

"Did you fuck?"

"No."

"Kiss?"

I blushed.

She clapped her hands together. "I knew it. Tell me everything."

I raised my stopwatch. "Can't, time's up. Last set."

"What?"

"Do it."

"It was fucking easier toilet training Annabelle than it is getting gossip out of you," she grumbled before once again completing the exercise.

When we were finally sitting in the sand and stretching, I decided to offer up some information without any bribery attached. Mae had worked hard, after all.

"Robin wants to take me out again."

"Yeah?" She smiled. "You must be a good kisser."

I glanced down, playing with grains of sand.

"What about Dominic?"

My hands froze. "What about him?"

"Have you seen him?"

After standing and brushing the sand off my shorts, I began packing away the equipment I brought with me. "We saw each other yesterday." Out the corner of my eye, I could see Mae watching me. "And that was the first time I'd seen him since last Sunday."

"Is he meeting you for a run after Annabelle and I leave, like last week?"

"Probably not." I sighed and then bent to collect more gear.

"How come?"

"Mae, I thought you wanted me to concentrate on Robin."

"I do."

"Then why are we still discussing Dominic?" I hastily blinked back the tears that threatened to spill.

She shook her head sadly. "Oh, babe."

"Enough. Just help me lug this stuff to the car, will you?"

"Okay, okay." She crouched down next to her daughter who was in the process of chewing the leg off a Transformer. "What are you bringing home today, gorgeous girl?"

Annabelle spat out the appendage and held up a stuffed giraffe with the sand encrusted fingers of her other hand. "This one."

Smiling, Mae helped Annabelle and her new acquisition to their feet. "C'mon, let's help Auntie Riley pack up."

I raised a questioning eyebrow.

"What? It's not as though I've got any family who'll actually talk to me." She grinned. "You're it."

"Great."

Mae smiled at my less-than-impressed expression before turning toward the car park with a pile of toys in one hand and Annabelle in the other. "Let's get this crap back to your car then, sis," she called over her shoulder before striding off.

****

Dominic didn't show. And it was strange because all week I craved solitude and freedom, I wanted nothing more than to be able to take off at a sprint along the shoreline and leave the rest of the world behind me. But when I finally got my space, when at last I was surrounded by silence, I wanted to fill up the empty void with him.

Bloody hell.

Once I finished my run, I sipped from a bottle of water in my car as I checked my phone for any new notifications. Okay, so I may have been secretly hoping Dominic had called or left a message explaining why he didn't come to meet me, and to be fair I did receive a message, just not from him.

Grace was heading to Melbourne.

I checked the time on my phone. Actually, she was probably already there—with Levi. Apparently, they were both representing G's school at a weeklong educational conference being held there. I tried to feel happy for her, truly I did. After all, this was an excellent opportunity, both professionally and romantically. But I needed her. Badly. And the morose part of me hated the fact that she had left when I wanted her most.

How selfish is that?

Over the past week, we had intermittently messaged each other, asking how things were going; however, it was nothing compared to the way we usually interacted. Before I visited Hell on Earth, we saw each other every day and I missed the way Grace cut through other people's bullshit. She had this uncanny knack of being able to plow through the emotional minefield I always found myself stranded in. I needed her here to help me. I needed her to say if I was acting like a fool, God only knew she would.

Clearly, that was not an option, so I tried

something different. When I got home, showered and dressed, I decided to take the Doctor Powell approach. I mean, it always worked really well during my sessions with her so what could go wrong now? I took a deep breath. It was decided, I was going to deconstruct my emotions objectively and without catastrophizing my current predicament. I was going to think logically and methodically. In other words, I was going to sort this crap out.

It didn't work.

Two boxes of Kleenex, a block of chocolate and countless cups of peppermint tea later, I gave up. It was probably for the best, unlocking Pandora's Box and eyeballing the contents should only be done under professional guidance anyway. Unsurprisingly, I tended to react irrationally toward my own feelings. So, until my next appointment with the good doctor, I decided to revert back to what I knew best—The Distraction Method. Only this time with less alcohol.

I called Brea, and we organized a girls' night out for later that evening. She was working at The Hole but would finish up relatively early, so I was going to head in and have a few drinks with her—only a few, mind you. Once that was planned, I thought I would feel better, but I didn't. I still felt … off. Sighing, I made a momentous decision. It was time to bring out the big guns.

I was going to clean.

Everything.

And I did.

From the cook top stove, to behind the washing machine, from the carpets, to the curtains. For hours, I sparkled the shit out of the apartment. I scrubbed until my hands were raw, vacuumed until my back hurt, and polished until I could see my own bedraggled reflection in every reflective surface.

But it still didn't help.

After taking yet another shower and then collapsing on the couch in black yoga pants and a pink fitted tank top, I decided enough was enough. I needed my best friend.

It took her ages to answer the phone but at last I heard that familiar voice. "Hey, Riley."

She sounded strange, but I was too caught up in my own emotional turmoil to comment on it. Instead, I cried, "Finally, I thought you were never going to answer." Granted, not the most welcoming hello, but I was desperate.

"Sorry, what's up?"

I let out a long breath, wanting to tell her everything about Dominic. I wanted to tell her about the time we spent together and how I was already missing him. I wanted to explain how his touch made my skin come alive and his voice made my body tingle. I wanted to articulate how he comforted me when I truly needed it and how his anger felt like a knife wound in my side. I wanted to tell her I was in too deep. So deep, I couldn't see my way out anymore and I needed her here to guide me.

But I didn't.

I couldn't get the words out.

So, when Grace asked, "Riley, what is it?"

I pathetically replied with, "I miss you, G. It's been a shitty week," and my heart tore a little because I wasn't being entirely truthful.

After that, we spoke about my mum for a while and I mentioned how Brea and I were hanging out later. Only, the more I spoke around the topic pulsing at the forefront of my mind, the more upset I became. Grace seemed to sense this change and after an exceptionally long pause where neither of us spoke, murmured, "Riley, love, that's not all, is it?"

Her kindness broke me. Sobbing, I choked out, "No." However, before I could offload my emotional baggage, there was a knock at the front door so I quickly ended the call by promising to ring her back. Scrubbing my face with my hands, I attempted to wipe away any evidence of tears but soon gave up after spying my disheveled reflection in the window—it was a lost cause.

Once the door opened, all thoughts of my abysmal appearance immediately vanished.

What the fuck?

I was inundated with what was surely the largest bouquet of roses in the history of horticulture. I mean, they took up the entirety of the entryway.

Wow.

They were beautiful. There was a decadent assortment of colors and varieties, each of them striking. My eyes traveled over the petals. Some were ruby, pink, auburn, white, cerulean, mauve, and my absolute favorite, the color of golden sand. From behind them peeked a modest-looking Robin. "Hey."

I stared open-mouthed at him but after a short pause, managed to imaginarily thwack myself on the upside of the head so closed it again. "Hey."

We looked at each other for a while before I realized he was shifting uncomfortably under the weight of the flowers.

I opened the door wider. "Shit, I'm sorry. Please, come in."

"Thanks." He moved past me and placed the extravagant gift on the countertop in the kitchen. I kid you not, the vase took up most of it. The small room filled with the sweet fragrance of the blooms and I breathed in deeply. Robin turned to face me. "I didn't know which ones you liked so—"

"You hedged your bets and bought all of them?"

He smiled. "Yeah."

I took in the bouquet and then the man who had given them to me. Both looked … damn fine. Robin wore casual blue jeans and a white t-shirt, it hung off his lean frame in a way which made me want to pull up the cotton material and glimpse the naked body underneath.

I'm such a pervert.

I had never noticed before, but Robin was fit, really fit. Not bulging muscles and ripped torso fit, more like well-defined and proportioned physique fit. It was nice.

Clearing my throat, I murmured, "Thank you, truly. But you didn't have to go to all this trouble." I gestured to the bursting assortment of color and foliage next to us.

He took my hand, drawing me closer. "I had a great time last night, Riley." He frowned. "But after our kiss…" I flushed and Robin looked at me closely. "Did I do something wrong? Did I move too fast? I thought I read the situation correctly." He gave a crooked smile. "And I've never had any complaints about my skills before."

Shaking my head, I laughed. "Don't worry, your kissing skills are great." I looked down at our entwined fingers. "I'm sorry for weirding out on you, I really enjoyed our date." Then I gazed up at him again. "It's been a shitty week, that's all." Yeah, using the same line I had given Grace not ten minutes before was lame, even by my standards.

Robin nodded and didn't push me further. I was so grateful I stepped forward, gently pressing my lips to his. "Thank you for the flowers."

He smiled at me. "You're welcome." After disentangling his fingers from mine, he checked his watch, rolled those warm hazel eyes and shifted back, breaking the spell. "I'd better go, I need to drop past the hospital and check on a patient."

As I walked him to the front door my mind ticked over something that had been bothering me since he arrived. I wanted to ask Robin something but wasn't sure how to go about it without sounding ridiculously impolite. Eventually, I gave up and instead blurted, "I don't want to appear ungrateful or anything but," I paused. "How did you get this address?" There was no point in attempting to hide my epic blush so I continued on in a rush, "I mean, I know I gave you my parents' address when we bumped into each other at work last week, but…"

Robin laughed and then leaned in, giving me a soft peck on the cheek. I shut my eyes briefly, breathing in the scent of him. He smelled fresh, like a citrus tree after a heavy rain.

Swoon.

After straightening up again, he replied, "Mae gave it to me."

"Oh."

That cute dimple made an appearance as he gave me a quick wink. "Can I take you out next weekend? I won't be on call at the hospital."

I shook off any murderous tendencies toward my overly helpful friend and smiled. "I'd like that."

And with that, he left, along with my despondency.

Chapter Eight

Breaking,
Holding,
It's not safe,
No more.
—MONDEZ, "Distance"

Hours later, I was sitting on a cracked leather barstool, happily chatting with Brea in between her customers. I had successfully discouraged the advances of no less than three tattooed Romeos, proving my canary yellow sundress, studded ankle boots, and black leather jacket combination was a hit. My fourth beer was going down well and that, combined with the heavy rock music emanating from the stage, meant I was well on my way to feeling chipper. Well, until I suddenly stopped and cursed out loud. "Shit."

Brea looked up from the bourbon she was pouring. "Everything all right?" She had to raise her voice to be heard over the epic guitar solo on stage.

"I forgot to call G back." I held up my index finger, indicating that I'd return in a minute, and left to find a quieter spot to make the phone call.

I hoped she wasn't pissed at me.

The dingy, poster-clad hallway leading to the toilets was going to have to do. So I rested my back against a classic Deftones poster from the late nineties and propped my left foot up behind me for balance.

Was I drunk? I didn't normally need any extra stability...

Just like last time, it took her forever to answer the phone. "Hey."

"Hey, G," I yelled a little too loudly. I'd have to monitor my vocal projection if I didn't want to deafen the poor girl.

"Having a good night at The Hole?"

She knew me well, and to be honest, I really was enjoying myself. Since Robin arrived at the apartment with the world's most aromatic gift, it felt like a dead weight had been lifted off me. At last, a decision had been made in regards to my love life and the best part was I didn't even make it because Robin had done it for me. Yeah, avoidance was something I needed to work on in the future—ironic, I know. Anyway, I wasn't going to waste any more emotional energy on a certain classic-car-driving-overtly-muscular-and-unpredictably-moody musician, no matter how moan-worthy his hands were. I was officially done with Dominic.

Finished.

It felt liberating.

"I'm having an amazing night," I squealed. Okay, so my eardrum detonator was probably the alcohol talking.

I needed to stop drinking.

As Grace and I continued talking/shrieking however, I noticed that something wasn't right with her. Like, at all. Her answers were clipped and her tone was somber—never good signs when she was concerned.

"G, what's wrong? How come now you're the one who's about to burst into tears?"

But she tried to evade my questioning which made me even more worried. I mean, if she couldn't talk to me, then who could she offload her problems to? Another whiskey bottle? Hell no. Thankfully, after some direct prodding, it all came to light.

Turned out, Grace thought I was romantically interested in Levi. She had been purposefully keeping him at arm's length despite her obvious feelings for the guy and therefore prioritized her friendship with me over her own happiness.

I never loved her more than I did in that moment.

And luckily, I could fix the problem. So, after several accusations on her part, like, "You were making doe eyes at him while almost force feeding him a damn smoothie," and explanations on my end, such as, "G, I don't like Levi. Well, not like *that* anyway," we finally got it all sorted.

Thank God.

After which time she quickly hung up the phone, no doubt to rush back to her man for some crazy make-up sex. Okay, I was envious. It had been ages since I'd been intimate with a guy and even longer since it was with someone who I actually connected with.

Let it go, Riley. Tonight is all about having fun.

As I pushed myself off the wall, I noticed that the alcohol running through my body left me feeling loose and frisky, the heavy drumbeats made me want to bump and grind, and if Robin didn't send me an amorous text within the next fifteen minutes I was actually going to explode.

Not the best recipe for a girls' night out.

Tucking the phone into my jacket pocket, I made to move. But stopped. Stared. And quite possibly drooled. All the breath suddenly left my body in a loud gust because standing at the entrance of the hallway was Dominic.

What was he doing here? Fuck me, but he looked edible.

I quickly put my hand out to rest against Chino Moreno's face. The lead singer from Deftones was going to have to help me stay upright because I could not trust my legs to do it on their own anymore. Once Dominic spotted me, his eyes flashed with recognition before transforming into a dangerous simmer.

Uh oh.

He took a step forward and my gaze unabashedly roamed his body.

Yeah, I really needed to stop drinking. I wouldn't feel this horny if I was sober.

His light brown hair looked like someone had just run their fingers through it and I bit my lip at the slight growth which peppered his strong jaw. He wore those scuffed combat boots I loved, some eye-watering black jeans and a grey V-neck shirt with the sleeves casually rolled up his forearms.

Sweet Jesus. The guy needed to come with a warning label.

Shaking my head, I forced one wobbly foot in front of the other in an attempt to get out of the suddenly microscopic hallway.

Don't do something you'll regret, don't do something you'll regret, don't—

"You lied to me."

My head whipped around to stare at him, *Exorcist*-style. "Excuse me?"

"You lied to me."

"I've never lied to you."

He scowled. "Right. You just 'forgot' to tell me about your fuckin' boyfriend."

I stopped for a moment, trying to get the alcohol-clogged gears in my mind working again. "I don't have a boyfriend," I said slowly.

What the hell was he talking about?

And then it clicked.

Ah, Robin.

Well, it was true, I didn't have a boyfriend. It was too early for Robin and me to call ourselves a couple and we hadn't yet discussed exclusivity either, so as far as I saw it, he was a ridiculously thoughtful guy I was casually dating.

Dominic gritted his teeth. "You looked pretty close with that loafer-wearing pussy last night."

Well, then.

I took a step back, trying to figure out where all his anger was coming from.

Was it possible...? Hang on, was Dominic *jealous*?

I am ashamed to say, my insides melted and I suddenly wanted to skip my way around The Hole singing jaunty tunes—crazy, I know. But if Dominic was jealous, then he liked me.

Liked me.

Dominic Mondez, universal womanizer and celebrated player, saw me as more than a vagina. Okay, so his affection was presently residing under a shitload of spite, hostility, and the possible lingering remains of some woman's cheap perfume, but it was there nonetheless.

Clearly, Dominic wasn't interested in the reasons behind his rude behavior, he just wanted me to pay for the inconvenience of feeling anything at all. He stalked closer, a predatory look masking his flawless face. "Tell me, Riley." The gap between us was closing fast. "How long have you and that prick been together?" He lowered his voice. "Weeks?"

I gasped.

"Months?"

My gaze narrowed.

"Years?"

My fists clenched.

There was no denying it, even when being a complete asshole, Dominic was still the most breathtaking sight I had ever seen. He was an electrical thunderstorm, all dark clouds, crackling energy, and potentially lethal lightning strikes.

My back hit the wall with a dull thud. Dominic glowered at me and swallowed when I bit my bottom lip. Deliberately, he pushed the leather jacket off my shoulders and let it drop to the floor.

Anger simmered in my belly.

Oh, no, you don't.

"When he touches you," he murmured, slowly trailing calloused fingers down my arms. "Does your skin flush scarlet like it does for me?"

Don't you dare punish me for something I didn't do.

His eyes flicked to my cleavage, it rose and fell with frantic breaths—*fuming*, frantic breaths. Nothing else.

I won't feel guilty for going on a date. I won't.

Dominic placed his hands on either side of my neck and I inhaled sharply when his knee forced its way between my legs, shifting them apart.

I've seen you with God knows how many women? Screw you, buddy. Screw—

He pressed his hips to my stomach and I felt him hardening against me. A low growl sounded, I think it was me.

"When he touches your body, does your pulse jump like it does for me?"

This whole friends thing was officially fucked. Fucked. I was going to kill him or jump him, not sure which but either way, it wasn't going to be pretty.

He leaned forward until his lips hovered enticingly close. "And when his mouth is on yours—"

I didn't let him finish.

I'd had enough. Of the innuendo, the misunderstandings, the abstinence, everything. In that moment I was sober enough to know better but too drunk

131

to care. This man was a spark to my gunpowder and he was going to feel the blast.

Consequences be damned.

I reached up, delving my fingers through his disheveled hair and then pulled down. Hard. Dominic's breath hissed through clenched teeth as his head snapped back, eyes flashing fire. Then, directing his face close to mine once more, I not-so-gently nipped his bottom lip. "I've never lied to you."

Dominic's knee involuntary spread my legs wider. I was wet. So very, very wet.

Not thinking, just doing.

"I. Don't. Have. A. Boyfriend," I repeated. Somewhere, from the back of his throat came a threatening snarl. Whatever. "I went on a date, a first date. Deal with it."

Dominic's nostrils flared. "Since we're being honest," he growled, "I'm on a first date right now."

I rolled my eyes. Surprisingly, this news didn't upset me. Heck, the fact his body was pressed against mine spoke volumes of his interest in his date. So, there was no point in denying it any longer, the line between friends and … whatever the hell we were currently, had been crossed. Who was I kidding? That sucker had been doused in kerosene and set alight with a gigantic flamethrower.

You see, from the very first moment our lives collided we ignored the bleeding obvious—our chemistry. More than that, we also refused to admit the undercurrent of genuine affection we felt for the other too. And Dominic cared for me; as much as he hated to admit it, he did. I knew it when he walked me back to my car the first day we met, I knew it when he didn't judge me for my stupid actions last week, and I knew it when he held me close on Friday afternoon. I knew.

So, rather than knee him in the balls, I tugged down on his hair in warning. "Yeah? Didn't take you for the dating kind. How's it working out for you?"

He ground his hips against me and I moaned. "Fuckin' shit."

"Anything I can do to help?"

"Hell yes."

And with that, he lowered his head, his mouth claiming mine. The moment our lips touched, we stared into each other's eyes, shocked. For a good five seconds, neither of us moved, we were too busy trying to figure out what the heck just detonated. But then my eyelids flickered closed and I surrendered, to the heat, the blaze, the burn.

To inevitability.

Oh. God.

Dominic's lips devoured mine. "Fuck, Riley. You taste…" And he groaned, delving his tongue inside. The exquisite sensation of it exploring my mouth and then running across my front teeth before licking the underside of my top lip left me breathless. Utterly. Breathless.

The man kissed me like his life depended on it, like he was drowning, and I kissed him back pretending he could be saved.

One of Dominic's hands traveled from my neck, down to my breasts. My nipples were all but laser beams so wordlessly I arched my back, offering myself to him. When his palm cupped and kneaded my soft flesh before pinching the taut peaks, I moaned into his mouth.

He sucked in a sharp breath. "Knew it'd be like this," he muttered, between hot, wet kisses. "Fuckin' knew it." His fingers skimmed over my ribs and around to my ass. Groaning, he squeezed it. "From the moment I first saw you, I… Jesus."

My hips bucked, and I moaned far too loudly,

much to the amusement of people walking past. Not that I cared, I was pretty sure dry humping wouldn't result in a public indecency arrest. So, Dominic could do whatever the hell he wanted with me, the sensations he conjured were too phenomenal to stop.

Thankfully, he didn't.

Oh, no, clearly the man wanted to see me come apart because his hand purposefully glided down my bare thigh and when he reached the back of my knee, hitched my leg up to wrap around his hip. He ground into me.

"Damn, Riley."

Fuck, fuck, fuck.

I broke away, my head tipping back against the wall as I felt just how much Dominic wanted me.

Quite a lot, it seemed.

The jean-clad hardness of his cock rubbed against the lace-covered softness of my clit, and as he licked his way down my neck, light flickered before my eyes. I dug my nails into his shoulders. "*Dominic.*"

I was going to come. Swear to God, if he didn't stop doing that thing with his tongue and if I didn't stop grinding up against him like some cowgirl at a rodeo, it was going to be all over within the next thirty seconds. And he hadn't even been inside me yet.

Fucking hell.

"What are you doing?"

Dominic's head whipped up. Standing at the entrance of the hallway with hands on her hips was a tall, tan, shapely blonde. Her skin-tight black dress emphasized large breasts, a tiny waist, and generous hips. She looked stunning, she also looked furious.

Stepping away from me, Dominic adjusted himself before running a hand through his hair. I hastily pulled my dress back down and bent to collect my leather jacket, pulse still racing.

Well. This is awkward.

"I'm going to ask you one more time, what the fuck are you doing?"

My eyes were pinned to Dominic's stony profile, imploring him to look at me. When he eventually glanced my way, his usually piercing stare had turned flat, empty.

Don't you *dare* walk away from me.

He shifted his gaze back to Angry Amazon Woman. "Nothing, I—"

My heart sank. No, scrap that, it plunged face-first onto a rusty shank wrapped in barbed wire, there might even have been a taipan oozing hydrofluoric acid thrown into the mix.

Asshole.

"Let's just get out of here, Amelia." He strode forward, grabbing the girl's elbow and steering her into the throng of revelers. She glared pointed daggers both at him and then at me, the whole way.

I just stood there, numb, staring at the scratch marks on the back of his neck as they receded from view, wishing beyond hope they would turn septic. After pressing trembling fingers to swollen lips and fighting back an onslaught of angry tears, I shook my head.

Girl, you played with fire. What else did you expect?

Never again.

No. Fucking. Way.

That familiar sense of abandonment washed over me as I thought back to an earlier time.

"Don't go."

Will's brown eyes were soft. "Babe, you know I have to," he murmured.

"No, you don't."

"Yes, I do. I've already accepted the job. It'll only be for twelve months and then I'll be back, you'll see.

Come on, we need this."

He wiped away the tears which trickled down my cheeks and then kissed the droplets off his fingers. He was forever doing that, being ridiculously romantic without even trying. Even in my emotionally fragile state I still managed a mild swoon. Stupid gravity.

"We'll make it work," he assured me. "We'll talk, text, FaceTime. We'll be in contact so much you won't even realize I'm gone." His smile was almost convincing.

Almost.

I nodded as a nasal voice crackled over the loudspeaker, announcing his flight and I instinctively clutched his t-shirt tighter. "Will."

"Babe, I'm telling you, we're gonna be okay."

In an attempt to maintain some semblance of rationality, I let go and took a step back. Granted, it was a small one—heck, an ant would have made more progress—but it was a step, nonetheless. Will gave me one last smile, a quick peck on the cheek, and then rushed toward his gate.

A minute later, he was gone.

Twelve months later he was still gone.

He never came back.

When I eventually pulled myself out of that unhelpful reverie and stumbled, zombie-like back to the bar, I noticed the swarm of thirsty rockers demanding refreshments had multiplied considerably. Brea looked swamped.

She saw me loitering by the trays of dirty glasses on the right hand side of the bar and moved over. "Girl, I'm so sorry. Corey's gone home sick so I need to pull a double shift to cover for him."

I gave a weak smile. "It's fine, really. We'll catch up another time." I shrugged. "To be honest, it's probably best I go home anyway."

Brea eyed me closely and nodded. "Yeah. Take a taxi, okay? I don't think you should drive."

"I'm fine, you just focus on that." I indicated with my head to the crowd that had started to grow restless in her absence. Anyone would have thought they needed a twelve-step program with the way they eyeballed the glinting bottles behind her.

We said our goodbyes and I pushed my way through the sweaty bodies standing between me and the front entrance. The room had grown hot and stuffy with so many people pressed up against each other and my fuzzy brain craved fresh air.

As soon as I stepped out into the crisp evening, I shut my eyes and threw back my head, breathing deeply. The muffled sounds of thumping drums and heavy guitar riffs emanated from inside The Hole but for once, I was glad to be leaving.

What a clusterfuck of a night.

I exhaled. How had it gone from a few innocent beers with Brea to dry humping a commitment-phobe? Opening my eyes again, I shook my head, resolute. That man wielded way too much power over me, it was like he flicked the switch to my crazy button. I had to keep my distance, my sanity depended on it.

Scanning both my left and right, I swore under my breath. Great, just great. No taxis. I thought for a moment and then moved unsteadily toward my car.

Don't do it, Riley.

I knew it wasn't a good idea and up until that point, I had never even considered driving drunk before in my life. But I wanted to go home. More than anything in the world, I wanted to crawl into bed and never leave it again. At least, not until the memory of Dominic's skillful lips faded into oblivion, which to be fair, would probably take an eternity anyway. So, standing in front of my car, I pulled the keys out of my jacket pocket and stared down at them.

"Don't even think about it."

I jumped with a start, spinning around so quickly, the keys flew out of my hand. They were plucked out of the air by none other than the last person I ever wanted to see again. Dominic must have been watching from the shadows the entire time I had been standing there contemplating my decision. To be honest, I wasn't sure whether to feel secretly pleased or disturbed.

He stepped out of the darkness, the light from a nearby streetlamp illuminating his hard features as they materialized, piece by mouth-watering piece. I shivered.

He's a dick, Riley. Don't forget that.

After somewhat recovering from my fright, I narrowed my eyes at him. "Give me back my keys."

"No."

I took a step forward, grounding out, "Give them back, Dominic."

Dominic moved closer, so close in fact I could feel his warm breath brush my cheeks. Ignoring the way my heart traitorously responded to these unintentional air caresses, I glared up into his annoyingly handsome face. He looked as angry as I felt.

"I said, no," he repeated.

Throwing up my arms in exasperation, I cried, "Why are you even here? Have you been put on this earth to punish me for shit I did in a past life? Because I sure as hell haven't done anything cruel enough to deserve you in this one."

Dominic stared at me and the intensity in his gaze caused me to take a step back. A range of emotions flickered across his face—irritation, resentment, lust, need, bewilderment, fear—it was like watching a slot machine which could explode at any moment. Finally, he settled on resignation. "I deserved that."

I ducked my head, the fight draining away from me as quickly as it came—it was too exhausting. With eyes downcast, I mumbled, "No, you didn't." Taking a deep breath, I gazed at him again. "I'm sorry for what I said. I didn't mean it, truly."

Dominic groaned and scrubbed one hand down the side of his face. "Fucking hell, Riley."

"What?"

But instead of annoyed, his eyes were gentle. "Angel, you're gonna get eaten alive out there."

"Out where?"

He gestured vaguely to the car park and road beyond, but I knew what he meant.

So, glancing away, I crossed my arms and muttered, "I can take care of myself."

Dominic snorted, before indicating to his car parked nearby, I hadn't even noticed it was there. "C'mon." He strode toward it.

My feet didn't move.

Dominic must have sensed my refusal because he stopped and turned around. "Come on, Riley."

"No."

His eyes narrowed. "Get in the car."

I shook my head.

He strode panther-like toward me, his eyes dark. I swallowed but remained still. After all, I needed to put some distance between the two of us, so there was no way in hell I was getting in a car with the man.

When he towered over me, I refused to tremble. I also refused to acknowledge the heat that somehow pooled in the base of my stomach.

"We can do this the easy way or the hard way. What's it gonna be?"

I glared up at him, defiant to the last.

"All right then." He gave a wicked grin before picking me up and throwing me over his shoulder like I weighed no more than his electric guitar.

"Put me down," I squealed, kicking my legs against his torso and pummeling my fists into his ass. Laughing, he gripped me tighter, restraining my lower body before slapping me soundly on the backside with an open palm.

I froze.

"You did not just do that."

His answering snicker refuted me. However, before I could retaliate, a car door opened and I was unceremoniously dumped in the passenger seat. Dominic moved to the drivers' side of his Thunderbird and climbed in beside me. I cursed myself for letting him cop an eyeful of my exposed upper thigh, so hastily pulled the hem of my dress back down.

"It's a bit late for modesty, angel." He smirked.

As he started the vehicle and sped off down the street, I thought up thirteen creative ways of wiping that stupid grin off his gorgeous face. And it wasn't until I'd hierarchized them all—tying him up and forcing him to watch me set his guitar alight was my number one pick— that I realized where we were. Confused, I looked around, we were almost at my apartment.

Strange, I didn't give him directions.

"How do you know where I live?"

He looked across at me. "I drove Gracie and Levi to the airport this morning."

I raised my eyebrows at the nickname he had given Grace, she would have hated it. "Seems like everyone knows my address these days," I muttered.

"What do you mean?"

"Well, first Robin and now—" I stopped, my gaze flying to his before shifting away again.

Shit, I said too much.

"Who the fuck's Robin?"

I stared out the window, refusing to meet his eyes.

Dominic swerved to the curb and killed the engine. He then turned to face me, his broad shoulders taking up so much space they somehow made the cabin feel small, insanely small, intimate even. Well, maybe if it weren't for the testosterone streaming out his ears like storm water down a drainpipe.

"Is that the name of the pretty boy you were mouth-fucking last night?"

I glared at him, ignoring the fact that his fists were clenched so tightly the whites of his knuckles showed. "Don't you dare." His eyes flashed fire. "After the way you treated me tonight, you're lucky you're not castrated."

He scowled.

I scowled.

He leaned forward, growling.

I leaned forward, glaring.

After an epic stare off, which I totally won because he blinked, I spat out, "By the way, where's your date?" The last word tasted like bitter coffee and I had a sudden craving for peppermint tea.

"Not here."

"Well, in that case," my voice dripped with so much sarcasm I was surprised the car floor wasn't saturated with it, "why don't you make a move on me again, huh? I mean, it worked out so brilliantly before. Hey, maybe we'll drive past some other woman you're hot for and you can leave me on the side of the road this time? You know, mix it up a little?"

"Cut the bullshit, Riley. I didn't start what happened between us at The Hole and you know it."

"You've got to be kidding me."

"Hell no. Are you honestly saying you didn't shove your tongue down my throat?"

"Are you honestly saying your hands weren't all over my ass? For Christ's sake, Dominic, your touch short-circuited my brain, what was I supposed to do?"

"Leave me the fuck alone, that's what."

"I was trying to leave you alone, believe me, I was. But you're everywhere, Dominic." My arms flailed around me like the shock reflex of a newborn baby. "You're in my head all the time and just when I think I can deal with the messed-up emotions you create, you show up looking like a goddamn orgasm personified." I was so worked up I was panting. "Then you have the audacity to kiss me, *kiss me*, Dominic. And of course, it was the best kiss of my life, wasn't it? I mean, this wouldn't be the headfuck to end all headfucks without that bombshell annihilating my sanity completely."

Dominic turned away, his jaw working. He was silent for a long time.

"Perfect. Just perfect." I stared at the console, disgusted at how much I divulged and how little he admitted in return.

Guess I was the only one who found the situation exasperating.

He muttered something under his breath.

"What?"

"Forget it."

"What did you say?"

"I said, forget it."

I officially lost my shit. Big time.

"*What did you say, Dominic?*"

Now, I wasn't normally someone who yelled. Heck, I avoided confrontation like it was herpes, but this man had pushed me over the edge time and time again. I was sick and tired of the free-fall.

Turned out, I wasn't the only one.

Rounding on me, he roared, "*I said it was perfect*." His eyes were anguished like the words were being ripped from his chest. "Your damn lips, your taste, the way your body fit mine like it was fucking made for me. It was all perfect." He took ragged breaths while I sat there, stunned. Dominic's voice almost broke as he continued, "You think this is hard on you, Riley? Well, it's fucking hard on me too. You make me feel things I don't want to feel, you make me believe things I don't want to believe, and you make me want what I sure as fuck don't deserve." He closed his eyes for a moment before continuing. "I'm not a good man, I'm not, but when I'm with you…" Dominic opened his eyes again and his gaze looked so lost and bewildered I actually forgot to breathe. "I can pretend to be one, even if it's only for a short while." He shook his head. "Thank fuck Amelia showed up when she did and reminded me of who I was—who I am."

"Why?"

But he didn't answer, so we remained in the darkness for a long time, each of us lost in thought.

I leaned back against the leather seat, God, I felt tired. The alcohol had worn off and I was left with a throbbing head, aching limbs and a heart that was so confused it barely remembered to beat. At last, I rubbed weary eyes, murmuring, "What are we doing, Dominic?"

He turned to me, his gaze despondent. "Nothing. We're doing nothing. You're dating a fucktard, I'm baggin' women, and that's just the way it is." With a heavy sigh, he gunned the engine and we drove the rest of the way to my apartment in silence.

I honestly thought that was the last time I would ever see Dominic, but fate, the fickle creature, had other plans.

Chapter Nine

Separate,
Does this feel right?
Stop holding on,
Don't let go.
—MONDEZ, "Awoken"

"Wow. You weren't joking when you said he bought the entire florist." Mae leaned in to smell the blooms.

There was no doubt about it, the bouquet still looked as beautiful as it did when Robin delivered it yesterday. However, when I first awoke that morning I needed to open a window because the smell gave me a headache.

Way to be ungrateful, Riley.

Despite my misgivings, Mae seemed to enjoy their sweet fragrance. "Nice." She looked back at me. "They must have cost more than my annual salary."

I grimaced. I'd been trying not to think about how much money Robin spent on me. For some reason, doing so made me feel uncomfortable, guilty even. Never a good sign.

After taking a final sniff, Mae turned around to face me. Strangely, she then proceeded to look me in the eyes for a good thirty seconds without saying a word, not one. It was seriously unnerving. So much so, I quickly grabbed a dishcloth and started wiping the already pristine cooktop like it had an inch-thick layer of residual grease.

"Okay, out with it."

"Huh?" My air of nonchalance was somewhat sabotaged by my frenzied strokes.

"Riley, you've almost rubbed off the label."

I swore under my breath when I realized she was right.

"You've seen Dominic again, haven't you?"

My startled eyes flew to her shrewd ones.

"For beguck's sake, Riley," she groaned.

"Beguck? Mae, that's not even a word."

My friend's gaze shifted to Annabelle. She was sitting cross-legged on the lounge room floor, having a tea party with her giraffe, the TV remote and a cushion. Mae's eyes moved back to mine. "Little Miss over there dropped the f-bomb at daycare. Now whenever I go in to pick her up, her primary carer gives me these judgmental looks." She shrugged one shoulder. "Figured I might as well curb my potty mouth before Annabelle says something worse to her, like how the old witch has a beard."

I squeezed Mae's hand comfortingly. "You're an amazing mum, don't let anyone make you think otherwise. Besides," I moved to the cupboard and grabbed some teacups, "isn't swearing a rite of passage or something? I'm sure every child says something embarrassing growing up. God knows I did, Mum still reminds me of all the shi—" Thankfully, Annabelle hadn't heard my almost-profanity "—*things* I said when I was younger."

"Maybe." Mae shook her head. "Anyway, back to the original topic. Did you or did you not see Dominic again?"

I sighed. That girl was as single-minded as a customs dog at border security. While turning on the kettle, I nodded. "Yes, but it's not what you think."

"Really?" She totally nailed the whole me-and-my-raised-eyebrow-don't-believe-you glare.

"Yes, really." I placed a peppermint tea bag and

145

some honey in each cup. "I honestly had no idea he was going to be at The Hole last night."

"Hang on," Mae interrupted. "Isn't The Hole a dive bar? What the hell were you doing at a place like that?"

"Brea works there and each weekend they play local live music." I gave a half-smile. "It's fun."

Her eyes immediately narrowed. "What type of live music?"

"Seriously, Mae? Does it matter?"

"You know it does."

I gave an exasperated sigh. "Fine, they play rock music. Heavy, loud, dirty, rock music. Now, do you have any other questions, Mum?"

"Just one … is Dominic in a rock band?"

My mouth opened and closed while I frantically tried to think of a way to divert the conversation but eventually just gave up and accepted the unavoidable. "Yeah."

"Christ."

The way she pronounced the blasphemy immediately took me back to when I was a child.

"Ouch."

Mummy came running over to where I was laying flat on my back in the entrance hall. "Christ, baby girl. Are you okay?" She crouched down next to me and her eyebrows did that crinkly thing again. She must have been scared. The last time she looked like that, I'd bumped my head on the side of the pool and blood ran everywhere.

Slowly, I sat up, rubbing my elbow. "I think I need a Band-Aid." My eyes were hopeful.

Mummy smiled down at me and my belly went all warm, like melted honey. "I think you'll be okay, love," she murmured. "But this on the other hand," she held up the offending toy car, "isn't quite so lucky."

I regarded it carefully. She was right, two of the wheels had fallen off and a window looked cracked. Instinctively, I started nibbling my bottom lip.

"How did it happen?"

Staring down at the white porcelain tiles, I mumbled, "I just wanted to see how fast I could run from the kitchen to the dining room. I didn't see it, promise."

When I finally managed to look her in the eyes again, she gave me a soft smile. "He's going to notice."

My voice trembled. "Am I in trouble?"

Mummy sighed. "You will be if we don't check the remainder of your running track. Goodness knows what else has been left lying around this house. Rose should have picked up all of these toys yesterday."

I winced, hoping our new housekeeper wasn't going to get into trouble because of me.

"Come on." She held out her hand to me. "Let's go look."

My smile was wide as I clasped her fingers, babbling excitedly. "Once we've tidied up, do you wanna time my lap? Reckon I'll be able to go really fast."

Annabelle's enthusiastic rendition of Happy Birthday—I think it was directed at the cushion—brought me back from my thoughts. I shook my head and a short while later, Mae and I were comfortably seated on the couch, cradling our cups of tea.

"So what happened when you saw him?"

I took a small sip, desperately trying to tame the blush that threatened to flood my cheeks. "We, ah, bumped into each other by accident."

My friend nodded encouragingly.

"And…"

Mae placed her cup down on the coffee table with a decided thump.

"Relax, it was just a kiss." I tried to push away the memory of Dominic's fingers branding my skin, of his tongue stroking mine, of his hard, pulsing, throbbing—

"Riley."

"Sorry." I internally slapped my own face. There was no stopping the scorching burn which worked its way across my cheeks that time. After taking a deep breath, I continued. "Anyway, nothing much happened because his date interrupted us."

Mae's mouth actually dropped open. "His *date*?"

I nodded, hoping her verbal lashing would be somewhat subdued on account of her daughter playing nearby and all.

"He was on a date with another woman when he kissed you?" The girl looked beyond incredulous. "Are you begucking serious right now?"

"Well, I guess when you say it like that—you know, all shocked and everything—it sounds pretty bad."

"You think?"

I sighed and took another sip of tea.

Mae leaned forward and picked up her cup before taking a mouthful, only to spit it back out again, exclaiming, "Oh, my God, that stuff's awful." Her horrified expression was hilarious. "It tastes like a tree just threw up in my mouth."

"Want me to make you a coffee?"

She nodded.

By the time I sat back down again, handing Mae a double strength coffee that even Grace would have been proud of, I noticed she was looking at me strangely. "What?"

"I get it."

"Get what?"

"The fascination with Dominic. I mean, the guy's sex on legs, he's in a rock band, he clearly knows his way around women and he's not afraid to go after what he wants. So I get it." Her eyes gentled. "The only problem is, I don't think you do." She shook her head sadly. "He's gonna tear you apart, love."

I suddenly found my fingernails incredibly interesting.

After a minute, she murmured, "Is he good to you?"

My gaze flicked to hers. I wanted to tell Mae that yes, Dominic was very good to me, but that wouldn't be entirely true. I mean, in part he was good to me, there was no denying it. However, in other ways… Well. He warned me I was going to get hurt, and last night he followed through on that threat. Dominic walked away with another woman despite knowing in his heart our shared connection was pretty damn phenomenal. He left me feeling vulnerable, exposed and, well … used.

Therein lay the answer.

So, shaking my head, I mumbled, "No, he's not good for me."

"Right. So, when you see him next what are you going to say?"

"I don't think I will see him again."

She snorted.

"Seriously, Mae, I won't."

"Amuse me, Riley. Let's say you hypothetically bump into him at the beach or The Hole, what do you tell him?"

I glanced briefly at Annabelle before replying. "I tell him to leave me the beguck alone."

"That's my girl."

As soon as Mae and Annabelle left, I quickly changed into some running gear, grabbed my water bottle and froze. "Crap."

Dominic still had my car keys.

Despite ceremoniously handing over the set for my apartment last night, he refused to give back those for my convertible. I wanted to feel angry with him, but in truth he made a mature decision, despite it being an inconvenient one. The only problem was, now I had no mode of transportation. Just as I was about to scroll through my contacts list and give him one heck of a grumpy phone call, I heard that familiar faint rumble in the distance. I locked up the apartment and raced down the stairs, water bottle in hand. By the time I made it to the communal car park at the base of the building, Dominic had already pulled up.

Peeking behind me, I noticed the telltale movement of Mrs. Jenkinson's lavender curtains. She was going to have a field day gossiping about this—well-behaved Riley Sears jumping into a beast of a car with a Herculean-sized man. It would get her through the next three days for sure. Oh, well, at least the sprint upstairs to old Mrs. Theolara's front door would increase her heart rate. In fact, if I thought about it from that perspective, I was actually giving the woman an impressive cardio workout. I smiled, no longer feeling the suffocating weight of her prying eyes and instead commending myself on my good deed for the day.

After slipping into the passenger seat, I took a deep breath and glanced across at Dominic.

Yikes.

He looked good, insanely good, like, I'm-going-to-have-you-every-which-way good.

If only.

I swallowed.

With a cerulean blue t-shirt stretched tightly across an obscenely broad frame, black basketball shorts outlining his strong, muscular legs and a dark cap facing backward, I had to consciously tell my brain to function.

For real. Which probably accounted for why I had to clear my throat a few times before any noise came out. Eventually, I managed to squeak, "Hey."

"Hey."

I'm embarrassed to admit the brief sound of his deep, gravelly voice made me literally squirm in my seat. A sudden ball of tension materialized at the base of my stomach and I knew exactly what it would take to rid me of it.

Dominic. Naked. Fucking me senseless.

Oh. God.

I took another deep breath, forcing all the sexy thoughts to the back of my mind. With superhuman will, I held out my hand, gesturing with my fingers for him to hand me back the keys.

Dominic's eyes narrowed. "You need to promise me never to pull that shit again, Riley. Wanting to get behind the wheel drunk? What the fuck were you thinking?

Okay, so scolding me like a two-year-old worked brilliantly at diffusing my raging hormones. I glared at him, refusing to answer.

"I'm not bullshitting when I say I'll impound your car if it happens again."

I rolled my eyes. "You can't confiscate my car, Dominic."

"The hell I can."

The tight clench of his jaw and pointed stare told me he was serious, deadly serious. I looked away, my heart pounding. "Fine."

"Fine, what?"

Turning back, I snapped, "I promise never to get behind the wheel after I've been drinking. Happy?"

"No." But he dropped the keys into my outstretched palm anyway.

"Thank you," I murmured.

We drove to The Hole—you guessed it—in silence and after quickly changing vehicles, I gave a long sigh of relief. While speeding along the coastal highway, I made a conscious effort to ignore the fact that Dominic had refused to utter another word to me after his verbal reprimand, yet waited until my car safely pulled out of the parking lot before accelerating toward the beach himself. It wasn't easy; I mean, the man was a walking contradiction for God's sake. He was both sunshine and storm clouds, flame and frost, kind and cruel—it was confusing as hell.

Which was why I had to stop seeing him. The whole conflicting emotions thing had officially run its course and it was time to move on. So, in my head I repeated over and over again the phrase I had given Mae.

He's not good for me. He's not good for me. He's—

If only my body would listen.

When I eventually made my way down the wooden stairs leading onto the sand, Dominic was already there, waiting. He stood facing the water, which today appeared grey and wild. Dark clouds hovered menacingly above and I rubbed my arms as a salty wind whipped the ocean spray across my exposed skin, stinging me.

Just get it over with, Riley. Pull up your big girl panties and tell him it's over.

I moved to where he stood and gazed up at his closed profile.

So complicated, so beautiful. Why do you have to be so beautifully complicated?

Steeling myself, I murmured, "We need to end this charade, Dominic." He blinked. Honestly, it was the only sign which proved he heard me at all. "We can't just be friends, you know it and I know it."

He turned to me, his blue eyes mirroring the tempestuous sky above.

"And we can't be more than friends either. I mean, I don't want a casual hookup and you don't want a committed relationship."

"You're right, I don't."

Why? For the love of God, *why?* What the hell caused you to feel this way?

But I remained mute on that subject and instead continued with, "So, we need to make a mature decision and do what's best for both of us."

Dominic's gaze morphed from stoic to predatory as he stepped closer, crowding my personal space. I really didn't mind. In fact, my heartbeat loved it a heck of a lot and it took everything I had not to throw myself at the man and rip his t-shirt off with my teeth.

"What's best for us, angel?" Dominic's low voice spoke directly to my pussy.

"I…" I swallowed, clenching my thighs together. "I think we should stop … ah, hanging out."

"Do you?" He bent his head, his nose skimming down my neck and across my collarbone, inhaling deeply. "Are you sure about that?"

I reached out, grasping his biceps—man, they were huge—as my head rolled back and sensation overtook common sense. "Not really."

Dominic gave a low chuckle before nipping my flesh—I gasped. "Didn't think so. You sure you can handle not seeing me anymore?"

I nodded, I think. It was hard to tell with my breasts crushed against his chest.

"Seems to me, your head is saying one thing but your body is saying another." His tongue lapped the spot which only moments ago stung from his teeth and my grip on his arms tightened.

"I'm not sure of anything anymore," I whispered. "I can't think when you're this close to me."

There was a brief pause. Dominic swore under his breath before releasing me from his hold. After taking a deliberate step back, he turned away, raking tense fingers through unruly hair, studying the turbulent ocean.

"Dominic?"

Nothing.

I moved closer, placing a tentative hand on his shoulder. "What's going on?"

When he turned back to me, his face wore a mask of indifference. I swear, a bowling ball to the stomach couldn't have done a better job at stealing my breath. "You know what? You're right. We need to stop this."

It took me a minute to pull myself together and then another few to gather my confused thoughts, but when I did, I muttered, "It doesn't matter anyway, I'm on an afternoon roster for the next two weeks so it's unlikely we'll see each other again."

Piercing blue eyes burned my skin. "When are you running?"

"Early morning."

"What time?"

I told him and he nodded, his jaw working hard. We were quiet for a moment longer and both of us watched as a gull swooped from the stormy sky above down to the wild ocean. It dived for a fish but seconds later struggled its way back into the air again with nothing in its beak. Entranced, we watched it. Over and over again it plummeted, over and over again it rose unsuccessful. The continual failure broke my heart.

Turning my back on the bird, I murmured, "Ready?"

"Yep."

And we took off down the beach.

Over an hour later, Dominic and I were back where we started. Panting, we trudged our way off the sand and up the stairs. It had been an intense workout. We each pushed the other harder than we had before and even stayed longer in the secluded cove completing challenging strength exercises despite the crazy weather. I for one dragged my feet with each step, though not from exhaustion, I just didn't want to say goodbye.

Fool that I was.

When we reached our vehicles, I grabbed my water bottle and took a sip. Dominic looked at me as though he was dying of thirst, so I offered my drink to him. With a half-smile, he took it, but not before our fingers touched. Whether it was on purpose or accidental, I couldn't be sure. What I could be sure of, however, was the way my skin hummed at the contact. Yes, *hummed.* A thrilling tingle wound its way up my arm like a vine slowly unraveling and I determinedly stared down at my running shoes so as not to give away how much his touch affected me.

Shit timing.

"Thanks."

My head shot up and Dominic grinned at me—at least the exercise helped improve his mood. His eyes were clear and his lips quirked up in the corners. My female parts swooned.

I mumbled something similar to, "No problem," put the bottle back in my car, and then stood there, awkward.

Well, this sucks.

Taking a deep breath, I murmured, "Guess I'll see you around then." My attempt at a genuine smile was pathetic by any standards but I found it impossible to feel pleased when my heart hurt.

Dominic's look turned serious, he reached out and gently cupped the side of my face. Instinctively, I leaned into it, shutting my eyes and trying not to cry like an idiot. A calloused thumb running over my bottom lip forced my eyes open again, and I watched as his gaze roamed my face as though committing each feature to memory. He leaned forward, brushing feather-light kisses on my cheek, nose and eyelids, while I just gripped his t-shirt like it was my lifeline.

God, even after a run he smelled amazing.

It was true. The earthy, minty scent of Dominic had me inhaling him like a turbocharged vacuum cleaner and I bit my lip when he whispered in my ear, "See you around, angel."

Before I knew it, he broke from my grip, turned and climbed into his car. The engine roared and not long afterward, he sped away. I honestly couldn't tell if he looked at me in his rearview mirror because my vision was blurred by tears.

****

I chose not to sulk for the rest of Sunday. After all, if there was one thing my witch of a mother taught me it was self-pity wasn't going to change anything. It certainly didn't change her indifference to my unhappiness growing up, that's for sure.

Since the apartment was already the cleanest it had ever been thanks to yesterday's distraction method, I decided on a different approach for the remainder of the afternoon—I was going to organize. Everything.

And boy did I ever.

Nothing was safe, not the cutlery drawer, the wardrobe, the linen cupboard, not even the black abyss under the laundry sink. By the time I was through, everything in the apartment had been systematically reordered, restructured, and redefined. I even color-coded random objects in case the size differentiation groupings were not obvious enough.

So with heavy music blaring and my hands kept busy, I did an awesome job of not thinking about Dominic. I even went a whole fifteen minutes without picturing his ruggedly handsome face at one point.

Awesome.

Sadly, the same could not be said for when I closed my eyes that night. Apparently, my subconscious thought it a great idea to stream images of Dominic into a full-length feature film. Needless to say, sleep was impossible. Instead, I was tantalized with montages of Dominic laughing, scowling, staring, running—heck, even grinding himself up against me—it was torture of the worst kind.

Yeah, trying to forget him sucked.

When I finally rolled out of bed the next morning, I was groggy and irritated, ridiculously so. The last thing I felt like doing was exercising but experience told me that this was when I needed it most. After pulling on my running gear and eating one-third of a banana—trust me, it makes all the difference—I drove to the beach.

The previous day's stormy weather had cleared, leaving the morning sky a textbook blue. There was not a cloud in sight, it was as though the harsh wind and raging waves were nothing more than a figment of my imagination. I took a deep breath. God, I loved the beach. It didn't matter if I started from the same spot and religiously followed an identical route, each day looked and felt completely different. In fact, I was so caught up in my musings that I almost missed the red and white Thunderbird parked nearby.

Almost.

My steps faltered. Yep, that was definitely Dominic's car all right. "What are you up to?" I mumbled to myself while making my way down to the sand.

Unfortunately, I couldn't ask the man in question because he was nowhere to be seen. So I shrugged my shoulders, pushed all confusing thoughts aside and promised myself not to think about that human-sized paradox anymore.

And surprise, surprise, it didn't work.

Not when I took off at an easy jog, not when I increased the tempo midway through my workout, and definitely not when I saw Dominic pumping out some push-ups in the secluded cove at the other end.

Shit.

Once I reached him, I tried ridiculously hard to appear nonchalant and when that didn't work, I even attempted annoyed irritation. But it was impossible. His muscles were rippling in that hypnotic way of his, and those eyes… Well, let's just say I had an itch only he could scratch. Oh, to hell with metaphors, I wanted to throw myself on top of the guy and fuck him senseless.

Oh my God, what's happening to me? I'm turning into a pervert of the worst kind.

I took a deep, albeit ragged, breath. "What are you doing here, Dominic?"

Good, just the right amount of suspicion but with no evidence of carnal lust. Totally nailed it.

He grinned up at me, a mischievous glint in his eyes that I did not trust at all. My knees may or may not have wobbled. "What's it look like? I'm exercising." With that, he stood, winked, and headed back along the beach at a loping run. He even had the nerve to call over his shoulder, "Later," three strides in.

Unbelievable.

****

The events of that morning were still turning over in my head hours later. I was sitting in the cramped office at work, staring absently down at the proof of birth documents which needed to be filled after the arrival of little Millie-Kate not an hour ago. Normally, they would have taken me all of five minutes, but I was pretty sure I had been staring at them for a good forty. Clearly, Dominic's appearance at the beach had thrown me. I mean, I could not stop thinking about him. What was he doing there? Why did he wait in the car park until I got back to my convertible before driving off? And why the heck didn't he wave back?

My head was spinning.

It made no sense. Not his behavior, his words, his intentions, nothing. Was this his idea of a joke? If it was, I must have been the brunt of it because I totally missed the punch line. All I knew was seeing him again left me confused, intrigued and hornier than a Texas Longhorn bull.

Jesus.

"Need any help?"

I jumped and then squealed.

A warm hand rubbed my knee. "Sorry, Riley. I didn't mean to frighten you."

I bit my lip because Robin had crouched down beside me. In fact, his soothing gesture did a heck of a lot more to my hormones than he probably intended.

"You okay?"

Turning, I gazed into concerned caramel eyes. They were level with mine and oh-so-close.

I really need to get laid.

Flushing, I pressed a hand to my thumping heart and tried to pass my sudden breathlessness off as something far less carnal. "Sorry, I was miles away."

He looked at me. "What's on your mind?"

Sex. Lots and lots of sex.

But I bit my lip before smiling innocently at him

159

instead. He was so sweet and so very, very handsome. Those eyes were liquid gold, they promised slow, sensual lovemaking and an earth shattering orgasm at the end of it.

Focus, Riley.

I shook my head. "Nothing really. It's just ... one of those days, I guess." I shrugged one shoulder before changing the subject. "You're not wearing your scrubs."

"No deliveries today. I'm just here to do a few postnatal examinations before I head back across the road."

I nodded, my gaze flitting over his fitted white business shirt and charcoal suit pants. The material stretched tightly over his shoulders and tapered in at his narrow waist; I couldn't help but think the entire ensemble fit him like a really expensive glove. Acting on impulse, I reached for his black tie and ran the length of the textured fabric through my fingers. "I like this," I murmured, tugging it gently.

Riley Sears, what are you doing?

Oh, fuck it.

Robin's eyes darkened, and I heard a sharp intake of his breath as I pulled him closer. He momentarily tensed as our lips met but soon relaxed into the kiss. When my tongue sought entry, he gave an adorable low growl before opening his mouth wider. I gently licked and stroked him, growing hotter, more demanding with each caress. It was not until my fingers crept to his collar and I hungrily loosened his tie before moving down to slowly unbutton his shirt that he made an anguished groan before pulling away.

"Jesus," he gasped.

Shit.

Robin stood and strode to the other side of the small office. I could hear him straightening out his clothes but kept my eyes down, staring at my fingers. To say I was shocked at what I had instigated and how far I would have gone if he hadn't stopped me, was a massive understatement.

After a moment, Robin said, "Riley, don't get me wrong, that was… Wow." I looked up as he ran a hand through his ruffled hair. Moving back to crouch down by my side again, he clasped my hands in his. "But I don't think it's a good idea to mix business with pleasure. Anyone could have walked in on us. They could have reported it and in the blink of an eye, ruined both our careers." Robin's smile was gentle. "Let's not jeopardize everything for the sake of a stolen moment, okay?"

He was right, of course. My actions put him in a potentially explosive situation which could easily have backfired, and it was lucky he put an end to it when he did. I really needed to chill the fuck out, like, stat. So, nodding, I mumbled, "I'm sorry, Robin. I should never have… God, this is embarrassing."

He tucked some wayward hair behind my ear, his touch soft, and grinned. "Don't be. Now I'm really looking forward to Saturday night."

I gave him a returning smile even though my heart wasn't really in it. "Yeah, me too."

Chapter Ten

When we survive,
Tell me your name,
Just so I know,
That we're closer.
—MONDEZ, "Closer"

Dominic was at the beach again on Tuesday morning. Similar to the day before, I pulled up and saw his Thunderbird in the car park. Once again, I promised myself not to think about him as I exercised, only to spy him at the cove and then watch, confused, as he darted off back the way he came.

He was doing my head in.

So much so, that during my lunch break at work, I found myself literally tearing into an Asian salad. It didn't stand a chance. I was seated at the cafe downstairs and had been giving myself an internal lecture about the futility of overanalyzing Dominic's behavior as I ate/stabbed. While I was at it, I also decided to berate myself for breaching the staffing code of conduct the day before. Just the thought of what I'd done to poor Robin made me attack random ingredients with a violent gusto. My vigor would have impressed Stalin himself. Needless to say, I was irritated, embarrassed and so desperate for an orgasm it was bordering on a physical debilitation.

Thus, the culinary carnage.

Mae plonked down opposite me. She looked at my bowl, her brown eyes inquisitive. "What's your deal?" She indicated to the cabbage leaf I had just finished shredding into a gazillion pieces.

I sighed, threw down the knife and fork, and instead focused my wrath on the brownie I bought for dessert.

She stared at me. "You didn't tell Dominic, did you?"

"I told him."

"So what's with the gastronomic abuse?" She gestured to the mess I was now making of my slice. Normally, I would not have wasted a crumb, but today I either wanted to punch something or mount someone, so ripping apart some food until it was dust in my hands seemed the safest alternative.

"He didn't listen." I scrunched my forehead. "Well, that's not entirely true. I mean, he did listen but then again, he didn't…"

Mae picked up her sandwich. "Riley, I've got no idea what the fuck you're talking about." She took a large bite.

I sighed, discarding the brownie remains and wiping my fingers on a napkin. "I told him we needed to stop seeing each other."

"Right," she mumbled around a mouthful.

"And then I said we should be distant friends."

She swallowed. "Okay."

"But when I got to the beach yesterday, he was there. And when I showed up again this morning—" I spread my arms wide.

"He was there again," Mae finished. "Got it." She shook her head. "I can't believe he's still running with you."

"But that's just the thing, Mae." I leaned forward. "He didn't run with me. He was down at the beach before I arrived and waited in his car until I got back. So technically, he did what I asked."

She took another bite and chewed, her features thoughtful. "Hang on, how did he even know what time you were getting there? I mean, we're on afternoons this roster."

I looked away, mumbling, "I might have, ah, accidentally mentioned it on Sunday."

"Rookie mistake."

Nodding, I muttered, "Trust me, I know." I rubbed my fingers across tired eyes, suddenly exhausted. "What's he doing, Mae?"

She shrugged one shoulder.

"Why is he doing this? Running is my thing, you know? I need it to clear my head, but now it's like he's there all the time." I sighed. "I just don't understand."

"Ask him."

I stared at her as though she had just spoken Dutch.

"I mean it, Riley. This man's fucking with you and what's worse is you're letting him. So when you see him tomorrow, grab him by the balls, stare him in the eyes and demand a goddamn answer."

Nodding slowly, I murmured, "That's a good idea. I mean, apart from the ball-grabbing part."

"Of course it is. Now, rather than decimate what's in front of you, how about you actually eat it?"

I smiled, ravenous. Scooping up a forkful of brownie, I popped it in my mouth and moaned in unabashed delight.

Delicious.

****

The next morning, I was determined to confront Dominic. I was going to be calm, firm, assertive—I was going to get answers. However, as soon as I pulled up at the beach, I knew something was up. The man in question was pacing in front of his Ford while muttering into his phone. When I stepped out of my convertible, his eyes found me and something in my stomach shifted. Something big. He ended the call, contemplated me for a moment and then strode over to where I stood.

Now's your chance, Riley. Don't back down now.

He stopped only a foot away.

Yikes. What's with Mr. Intensity?

But I lifted my chin, refusing to become distracted by the molten heat that spread through my limbs and the way his breathing accelerated when he took in my tight running shorts. "Dominic, we need to talk." My voice barely even wobbled.

So far, so good.

"We will. On the plane."

"Look, I don't know what's—" I paused, his words finally registering. "Plane?"

He grinned at my confusion, it was equal parts gorgeous and frustrating. "We're flying to Melbourne this afternoon so you need to go home and pack."

"What?"

"Levi just called, a friend of ours wants Mondez to support them at a gig they've got lined up for tomorrow night. The band that was going to play pulled out, so the boys and I are heading over in their place."

"That's … ah, great." I paused. "Where do I fit in exactly?"

"Levi doesn't want Grace by herself while we're on stage, so you're coming too."

Oh. So, Dominic doesn't want me to go, Levi does.

Ouch.

Now, don't get me wrong, I really wanted to see Grace again. In fact, I missed her so much it hurt. We had not spoken in what felt like years and being with her would ground me from all the craziness of the past few weeks. I was sure I would be able to negotiate my shifts at work. After all, I never took time off so had plenty of leave owing. But Dominic's attitude annoyed me, a lot. I was sick of his arrogance and his games, I refused to play anymore.

"I'm not going."

He stared at me.

"I mean it. I'm not going, Dominic."

He narrowed his eyes and stepped in close. "Yes, you are."

"No. I'm. Not."

He gritted his teeth. "The tickets are already paid for and I'm picking you up from your apartment in one hour. So quit arguing, get that fine ass in your car and head on home to pack."

I threw up my arms, exasperated. "Can you stop bulldozing me for one second? First, I ask you to stay away and you completely ignore me." My entire body blazed. "And now you're ordering me around like I'm a foregone conclusion." I poked him in the chest, it was rock hard. "Well, I'm not, okay? Just because you and Levi snap your fingers doesn't mean I'm going to come running like a fucking lackey."

Blinking back frustrated tears, I mumbled, "Just give me some space, Dominic. Let me breathe, please." I hated how my voice broke on the final entreaty.

Instead of moving away, Dominic did the exact opposite. He wrapped himself around me and one strong arm clasped my waist while the other hand cradled the back of my head. Goose bumps broke out where he touched me and I didn't even bother suppressing the shiver that tingled its way down my spine. After burying his hands in my hair, he tugged on it gently. "I can't."

I hugged him back, even tighter if it was at all possible. His fresh scent disorientated me and I found myself clawing his back, whispering, "You have to."

"I know. But not today."

We continued to hold each other and despite the

obvious contradiction between our words and actions, for the first time in over a week, I felt calm. Peace slowly descended over me like a comforting blanket and seeped warmth through my extremities, relaxing me completely. I sank against him with a sigh.

"Please, Riley."

I squeezed my eyes shut.

"Come to Melbourne with us … with me."

After a moment's hesitation, I murmured, "Okay."

It was official, I was lost, and I hated the sensation because it reminded me of one year ago.

"I won't be long," I promised Phillip, giving him a final, lingering kiss.

"No problem." He brushed his lips against mine once more. "I'll go get some gas, double-check we've packed everything and then meet you back here in half an hour." He pulled away slightly, totally rocking that boyish grin of his. "Can't wait to start a new life with you, Riley."

My heart melted, molten-magma style. "Me neither."

Can this guy be any more perfect?

I shook my head. This was no time for waterfall impersonations, I had shit to do, like, say goodbye to Grace. It wasn't the best timing, particularly with her father passing away only a couple of months ago, but she seemed genuinely happy for Phillip and I. Heck, she'd even not-so-subtly told me to quit putting my life on hold and instead go out and do something with it. She was right, of course. But my stomach still tied in knots when I thought about not seeing her for… To be honest, I really couldn't think about how long it would be without bawling my eyes out.

Grace didn't answer her door. Well, not after the

first hundred or so knocks, anyway.

"*Strange,*" *I mused, unlocking the apartment with my spare key. "Hello?" My voice rebounded off bare walls and echoed through the empty rooms.*

Bare walls? Empty rooms? What the hell?

"*Grace?*"

Moving through the entryway, my gaze flicked first left then right, finally coming to rest on my best friend. She was sitting on the floor where the couch used to be, her back resting against flaking cream paint. Those short legs of hers were stretched out and crossed at the ankles and she was staring straight ahead, her expression blank. It looked like she was watching TV, only there was no television to look at because that too was gone.

"*What's going on?" I ran over and crouched down next to her. "G?" Pushing dark tangled hair away from emerald eyes, I tried to get a closer look. She didn't look good; I blamed the almost empty whiskey bottle sitting close by. "G, what is it?"*

It took her forever to respond and when she did, she simply mumbled, "Serena left."

Cradling flushed cheeks in my hands, I gently turned her head until she was looking at me. "I can see that, but why did your sister leave? Did you guys have a fight or something?"

Grace didn't answer, she just stared, her gaze empty.

Sighing, I asked, "Where's Dylan?"

"*Dunno.*"

"*Oh, G." I slumped down next to her.*

Dylan was an asshole, there was no doubt about it. He was a complete and utter waste of space. So to be honest, I wasn't exactly surprised that he conveniently disappeared when his girlfriend needed him the most. It was just the kind of dipshit he was. But Serena leaving was something different altogether. I shook my head, beyond confused.

Grace started slipping sideways, so I carefully lay her down in my lap, stroking her hair. It wasn't long before the silent tears which must have stained her cheeks dampened the material of my jeans and my heart broke into millions of tiny pieces for her.

I couldn't leave.

Not now.

I couldn't abandon my best friend when everyone else around her had. Sighing, I shut my eyes and rested my head back against the wall.

Maybe one day Phillip will forgive me.

****

Thump.

The sound shocked me from my not-so-pleasant trip down memory lane. I stopped and listened.

Thump. Thump.

"Shit." After turning off the tap, I scrambled out of the shower and hastily dried myself with the first towel I could find.

Thump. Thump. Thump.

"Coming," I called, padding to the front door. Swinging it open, I was met with hostile blue eyes. "Am I late?" I went to check the time on my watch before realizing I had taken it off. Obviously. Since I had been in the middle of a shower and all. I sighed, my arm falling uselessly back to my side again. Dominic seemed to have that effect on me.

The door slammed shut. I glanced up, surprised to see him leaning heavily against it.

"Fucking hell, Riley." His gaze was harsh.

"What?"

"You're bullshitting me, right?"

I took an involuntary step away from the fuming

pile of brawn, completely mystified at what had pissed in his shoes this time.

He rolled his eyes at my blatant incomprehension. "Never answer the door looking like that." He gestured to my near nakedness, and I tried not to notice how the pulse at the base of his throat jumped. No, *leaped*. There might even have been a bungee rope involved.

My gaze dropped down. The fluffy white towel left little to the imagination, it was true. It barely covered my breasts and mid-section let alone... Anyway, he hadn't exactly given me a chance to dress and I was about to tell him so—I even crafted a witty rejoinder in my head—only, when I looked into his eyes again words failed me.

Everything failed me.

Well, everything except for my vagina, of course. There seemed to be a welcome party kicking off down there, complete with balloons and streamers.

I swallowed. Loudly.

The tension between us shifted. I could tangibly feel the energy surge, pulse and crackle as the surrounding air grew denser. Magnetism sparked, fizzed and ricocheted between his body and mine until we were connected by what felt like hundreds of pulsating electric currents.

Whoa. I mean, uh oh.

The guy looked at me as though he was on death row and I was his last meal. I clenched my thighs together, blushing at how soaking wet I had become.

I'm gonna need another shower at this rate. God, I hope he doesn't notice.

His pupils dilated.

He noticed.

Crap.

And if it was at all possible, he suddenly looked

even more famished.

Someone needed to feed the poor man.

Dominic licked his bottom lip, shaking his head. "The things I could do to you."

Okay, so his erotic admission did not exactly help matters in my downstairs department. In fact, it made things a heck of a lot worse because I could have sworn one of the revelers at the welcome celebration let off a party popper.

I needed him. On me, in me, whatever.

Now.

"Do them. All of them."

Did I actually just say that? Out loud?

His gaze darkened.

Yep, sure did.

"I mean it, Dominic. I'm not in the mood for games, so either man up and show me what you want to do to me or leave."

"I'm not leaving."

Smiling, I inched closer, my voice huskier than usual. "Glad to hear it."

He shook his head. "You don't know what you're asking."

I moved until I was pressed flat against him. God, he felt good. And his smell… I let out a soft exhale. "Yes, I do."

Slowly, I skimmed one hand up his bicep, amazed that the simple gesture could have such a profound response. Dominic bit back a groan and I felt his erratic heartbeat pounding under my palm as it flittered across his taut chest. Even his mouth parted when I snaked my hand around the back of his neck.

Wow.

"Angel, I don't—" He growled when my fingers delved into his hair. It was by far the sexiest sound in the

171

whole world. It echoed within me, awakening every last particle that was not already on the verge of a catastrophic meltdown.

"The other women, they know what they're getting themselves into. They can walk away, but you—"

Despite trembling legs, I stood on the balls of my feet, my lips a hairs breadth away from the mouth he wanted to deny me. Mint. Always mint. My goddamn favorite. "I'm not a child, Dominic."

He hesitated, his piercing blue eyes searching mine.

And to be fair, he had good reason to. After all, did I know what I was doing? Not really. Was it all going to end in disaster? Probably. Would that stop me? No. Heck no. I needed him too badly.

"Kiss me."

He did. With a strangled groan, his lips claimed mine. It was as though someone turned the radiator dial up to eleven because an inferno engulfed us and I could feel the burn. I relished it. It felt powerful, raw, beautiful.

Fingers, hands, lips and tongues, they were everywhere yet nowhere. Close yet distant. At some point I must have climbed the man like a ladder because my legs were wrapped around his lean waist, strangler vine style. There was a moan—his or mine, I couldn't tell.

Movement. We were moving.

Crash.

The pungent smell of crushed rose petals filled the apartment.

Right. The kitchen.

I was hastily placed on the countertop, it had been cleared. A low voice rumbled, "Lie down, angel." I clamped my eyes shut, fearful that if I opened them again, none of this would be real.

Thank you, God.

Goose bumps broke out over my skin at the sharp coldness of laminate against my bare shoulders. I gasped but laid there regardless. Truth be told, I would have done anything for Dominic in that moment—a bed of nails? No problem. Terrifying but true.

With a sinful growl, he kissed me again, deeply.

My head spun, my skin blazed and when Dominic's lips left mine I whimpered. I kid you not, the lack of contact shot through me like a lance.

"Shhh," he crooned, as his hands skimmed down my neck and worshiped my cleavage. Those talented, dexterous fingers left rivers of molten heat burning me from the outside in. When they finally reached the towel, there was a short pause and to be fair, I was surprised the damn thing was still on. However, after a ragged breath, the material opened and fell away. I lay naked before him.

"Jesus fucking Christ." Dominic's hungry eyes roamed my body, his jaw working hard. With an anguished groan, he dropped his head, capturing one of my hard pink nipples in his mouth. It was lucky the sucker didn't asphyxiate him, I was that turned on.

Sweet Lord.

I cried out, arching my back and reaching down to grasp his hair, desperately needing something to hold on to. His merciless tongue teasing my pebbled peak had me seeing stars where the off-white ceiling plaster used to be.

"So. Fucking. Good." Dominic hummed, systematically alternating between licks, nips and sucks.

"*Dominic.*"

A large hand kneaded my other breast, its calloused fingers grazing my sensitive skin, sending shockwaves through my body. Finally, his mouth broke away from its sensual onslaught. He palmed both, pushing them up and together before licking the valley

173

between with a surreptitious swipe of his tongue.

"Dominic, I need you. I—"

"I know, angel." He chuckled, shaking his head. "So fucking glad I rocked up when I did."

As his mouth descended on me once again, my hands slid down his back. Dominic moaned softly before nipping my soft flesh. I almost sobbed. Not at the way his teeth sank into the underside of my breast—that sensation went so far beyond good it turned holy—but at the way his firm muscles contracted and elongated under my exploratory touch. It was insane how strong he was, how perfectly formed. Truly it was.

At last, I reached the hem of his t-shirt. Gripping tightly, I yanked the material up and over his head in one fluid motion.

Dominic recovered from the shock of my unexpected movement to grin down at me. "You could've just asked."

I was mute. Honestly, there were no words. In the name of all things logical, there was nothing to be done except ogle the man.

And ogle I did.

Holy. Fuck.

A half-naked Dominic standing between my open legs was the most delectable sight I had ever seen. If only I had a camera.

I shook my head.

Dominic's eyes grew pained. "Don't."

"What?"

"Don't look at me like that."

"Like what?"

But he didn't answer. Instead, he dipped his head and kissed his way down my ribs and stomach, his touch ravenous, his lips unforgiving. The overall effect teetered the precipice of exquisite pleasure and pain. My eyes widened as he intentionally placed first one, and then the other of my legs over his broad shoulders. Pausing, he stared at me, his eyes so dark they were almost black. "You might wanna hold on."

The guy was deadly serious.

So I gripped the edges of the countertop, almost certain there would be indents by the time we were finished.

Fuck. Fuck. Fuck.

Dominic's fingers deftly slipped between the slick skin of my pussy before moving downward and sliding inside. Deep inside. "Christ, Riley," he groaned.

I moaned. A lot.

His fingers rhythmically worked me, and I almost came on the spot when his mouth lowered, his tongue at long last darting out, lapping my clit.

Oh, my God.

Dominic purred while his lips, tongue and fingers played me like some grand maestro. And that wickedly talented virtuoso knew my every want and need before I even recognized it myself—he was a freak of nature. At times he grew tender, his hot tongue softly caressing my swollen flesh. While at others he was merciless, his mouth voraciously gorging itself on my willing pussy.

And throughout it all, I moaned, writhed and bowed, never entirely sure if I was trying to escape the pleasurable anguish he elicited or exacerbate it. Either way, heat unfurled at the base of my spine and slowly spread its way through my trembling limbs.

This was going to be one heck of an orgasm.

"Dominic."

He groaned.

"Dominic, I'm—"

"Let go, angel. Let me feel you come against my mouth."

I came.

With a sharp, anguished cry my entire body detonated. Head back, eyes closed, wave after wave of exquisite release surged through me, annihilating me completely.

"Fucking gorgeous."

I barely registered his voice, it seemed so far away. I just lay motionless in a hazy, semi-comatose state, trying to gather myself together after that epic obliteration.

And then it all changed.

My body gradually registered an empty coldness because Dominic no longer stood where he had moments before, and even though the towel was miraculously wrapped around me once again, it retained no warmth.

I sat up.

My hair must have been a disaster, but it was nothing compared to the carnage on the kitchen floor. Roses, petals, stems, leaves and broken shards of glass were scattered everywhere. It looked like a horticultural massacre of the worst kind.

Sorry, Robin.

Oh, my God, Robin. What must Dominic think of his overenthusiastic declaration?

I honestly couldn't tell because his back was to me, though it seemed he had only noticed what lay at his feet. Regardless, I could distinctly see the tension in his coiled muscles and came to the conclusion that whatever he was thinking, sucked. Hardcore.

"Dominic?"

He remained motionless.

"What's going on?"

Nothing.

I clambered off the countertop, clutching the towel close to my chest. After placing a hand between his shoulders I was shocked to discover his skin had turned cold. "Hey."

"Get dressed."

The abruptness of his voice gouged me like a knife wound, piercing deeply. Surely, an artery had just been severed? I mean, how had we gone from molten heat to arctic blizzard in such a short space of time? I was so confused.

"I said, get dressed. We need to leave."

Turning away, I blinked furiously and stumbled back to my bedroom, completely unconcerned if my feet were torn to shreds by the splinters of shattered glass scattering the floor.

I'm not going to cry, I'm not. I won't give him the satisfaction of my tears.

I took a steadying breath.

Dominic Mondez can go fuck himself.

Chapter Eleven

I'm losing this game so…
No rules,
They make no sense anyway.
—MONDEZ, "Rules"

Dominic and I sat through yet another long and awkwardly silent car journey, though this time to the airport. Each of us was cocooned in our own bubble of spite-filled hurt, refusing to be the first to burst it by speaking. And what happened once we arrived… Well, let's just say it was weird.

As soon as we dropped off Dominic's guitar and our luggage, we headed to the bar and walked up to two of the most breathtakingly handsome men in the airport. They were leaning against a wall, looking all gorgeously self-assured. Of course, I recognized them, one was the drummer and the other the bass guitarist from Mondez. On stage they were a visual feast for the eyes, but in person—sigh—they were an all-you-can-eat buffet.

As soon as Dominic saw them, he transformed into a completely different person. And I mean completely. The man I knew, the one who had turned taciturn and distant lately was suddenly *poof*, gone. Instead, before me stood the physical embodiment of jovial cheerfulness.

It was painful to watch.

"Finn, Tyler," Dominic boomed. He slapped the taller one on the shoulder before dragging him in for a rib-crunching man-hug. This guy had blond shoulder-length hair which hung in the kind of loose waves a hair stylist would have been proud of. Anyway, he eagerly reciprocated said man-hug with plenty of fist-pumping and body-shoving in return. With all the exuberant arm flailing, I noticed that both of his were completely covered in tattoos. They looked amazing.

The shorter guy—Tyler, I think—had blond scruffy hair and forest green eyes. Where Finn was covered in ink work, this man showcased more piercings than I ever knew existed. Not only did he have an eyebrow ring, but there was a nose, lip and spacer earring too, the combination looked sinfully hot. As I stared at him longer, I came to the realization that he was not short at all, he just appeared so next to the two gigantic mounds of hunk and muscle next to him.

How am I going to get through this flight without completely embarrassing myself? I mean, they are three of the sexiest guys on the face of the planet, for God's sake. This is going to be such a disaster.

Sadly, before I could turn and run, I noticed something odd. Both Finn and Tyler kept shooting furtive glances my way and it stopped me dead in my tracks because it could only mean one thing.

They had no idea who I was.

They did not know I was heading to Melbourne with them, they did not know Dominic and I saw each other nearly every day. Heck, I bet they did not even know I was Grace's best friend.

They did not know me at all.

Surely, Dominic mentioned me at some point? Surely, my name came up in conversation? I mean, men talk, right? So, whatever happened to the, "Hey Dominic, you stalking or acting like a total dick toward any impressionable girls lately" conversation?

It had not happened.

Wow. What a blow to the self-esteem. Doctor Powell was going to have a field day with that one. She would be able to deconstruct my emotional vulnerability for at least two sessions, I was certain.

I sighed, choosing to stand slightly apart from them while suddenly finding the loose thread on my red cashmere top extraordinarily interesting. Finally, Finn turned to Dominic and asked, "That your girl?"

My head shot up. "Oh, he's not—"

"She's not—"

Both Dominic and I froze, refusing to look at each other. I tried to pretend our hasty denial was not yet another nail in our relationship's already fastened coffin, but I still could not stop the twinge of hurt that pierced through me. Again. This was shit, and I was now pretty sure the color of my sweater matched my face.

I actually want to die.

Tyler's shoulders started to twitch and it wasn't long before he was laughing so hard I could actually see his tonsils. And tongue ring.

Dominic sighed and half-heartedly gestured for me to move closer. I gritted my teeth and did as he asked, though only because I was tired of being laughed at. So, standing at a respectful distance from the guy who not an hour before had had his head between my thighs, I murmured to the two men, "I'm Riley, it's nice to meet you."

Tyler finally calmed down enough to speak, though his smile was wide. "Hey."

I gave a weak wave.

"Finn."

Turning, I faced what was surely the delectable combination of a seventies rock star and an underwear model. With a strong, angular jaw peppered with light stubble, lush lips, high, angular cheekbones and a straight nose, the guy was simply gorgeous. His most arresting feature were definitely his eyes, they were grey, and I'm talking, soulfully so. They were the kind of eyes that demanded your deepest, darkest secrets, yet shared nothing in return.

I needed to keep my wits about me with this one.

Bizarrely, despite all their combined sexiness, neither Finn nor Tyler made me feel even an inkling of what Dominic did. It was like he was true north and I was a compass needle, I could not see anything else.

Fuck my life.

Anyway, the man in question shifted impatiently next to me. When I finally broke eye contact with Finn and looked over at him, he was glaring.

"Let's go." He turned on his heel and stormed off in the direction of our departure gate.

This was gonna be a long flight.

I didn't know whether to be relieved or insulted that Dominic and I were not sitting directly next to each other. There was an aisle between us, but it might as well have been the Amazon River for all he cared. You see, there was a gorgeous redhead pressed firmly up against his right-hand side and she had two of the largest breasts in the history of mammary glands. I kid you not, they were huge. She also seemed quite proud of her bulging assets, using them at every opportunity to oh so casually brush up against Dominic's arm.

She was going to wear a hole in his sweater if she wasn't careful.

The guy was in heaven.

I, however, was in hell.

Mostly because as soon as we seated ourselves he turned his back on me and engaged her with inane conversation. Like, for the entire three and a half hours. Redhead seemed more than pleased with the attention. I hated her instantly.

To my right sat Finn and Tyler, the latter put on some headphones as soon as we sat down and the sounds of heavy rock beats emanated from his direction for the remainder of the flight. The former sat silently, staring at his hands as though deep in thought. Or was it prayer? I really wasn't sure. I just hoped he was not a nervous passenger because I had enough pent-up anxiety to fill the cabin as it was.

I tore open the in-flight magazine. Normally, the images of exotic destinations and beautiful people transported me to my happy place, but today they just pissed me off. After all, it was hard to concentrate on sea villas in Bora Bora when every few minutes a deep chuckle, followed by a shrill, giggling squeal pierced my eardrums.

Redhead was fucking annoying.

I slammed the magazine shut. God, I needed a holiday, one without rock musicians and their voracious, womanizing ways. No, scrap that. I needed a complete life overhaul. Maybe if I moved far enough away from Dominic and my parents I would start to feel sane again? Doctor Powell might call it avoidance but I thought the term *self-preservation* much more suitable. It didn't matter really, we would be able to debate the label during our session on Monday.

I was not looking forward to it.

In my peripheral vision, I noticed cool grey eyes assessing me. "You all right?"

Looking at Finn, I shrugged one shoulder. "Sure."

He stared at me for a long time, silent. It was unnerving, and I suddenly felt the need to clean something.

Unfortunately, there were not any grimy surfaces nearby, so I started to babble instead. "Look, it's complicated. I mean, I'm good, but on the other hand, I'm not good. I'm just … you know … half-good." I groaned, throwing my head back against the seat. "I don't even know what I'm saying."

Thankfully, Finn ignored my verbal diarrhea and changed the topic instead. "You've really done a number on him."

I glanced at Finn but his stare was directed at Dominic. His back was to us and he was in the process of laughing at something Redhead had said, my stomach tightened to the point of agony.

"He looks perfectly happy from where I'm sitting."

"Then you can't see it."

"What?"

"Desperation. I'm surprised you can't see it, it's obvious." Finn's eyes met mine, his gaze so direct I had to force myself not to look away. "Dom needs a woman on his cock, Riley."

I blanched at his directness, my cheeks no doubt flushing crimson. "Well, he's not far off it," I returned, referring to Redhead. The bitterness in my voice was telling.

Finn's gaze softened. "He needs a good woman, Riley. That woman with him now? I've seen him with girls like her for most of my adult life. He fucks them and leaves them before they can fuck him over." He shook his head. "It's sad."

I looked back at the woman who was shoving her cleavage into Dominic's face and was surprised to find him still breathing. Not that he seemed to mind. In fact, I was sure death by breast asphyxiation was top of his Most Awesome Ways to Die list.

"You like him."

My startled gaze flew to Finn, who was watching me closely.

Am I really that obvious?

His eyes were clear and so perceptive I was sure

he could see straight through me.

Sighing, I whispered, "I don't want to."

"But you do."

I nodded.

"Dom's a broken man, Riley." I raised an inquisitive eyebrow but Finn shook his head. "Not my story to tell. All I can say is he's been through more shit in his twenty-four years than some people get in their entire lifetime." He stared at me. "I'm not defending him. I love the guy like a brother but he can be a complete asshole to the people he cares about." He shrugged. "It's messed up, but true."

I shifted in my seat, uncomfortable at the astute gaze roving my face. Honestly, I might as well have cut my heart out and handed it right on over to the guy for inspection.

"I hope you know what you're doing." Finn's gaze shifted to Dominic again and mine followed suit. "Because he hasn't a fuckin' clue."

Finn's last statement took me back to a time when I felt equally lost.

I woke up screaming. Again. For the third night in a row, the faceless people of my nightmares pressed against me, blocking me, stopping me from finding him.

My brother.

God, I missed him. I wished it was all some practical joke and he would pop up from behind the couch like he used to when we were little. But he didn't. He was gone, and despite everyone's best efforts, he was gone for good.

I prayed he was okay.

"Mummy?" I whimpered into the darkness.

"Shhh, child." Rose's head popped up from the temporary cot at the foot of my bed. Ever since The Day Everything Changed, she set herself up in my room.

Usually, I felt calmer knowing she was there, but not that night. As I woke from yet another nightmare, a large part of me desperately wished she did not have to be there in the first place.

"I want Mummy."

Rose heaved her large bulk up off the single mattress with a dramatic groan and waddled over to where I sat shivering under the goose down blanket. "Darlin', your mamma needs her rest," she crooned as the bed dipped under her weight. "Let her sleep. It's been hard for everyone."

I was cradled against her side as she hummed a lullaby I had never heard. Eventually, the soothing lilt of the song relaxed me and I sagged against her, exhausted. I felt safe with Rose, she didn't stare at me with dead eyes and scowling lips like the rest of the household. She didn't grow quiet the moment I stepped into a room or turn away as though the sight of me was too painful to bear.

I messed up, I knew that. With every ounce of my nine-year-old body, I wanted to make things right, truly I did. But I couldn't, he was gone.

Mum hated me.

Dad ignored me.

And it was all my fault.

****

The remainder of the flight passed in a blur and I was thankful to finally disembark. To be honest, I was even more grateful to see the back of Redhead at the luggage carousel—petty but true. I scowled as she sauntered away with her leopard-print suitcase and a satisfied sway of her hips after slipping Dominic her phone number. However, by that point, all the guys were in total band mode, so he merely nodded, shoved the business card in his jeans pocket and then spent the next forty-five minutes taking careful inventory of all the equipment piled in front of him. They had piles of the stuff. From guitar picks to traps case, speaker heads to foot pedals, those men had not taken any chances because they brought everything. And I had nothing to do except sit on my Louis Vuitton bag, watch and wait.

So, watch and wait I did.

Just as Finn finally gave the all-clear on the last symbol in his drum kit, yet another beautiful woman—this time a brunette in her early twenties—hurried over. "So sorry I'm late," she panted.

It took Dominic all of five seconds to envelop her in a hug, though something in her playful squeal and gentle laughter immediately set me at ease. They were friends, good friends, nothing more.

I liked her.

Once she was let go, Tyler embraced her, followed by Finn. I could not help but notice the faint color staining her cheeks when she and the drummer held each other a bit too close and for a moment too long.

Interesting.

Dominic and Tyler did not notice, or if they did, did not seem to care. I, on the other hand, was very curious. After all, any woman who could get under the skin of a man like Finn must be pretty remarkable.

When the man in question took her hand and steered her over to me, I pretended not to have been scoping them out and quickly stood.

"Katrina, this is Riley."

"Hey." Katrina smiled and a cute dimple appeared on her left cheek. If it wasn't for the ripped jeans, dark woolen knit sweater, and black leather jacket, I would have described her as adorable.

"Hi." I grinned back.

Finn shared a look with Katrina. "She's with

Dom."

"No, I—"

"She's not—"

Dominic and I glared at each other, and then at Finn. His grey eyes held a mischievous glint which I did not appreciate at all.

Katrina's gaze darted between Dominic's and mine, shocked. "I can't believe it," she murmured.

I had no idea what she was on about and thankfully did not have time to ponder it further because Tyler rounded us all up like stray cattle and herded us outside.

It was freezing.

Instinctively, I wrapped a free hand around my upper body, trying to maintain as much body heat as possible while pulling my suitcase behind me. I had heard Melbourne was cold, but I did not expect it to be so bitter in late spring. Sadly, the wind cut straight through my cashmere and all of my warmer clothes were unhelpfully color-coded at the very bottom of my luggage.

Cold. So cold.

A huge black hoodie was thrown in my face. "Put it on."

I glared at Dominic.

Can the man be any *ruder*?

"I'm fine."

"Wear the fucking hoodie, Riley."

Tyler, Finn and Katrina had moved over to where Katrina's olive green Savana was parked in the express arrivals lane. It was a timely coincidence because none of them would witness me taking my momentary insanity out on the man standing next to me. A perfect crime.

I turned to face Dominic and tried to ignore the way his short-sleeved t-shirt clung to obscenely protuberant biceps, I was in half a mind to cover them up

187

myself. "What's with you?" I hissed. "Why are you being such a jerk?"

He stepped closer, blue eyes narrowing, and I hated how my knees trembled—from the cold. "I just gave you my hoodie because you're freezing your tits off and you're calling me a jerk?"

I stood tall. "Yes, I am. You're a jerk." Then, poking him in the chest with my index finger, I angrily spat, "A. Big. Fat. Jerk."

"I'm fat too, huh?" His eyes softened.

"Obese," I snapped.

I was making no sense, Dominic knew it and I knew it, but damn if I wasn't angry with the guy. I had just watched him chat up another woman after he went down on me in my own kitchen, for God's sake. Who did that? And then I stupidly admitted to one of his band mates how much I liked him.

It was humiliating.

I was humiliated.

Thus, the stupidity.

His hand delved into my hair, cradling the back of my head and I bit my lip. "Put on the hoodie, angel." Dominic's voice was gentle but I looked away, blinking back the tears that threatened to spill.

After a minute, I relented and he helped me into it. The sweater was huge. His earthy scent lingered on the fabric and waves of nostalgia rolled over me. I suddenly yearned for the beach, for a time before my heart felt so wrung out and exposed. Shaking my head, I fixed my disheveled hair and then glanced up at Dominic again. He looked pained. With a noisy exhale, his thumb skimmed over my damp cheeks.

I did not even know I was crying.

"C'mon, let's go."

I blinked, wiped my eyes and then looked from

him to the others. "Aren't we going with them?"

Dominic shook his head. "Need to check-in with my bro first. I'll meet up with those guys later."

"Oh, okay."

He grabbed his gear and indicated to the taxi waiting nearby before striding off. I nodded and followed suit. After a few steps, I glanced back, Finn was watching me closely. His eyes were unreadable, but even from a distance I recognized the concern written all over his features. Ignoring this, I turned and walked away.

****

We stepped into the hotel lobby where Grace and Levi were staying and I liked the place immediately. So much so, that I decided to book a room for the remainder of my stay. To be honest, having my own space was probably the wisest decision I had made in a long time and since Dominic was crashing at his aunt's, I was guaranteed it.

Yay, me.

Moments later, we moved into the lobby bar called Oblivion. There were low patterned couches surrounding circular wooden tables, each with its own twinkling tea light candle placed in the center. The soft, atmospheric music wafted through ceiling speakers and helped create an aura of unassuming elegance. I bit back a smile; Grace must hate it. Not that it would stop her from drinking here, though. If nothing else, the girl was pragmatic when it came to her alcohol.

"This place is shit."

I turned to glare at Dominic. He was leaning against the bar, his elbows resting on the polished auburn wood with a beer in hand. After shooting a furtive glance at the barman, I hissed under my breath, "He'll hear you."

Dominic snorted, not in the least concerned.

Fortunately, the barman was busily restocking the spirit bottles. It was like he knew Grace was coming.

When I looked back, Dominic had his phone out and was texting. I gripped my own drink tighter, determined to remain silent.

It was useless.

I crumbled almost instantly.

Clearly, patience was not a strength of mine. So, referring to Redhead, I muttered, "You don't waste any time, do you?"

I hated the bitterness in my voice, it irritated me, and Dominic's uncommunicative response made my ire even worse. So, picking up my beer, I made to leave.

"What the fuck's your problem?"

I turned around. "Excuse me?"

He moved to tower over me and I was hit with a waft of mint. Angry mint. Heck, I could even see my own furious reflection in his eyes he had moved so close. "I said," he slowly enunciated, "what the fuck's your problem?"

Lifting my chin, I retorted, "I can't believe you messaged that girl, and what's worse is I seriously can't believe I care. But I'm standing right in front of you, for God's sake." My voice caught, emotional turmoil was beyond exhausting. "Don't you see me at all?"

Dominic took the bottle from my hand and placed it on the bar, his jaw working hard. "I see you," he replied, his voice deadly quiet. "Fuckin' hard not to." After a brief pause, he seemed to collect himself and asked, "What girl?"

I groaned. "You're kidding me, right? The redhead who was all over you on the flight out here. The one with the enormous—" I stopped, blushing.

Dominic was silent for a moment, so I took the opportunity to take off his gigantic sweater, fold it carefully and then press it against his solid chest. "Here." I honestly could not deal with him anymore, I just wanted to go upstairs and either drown myself in the bathtub or drink myself to death—either option was fine with me.

He made no move to take it back.

"I didn't text that chick, I texted Levi."

My eyes flicked to his and after searching his face for a solid minute, I knew he was telling the truth. There was a sincerity in his features I trusted instinctively, though whether my faith in him was misplaced or not remained yet to be proved. Regardless, a pent-up breath escaped me. "Oh."

Dominic's gaze narrowed. "What do you care, anyway? You've got a boyfriend, remember?" He spat the word as though it were a fly in his beer.

"No, I don't."

"The pussy bought you a goddamn rosebush, he's your fuckin' boyfriend."

I placed the sweater on the bar next to my drink and turned back to Dominic. "Look, I'm not gonna lie, Robin's a really sweet guy—"

"Don't say that asshole's name to me."

His torso heaved with ragged breaths so I placed placating palms flat against him. Yeah, it was disturbing how much I craved physical contact with the man. I shook my head. "We've been through this already, Dominic. He's not my boyfriend. Look, he went overboard with the flowers, I'll admit." He growled, and I bit back a smile. "But to me, he's nothing more than a nice guy who likes to deliver scented gifts after a first date."

"Yet."

I stared at him, confused.

"He means nothing more to you, yet." Dominic's eyes were piercing and I swear, in that moment he saw my very soul.

Wow.

We both stood there, staring at the other for God knew how long. The air grew denser, our pulses raced and Dominic's hands covered mine like it was inevitable we were going to be torn apart.

"This is bullshit."

"I know."

"We should have just fucked when we first met. Got it over with."

I bit back my reply.

"Now we've got all this other shit in the way."

"You mean, emotions?"

Dominic looked like he was in physical pain. "I hate this, Riley. Really fuckin' hate it."

I shut my eyes, willing his anguished voice to have been a figment of my imagination. Willing my own pathetic heart ten times stronger so it could pack up its bags and get the hell out of there. There was no doubt about it, falling for the emotionally unavailable sucked hairy yak balls.

He groaned and crushed me against him. I buried my face in his neck and wound my arms around him, virtually cutting off any air supply. To be fair, we didn't need it, without the other we struggled to breathe, anyway.

Strangely, despite the desperate, cruel way we clung to each other, the contact felt so comfortable, so reassuring, so … right. I sighed. And then started, because Dominic flung me to the side just as quickly as he reached for me.

It was the story of my life. Clearly, I needed a new one.

"Gracie, Dickwad."

He had done it again. Dominic turned from Mr.

Deep and Meaningful to Class Clown in under five seconds. His bipolar was seriously messing with my equilibrium. Which probably accounted for why it took me so long to gather my wits together, shove his sweater into my oversized handbag and slowly make my way over to where Grace was threatening Dominic with physical violence.

Man, I missed her.

In fact, she must have already punched Dominic because her right arm looked pretty sore, she was rubbing it while glaring up at him.

"How about I take a look at that arm for you?" I asked.

Grace instantly threw her arms around me, crying, "Riley," and I hugged her back. It was the warmest greeting I had received in a very long time. "It's so good to see you." She moved away slightly, her eyebrows creased in confusion. "Hang on, what are you even doing here?"

Oh, you know, tormenting myself with the unattainable. The usual.

I bit back a snort.

Instead, I plastered on my most winning smile and said something about wanting to watch the boys play, blah, blah, blah. It was partly true, and I really was thrilled to see her again, I just wished… Never mind.

Anyway, after I finished my spiel, Grace turned and smiled adoringly up at Levi.

Whoa.

Is Grace…? Oh my God, is she *in love?*

Grace Anne Thompson, serial man-hater, skeptic of anything with two legs and a penis, was in love. It was illogical. My world officially shifted and resettled slightly left of center. And during said realignment, I not-so-subtly tried to wipe the incredulous grin off my face. She was my best friend, after all, I was ecstatic for her.

Dominic stepped closer to Levi and I was once again reminded of their similarities—physical similarities. Emotionally, Dominic lagged behind somewhat. Anyway, both men sported the same tousled hair, strikingly blue eyes, and plump, kissable lips. It was a mirror image of the sexiest kind. However, the main point of difference was when Levi gazed at Grace with open reverence. He did not hide it, fight it or pretend their connection was not real. In fact, it looked like he was still pinching himself about the whole thing.

It was beautiful, and I was so fucking envious.

I was not the only one who noticed either.

Dominic must have picked up on the pulsing vibes as well because after a quick game with Levi of "Which Girl Are You Bagging?" he started hooting with laughter when he discovered it was Grace. Once his hysterics subsided, he began yet another round of man-hugging and back-slapping.

It made no sense.

I mean, how was it that he became unbelievably excited for his brother's happiness, yet remained determined to experience none of it himself? The strangest part was, he seemed genuinely thrilled for Levi, his eyes shone in that arresting way of his, and he gave Grace even more shit than usual. He was stoked.

I shook my head.

A split second later, Dominic transitioned effortlessly back into band mode and turning to his brother, asked, "Ready to go?"

"Now? But where's Finn and Tyler?"

Dominic explained that they were all meeting at The Ruby Room. I watched, envious, as Levi said a passionate goodbye to Grace. He had fallen for her, hard. I only hoped she would not freak out, run off, and break the poor guy's heart.

Turning to Dominic, I noticed he was making exaggerated doe eyes at Levi. I scowled up at him—what an ass—but he just quirked a half-smile at me, winked, and I spent the remaining few minutes of us all standing together trying to calm my own fickle heart.

Stupid thing.

Once Dominic and Levi finally left, Grace turned to me, her green eyes disbelieving. Referring to Dominic she said, "You had to sit next to that the whole flight over?"

I sighed. Even though I had not technically been seated next to Dominic, it still felt as though I had my fill of the contradictory man for one day. And then some. So, nodding, I murmured, "Yeah."

Grace shook her head. "Girl, you deserve a drink. Come on, let me introduce you to Patrick. He'll pour you something strong enough so you can forget all about him." She strode toward the bar.

Following close behind, I muttered under my breath, "I highly doubt it."

****

For the next few hours, Grace and I sat in the lobby bar where we drank, ate, and gossiped. It was exactly what I needed. She had this steadying, no-nonsense way about her which, after the tumultuous past two weeks, was a refreshing change, let me tell you.

Patrick, the bartender, seemed nice. He and Grace were on friendly terms which was both hilarious and slightly disturbing. I mean, the guy knew her name, drink of choice, and even remembered to pour her double shots. She, in return, remained polite and I even heard a, "Thanks," at one point. Luckily, I was already sitting down because I might have fallen over otherwise.

Sadly, Patrick spent most of the evening talking

about himself. If I was going to go all Doctor Powell on him, I would say he was overcompensating for low self-esteem. So, not wanting to appear rude, I smiled and nodded but secretly wished he would just go away.

We were about to manage our escape when Patrick gave me his number on the back of a coaster. Grace smirked, and right on cue, I blushed. Of course I was flattered, who wouldn't be? The man was tall, dark-haired, and easy on the eyes. But I had more than enough crap to deal with as it was, so slipped the coaster into my handbag with every intent of throwing it away the first chance I got.

I hadn't yet seen my hotel room. After checking in, the concierge had taken my suitcase upstairs and Dominic resolutely steered me into the lobby bar instead. So, once the elevator doors opened and Grace and I stepped across the threshold of my suite, I stopped. The place was gorgeous. And I mean, *Interior Design Magazine* gorgeous. Even Mum would have approved.

I somehow managed to score a corner suite on the top floor. Meaning, there was floor to ceiling windows on two sides with awe-inspiring views of the Melbourne skyline at dusk.

Wow.

A luxurious marble bathroom, complete with pool-sized Jacuzzi and heated towel bars was just to the right of the entrance. At the end of the short, wood-paneled hallway was an opulent sleeping area in neutral beige with pops of rust-colored accents. The bed, which faced floor-to-ceiling windows, was surely two king-sized mattresses fitted together. In all seriousness, the thing was enormous. And when I looked closer, the windows opposite were actually glass-paneled doors leading to a private balcony that overlooked the cityscape. It was fitted with a U-shaped wooden bench at one end, simply oozing with ornate cushions.

An open doorway to the left of the bedroom heralded a second living area, complete with dining suite, one of the largest sofas I had ever seen facing a state of the art entertainment system, some more glass sliding doors, and a continuation of the private balcony from the bedroom.

All in all, pretty spectacular.

Grace whistled in appreciation as I attempted to pick my jaw up off the plush carpet and shepherd her into the second room. Curling up on the ridiculously comfortable couch, I watched her as she sat down next to me. "Okay, spill."

She tried to look innocent but failed. Dismally. "Spill what?"

I was having none of it, and after an academy award winning speech outlining how she cruelly left me—her one and only best friend—in the dark about her blossoming relationship with Levi, she finally relented and told me everything.

Un-be-lievable.

What an awesome story.

When she finished, I just stared at her, completely flabbergasted. "So, you're telling me that after twelve days, you guys knew you were in love?"

She at least had the decency to appear sheepish. "We knew after eleven, actually."

I stared for a moment longer and then launched myself at her, squealing like a teenager recounting their first kiss. Honestly, I could not have been happier for her. Grace had experienced so many hardships over the past two years and I was ecstatic someone worthy of her had seen past the brittle outer shell she wore like armor and discovered the awesome woman beneath.

After some well-deserved gloating on my part—

after all, I knew they were perfect for each other from the very beginning—and a not-so-subtle inquiry into their sex life, I was once again clapping my hands with glee while bouncing up and down on the sofa.

Living vicariously through others was brilliant.

However, a thought suddenly struck me and I quickly sobered. Checking the time on my watch merely confirmed it, I was being selfish. There I sat, hoarding Grace all to myself while Levi was probably going mad from the toxic combination of worry and pent-up sexual tension.

"It's getting late. I need an early night if I'm going to hit the gym tomorrow morning." Grace rolled her eyes. "And I don't want to keep you from your next orgasm."

That got her attention. I could not hide my smile when she looked at the time on her phone and agreed with me. The girl was smitten, it was adorable. Not that I would ever admit it out loud, of course. God knew I would never wake up again if I did.

Not long afterward, the door to my suite clicked shut behind my best friend. I wandered through the two lavish rooms and eventually found myself wrapped in a soft woolen throw blanket standing outside on the balcony. I gazed up at the night sky; it was hard to see past the skyscrapers to the stars above, but eventually I found them. They were glinting away, unfazed by all the noise and chaos below. My eyes sought out the largest one, it sat apart from the others, almost scorning their presence. Closing my eyes, I hugged myself tightly, took a deep breath and made a wish. After a long exhale, I opened them again, turned away from it all and made my way back inside.

Weeks later, I could have kicked myself for tempting fate in that way.

Chapter Twelve

I can't feel you there,
Too far.
I can't see you there,
So far.
Come closer.
—MONDEZ, "Stranger"

I awoke feeling oddly restless the next morning. It was strange really, considering how soundly I'd slept in my gargantuan bed. So, after a quick, healthy breakfast downstairs, I changed into my workout gear before hitting the hotel gym.

It sucked.

Okay, so that may have been a slight over-exaggeration. I did not hate the exercise and I did not hate the gym itself either, it was just horrible being restrained within those four walls while running on a treadmill. I missed the wide expanse of coastline, the salt-laden wind as it whipped sea spray onto my skin, I missed … the freedom of it all. Running in the same spot and staring at insincere women gossiping on a morning talk show just did not do it for me.

Which was why, after my run and subsequent shower, I did not feel that sense of calm I had been chasing. Instead, I felt jittery, frustrated, and restless. It was therefore not surprising then, that once dressed and wrapped in a warm jacket, I headed down to the concierge, grabbed a map of the city and strode outside.

A short taxi ride later, I was standing at the entrance of Melbourne Zoo with a ridiculously cheesy grin on my face. It had been years since I visited a zoo, not since middle school when we went for a photography excursion. Granted, I spent most of my time trying not to get shat on by exotic birds in the walk-through aviary, resolute on taking the perfect shot of a Red-Knobbed Hornbill, but thankfully the experience had not lessened the appeal years later. There was something about the raucous sounds of the animals as they called across the park claiming their territory that I loved. It promised adventures in far off places, it promised discovery, it promised … new beginnings. And right then, a new beginning was exactly what I needed.

Just as I was about to walk through the entrance, my handbag vibrated and rummaging around inside it, I searched for my phone.

Bootycall: **Where are u?**

I really needed to change Dominic's name profile.

Me: **Don't judge me but I'm at the zoo.**

Bootycall: **k wait up I'll b there in 5**

Right, then.

That restlessness which had all but abated suddenly made an epic comeback, like, *The Lord of the Rings* style. In 3D. My stomach churned, rolling with angst-coated excitement, and I hated the way my eyes kept searching the crowds of schoolchildren and tourists for my walking enigma.

My walking enigma?

Uh-oh.

However, before I could give myself a stern lecture on forming lasting emotional attachments with emotionally comatose men—particularly those of the musician variety—he was there.

Oh, my sweet Kestrel.

Dressed in a red and black checkered button-up shirt, pulled so tightly across his broad shoulders and well-defined pecs I actually thought the material was going to burst open to a Beyoncé song, was the physical manifestation of male perfection. Dominic's black jeans hung mouthwateringly low and the way they hugged his narrow hips made me want to lick something, anything. A buffalo would have done the job right then.

He sauntered toward me, his predacious crystalline eyes making my breath catch. Literally. I mean, I actually had to remind myself to breathe.

In and out. In and out. In—

"Hey." That half-smile of his made my knees tremble.

Focus, Riley.

I gulped before croaking, "Hi."

His grin grew wider. "Nice outfit."

My eyes dropped down to black ankle boots, a sixties-inspired red skirt—it only just made it midway down bare thighs, don't judge—a tight black sweater and a fitted cream woolen jacket. I left my hair down, on account of the woolen beanie perched snugly on my head. It all seemed okay when I looked in the mirror that morning. However, the way Dominic licked his lips—as though I was a gazelle and he was a cheetah—seriously left me wondering.

Upon meeting his eyes once again, I blushed, murmuring, "Thanks."

Dominic grabbed my hand. "C'mon, I wanna show you something." He threw some cash at a disgruntled teller and led me inside, but to be honest, I paid little attention. In fact, I was so busy reeling from the tingling feel of his strong, possessive hand pressed against mine, I could not do anything except stumble after him.

Numerous twists and turns later, we walked into a darkened alcove. Before us stood a wooden bench facing a large glass window. It was surrounded on three sides by imitation rock and the overall effect was like peering through a mountain crevice to a woodland clearing. There were tightly knit trees to the left and a shallow, trickling river separating it from the sloping pasture on the right. Well, until the whole enclosure was interrupted by a rendered seven-foot wall. Subtle.

I let go of Dominic's hand and moved toward the glass. "What lives here?"

"A sun bear."

"A what?" Turning to face him, I raised my eyebrows.

Fuck, he's hot.

I shook my head. "Okay, I've got two questions."

He looked at me, his blue eyes impenetrable.

Will you get naked with me? And—Damn it, *Riley, focus.*

After clearing my throat, I asked, "One, what's a sun bear? And, two, how did you even know it was here?"

Dominic turned and made his way over to the bench before sitting. He stretched long legs out in front of him, crossing scuffed boots at the ankles.

I spun around, with a very attractive so-are-you-going-to-tell-me? look on my face.

"A sun bear is the smallest of the bear species," he began. "It has a patch of fur on its chest, kinda like a rising sun, which is where it gets its name—"

He was about to go on but I raised one hand. "Hang on, what's with the David Attenborough impersonation? How do you know all this stuff?"

Dominic indicated to the sign attached to the faux rock just to my right, a self-satisfied smirk on his face.

I blushed and turned my back to him, pretending to search for the creature but in reality taking deep breaths in order to get my embarrassment back under control. Once assured my face was not the color of a red panda, I threw over my shoulder, "You didn't answer my second question."

Dominic was silent for a moment. Just as I was about to give up and go in search of a Hippo, he murmured, "Auntie Val brought all us boys here once, when I was a kid."

I stared at his reflection in the glass, his head was down and he was systematically clasping and unclasping tense hands. He sighed. "Mum, Levi, and I first came to Melbourne when I was six. It was a spur of the moment thing, not planned at all. She never said why we packed up and left so suddenly, but it must've had something to do with Dad. They were at each other's throats the night we took off."

"Over the years, we ended up visiting Auntie Val more and more often, reckon at least eight times before I turned sixteen. Anyway, the boys and I used to run riot in her house. We'd all jump on her instruments—she was a kickass music teacher—and pretend to be rock stars." He gave a small smile and I reached out to rest against the glass. I wasn't swooning, honest. I was … resting.

"It got pretty loud and we didn't know what the fuck we were doing so it must have sounded like shit."

Once I trusted my legs enough, I turned to face Dominic, completely mesmerized by the stranger finally being revealed to me.

"Anyway, one day we pissed her off real good because she shoved us all in the car and then let us loose on this place." Dominic looked up and our eyes caught. I held my breath, in all seriousness, his vulnerability was the most beautiful sight I had ever seen. Awe-inspiring sunsets and spectacular mountain peaks had nothing on him.

Not a thing.

He did that half-grin thing and I exhaled. "It

doesn't get busy in this part," he continued, "and I remember wanting to disappear for a while."

He was right, this part of the zoo was quiet. Probably because most people were off admiring the lions and tigers, rather than searching for what appeared to be mythical sun bears. After all, since entering the alcove, I had not seen a single soul, furry or otherwise.

"What about you?"

I started. "Huh?"

"You never talk about your past." He paused. "Or your family." Dominic stared at me, his gaze unflinching.

I glanced away, immediately uncomfortable.

Jesus, where do I start?

Looking down at my hands, I noticed they were subconsciously wrapping one of the loose threads from my jacket around a pearl-colored button. My fingers trembled slightly.

Shit.

Letting go, I attempted to feign a confidence I really did not feel. "What do you want to know?"

"Whatever you wanna tell me."

It took everything I had to bite back a hysterical laugh and I found myself once again facing the enclosure, searching for the four-legged creature which refused to show its sweet self. My eyes shifted left then right, hunting for it, for a distraction. Anything.

Nothing.

Double shit.

"All right then," he conceded, after what must have been an epic silence on my part. "Tell me about your mum."

I swore under my breath.

There was a moment of quiet on his end—I was rhythmically thumping my head against the cool glass—followed closely by, "Come here."

My feet responded before my head had a chance to catch up and before I knew it, I was standing in front of him.

"Sit down."

After taking a deep breath, I perched myself on the edge of the wooden bench and squealed in surprise when Dominic scooped up my legs and lay them across his lap. My eyes widened as he wrapped one arm around my shoulders and pulled me in close until my cheek was flush with his chest. A moment later, his chin rested on top of my beanie.

"Better?"

Not gonna lie, I breathed in eu de Dominic until my lungs almost burst. It was without a doubt, the best fragrance in the world—I'd make squillions selling it. Slowly, I exhaled and my body slumped against him, finally relaxed. "Yeah."

"C'mon then, tell me about her. I'm getting old here, angel."

There was a resounding slap of my hand against taut muscle and a corresponding chuckle when I agitatedly shook it to ease the sting. Dominic brought my hand up to his lips and kissed my palm, the sting consequently died and a tingle was born.

I may or may not have sighed.

Might as well get this over with. After all, if his lips go anywhere near me again, this conversation is going to head in a completely different direction.

So, steeling myself, I blurted, "Mum hates me."

He stilled.

"I'm serious, she does."

"Why?" His voice was low, dangerously so.

"I—" Swiping imaginary dirt off my skirt, I continued, "I lost something of hers, a long time ago, and she's never forgiven me."

"What do you mean?"

I shrugged one shoulder—the one not nestled against his warm torso—refusing to elaborate further.

Dominic's fingers circled my back and I had to consciously stop myself from purring, Burmese cat style. "Why won't she forgive you?"

After a minute, I whispered, "It's easier, I guess, holding onto the hate. She doesn't have to deal with it, process it, you know?"

"Have you?"

"What?"

"Processed it."

"Yeah." I sighed. "It's taken a heck of a long time and countless hours in therapy, but I've made my peace with it." I gave a harsh laugh. "Now I'm just dealing with the side effects."

"What about your dad? Where does he fit in all of this?"

"Dad's not around much. He… He likes to keep busy."

I could feel Dominic nod in understanding. We were both quiet for what felt like ages before he murmured, "My dad's in prison."

Pulling away from him, I stared into his face, shocked. "Dominic, I'm so sorry."

"I'm not. He's a fuckin' asshole."

Okay, then.

Reaching up, I tenderly soothed the tension lines on his face until he shut his eyes and leaned into my touch. A faint smile appeared and my stomach flipped like it was performing at a national gymnastics competition—perfect scores all around.

"Must be hard on your mum."

"Mum's dead." Dominic's eyes remained closed, and for once, I was glad. If he opened them, he would have seen the true extent of how this news affected me.

A lot.

Too much.

Uh-oh.

"Stop it."

"Stop what?"

"Feeling sorry for me. I've already dealt with her death so don't waste your sympathy."

If it was at all possible, I now felt even worse. However, I didn't want to push the matter further and risk him never opening up to me again, so remained mute.

"I've been thinking." His eyes were still closed but there was something in his voice that sparked my interest.

"Mmm?"

"About our problem."

"Problem?"

Blue eyes crashed into mine and my heart somersaulted its way to victory—I was officially national gymnastics champion, there was a trophy and everything.

Oh. That problem.

"We need to fuck. Tonight. Get it out of our system, you know?"

I blinked.

"I mean it. Once I've been inside you, all this," he gestured to the space between us, the one jam-packed with The Great Unsaid, "will be sorted."

Nothing. I had nothing. I mean, how could the man go from the topic of death to sex without flexing a muscle? And how could I get the mental image of Dominic thrusting himself deep inside me out of my head?

Sweet baby Jesus.

My cheeks flamed beetroot, I was officially a flamingo's dinner.

Dominic moved my hand from his face to his chest. I watched, mesmerized, as my trembling fingers slowly journeyed down his torso, abs and stomach. There was a strong possibility I moaned out loud when my palm cupped his hardening erection, it felt superb.

"Fuck yeah," he groaned, shifting against me. "Do you want my cock, angel?" He leaned forward, nuzzling my jawline and setting off a pyrotechnic display in my panties.

"Want it to feast on your sweet pussy?" He licked my earlobe and I almost exploded.

"Yes." A wanton voice I didn't recognize panted back. "Hell yes."

Dominic's hands shot to my face. He cradled my cheeks, angled my head, and then feasted on my lips as though it were an all-you-can-eat buffet.

Whoa.

Holy. Fucking. Whoa.

It was official, this man owned me.

Completely.

With a stifled moan, I threw all caution somewhere in the general vicinity of the Ocelot and deepened the kiss. Wrapping my arms around his neck, I drew him closer, deeper, delving my tongue inside.

Dear God.

My body ignited with burning need and it was then I came to a decision, if something did not happen soon—preferably in the Big O department—I was actually going to spontaneously combust.

Boom. Gone.

No more Riley.

Just like before, Dominic sensed my growing angst and knew exactly what I needed. "Wanna taste?" he growled between scorching kisses. "A taste of what's to come?"

I nodded and with a low groan, one of his hands moved to my upper thigh. Slowly, deliberately those deft fingers of his slid under my skirt.

I moaned. And so help me, shifted my legs farther apart, encouraging his fingers higher.

Dominic's hand glided across sensitive skin, leaving goose bumps trailing behind. At last, his touch flitted over the damp lace of my panties and I jolted—extremely thankful for the vise-like grip I had on his neck. He maneuvered the material to one side and without further preamble, slipped thick fingers through my slick folds before sliding two of them inside. "Fuck, angel," he groaned. "You're so ready for me."

Yes. Yes, I was.

And as his fingers rhythmically pumped me, I could hear the blatant evidence of my carnal want. If I wasn't so turned on, I would have felt seriously embarrassed, but as it was, his thumb systematically worked my clit so expertly I could not even see straight, let alone blush or pull away.

Honestly, my world concaved around me until there was nothing left except total blackness randomly interspersed with reflective, sensation-fueled light. Oh, and Dominic. Of course, there was Dominic. He was everywhere, it was insane.

Our movements became frantic, desperate with desire. "Need. To. Be. Inside. You," he muttered between hot, wet kisses. "So—"

Footsteps.

"Fucking."

More footsteps.

"Much."

"Okay ladies and gents, here we have the sun bear exhibit—"

I gasped, my eyes wide with horror. Entering the

alcove was a group of seven or eight visitors being led by a khaki-clad tour guide with a ridiculously cheerful voice. It grated on my raging hormones and irritated the bejesus out of my almost-orgasm.

"Jacket," Dominic instructed. "Now."

Looking down, I quickly rearranged my jacket so it covered all evidence of Dominic's exploration—his fingers were still inside me—and my obvious disdain for public decency.

With a flurry of pointed hand gestures, Chirpy Khaki Woman began her well-rehearsed spiel, "The sun bear is found in the tropical habitats of Southeast Asia—"

"Dominic," I whispered frantically. "We can't—"

"Shhh," he admonished, his grin wicked. "Of course we can."

My eyes widened even more—they were going to pop right out of my skull if I was not careful—and with a stifled groan, Dominic's fingers once again began their slow, sensual onslaught on my Victoria Falls.

"Fuck," I breathed, gripping his shirt as though I was going to keel over and die from pure arousal induced stupidity. There was no denying it, I was one part terrified and three parts the most turned on I'd ever been in, well, ever.

"Tonight, angel. We're gonna fuck tonight."

Dominic's low promise had me biting my bottom lip. I was shocked at my wantonness, yet instinctively opened my legs wider for him—thank God for the jacket.

"Sweet, filthy girl," he growled in my ear as his thumb once again skimmed over my clit. I bit down harder. "I'm burying my fingers deep inside your wet pussy not three feet away from random strangers and you're fuckin' lovin' it, aren't you?"

The tour guide kept chirpily yakking away to her disciples.

"You love how I make you feel."

I honestly didn't hear much of her well-practiced lecture on account of the devil in my ear and all. However, in between his wicked comments, I registered small snippets, like, *"Lives an insular life."*

"You want me to keep touching you like this."

"Reclusive."

"Even though someone might find out."

And, *"Stocky, muscular build."*

"Bet that fucker with the camera knows what we're doing."

I tried to distract myself but was too busy staring, dumbstruck, at the man who was about to make me give the howler monkey a run for its money in the decibel department.

Dominic's eyes darkened when he saw my expression. "Shit, Riley. You're gonna come."

I nodded, absolutely terrified that any more movement on my part would be the cause of my complete undoing.

"Fuck," he groaned, then licked his lips and shifted in his seat. "I'm so goddamn hard right now."

"Not helping," I silently mouthed.

The tour guide continued, "Unfortunately, I think our sun bear's in hiding today."

"Dominic, I can't—"

"I can't seem to find him. Never mind, it's still vitally important we encourage authorities around the globe to—"

"I'm going to—"

"Do more—"

"More, Dominic—"

"To protect this species."

I bit back an anguished groan, almost carving a chunk out of my bottom lip in the process.

Finally, she changed the topic and gushed, "Well, I think we're about done here, guys, but next up is the snow leopard. Follow me."

It took a strength of will I never thought I possessed to hold off until the last of the stragglers followed Chirpy Khaki Woman out the alcove. But as soon as they did, I threw one leg over Dominic's lap and straddled him. Grabbing his face, I kissed him with an unparalleled ruthlessness, rocking my hips against his hand and chasing the sensation that he effortlessly wrought on my unsuspecting pussy. Throughout it all, Dominic was relentless. His tongue sparred with my own, his thumb expertly massaged my sweet spot and his fingers rhythmically stroked me until I was so full of ricocheting sensation, I didn't know where he ended and I began.

Boom.

Detonation.

Wave upon wave of exquisite pleasure crashed through me as my body came alive under his touch. Light fractured, sound fissured and my limbs quaked from the intensity of it all. And still, Dominic touched me. His fingers continued on and on until the last of my shudders finally subsided and the roar in my ears gradually morphed into a soft, simmering hum.

"Christ, angel."

Dazed, I lifted my head from his shoulder to stare vacantly at him.

"You bit me."

"I—what?"

"Never took you for a biter."

I shook my head. "I didn't."

But he continued on as though I hadn't spoken. "I mean, a screamer, sure. But not a biter."

Dominic gently removed his fingers from inside

me and held my gaze as he licked each of them in turn, growling in pleasure.

Christ, that's hot.

I, meanwhile, invested all of my focus in readjusting my sodden panties rather than begging the man for round two. After getting myself sorted, I pulled the shirt collar away from his neck, gasping in horror. He was right, a perfect imprint of my teeth stared back at me.

I slapped a hand over my mouth, exclaiming, "Holy shit, I'm so sorry." The red panda had nothing on me now, I'm sure my face was more fluorescent than it had ever been.

"I like it."

I froze. "You, ah, you do?"

He grinned. "You keep surprising me, angel. It's fuckin' awesome."

"Oh." I had no idea how to respond to that. I mean, really, what was there to say? Looking down, I indicated to the protruding bulge in his jeans which made my fingers itch and my mouth salivate. Okay, a lot. It salivated a lot. "How are you going down there? Do you need a hand with anything?"

His grin grew wider but then turned rueful. "Can't believe I'm gonna say this, but I'll need to take a rain check on that blowjob. Sound check's in an hour and I need to get shit ready."

Downcast and pretending not to show it, I clambered off his lap while attempting to straighten the remainder of my outfit. The need to keep my eyes averted and hands busy proved overwhelming.

My face was unexpectedly swiveled toward Dominic. "I meant what I said though." His gaze was steady as he held my cheeks in his large palms. "We're gonna fuck, tonight."

Be still my beating heart.

213

I blinked. Once.

"Riley?"

Twice.

"You all right?"

Three times.

"You're not breathing."

Dominic's concerned voice cut through my lust-induced fog and a loud gust escaped me. Shaking my head, I mumbled, "Oh, um, right. Yeah, I'm okay. Thanks."

The wicked half-smile was back and he drew my bottom lip into his mouth, sucking on it. After releasing it, he murmured, "It's gonna be fuckin' amazing. You'll see."

The scary part was, I believed him.

Chapter Thirteen

If I make a mistake,
If it hurts,
Am I alive?
Is something there?
—MONDEZ, "Rules"

Back at the hotel, I was laying still, dazed, on the private balcony when my phone rang. To be fair, the sun heating my skin and cushions nestled against my back, probably accounted for why it took me so long to answer. But eventually, I did. "Hello?"

Okay, so I'm drawling now.

"Hey, Riley."

I barely recognized the warm male voice on the other end of the line—multiple orgasms could do that to a girl—but finally it clicked. "Robin?"

He laughed. "You're sounding very relaxed, where are you?"

I scrambled upright, feeling first dizzy, and then shamefully guilty. In my post-lounging haze, I even glanced about me to reassure myself he was not hiding behind the sliding door or perched in the wall garden attached to the side of the building. Nope, no Robin.

Phew.

"Oh, um, I'm in Melbourne."

"Yeah? How come?"

"Ah, I'm here with my best friend. We're seeing a band tonight."

"Sounds great." I could almost hear him thinking. "Never took you for a music lover."

It proved almost impossible to bite back a snort.

Oh, Robin. If only you knew.

There was a short pause on his end and I took a moment to rub suddenly tired eyes. Stupid sunlight.

"I need to confess something, Riley."

My stomach dropped. After all, if previous experience served, a statement like that almost always precluded years of agonizing misery. "You do?"

"I do." I heard him take a deep breath. "I can't stop thinking about our kiss." He exhaled.

Kiss? What kiss?

It took some time, but finally, I sifted back far enough through my Dominic-saturated memory and remembered accosting Robin at work. I cringed. I also distinctly remember attacking his tie and shirt … before letting Dominic get his fingers on/in me, and all within a twenty-four hour period.

I'm seriously messed up. Doctor Powell's going to kick my ass.

"Ah, yeah. It was some kiss." I tried to sound sincere.

In all honestly, it was a perfectly good kiss. I mean, it had just the right amount of lip pressure, tongue penetration, and there was even a sexy guy attached to the other end of it. In fact, on its own it proved pretty damn great. So, there was nothing to complain about—*zilch, nichts, niente.*

I sighed.

Fucking Dominic.

Why did he have such absurdly delicious lips? Why did his dirty mouth do such wild things to me? And what the heck was with those fingers? They needed to come with their own caution sign. Seriously.

Robin continued, "So, I was wondering if you still wanted to go out on Saturday night?" His voice sounded uncertain and my heart immediately softened, I was such a sucker for vulnerability in a guy.

"Oh, um—"

"I was thinking of a sunset picnic on the beach. You know, wine, dips, cheese, I'll organize it. What do you think?"

I stopped. "Wow. That sounds … amazing actually." There was no avoiding the smile which threatened to overtake my face.

He chuckled and the sound of it made my stomach do that little flip thing. Robin was such a good man, he was thoughtful, romantic, generous, kind, emotionally available.

Hello, emotionally available.

What the hell am I doing? Just say yes already, it's only a second date for God's sake.

"So, I'll pick you up at seven?"

After the briefest of pauses, I murmured, "Yeah, thanks."

Once we said our goodbyes and hung up, I stared down at the black screen of my phone for what felt like hours, thinking.

I'm not cheating on anyone, I'm not. I mean, it's not as though Robin and I are together or anything, we're not Facebook official and we definitely haven't had The Talk. If we had, then of course I wouldn't look at anyone else let alone allow a promiscuous guitarist to finger fuck me. Twice. In one day.

Oh, God.

I honestly don't know what the heck is going on with Dominic and me, and I'd bet my running shoes he hasn't a clue either. But something has shifted; it's different between us now, I can feel it. We're in a deeper space, we're somewhere, I dunno—real. Or am I projecting? Does he really just want to have sex with me and be done with it? I can't believe I just thought that, now I need another run.

217

****

Grace looked amazing. There was a light in her eyes and a sway to her hips that I had not seen in a long time. Levi was going to get the world's biggest hug when I saw him next. And when we walked into The Ruby Room, I was not the only one who thought so either. Heads turned, gazes shifted, bodies pivoted, all because of Grace. Not that she noticed. She never did, and it was one of the attributes I loved most about her. Completely oblivious to all the stares, G led us straight to the alcohol and did not question the bartender when he ignored the guy standing next to her who had been waiting not so patiently for his bourbon. I didn't question it either; I was just thankful to have a beer in my hands.

The truth was, I had never felt so anxious. My stomach felt like a rollercoaster from the forties. You know, the rickety wooden ones that collapsed without warning or shot the cars through the sky, bullet-like, when the wind changed direction. My chest was home to a boa constrictor which mistook my torso for a lizard, and millions of tiny needles pricked my skin for the sheer fun of watching me slowly bleed to death. Not good.

"We're gonna fuck, tonight."

Dominic's dark promise kept circling my brain, one minute thrilling and the next torturing, my already confused heart. For the life of me, I did not know what to do. I mean, I knew what my body screamed at me to do—that was pretty damn obvious—but I also seriously doubted my vagina's ability to make an informed decision. And then there was Robin to consider. Good, sweet, honest Robin.

Jesus.

I finished my first drink in record time and quickly ordered another. Grace raised a questioning eyebrow but remained silent, thank the Lord. After I'd swallowed a good portion of my second beer, we made our way over to one of the raised metal tables flanking one side of the music venue and perched ourselves precariously on some stools.

"Okay, Riley here's the plan for tonight."

It took every restraint I had to swallow my beer rather than spit it out my mouth, Trevi fountain style. My eyes darted around the room, hoping to God that no one was witnessing my psychological episode. After all, an imaginary therapist sprouting wisdom inside a patient's head rarely—if ever—ended well.

"One: you're going to accept the emotions you're feeling as uncomfortable and perplexing, you're going to make room for them. They're shit, deal with it."

I hated Fictional Doctor Powell, she was just as ruthless as the real deal.

"Two: you're going to stop using alcohol as a numbing tool. It always ends in disaster, you know that."

My mind flashed back to the last time I had drunk too much and my cheeks instantly burned. Dominic. Pushing me up against the wall of The Hole, rubbing his hardness into my sensitive flesh, devouring my mouth with his tongue… It sucked when she was right.

"And three: you're going to breathe."

"Ah—"

"Don't interrupt me. You're going to breathe in the moment and make a decision which you know feels right. No more questions, no more internalized debates, you'll give yourself a migraine otherwise."

I sighed. Fictional Doctor Powell was right, and as soon as I admitted to myself the obvious reason behind her exorbitant hourly rates, she was gone. Probably for the best; I did not want to be diagnosed with multiple personality disorder as well. So, taking a deep breath, I grudgingly accepted the rollercoaster, boa constrictor and needles. I promised myself only one more drink and forced myself back into the present.

Huh.

The Ruby Room was actually pretty huge. The night was still early as far as live music went, which was why the venue wasn't yet packed out. However, there was a band already on stage and a handful of devoted fans standing in front of them, nodding their heads in unison to the rhythmic drumbeat.

The band itself—a five-piece I had never heard of—were decent. Their sound was heavy, loud and easily filled the cavernous space in front of them. They played on the raised stage of what used to be a theater and were blanketed either side by red velvet curtains partially masking painted black wings—I assumed they led to the green room backstage. Above the band hung exposed rigging with a lighting setup, and in front of them was the dance floor/mosh pit, interspersed with patrons laughing, drinking, and headbanging.

I loved it.

Tall, metal tables, like the ones G and I were seated at, lined both walls of the building, and behind us, tucked just to the left of the entrance, was the bar. I tried to figure out where the name of the place came from. I mean, wherever I looked, everything was black—black floor, walls, ceiling, stage. But on closer inspection, I realized the accents of the building—the splash back behind the bar, the beer coasters, restroom doors—all of them glistened ruby red.

Once again, life made sense.

Well, until I scanned the slowly swelling crowd seeking out the man responsible for my erratic heartbeat—the one that refused to calm the heck down despite fictitious Doctor Powell's advice. Turning to Grace, I yelled over the music, "Where are the guys?"

Her eyes scanned the room, but when she could not find them, she looked back at me and shrugged.

How could she be so calm? I mean, the guy she was in love with was somewhere in this venue, for God's sake. Why wasn't she searching behind every last whiskey bottle for him? Weren't her fingers itching? Weren't her feet tapping—and not in time with the music. Weren't her insides trying to do a fucking Houdini out her ear holes, like mine?

I shook my head. No, of course not. After all, Grace had her shit together, didn't she? Whereas I—obviously—did not.

I swallowed the rest of my drink, determined to act like a rational human being. However, my internal scolding must have taken longer than expected because when I looked up again, the first band had packed up their equipment and the boys from Mondez were making their way on stage.

Levi was first, his stride long and sure. Dominic followed close behind, sauntering over to where his foot pedal lay just right of the stage—my ovaries squealed in delight at the sight of him. I ignored them, mostly. Finn was next, meticulously arranging his Tama drum kit until satisfied with the placement. The guy seemed completely unaware of the collective sigh which burst forth from anyone with two eyes in their head. Tyler was last, his trademark smile strangely absent, and in its place a focused, determined look. Not that it detracted from his appeal. Heck no. If anything, this new dark edge blatantly added to it tenfold.

However, my gaze drifted back to the lead guitarist. Of course it did. Clearly, my eyeballs were rebelling against logic and common sense because when they landed on him—whoa—I drew in a sharp breath. Dominic was staring at me. No, scrap that. He was

221

beckoning me with a sultry come-hither-and-fuck-me gaze. I swear, the steel strings of his guitar miraculously freed themselves from the fret board and snaked their way toward me. They slithered around my lower back and tugged, summoning me closer, so I slid off the stool and moved.

One step.

What am I doing?

Two.

Can't stop now.

Dominic's eyes were even more brilliant under lights. The way they leisurely took in my chunky heels, high-waisted black shorts, white tank and leather jacket left me tingling all over. Even from where I stood in the crowd, I could see his pupils dilate and the pulse in his neck throb.

Sweet Jesus.

I couldn't breathe.

In all honesty, it felt like someone had vacuumed all the oxygen out of The Ruby Room. We were all actually going to die if a door or window was not opened within the next five seconds. It would be like a mass sacrifice to a guitar god, we would be on TV and everything. Parents would use the footage as a dire warning against intoxicating male musicians and the power they wielded over susceptible young women. The live music industry would cease functioning as a result and it would be all Dominic's fault.

I swallowed. The guitar strings strengthened, crackled and fizzed. Surely, the lead cable running from his guitar to the amp was an exposed live wire? Surely, that was the cause of all this mess? After all, what else could have generated the millions of thrumming, surging, ricocheting currents running between us?

And still he stared.

Oh, God.

I wet my lips.

A faint, *tap, tap, tap* filtered its way through my subconscious. Dominic blinked, looked over at Finn and the spell was broken. A gust of wind escaped me from the loss of contact and I suddenly felt the urge to cry, but there was no time for tears. Heck, there was barely enough time to brace myself before being hit with a cyclonic barrage of sound.

Holy. Crap.

Mondez's opening song was like a permission slip to cut loose. Completely. It demanded I forget everything other than the music surrounding me, and the hypnotic rhythm it produced. It compelled everyone in the crowd to dance, laugh, *live*. So we did. Grace and I rocked out to the dirty guitar riffs, we grinned like crazy to Levi's vocal caresses, and we threw our heads back—drinking the night in—while moving to the cadenced reverberations of sticks on skins.

It was the best hour of my life.

Well, up until then at least.

I mean, beside me was my best friend, in front of me was a musical phenomenon, and surrounding us were more and more people keen to get in on the action.

Fucking brilliant.

When the final strum of the last song echoed its way through the speakers, G and I screamed like there was a combined whiskey and chocolate sale at our local shopping center. The guys smiled, waved and made their way off stage, no doubt to partake in a gigantic man-hug and congratulatory fist pump—or ten.

Grace wiped a sheen of perspiration off her face and asked, "Drink?"

I lifted the bedraggled mess of what used to be my hair and fanned the back of my neck, nodding. "Drink."

We pushed our way through the crowd—the place was packed—finished our water and was onto our next round of drinks when Grace suddenly had her tongue down a man's throat. I assumed it was Levi on account of the six-foot-something sexbomb he was impersonating. That guy was definitely a method actor. It must have been the music, God only knew it made me want to hump something.

Looking down at my beer, I blushed, craving a small slice of the heat and pheromones on display in front of me. Unexpectedly, I was spun around and pulled up against a wall of solid muscle.

Oh my.

The beer was taken out of my hand and I watched, entranced, as Dominic tipped his head back, draining the entire bottle. Never had theft looked so damn fine. My heartbeat spiked—oh, the depravity, I was officially jealous of a cold beverage—and I bit my lip, determined to remain mute. Once finished, Dominic leaned around me, placed it on the bar and then slipped his fingers into the back pockets of my shorts, pulling me against him. Neither my stomach nor my pussy could ignore his growing erection and I bit back a groan, just.

Dominic must have seen the want in my eyes because his grin was wicked as he glanced at Levi—still busy—leaned forward and then licked his way from my collarbone to earlobe. The moment his cool lips touched my skin, my hands were in his hair, demanding more.

With an aggressiveness that shocked me, I drew his mouth to mine, unashamedly running my tongue along the underside of his top lip. Beer. Dominic. Heaven.

With a low growl, Dominic closed whatever gap was left between us and kissed me, really kissed me. His masterful strokes were hot, deep, hungry, exactly what I craved. "Damn, Riley," he muttered between a flurry of moist lips and tongue. "I can't get enough." More kissing. "Every fuckin' time. What are you doing to me? I just—" But he paused, and then tore himself away, panting.

"Dominic?" I puffed. "What's wrong? Why are you stopping?"

But he didn't answer, so I groaned in frustration. The heat in his eyes gradually cooled and was then gone, while in its place sprang cool detachment.

What the fuck's happening?

I did not like it. Not. One. Little. Bit.

Jesus Christ, Dominic, you were right here a second ago. Where did you go?

"Dominic?"

Nothing.

I reached out to touch his face, but he shook me off. Then, noticing my hurt expression, he sighed, threw one arm around my shoulders and quickly kissed the top of my head. It was like we were back in high school playing the age-old game of What the Hell Is Wrong with You? I hated it. Clearly, my rulebook was somewhere in the bottom of my locker.

"Get a fucking room already."

I started. Even to my own ears, Dominic's voice sounded … off.

Levi turned to look at his brother as Dominic continued. "People don't want to have to look at that shit, we're trying to have a good time here." I think he was aiming for mockery, but his words definitely came out bitter.

My heart sank, with every passing second he was drifting further and further away from me.

"Now that your dick's back in your pants, Casanova, let's go watch Adrift play, huh?"

Thankfully, Levi did not seem too fazed by

Dominic's bipolar behavior. He just lowered Grace to the floor, took her hand and followed me as I trailed behind the storm cloud back to the mosh pit.

We stood just behind the mass of thrashing bodies hurling themselves at each other, it was intense. The music was loud, the fans screamed louder, and I looked at the stage to see who was responsible for the mayhem.

Wow.

Katrina was good.

She held the mic between both hands, her reverberant, husky voice easily carrying throughout The Ruby Room as she rocked the heck out. The girl looked amazing, and I'm talking front-cover-of-*Rolling-Stone*-magazine amazing. I blamed the ripped jeans, tight black tank top, and mane of wavy brown hair. Oh, and her voice, definitely that too. Up on stage, it looked like she owned the place, like this very moment was exactly what she was put on this earth for.

I sighed. If only I had found what I lived for, if only I had the guts to—

"Ouch." Turning, I glared at the woman who stepped on my foot in what were surely steel-capped boots. She jostled past, pushing me up against Dominic in her haste. Mascara ran down her face and an aggrieved guy with a Mohawk stalked not far behind—I barely noticed. Instead, I found myself in a state of complete shock. I blinked and then looked down.

Dominic held my hand.

My eyes flicked to his face, he was staring unseeing at the stage, almost like he could not believe it either. But he didn't let go. Despite the pounding drums, blaring guitar pickups, Katrina's throaty voice and the blatant pandemonium directly in front of us, his fingers remained entwined with mine.

I had never felt so calm.

I smiled, my heart doing a strange arabesque-type movement. Dominic's eyes slid to mine and a wry half-grin tugged the corner of his mouth. He shook his head slightly, warning me not to draw attention to what we were doing—like anyone would notice or care—gently squeezed my fingers and then turned his attention back to the music.

I did not hear a single note after that. Hell, I could not do anything except beg my cursed knees to do their job as his thumb rhythmically brushed the über-sensitive skin on the inside of my wrist. And when the last song of the set finally faded out, there was a light in Dominic's eyes I had not seen since we were at the zoo. He was back. My Dominic was back. All it took was insanely heavy music and some physical contact from yours truly.

Who would have thought?

In fact, he was in such fine form that he pointedly glanced from Katrina to Levi, joking, "Cold shower anyone?"

Tearing my hand from his, I glared up at him, willing him a crumpled carcass at my bruised feet. Dominic just smirked, and I fought the sudden overwhelming urge to wipe that stupid sexy grin off his face … with sandpaper.

While Levi and Dominic went backstage to congratulate the guys from Adrift, Grace and I waited—not surprisingly—by the bar. I kept my promise to Imaginary Doctor Powell and stuck to good old-fashioned water, while G downed yet another whiskey.

"You okay?"

My head shot up from the bottle in my hands. "Of course. Why?"

She stared at me for a moment before replying, "Because you're lying."

"No, I—" But I stopped because it was useless. G

knew me better than anyone, so it was pointless pretending. The thing was, as soon as I let go of Dominic's hand, the rollercoaster, boa constrictor, and prickly needles were back—with friends. Lots of them. In fact, they must have received a group rate or something because the full gravitational force of what Dominic and I were about to do suddenly descended upon me, plague-of-locusts style. I was a cacophony of emotional fragments, and each one of them stood in direct contrast to the other. Impatient? Yes. Excited? Sure. Horny? Definitely. But above all else, loomed fear.

I was scared shitless.

I mean, after tonight we would never be lovers again, and if I was being truly honest with myself, we would never be friends again either. There was no way I could go back to exercising with him every day knowing he had been inside me and yet was sleeping with other women. I was simply not wired that way. And yet, I could not give up the opportunity of finally being able to explore the physical connection we shared. If the two orgasms he gave me earlier were a movie preview, I wanted the whole damn feature film. For the life of me, the hour could not come fast enough. However, a large part of me never wanted it to arrive.

"Well?" Grace grabbed the drink from me—what was with people stealing my beverages—and placed it on the bar alongside her empty glass. She then turned back with a look of genuine concern, probably because I had been gazing blankly at her during my lengthy inner flummox.

"Oh, um. Look it's—"

"Ready to go, kitten?" Levi sidled up to G and tucked a strand of hair behind her ear. She smiled lovingly up at him and I could not glance away if I tried. The two were adorable, well, in an icepick-to-the-heart kind of way.

Grace's gaze met mine again. "Wanna come back to the hotel with us?"

"Eww, no thanks."

She laughed. "I meant to share a taxi, not a fucking bed."

"Either way, eww."

"Dom's already promised to take care of Riley." Levi nuzzled G's neck.

Yes. He. Has.

I somehow found the will to avert my eyes, though shifting on the spot did next to nothing to ease the sudden, unbearable ache between my thighs. "Yeah, ah, like I said, no thanks." Swallowing with effort, I continued, "You two head on back to the hotel and, um, have fun."

Grace was about to argue but I spun her on the spot and pushed her toward the exit. "Honestly, it's fine. Now go." And with that, they were gone.

I was on my way back to the bar when it happened. The sight of it made me stop dead in my tracks.

What the fuck?

Dominic was kissing someone.

Okay, so not kissing exactly—my subconscious might have overexaggerated slightly—but he was definitely leaning down and whispering in some random woman's ear while she giggled, fluttered her appallingly fake eyelashes, and then trailed manicured talons down his eight-pack.

So I counted them one time. What of it?

Anyway, Dominic indicated to talon girl to follow him and the two made their way backstage. Together. Her squeals of delight echoed throughout The Ruby Room while I just stood there with my mouth gaping open like a fucking idiot.

He was going to have sex with her. I mean, that was where he took his groupies, right? To the green room? It suddenly felt like my ribs were made of dagger-like thorns that punctured my lungs with each breath.

I had to get out of there. *Now.*

I practically bolted to the exit and was almost across the finish line when a strong hand gripped my wrist, detaining me.

"What's going on?" Finn's perceptive grey eyes took in my manic expression before glancing over my shoulder. "Where's Dom?"

"How should I know?" I spat, surprised by my vehemence.

But Finn just did that I'm-gonna-force-you-to-tell-me-the-truth-with-my-hypnotic-gaze thing and I immediately hung my head, defeated. The fight drained out of me, no doubt morphing into a puddle of gooey humiliation layering the sticky black floor.

"He's in the green room," I mumbled. Finn kept staring. "With some woman." More staring. "Blonde hair, tiny waist, hot outfit. She was all over him like an eczema flare-up." I glanced away. "I think."

He was silent for a long time before nodding once. "Right." Two seconds later, he strode toward the door just off stage.

I raced after him. "Finn, wait."

He ignored me.

Stepping in front of him, I put my hand to his chest, halting his progress. "Stop." He did, thankfully, so I took my hand away. "This isn't high school, he's a grown man who can make his own decisions." I looked away, muttering, "No matter how shitty they are." Turning my gaze back to one very furious Finn, I added, "I'm okay with it."

Another grey stare. He was going to burn a hole straight through me at this rate.

My voice only trembled slightly as I repeated, "I'm okay with it."

Finn let out a long exhale. "Fuckin' asshole."

I blinked back tears. "Yeah." And the small part of me that held onto any hope of a miracle between Dominic and I, shriveled up and died.

Which was why what happened next came as such a surprise.

Chapter Fourteen

Escape is useless now,
No one will survive,
No one.
—MONDEZ, "Distance"

I was on my third drink by the time the pounding started. At first, I thought it was my head, but when the door shuddered on its hinges, I knew it was not the alcohol.

"What the hell?" Clambering to my feet, I made my way over to the source of the noise.

Since returning to the hotel, I tidied the cushions on the balcony, rearranged the bath towels by size, and even reordered the minibar according to alcohol potency and calorie quota. Yeah, I was not in the best frame of mind. Not that any of it worked, mind you, because my heart hurt, body jittered, and head refused to do anything but tick.

Dominic. Tick. Talon girl. Tick. Their steamy sex in the green room. Tick, tick, tick.

Fucking hell.

So I took a long bath, slipped on my favorite silk nightie, and shrugged into one of the suite's fluffy white bathrobes—before drinking myself into oblivion. Doctor Powell would have to deal, I was desperate.

After opening the door, I was met with two blazing eyes. They scanned me from head to toe before a low voice growled, "Thought I told you never to answer the door like that."

"What are you even doing here, Dominic?" I retorted. "Just leave me alone."

Huh. The alcohol's kicked in.

But Dominic still glared, his jaw working hard. How he managed to make it both vulturine and sensual, I had no idea. The guy was a master at mixed emotions.

My grip on the door handle tightened, though not in response to his close proximity, that would be stupid. "Go away," I barked, shutting the door in his face.

Okay, so I tried to shut the door in his face. His palm flattened against the wood veneer, preventing me from actually doing it. And he also scorned my attempt at blocking the entrance on account of being twice my size and all. Easy as you like, Dominic pushed past, slammed the door, picked me up and then threw me over his shoulder like an inebriated sack of potatoes.

"Put me down."

He did. I was unceremoniously dumped onto the bed. Scrambling to cover myself with the robe, I crawled onto my knees to glare up at him. Only, it was impossible because he was pacing and a pacing Dominic was hot as hell, despite being a complete douche.

Left. One, two, three. Right. One, two, three.

Such a fine ass. I mean, jerk.

Finally, he stopped, raked tense fingers through his hair—a small part of me might have whimpered—and demanded, "Why'd you run out on me?"

I scoffed, crossing my arms and refusing to answer.

His eyes flicked to my now-exposed cleavage and then back to my face. I scowled at him, pretending his dilated pupils were nothing more than an irritating figment of my imagination.

Dominic moved closer to the bed. "Riley." His voice held a cautionary warning. One I really did not give a shit about no matter what my tingling spine had to say. "Why'd you leave without me?"

Silence.

"For Christ's sake, woman," he exploded. "My cock's supposed to be inside you right now. I'm supposed to be giving you the mother of all fuckin' orgasms—"

"You mean—" But I quickly snapped my mouth shut. After all, there was no way I was going to voice that question out loud.

Not that it mattered, like usual, he could see through me, anyway. "Angel." Dominic's voice turned pitying while I squirmed on the mattress trying to relieve the building torment between my thighs. "The other two orgasms you thought you had were just a warm-up. You ain't felt nothin' yet." There was a dark promise in his eyes which almost made me forget talon girl.

Almost.

"Come here," he ordered.

I swear, my body tried to launch itself into Dominic's orbit. There was even a moment when I gravitated forward slightly because, so help me, I really wanted to. But I didn't.

Wouldn't.

"You asked for it." He crouched low—jaguar style—and slowly crawled across the bed toward me. I, on the other hand, hastily scrambled backward like a crab with directional issues. When my shoulders bumped into the padded headboard with an ominous thud, my heart began beating at quadruple the normal rate. Clearly, it wanted me dead.

"Leave me alone, Dominic." I shut my eyes, pissed that the quiet plea did not even begin to sound convincing.

Stupid voice box. Fucking useless.

"No."

They popped open again and he loomed above me.

Whoa. So beautiful. Such a bastard.

His earthy scent hit me like a waft of cologne and I unashamedly breathed it in. Deeply.

Sweet Jesus.

"I'm not going anywhere," Dominic murmured, his voice deep and so damn sensual I grew breathless. "Not until you tell me why you left." His gaze dropped to my parted mouth, it seriously did not help.

So I avoided his eyes after that, they were simply too blue for my liking. And his lips. Well. They were another matter entirely. Let's just say there was an *open for business* sign where my vagina used to be.

"Look at me."

Damn it.

"Why are you acting like this?"

I tried to feel angry, truly I did. I tried to summon my inner Grace and tear him to shreds with well-chosen slurs about his intelligence or penis size. But I couldn't. For one, he was not stupid, two, his penis was, well, huge, and three, what was the point? It did not change the fact he slept with someone else. I swallowed, willing my eyes not to well up with tears. They did.

Christ.

And the bastard wiped them away.

Resigned, I took a shuddering breath and mumbled, "I saw you." My gaze flicked to his impenetrable blue stare and something in my stomach shifted. Something big. "You were with a girl and you took her to the green room."

"So?"

I stared at him, beyond incredulous. "So?" Pushing him off me, I sat up straighter, my face level with his. I did not want to suck his lips. "You had your fingers inside me this afternoon, you tell me you want your cock inside me right now, and yet you have a goddamn quickie in the green room with some random groupie? What the hell am I? The bread of a fucking sandwich? Is she the salad to my rye, Dominic? Is that what she is?"

"Shithouse analogy, Riley."

"You know what?" I yelled. "Screw you. Screw you and your stupid smile, your stupid hands, your stupid…" I threw up my arms, beyond livid. "Stupid *everything*." Turning, I went to climb off the bed, only the mattress was so large I suddenly wished I brought my analogy with me for a fucking snack on the way.

Dominic grabbed my ankle mid-crawl and the heated contact sent a shockwave directly to my center. I bit my lip. Ironically, I grew even more furious at how quickly he could diffuse my anger.

Don't you dare moan, Riley Jayne. Swear to God—

"You reckon I bagged that chick."

Kicking his hand away—and with any luck, those lingering aftershocks—I continued crawling in silence.

"You do, don't you?"

"Well, what am I supposed to think?" I shot over my shoulder. The look in his eyes made me pause, but I blinked, shook my head and continued the epic journey across the bedspread. "It wouldn't be the first time you took a woman backstage while I was around. Hell, it wouldn't even be the third time you hooked up with a girl right in front of me."

He followed, and I felt an intensifying heat building behind me. Both of us must have looked like a camel train in the fucking desert. His hand suddenly clamped down on my calf, stopping me from finally climbing off the side of the bed. Dropping my head, I begged my molten pussy to play nice with me. She didn't listen. Turned out, she was a cruel bitch who wanted what was owed.

Lord, give me strength.

Dominic's hand slid up my leg and right on cue, goose bumps formed. "Look, I might not be a spokesperson for committed relationships." Despite his low tone, I snorted. "But I'd never do that, Riley."

I faltered on the edge of the mattress, my heart in my mouth.

"Not to you."

And fell.

There was a tangle of arms, legs, hands and feet until I landed with a soft *oomph* on top of Dominic's chest. How he managed to hit the floor first I have no idea—I blamed his muscles, those babies must have weighed a ton. Anyway, after our epic tumble, we lay on the plush carpet of the hotel room floor for what felt like hours in silence.

What a disaster.

I rested my head against his heart, reassuring myself that he was still alive. Yep, those rhythmic heartbeats rang strong and true. His hand systematically caressing my ass was also a pretty strong indicator.

Finally, Dominic raised his head, his blue eyes searching. If he was looking for my dignity, it was somewhere back on the quilt. "You okay?"

I gazed at him, nodding and the room shifted slightly with the movement—alcohol, not concussion. "Yeah, you?"

"Yeah."

Tracing small circles on the fabric of his dark sweater, I gave in to curiosity and asked, "What were you doing in the green room? I mean, if you didn't take her back there to … you know."

"Fuck?"

I could feel a blush coming on and Dominic raised his hand, trailing the backs of his fingers down my cheek. The gesture did next to nothing to ease my embarrassment and that secret smile playing on his lips was seriously doing my head in.

"She wanted a copy of our EP, we brought some with us." He chuckled; the deep, throaty sound did dangerous things to me. "Could've just downloaded it from our website, would've been a hell of a lot cheaper."

"Oh."

And that was it, all the reply I could muster. Truth be told, I was ridiculously frustrated with myself. I mean, rather than drink myself senseless or channel my inner Alice from *The Brady Bunch*, Dominic and I could have been having passionate, soul-destroying sex. For hours. If my pussy had feet, she would have kicked me.

Dominic tucked some hair behind my ear, his voice teasing. "You're a jealous little thing, aren't you?"

I glared at him. "I'm not jealous." Then, looking away, muttered, "I just don't like sharing."

Strong fingers drew my face back and Dominic stared at me for a long moment. It was the strangest thing, when our gazes locked, the carpet, the bed, heck, even the hotel suite itself, disappeared. And I'm talking, completely.

It was just the two of us. We were drawn together by heat, desire and something altogether more powerful.

Whoa.

I could feel it. I could feel the connection. It was there in his eyes, his breath, his touch.

His heart.

In all honesty, I could have stayed wrapped in that little cocoon for hours, days even. Never before had I felt so existent. It was strange because for the first time in my life it felt like someone saw me, really saw me. Dominic moved past the illusion of perfection, he sidestepped the anxiety and crawled under the fear. None of that stuff mattered to him and it felt… Beautiful.

Finally, Dominic murmured, "There's no need to be jealous, angel." He swallowed. "I'm yours."

I inhaled—*is he serious?*

Then, as though realizing what he had said, hastily added, "For tonight. I'm yours for tonight."

And the spell was broken.

Christ.

I blinked and clambered off Dominic while he scrubbed one side of his face with his hand, muttering, "I need a drink."

Standing, I turned to face him. "The stuff you want is at the very back of the minibar." He raised a questioning eyebrow but I shook my head. "Don't ask."

"Right." Dominic got to his feet and strode off in the direction of the alcohol. "Want anything?" he called over his shoulder.

I shook my head. At least the room stopped moving. "No thanks, I've had enough. Maybe just some water?"

"On it."

A short while later, I was wandering aimlessly through the second room of the suite. I left the lights off—quite frankly, the darkness was soothing—and eventually found myself standing in front of the glass windows. The night was clear and, despite the many skyscrapers, if I craned my neck slightly to the left, I could make out the twinkling stars above. They were timeless. And I loved how all my insecurities suddenly felt so inconsequential, so unimportant in their presence. It was a nice change, let me tell you.

Strangely, my head was empty—I know right? There was no internal dialogue between myself and Doctor Powell, no conflicting tirades, no pep talk, nothing. It was so peaceful, like everything I had experienced in the past few weeks, all the contrasting emotions, angst and confusion had been leading up to this very moment.

I was ready.

Dominic and I were going to have sex. We were going to acknowledge our physical chemistry, revel in it and then move on with our lives. Okay, so that part I was not exactly ready for, but everything else I could deal with. Honest.

I sighed.

"You sure you wanna do this?"

I spun on my heel, my eyes wide—that guy had ninja blood. He stood in the doorway with a beer in one hand and water in the other. The light coming from the bedroom behind him cast his body in shadow. I could still clearly make out every contour of his face though, even in the darkness. God knows I memorized each feature often enough. His eyes were soft, his lips moist from recently taking a sip of his drink. A strange fluttering started in my chest the moment our gazes locked. I chose to ignore it. Mostly.

The only problem was, I could not answer him because I could not speak. And I am talking not a single word. Seriously, it was like my tongue had attached itself to the roof of my mouth with an industrial strength adhesive. I mean, in front of me was the physical embodiment of everything I never knew I wanted in a man—commitment issues aside—and yet he was willing to forgo his obvious desire if I truly was not okay with it all.

It was official, my pussy took over my brain.

Some might even say steamrolled.

The poor sucker did not stand a chance.

Without taking my eyes off him, I reached for the belt of my robe, carefully untying the knot with unsteady fingers. Even from where I stood, I could see Dominic's grip on his beer tighten. He knew my answer and he liked it, awesome.

With a heart thumping so loud I was sure he could hear it, I opened the material wide and shrugged it off my shoulders. It cascaded down my body and pooled at my feet. I lifted my chin, daring him to misconstrue my meaning. He did not. However, he did not come charging toward me—raging rhino style—like I thought he would either. Oh no. Instead, he remained where he was with eyes full of dark promise. Dominic took a long, slow drink from his beer while I watched, thirstier than ever before.

He really needed to get into advertising, Diet Coke would take him on for sure.

There was every chance I licked my lips as Dominic swallowed his last mouthful. He placed both drinks on the coffee table and then sauntered toward me, a dangerous smile tormenting my already waning equilibrium.

Sweet Lord, I might not make it 'til morning.

Dark jeans hung in the way I loved, his gray V-neck sweater strained against that strong torso, and with every purposeful step I found myself growing wetter and wetter. Surely, there would be a puddle on the carpet soon? Heaven only knew how I would explain that to housekeeping in the morning. I shook my head.

Focus, Riley.

Eventually, Dominic stood before me, his gaze a fiery caress as it traveled from my bare feet, up tingling legs, and over my sapphire silk nightie. The material felt cool against my heated skin as those blue eyes followed the curve of my hips and came to rest for a moment on my breasts. There was no point in denying it, my erect nipples could have cut through glass easily. Those girls relished his undivided attention and I did not blame them. In fact, I watched, mesmerized as the pulse at the base of his throat throbbed at the sight of them.

At least I wasn't the only one throbbing here.

His eyes continued upward, momentarily lingering on my parted mouth, brushing across flushed cheeks and finally, they met my own fevered stare.

Touch me. For the love of God, touch *me, Dominic. I'm going to explode if you don't.*

He leaned forward, his breath tickling my ear as he murmured, "You're a fuckin' wet dream, Riley."

I may or may not have moaned. Okay, I totally did. When he licked and nibbled my ear lobe, I honestly could not help a small mewl. When his lips traced along my jaw and finally found mine, I hummed. And when his tongue entered my mouth, exploring every last crevice… Well. Let's just say all bets were off.

Reaching up, I wrapped my arms around his neck, burying my hands in his hair and pressing myself flush against him. God, he felt good. My breasts crushed against his chest and the sensation of my hard nipples rubbing against his solid pecs sent unfettered pleasure coursing through me.

"Naked. Need to get you naked," I muttered between hot, frantic kisses. Running my hands down his torso, I reached for the hem of his sweater and tugged. Anyone might have thought I found his clothing offensive, and in part, it was. Dominic gave a low chuckle which did nothing to ease my growing lust-fueled psychosis, though helped me get rid of the cursed sweater. Once it was safely thrown out of sight, I stood back and admired.

Holy fuck.

Dominic's wolfish grin proved that my internal exclamation was not as private as I first thought. In fact, I was pretty sure I could still hear it echoing throughout the hotel suite. But I didn't care because in front of me stood the most breathtaking sight I had ever seen. Dominic's upper body had always been a draw card for me, but up close—I shook my head, trailing possessive fingers over each rise and dip of his taut muscles—Michelangelo himself could not have sculptured anything better.

"Christ, Dominic."

However, when I looked back at his face, I was surprised to see his expression had turned cynical. "It's just a body, angel. Just a shiny wrapper, nothing else."

He winced when my fingernails inadvertently dug into his skin. "No." My voice was adamant. "You're wrong." Dominic raised an eyebrow but I continued anyway. "It's so much more than that." I skimmed my fingers across his chest, marveling at how smooth he was. "It's your body, Dominic, the body of a good man." I paused before looking at him, murmuring, "And that makes all the difference."

Immediately worried I had said too much, I then kissed my way down his neck. When I reached it, my lips lingered just above the loud thumping of his heart.

There was a sharp intake of breath and my head was pulled back by the hair. Not painfully, just enough to put my body into sensation overdrive.

"Where did you come from?" Dominic's incredulous eyes bored into mine.

After a moment of silence on my part—I mean, really, what was there to say?—he brushed the pad of his callused thumb across my bottom lip. I opened my mouth, sucking it gently. When I wrapped my tongue around it, a stifled groan emanated from the back of Dominic's throat and when I nipped him, he made another sound entirely.

Fucking brilliant.

243

He removed his thumb, cupped my face in his hands and kissed me with a ferocity I never before experienced. Honestly, I had no idea where he ended and I began because it was like we became one writhing, desperate mass of want and need. And yet, I still could not get close enough, could not grasp the sensation I craved. It was driving me insane.

Like usual, Dominic knew what I needed and murmured into my mouth, "Back pocket."

Like a hawk targeting an easy prey, my hand dived into the back of his jeans and returned triumphant with a foil packet—though not before giving his delicious ass a quick once over. Pulling back slightly, I raised an eyebrow and flashed the condom. "I was a foregone conclusion, huh?"

He gave me one of those wicked smiles, the one that left me clinging to him since my knees suddenly forgot their purpose in life. "I was hopeful."

"There's only one."

"You know the rules."

"What if it breaks?"

"It won't."

Determined not to overthink the fact that we would never be intimate like this again, I shook my head and returned, faux brightly, "Better make the most of it then."

"That's my girl." And he slipped the spaghetti straps of my nightie off my shoulders, grinning as the garment fell to the floor. However, his triumph was quickly crushed. With pupils more dilated than I had ever seen them, he glanced back at me, growling, "No panties?"

It was my turn to smile. "Nope. I never wear any to bed."

Dominic groaned before dropping to his knees.

With his face pressed against my pubic bone, he breathed in deeply, mumbling, "Fuck. What are you doing to me, woman?"

My own breathing hitched as he placed one of my legs over his shoulder.

Hang on, is he going to—

"Can't get enough of this pussy, so pink, so perfect. It's all I've thought about for weeks. Drivin' me fuckin' crazy."

Oh, my God, he is.

I threw my head back as his long fingers slid through the soaked lips of my sex and with a low growl he delved them inside me. "Goddamn, Riley."

I moaned. Deafeningly.

His tongue darted out and hungrily lapped my clit.

"*Dominic*." Reaching down, I ran my fingers through his hair, scratching my nails along his scalp and rocking my hips in time with his rhythmic carnal assault. To say it was mind-blowing would have been the understatement of the century, millennium even.

Sweet. God. In. Heaven. This. Is. So. Good.

I hate to admit this but it took me all of three minutes to climax. Seriously, I could not help it. From the moment his mouth first touched my skin, I was lost. With each swipe of his tongue, each thrust of his fingers, and each guttural growl, my body came alive with sensation. It took over all other thoughts and feelings until I was a quivering, boneless mess screaming incoherently at the roof overhead.

By the end of it, I'm pretty sure I garbled something like, "Wow" or "Yikes." There was every possibility it verbalized as, "Wowkes." Yeah, not my most intelligent moment. Not that it mattered, of course, because Dominic was too busy drawing out my orgasm for as long as possible to notice. Thank fuck.

Once I calmed down, blinked and regained my focus, Mr. Orgasmatron kissed and licked his way up my trembling body, his lips leaving a wet trail of our combined desire. And when he took one of my nipples in his mouth, teasing it, tantalizing it until my fingernails left half-moon imprints in his shoulders, I almost came on the spot—again.

"Need you inside me," I moaned, as my back arched and a ball of tension began to build at the base of my stomach. "So much. Please, Dominic, I can't—"

He straightened up and stared at me, lips moist and eyes dark with heat. "You dropped something." In his hand he held the condom, I must have let go of it while he had his head between my legs. Understandable, given the circumstances. "Undress me and put it on."

The man did not have to ask twice. I attacked the button and zip of his jeans with a vengeance—hell, the Crusaders would have been proud of my dogged determination—and with a sigh of satisfaction, watched as his pants finally dropped to his ankles.

Dominic kicked off his boots, peeled off his socks and then stepped out of his jeans. Not that I paid much attention. Oh no. I was far too busy eyeballing the gigantic bulge in his black boxers, trying to determine how the heck it was going to fit inside me. Physics was never my strength at school and for once I wish I had taken an extra class.

"Dominic?"

He stopped, and after registering the trepidation in my eyes, gave a soft smile. Stepping closer, I felt his erection rest heavily against my stomach. I bit my lip. "Don't overthink it, angel. I won't hurt you, I'd hate it if…" He sucked on my bottom lip, took a breath, and said, "Reckon my cock was made to fit inside you."

So true.

With those words, the tension in my body dissipated and I kissed him back. "Yeah, I think you're right." My hands trailed down the ridges of his abs and played with the elastic band of his boxers. One finger dipped inside and brushed against soft hair, Dominic groaned, and I smiled against his mouth. After taking a deep breath, I delved inside, releasing him from his boxers and stroking the long, smooth length of him.

"Damn, woman."

Yep, there was no denying it, the man was big. But I was not nervous anymore. Instead, I relished his ragged breaths as I worked him, I welcomed the way he gripped my hips to the point of bruising. I did that to him, I was the one responsible for his pleasure, for his undoing.

It. Was. Awesome.

Taking the condom from Dominic, I grinned at his sharp intake of breath when I tore the packet open with my teeth. Throwing away the foil, I pinched the end, placed it over the straining head of his hard cock and slowly unrolled it down the shaft.

He growled. "Now there's a fuckin' sight. I love seeing your hands on me, angel."

I smiled but soon gasped when he picked me up, wrapped my legs around his waist and strode over to the dining table. With a single kick, one of the chairs flew across the room and I was carefully placed on the cold glass top. Without any further preamble, he spread my knees open, his hands trailing up the inside of my thighs until he found my pussy again. The sexiest damn smile I had ever seen lit up his face just before I dropped my head back and moaned.

"Want my cock inside you?"

"Yes," I breathed.

I felt him shift closer and the slight pressure of his

hardness against my entrance almost did me in.

"You sure?"

"Yes."

Still, he did not enter. "Really sure?"

My head snapped up and I glared at him. Now was not the time for games. "Fuck me, damn it."

Dominic's gravelly chuckle resonated directly with my center. "Whatever you say."

He entered me.

Oh. My. Sweet. Baby. Jesus.

"*Fuck.*"

I was thankful Dominic took his time slowly stretching and filling me because, in all honesty, there was a lot of him. And maybe it was his size or maybe it was the fact it was Dominic, but no other man had ever felt as good. It was like he crowded every possible space inside me, leaving nothing but him, me and this insanely pleasurable friction. When at last he reached as far as he could go—I swear, his cock hit my cervix—he mumbled into my shoulder, "You okay?"

I think I nodded.

"Riley?" I opened my eyes and the concern on his face almost broke me. "I need some words here, angel. Do you want me to stop?"

After wrapping my arms and legs around him, shifting him even closer, I whispered, "No, don't stop."

A gust of air escaped him. "Thank Christ." And we both smiled. "Wasn't sure if I could. Now hold on, shit's gonna get wild."

It did.

He pulled out, almost to the very end and then slammed back into me.

"*Dominic.*"

Over and over again his cock hit my sweet spot. I couldn't think, couldn't talk, couldn't do anything except drown in the pleasurable sensations he created.

It felt so fucking good.

And in no time at all, I once again spiraled out of control, my body shuddering and shaking with exquisite pleasure as another orgasm tore through me.

"The way you come apart in my hands—Fuck, angel. Can't get enough of it."

I blinked dazedly up at Dominic and he gave a wicked smile. "Reckon there's still another one inside you." And before I could object—half-heartedly, I grant you—he pulled out of me. Carefully standing me up on trembling legs, Dominic then spun me around, pressed down on the small of my back and bent me over the table.

"Look up."

It was safe to say, until that very moment I paid no attention whatsoever to the floor to ceiling gilded mirror hanging on the west wall of the hotel suite. But when Dominic wrapped my hair around his fist and pulled my head back, it was all I could see. We were all I could see.

Oh, my.

I blinked. Who was that woman with the sultry eyes glowing with pleasure? Who was that woman with the bruised mouth and glossy sheen of sweat coating her skin? No idea. I sure as hell had never met her.

"Fuckin' gorgeous." Dominic ran his free hand from my shoulder down the curve of my spine and across my ass. His fingers then deftly trailed along the back of my thigh until he reached my knee. In one fluid motion, he hitched it up until it was resting on the dining table, his pupils growing darker with each passing second.

He stepped back, and I watched his reflection as those enigmatic eyes took in my exposed pussy. Never before had I felt so desired. With a low growl, a muttered curse and a shake of his head, he moved closer, angling his straining cock at my wet entrance—I was positively dripping. Dominic teased me with himself before taking a deep breath and, in one swift movement, thrust inside.

I screamed. Not from pain, hell no, I screamed because the pleasure of him taking me so thoroughly felt that damn good. Seriously.

"Open your eyes."

Blinking, my fevered gaze met Dominic's lust-filled one in the mirror. His deep, purposeful strokes instantly creating a ball of tangled energy in my lower stomach.

"Jesus," I whimpered, almost certain this building orgasm was going to be the one I compared all others to for the rest of my life. They would suck in comparison, there was no doubt about it.

"Dominic, I can't—"

"Yes, you can. Watch." And he moved his fingers over my clit, skillfully rubbing the swollen nub in time with his deep thrusts.

My breathing grew erratic.

"Just look at you."

Light flickered before my eyes.

"Sexiest fucking sight I've ever seen."

Sparks of heat unfurled in my stomach.

"The moment I saw you, I knew. Knew I had to have you like this."

"Oh, God, I'm going to—"

"Your hot pussy is heaven, Riley."

"Dominic, please I—"

"It's clamped so tightly around my cock. Can you feel it?"

"I—"

"Tell me you feel it too."

"*Dominic*," I cried, as the orgasm to end all orgasms completely rocked my body, pulsing, throbbing and owning every inch of me to the core.

A minute later, Dominic came too. His deep roar a sound I wanted to bottle up and keep forever. We were still for a minute and I gazed at the mirror, fascinated as his features turned possessive yet soft in the aftermath of what we had done. Neither of us said a word as he eased out and helped me straighten up, we just stared at each other, our breathing labored. But our faces said it all, and the combined realization was a headfuck of epic proportions.

Once was not enough.

Chapter Fifteen

I see your conscience,
It's changing your words,
What I want you to say.
—MONDEZ, "Distance"

"So, did you do it? Did you finally do the deed?"

"Huh?" I shook my head, blaming the warm rays of sunshine and the lingering X-rated memories of my evening spent with Dominic for my lapse in concentration.

"Dominic. Sex. Did his cock enter your vagina?"

I blushed. "Jesus, Mae. You've got no shame, do you?" Her laughter echoed through the phone as I lay back on the sunbed, exhausted. Needless to say, I got next to no sleep last night and despite a lazy morning spent on the hotel balcony doing nothing but reliving every spine-tingling caress and toe curling thrust, I still felt tired. It also did not help when every time I moved, muscles ached in the most delicious way possible.

Sigh.

I needed a run. I needed some fresh air and the beach to clear my head. Maybe if I closed my eyes, ignoring the intermittent honking of car horns and occasional gusts of exhaust fumes from the streets below, I could pretend I was back in Geographe Bay? The sudden screeching of tires followed by the most elaborate use of the word, *fuck* I had ever heard interrupted my musing. I groaned. Nope, not a chance.

"Well?"

"You're not going to let this go, are you?"

"You mean, the fact that you left town with the hottest man alive without warning me? Hell no, I was rostered on with Tiffany, for God's sake. *Tiffany*, Riley. Longest eight hours of my life, that alone deserves some juicy gossip in compensation."

I grimaced, immediately feeling guilty for leaving Mae with the least intelligent midwife in the history of the universe. No exaggeration. "How was she?"

"Vacant. Like a walking, talking, breathing vacuum of nonexistent particle matter. How that woman ever got herself a midwifery degree is a fucking paradox I can't even begin to comprehend."

"Maybe it was through passion, dedication, and drive?"

Mae snorted. "If you're referring to her bedroom habits, then I'd say you were right."

"Mae."

"Speaking of…"

"Mae, I'm sure she—"

"How was sex with Dominic?"

I paused, caught off guard. "Oh, ah…" Then I blushed furiously, channeling my inner burns victim in the process. "It was…" After exhaling a long sigh, I finally admitted, "The most amazing experience of my life."

Mae squealed, and I quickly pulled the phone away from my ear, fearful for my hearing. "I knew it. Tell me everything."

Resigned to the inevitable, I did. I recounted from Dominic's unexpected arrival at my hotel room door, through to the lingering kiss just before he left a few hours later. To say they were the best few hours I had ever faced was officially the biggest understatement of all time.

"Wow."

"I know, right?"

"Wow."

"Mae, I get it. It was wow." Agitatedly, I ran one hand down the side of my face. "The only problem is, what do I do now?"

"What do you mean?"

"Well, it was jaw-dropping, categorically, one hundred percent the best sex of my life. I now want him more than anything else in my entire existence and I'm pretty sure he feels the same way, but unless Satan himself buys a snow plow, a relationship isn't in the cards for us." Shaking my head, I muttered, "At least, not with his stupid one-night-stand rule in place. I mean, who does that? And more importantly, why on earth would he do that?"

Mae swore under her breath.

We were both silent for a moment, no doubt pondering the ridiculous situation my libido had gotten me into. Yeah, I was totally blaming hormones instead of my nonexistent common sense. There was less guilt that way.

"I've got it."

"What? A debilitating crush on an emotionally comatose man? No, you don't, Mae. I do."

"No, I mean, I know how you're going to keep busy until your head catches up with your vagina."

"Okay, now you've completely lost me and can you please stop talking about my vagina? It's freaking me out."

But she continued on as though I hadn't spoken. "Remember when we both got blind drunk at our work Christmas party last year?"

I shut my eyes, refusing to dwell on the embarrassing memories from that evening. Why did she have to bring it up? The less I thought about that night, the better. "The one in Margaret River?"

"Yeah, when we had one too many red wines and

you ended up curled in a ball on my lap bawling your eyes out while I sang you Miley Cyrus lyrics."

I swore. A lot. Even the irate driver on the street below would have been impressed with my originality and flair.

"You went on and on about how you liked your job at the hospital but it didn't feed your soul."

Flashbacks to mascara smeared cheeks, red wine stained teeth and random pieces of toilet paper littered throughout my hair came to mind. I pressed fingers to my mouth, softly exclaiming, "Oh, God. I used those exact words, didn't I?"

I could almost hear her smile. "Yep."

I swore again.

"Anyway, you're going to do it. You're going to feed your soul."

"What? You're crazy. Mae, I really don't think—"

"No, Riley. No more bullshit excuses and no more thinking you're not good enough. Get that toned ass of yours off the couch and into gear. Make something awesome happen. Those new mums aren't going to exercise themselves, you know." She stopped for a moment. "Okay, so some of them might exercise themselves but they're the stupidly motivated ones, freaks of nature, ignore them."

Now it was my turn to fall silent.

Is it possible? Could I do this? Could I finally start living the life I've always wanted instead of the one I felt I should?

A tentative smile teased the corner of my mouth, growing wider and wider with each passing second. "You know what, Mae?" I murmured slowly. "I think you're right."

"Damn straight."

"It's time to feed my soul."

"Yep." Her mouth made a loud popping sound, emphasizing the 'p'.

"I'm gonna do it, I'm gonna start up an online personal training business. It's going to target new mums and will help them both recover from birthing and encourage them to get back into exercise again."

"Girl, you might want to work on a catchier job description. Just sayin'."

But my mind was whirling too fast to be offended. I had so much to do, I needed to research what was already out there, create a business plan that capitalized on a gap in the market, organize an innovative marketing strategy, contact a website designer... An exhaustive list began to formulate in my head and I was beyond excited.

"I've gotta go."

"That's my girl. But before you do, don't forget—"

But I had already hung up, my smile now a mile wide. With this new business venture, forgetting Dominic was going to be a breeze. I wouldn't have a chance to stop and take a breath, let alone pine after him like some lovesick teenager. I was going to get over him in record time. For real.

Famous last words.

****

The remainder of Friday was spent nose deep in my iPad. I brought it with me thinking I would be passing the time watching Netflix, not researching the personal training industry. But I was. And I loved it. Just the thought of being able to combine my knowledge of midwifery with a passion for exercise gave a thrill almost comparable to finally seeing Dominic naked.

Almost.

Anyway, I didn't even notice how many hours

had passed until the sky outside darkened and it suddenly registered—somewhat belatedly—that I had not even showered or eaten yet. To be fair, I really did not want to wash the smell of Dominic off my body. Yes, I was well aware this made me sound slightly obsessive. I mean, I knew we were never going to have sex again, so my subconscious kindly decided to prolong the moment until I would have to wash his heady, masculine scent off my skin. Sue me, I was rolling with it.

After a lengthy shower, I was toweling myself dry when a sharp knock sounded.

"Shit."

My eyes frantically searched the bathroom for something to throw on. Nothing. All of my clothes were unhelpfully packed in my suitcase in the next room and by the sound of the repetitive barraging, this person was not in a patient mood, at all.

"Double shit."

The knock thundered once again, though this time even louder if it was at all possible. It was a miracle the thing was still on its hinges. I ran into the hallway and, hallelujah, threw on the first thing I found that covered up all the essentials. Wrenching the door open, I wiped bedraggled strands of hair out of my eyes before freezing stock-still.

"Dominic."

Okay, so my voice sounded way breathier than intended and there was very little to be done about my already hardening nipples—those girls had a mind of their own whenever he was in front of them. I figured crossing my arms over my chest would draw attention to them, so cleared my throat instead, hoping the distraction would suffice. It didn't. His eyes leisurely scaled my body from head to foot, lingering hungrily on my breasts.

"What are you doing here?"

But he ignored me so I took his silence as an invitation to openly ogle him too. Dominic's short hair was wild, as though he had been running his long fingers through it, and there was sand-colored stubble peppering his strong jawline which I suddenly needed to feel between my legs.

Bloody hell, Riley. Calm your farm already.

I swallowed.

Dominic's tight black t-shirt practically begged me to tear it off his chest with my teeth, and those dark, ripped jeans had no place looking that damn fine. None at all, it was cruel.

I gave a soft moan. God, help me.

On his feet were scuffed combat boots and when my gaze finally flittered back to his face, those blue eyes of his were so dark they had almost turned cobalt.

Yikes.

"Nice outfit."

"Oh, I ah—" I stopped and looked down, realizing that in my haste I had thrown on the hoodie he lent me at the airport yesterday … and nothing else. Granted, it was big enough to reach midway down my thighs, but it suddenly felt like I was standing before him naked.

Maybe he has x-ray vision? Jesus, what a terrifying thought.

"Do you, um, want it back?"

"Fuck no. Looks better on you."

It was official, my downstairs department was a panting, slobbering mess. What a disaster. I was supposed to be getting over this guy, not futilely wishing he would lick every square inch of me. I shook my head, outwardly trying to maintain some semblance of rationality and calm.

"Do you want to come in?"

He nodded, and I stepped back as he walked past

me, not for one second believing the casual brush of his arm against my breasts was an accident. Cocky bastard.

Dominic moved into the second room and began pacing in front of the couch. Curious, I sat and watched him stalk—cheetah style—before me.

And watched.

And watched.

After ten minutes of silence, in which time I steadily grew more and more dizzy, I had had enough. As sexy as the guy was, I could not keep gawking at him like he was a runway model. "Okay, what's going on? You're wearing a hole in the carpet."

Dominic took a deep breath, and I tried to ignore the way his pecs expanded with the movement. "Jimmy wants us to record a full-length album."

I jumped to my feet, equal parts shocked and excited. "Dominic, that's amazing news, congratulations." I paused, mid-squeal. "Who's Jimmy?"

"Adrift's band manager. Nice enough guy, great taste in music." He smirked. "The boys and I had a meeting with him this morning. He wants us to stay on in Melbourne, record our album and then tour with Adrift over the summer."

I tried so hard to keep my smile in place as realization slowly dawned on me. "Hang on a second, you're staying here?"

He nodded.

"In Melbourne?"

He nodded again.

"And then you're going on tour?"

"Yeah."

"Oh." My heart pounded and I was pretty sure my smile turned into an alarming grimace-like contortion. "But what about afterward? You'll be coming home then, right?"

Dominic was silent, his impenetrable gaze locked on me and I hated not being able to read his expression. The skin on the back of my neck prickled, never a good sign. Finally, he murmured, "Riley, we're not coming home. We're moving over here, permanently."

It was lucky the couch was right behind me because my knees gave way and I dropped like a dead weight onto the cushions. "Oh, okay." I nodded, I think. "That's great. That's really, really," I tried to clear my throat before whispering, "great."

Dominic began pacing in front of me again, only I could not look at him. I could not do anything except stare at the white knuckles of my clenched fists while desperately begging the rising panic to dissipate.

It was not working.

"I've gotta do this, you know?" His voice sounded muffled and far away, like he was talking under water. "I love working on cars but it's not gonna get me where I want to be. I'm not gonna stay in some dead end job out of fear, I'm not some dumb punk too stupid to take a chance."

My vision grew dark and there was no escaping the rasping breaths which burned the back of my throat.

"I mean, think about it, Riley. When else am I ever gonna get this opportunity? I've got balls, damn it, I'm gonna fuckin' use them."

Maybe it was the reference to his balls, maybe it was the fact we would never run together or hang out ever again that had me wrapping shaking arms around myself. I wasn't sure. Either way, it felt as though I was going to fall apart if I did not hold my agony-riddled insides together. I swear, they hurt that damn much. It wasn't until Dominic crouched in front of me, his strong hands gripping my shoulders, that my muddled brain registered I had been rocking myself back and forth like some crazy woman.

"You all right?"

I barely heard him. My body was in the process of shutting down, my skin burned hot and clammy while my breathing—or lack thereof—turned into outright hyperventilation.

"Angel?"

I swear, my heart was going to explode it beat that damn fast, and the short, gasping breaths I barely managed did sweet fuck all to calm me down.

There was nothing but black.

It surrounded me, suffocated me and I was slowly drowning in its endless murky well, completely terrified.

This is it, I'm actually gonna die. Oh, the shame, I'm gonna haunt people for the rest of my days dressed in nothing but Dominic's sweater.

Far off in the distance, I heard muttered oaths followed by the sound of running water. There was sudden movement and then the painful sensation of pinpricks stabbing my body, everywhere. They hurt like hell. A harsh scream sounded and limbs thrashed, only they were restrained by a vice-like grip.

A grunt, followed by, "For fuck's sake, Riley, hold still," hissed in my ear.

It finally registered. Dominic held me under a cold shower, my back plastered to his front as his arms pinned mine to my sides and a stream of frigid water saturated us both.

I blinked beaded droplets out of my eyes and slumped back into his strong frame, shivering and exhausted.

"If I let go are you gonna kick me in the junk again?"

I did not even have the energy to reply and Dominic—I assumed—took my silence as agreement before releasing one arm from around me to change the temperature of the water so it warmed our chilled skin.

He slid down onto the floor, taking me with him. With his back against the charcoal tiles, Dominic positioned me between his legs and maneuvered my body until I was resting against his chest, my head on his shoulder. We both sat in silence for a long while—me slowly trying to pull myself together while Dominic… Well. Who knew?

But his deep, calming breaths and rhythmic heartbeat relaxed me until I felt composed enough to speak. My voice was soft as I whispered, "I've ruined your boots, sorry about that."

Dominic lifted his left foot, inspecting his sodden combat boot. "Shit happens." He placed it back on the tiles again as the water continued to rain down on us.

"And your clothes, I've probably ruined them too."

"They're fine, they'll dry."

"Not to mention—"

"Riley, it's fine. Forget about it." He let out an exasperated breath that tickled the side of my neck, before falling quiet once more.

I shut my eyes and let the warm water wash over me. Doctor Powell was going to give me so much grief when I told her about this panic attack. In the heat of the moment, I completely forgot everything she taught me. I sighed.

"Does this shit happen often?"

My eyes popped open. As much as I really did not want to go into detail about my anxiety, it seemed only fair to answer Dominic's question after what I had put him through. Poor guy, I probably scared the bejesus out of him.

I nibbled my bottom lip. "Not as much anymore. I

get the occasional one here and there, mostly when I'm tired or overly emotional about something but they're not usually so … epic."

"Not like the one you just had?"

I shook my head. "No."

"What would you have done if I wasn't here?"

I wouldn't have had a panic attack in the first place. *Duh.*

Rather than voicing that unhelpful thought, I shrugged one shoulder instead. After all, it was pointless upsetting him when he had gone to such drastic lengths to calm me down and heaven only knew if his junk was ever going to be the same.

Focus, Riley.

With a low growl, I was suddenly whipped around until I straddled Dominic's lap. My hands grasped his shoulders until my head caught up with the rest of me. Blinking away the dizziness, I noticed two blazing eyes piercing me with their stare. Once again, I had to remind myself to breathe—though for a very different reason this time.

Don't even go there, Riley. Honestly, it's a waste of time, energy and endorphins. Move the hell on.

Apparently, my fingers suffered from selective hearing. They traced the scowl lines on his face until his features softened under my touch. "Dominic, it's fine." I gave a small smile. "I see a psychologist who's given me some coping strategies and on the whole they're really effective."

His gaze narrowed, calling bullshit.

I grinned wider, wondering how someone as gorgeous as Dominic could be so ridiculously cute at the same time. "I just forgot to use them, that's all. But if it makes you feel any better, I'm seeing her again on Monday and will tell her about it, okay?"

He grunted. It was adorable.

"How is it that I'm the one comforting you, anyway?"

"Because I'm the one with a bruised ball sack."

I blinked and shifted slightly, registering the fact I was conveniently sitting oh so close to said ball sack. With no underwear on. Trying not to groan out loud became a priority, a top priority.

After clearing my throat a few times, I somehow managed to mumble, "Oops."

His lips quirked up in the corners but then instantly sobered. "I'm really fuckin' sorry for upsetting you like that."

Dominic's gaze was so genuine I had to look down. Only, as soon as I did, I realized I was staring at his package which—because fate was an eternal prankster who loved messing with my head—was clearly outlined through the soaked material of his jeans. I looked away.

"I just didn't want you hearing about it from anyone else. It would've been a dick move and I couldn't do that to you. To some other chick? Sure." He tucked a bedraggled lock of hair behind my ear. "But not you."

I shut my eyes, wishing he had not used the word *dick*. It seriously wasn't helping matters. In fact, the only thing I could now think of was how phenomenal his dick would feel thrust inside me, over and over again.

Bloody hell,

"Angel?"

My eyes popped open and I swear he read every filthy thought running through my mind like they were projected onto a big screen.

Dominic's grip on my hips tightened in warning. "Don't look at me like that."

But for the life of me, I could not stop. So I

continued, mesmerized by the droplets of water trickling down his face until they gathered on his bottom lip. I wanted to lick them off with my tongue, one by one.

I wondered if they would taste salty, like his skin.

He shifted beneath me and I felt his hardening erection. If I leaned forward slightly it would, by pure accident, rub against my exposed clit. I bit back a moan.

"Dominic," I whispered. "I just—" I moved until my face was a hairsbreadth away from his, my eyes trained on his mouth. "I need to kiss you."

Dominic groaned and then swore. When he next spoke his voice sounded broken. "Angel, I can't. You know the rules, I can't fuck you again."

"Shhh," I crooned, before darting my tongue out and licking the water droplets off his full lips.

He hissed.

Dominic tasted like heaven, absolutely divine. "I didn't say anything about fucking. It's just a kiss, nothing more."

But I was lying.

Oh, boy, was I lying through my teeth. And as soon as our mouths touched, he knew it too. Only, by then it was too late. The spark ignited, the flame caught, and an inferno engulfed us both.

Chapter Sixteen

This emotion hurts deeper,
And when I hold on,
We feel here in this moment,
All we've wanted for so long.
—MONDEZ, "Moments"

Dominic was the first to pull away. He pressed his forehead against mine, breathing heavily. "What the fuck are you doing to me? You're breaking me, Riley. You're tearing me apart."

I shook my head, pushing my breasts against his chest, needing to get closer, inside him somehow. It seemed to be the only place I felt sane.

He reached out and skimmed calloused fingers down my face until they brushed over my swollen and bruised lips. After gathering the droplets of water that gathered there, he then placed his fingertips in his mouth and sucked.

Sweet Lord.

I couldn't look away if I tried. Instead, I found myself squirming on his lap until he let out a low growl. Was it a warning? A promise? I couldn't say, though God and sundry knew what I wanted to happen within the next five minutes. Rules, anxiety, and future complications be damned, I was all in.

"I want you," I murmured, for once not surprised by my brazenness. For some reason, Dominic brought out the truth in me, plain and simple. And in that moment there was nothing I craved more than the feel of him inside me once again.

"I think about you," I continued, watching his eyes grow darker with each word. "All the time. I think of us together, like this."

His pupils fully dilated. Not gonna lie, the effect I had on him felt pretty damn good.

"Angel, there's nothing I want more than to be balls deep inside you right now. I want to fuck your sweet pussy until it milks my cock, I want to hear you scream my name, but I can't, and you know it. I'm a fuckin' broken man."

I kissed him, long and deep. I kissed him until he buried his hands in my hair, pulled my head back by the roots and ground me against his straining cock.

"I know you can't," I whispered. "I just… It's killing me, you're killing me."

Dominic groaned as one of his hands trailed down my neck and came to rest on my breast. It felt full, swollen, practically begging for his mouth—the hussy.

"I remember what it felt like," he growled, his thumb flicking my nipple as I gasped in surprise. "I remember how tight and wet you were, how your greedy pussy took all of my cock and still begged for more."

He shook his head before turning his attention to my other breast, kneading and molding it with his large hand. Those hands were going to be the death of me, no question. I might as well have typed up my eulogy then and there—gotten it over with.

"I remember the noises you made and the look on your face when you came."

I moaned. Loudly. Honestly, I couldn't help it. Between those magical hands and that dirty mouth of his, I was officially a pile of orgasmic goo.

"It's burned into my fucking brain." Dominic's hand then deliberately skimmed down my stomach and pushed its way under the sodden hoodie. His fingers caressed the lips of my exposed pussy, essentially short-circuiting every nerve ending in my body and rational thought in my head. I threw it back, desperate for more.

After a pleasure-filled minute, my gaze returned to his. "I remember the way your cock filled me, stretched me, owned me." I whispered against his lips, "You owned me, Dominic."

With an anguished groan his fingers slipped inside.

I cried out before sighing, "Just like you're owning me now."

Dominic's fingers pumped me while I slowly rotated my hips and murmured in his ear, "I need you, just for tonight. Please, can we … can we pretend it's our first time?" I pulled back to stare at him.

Silence.

Heat.

Crash.

Our lips collided. I swear, he stole my breath, my sanity, my very existence. When his lips claimed mine, the world receded, when his tongue possessed my own, there was nothing but stars. Nothing but heaven, hell and purgatory in between. Oh, and Dominic.

Contradictory, unpredictable, all-consuming Dominic.

He was everywhere, everything. Strangely, this awareness was both life-affirming and soul-destroying in the same breath.

Lord help me, I'm lost.

I peeled his t-shirt up and over his head, not allowing any time for second thoughts. Not that he seemed to be having any; his deep groans and ruthless tongue left little room for hesitation. Not to mention his fingers massaging my clit and then systematically filling my pussy until I thought I was going to explode. Yeah, we weren't stopping anytime soon.

I marveled as my hands stroked his pecs and

worshiped those chiseled abs. "I love your body," I murmured. "I love how it feels under my fingers."

Dominic yanked my own sodden sweater off. He leaned back against the tiles and stared at me revering him. His gaze traversed my face, breasts, hips, with every passing second, his breathing accelerated and the pulse in his neck throbbed. It was lucky I was already naked because there would have been no way in hell my clothes could have survived the fire in his stare for a second longer. They would have incinerated, for sure.

Reaching around behind me, he grasped my ass, squeezing it, drawing me closer still. "I love the way you fit perfectly in my hands." He squeezed again and I moaned. "You were fucking made for me, Riley."

Hot, wet kisses trailed down my neck and across my collarbone. "I love how you taste," he muttered, continuing his sweet torture. "Like motherfucking strawberries."

It was official, I had to have him. Enough with the polite shit, that ship had sailed the minute his fingers dipped inside me. Reaching down, I gripped his cock through his jeans. "I love the feel of you. You're so hard, thick, perfect."

Dominic groaned and nipped my neck, I would have a mark in the morning. The thought gave me a dark thrill I had no intention of psychoanalyzing.

"I love how you're always so wet for me."

I gasped and gripped him tighter as he pinched my clit. The man was going to have me screaming his name in next to no time if he was not careful. I only hoped the acoustics in the bathroom did not cause the mirror to shatter.

"The feel of your juices dripping down my fingers? That's fucking perfect, angel."

With my free hand, I cupped the side of his face

and took a deep, steadying breath, trying desperately to hold off for a bit longer. There was something important I had to say. Once I felt like I had my impending orgasm under control, I whispered, "I love your eyes. The way they see me, the real me."

It was true. Despite all the crap we had been through, Dominic was the only man who truly knew me. He saw the flawed, awkward woman I was and encouraged the courageous, determined woman I wanted to be. And for once, I was okay with it, I was okay with another person knowing the truth. After all, this man did not expect me to be perfect, he expected me to be authentic and that made all the difference.

Sadly.

To say my heart was screwed was the most obvious statement in the history of the universe. Not that this realization made any difference to what we were about to do—hell no—I was in way too deep to stop.

Dominic looked like he wanted to say something too, his mouth opened but then quickly closed again before formulating any words. Instead, he grasped me tighter and growled, "I love being inside you."

I shook off the fact he had probably said the second thought that came to mind rather than the first and instead replied with, "I love you being inside me too." After all, it was true. There was nowhere else I wanted him to be.

My fingers unzipped his fly and freed him from his boxers in a dexterous move which would have shocked my sensibilities if they were not already clouded in a sex-starved haze. When I gripped the base of his hard cock, Dominic's eyes rolled back in his head and he hissed, "Jesus, woman."

I worked the shaft, relishing the feel of his silken skin as it moved under my fingers. When he groaned I took note of what I was doing so I could do it again—and again and again. I could not get enough, pleasing him turned into the strongest aphrodisiac I ever encountered. Fuck oysters, they did not stand a chance.

When I teased the head, Dominic swore before gripping the back of my neck with one hand—thankfully not the one pleasuring my pussy—and crushed his lips to mine. We kissed for what felt like an eternity and I marveled over the fact that if it were not for our hands on each other, he would no doubt be impaling me with his cock.

I really wanted his cock.

There was a distinct possibility the man in question read my mind because he broke away from the kiss, removed his fingers from inside me and slipped them into my mouth. With a moan, I sucked them dry—not at all minding the tangy taste of myself on his skin—and pretended they were him. He cursed again.

With the taste of myself on my tongue, I cupped his face with both hands, leaned forward and kissed him. Ruthlessly. The poor guy did not stand a chance. I licked his lips, massaged his tongue, and explored his mouth. Hell, I staked territory.

Mine.

That's what each deliberate swipe of my tongue declared.

You. Are. All. Mine.

A low growl emanated from deep inside Dominic's chest and with one fluid upward thrust of his hips, he entered me. Guess I was not the only one who needed to stake a claim.

"*Fuck.*"

"Fuck," I groaned back, completely overwhelmed by how phenomenal he felt, how full, how right.

We both stared at each other until I slowly began

to rotate my hips, craving the friction of his cock against my sweet spot more than my next breath, or five.

"Damn, angel. Fuckin' love the feel of you."

Spurred on by his admission, I increased the pace, brokenly murmuring, "Me too. God, I love the feel of you too."

Dominic clasped his hands over my hips, controlling the pace, the depth, the extent of this pleasure-fueled torture. And the sensation built. Oh, fuck, did it build. We fed off each other's gasps, cries, and pleasure under the cascading water of the shower.

Steam.

Heat.

Desire.

Need.

Our bodies moved seamlessly together, perfectly synchronized. Honestly, it was like we had done this a million times before. Finally, when I could not take it any longer, I whimpered, "Dominic," but could not continue because my orgasm was about to erupt and it became impossible to formulate any words.

He thrust deeper inside me, his voice harsh, "Christ, angel."

Our eyes locked.

"Dominic—"

He gripped my ass. "Riley—"

Holy. Shit.

After registering the look in his eyes, the mother of all orgasms tore through me and I let go. My body was torn, wrecked and annihilated with a pleasure so acute, so concentrated, I truly was not sure I would survive it.

From somewhere far away I heard Dominic bellow my name and seconds later felt his cock twitch before a burst of hot cum released inside me.

In the aftermath, with my head buried in his neck

and his heart thundering against my chest, a series of truths suddenly hit me like a wrecking ball to the face.

Boom.

We had unprotected sex in the shower.

Boom.

We were never going to see each other again.

Boom.

I was in love with Dominic Mondez.

Boom. Boom. Boom.

****

After carefully placing our saturated clothes on the heated towel bar in the hopes they would dry, Dominic toweled me off and wrapped my sated body in one of the hotel robes. Sadly, he then proceeded to cover up his own male perfection in the other one and it was only when he noticed the scowl on my face that he winked before kissing the tip of my nose. I had no idea how he did it, but that man could rock a white robe like nobody's business.

We did not talk much after that, just ordered some room service before eating it in amicable silence in bed. It was nice, a much-needed change of pace.

Once finished, Dominic cleared away the dishes before turning off the lights and coming back to where I sat cross-legged in the middle of the bed. He lay down, pulling me in close until we were spooning. Never thought I would see the day, the man actually liked to spoon. Not that I was complaining—heck no—the intimate gesture was the icing on the subliminal cake that was the past two hours. And of course, our bodies aligned perfectly. I sighed.

Fate was officially on my shit list.

That bitch was going down.

I tried not to think about the irony behind finally experiencing intimacy with Dominic on the same night he told me he was moving across the country. I tried not to decipher the raw emotion on his face when we both came. I tried not to think, period. I was over it, it hurt too much.

So instead, I snuggled in closer to the warm wall of towel-wrapped muscle behind me and smiled when Dominic's cock hardened against my ass.

"Bloody hell, woman," he growled low in my ear. "Can't get enough of you."

"Maybe I can't get enough of your cock. You ever thought of that?"

He bit down on my earlobe and I moaned softly. "Be careful what you wish for, angel."

I rolled over until we were so close I could see the lights from the buildings outside reflected in his gaze. "I wish you'd fuck me again," I whispered. His muttered curse spurred me on. "I want to wake up tomorrow aching in the best way possible, I want it to be a reminder of you long after you're gone."

Dominic's eyes dropped to my mouth when my tongue moistened suddenly dry lips. What the hell kind of woman had I turned into? Since when did polite, well-mannered Riley Sears talk dirty? Had we suddenly entered an alternate universe or something? Apparently so.

"You're really moving over here, aren't you?"

"Yeah."

"Then take me again."

His hips rocked against me and I gasped, the friction felt sensational. "As much as I want to, I've got no business being inside you without a condom."

"Bit late for that, isn't it?" Chastened, Dominic looked away, but I drew his face back to mine with a smile. "It's okay, I'm on the pill and since I've never had unprotected sex before, I know I'm clean."

But his haunted look remained. "I haven't gone bareback in almost four years. Not since Allie."

"Who's Allie?"

Seriously, Riley? You actually want to go there?

Luckily, Dominic ignored my ill-timed interruption and did not seem to notice my internal chastisement. "Even then it was only once and I sure as fuck got tested afterward. Had to, to find out—" He let out a long breath.

"To find out what?"

But he shook his head. "Doesn't matter, that shit's in the past."

"You sure about that? Because I swear I can feel the weight of it, like another person in this bed."

He squeezed my hips, drawing me closer. "Ain't no one else here except you and me, angel. That's a promise." His hand slipped around to my ass, cupping it. "Don't know what it is but you always make me forget the fucked-up shit life has thrown at me."

"You make me forget too."

His lips were gentle as they teasingly caressed mine. "One day you're gonna tell me all about it."

"Only if you do the same."

He stared at me for a long moment, his eyes searching. Finally, he murmured, "Deal."

"Toby?" I screamed, before taking another deep breath. "Toby?" I spun in frantic circles searching for my brother, only the deafening sounds of the carnival swallowed my voice until it sounded like nothing more than a mere whimper.

Everywhere I turned there were people, so many people. They were smiling, laughing, hugging, running— it was like a macabre freak show sent to torture me—and I could not see him anywhere. I desperately searched the throng of revelers but there was no sign of his Batman t-

*shirt or navy blue shorts. There was nothing but
confusion, chaos and the tinny sounds of carnival music
crackling over a loudspeaker.*

*I only turned my back for a minute. Honestly. The
sideshow we stopped at was offering a superhero
costume as the main prize and I knew Toby would love it.
So, I had been asking the bored teenager running the
stall what the rules of the game were. Only, when I
turned back to ask if Toby wanted to play, he was gone.*

Gone.

*My stomach plummeted to the soles of my feet and
tears began to stream unchecked down my face as I
haphazardly pushed my way through the crowds of
people. And with every step, I felt it—a slow, ominous
dread creeping up my spine, slinking around to my chest
and squeezing my thumping heart. Tightly.*

I had lost my brother.

He was really, truly gone.

Mum and Dad were never going to forgive me.

****

I must have fallen asleep. As much as I wanted to
stay awake and continuously gorge myself on Dominic,
my body could not keep going. It must have been the
orgasms, and boy there had been many, so many in fact, I
lost count after the fifth time Dominic entered me. Since
we were not going to see each other again—God, I could
not even think about it without my stomach knotting—
Dominic wholeheartedly threw his *I never sleep with the
same woman twice* mantra out the window.

Best. Night. Of. My. Life.

Sadly, like all good things, it ended.

When the sunlight streaming through the open
curtains woke me the next day, there was no warm,
muscled body wrapped around me, no deep voice talking
dirty in my ear, no … anything. Instead, there was an

indent where his head had rested on the pillow next to mine and the scent of his skin on the sheets. I may or may not have burrowed my head into them before inhaling like a drowning lunatic.

Pathetic.

After scolding myself for a solid ten minutes about the stupidity of my actions, followed by another five on the ridiculousness of harboring strong feelings for someone who refused to admit his own, I dragged myself out of bed and gave Grace a call. After all, with everything that had gone down, she was probably in worse shape than I was.

"Yeah?" she croaked, after picking up the phone.

Yep, the girl sounded like shit. "G, you okay?"

"No. Levi's staying, Riley. In Melbourne. They're all staying and I can't... I just—" She sobbed and my heart broke for her. This was the first time Grace allowed a man into her life after Dylan royally fucked her over twelve months ago and the thought of her dealing with this situation on her own brought out my protective side, big time.

"You're going to be okay, G. You and Levi are in love, anyone who has seen the two of you together can tell it's meant to be. You'll make it work somehow, I know it."

There was a loud sniff on her end of the line.

This was exactly what I needed. Distraction 101. "Right, you're heading home today, aren't you?"

She mumbled something comparable to a yes.

"What are your flight details? I'm going to swap mine so we can fly home together."

Once I promised to meet her down in the lobby in just over an hour, I went about reorganizing my life. My flight was changed, my belongings were packed and finally, after not being able to put it off any longer, I washed the lingering remains of Dominic off my skin in another hot shower.

Don't overthink it, just move on. It was time.

And it was. As much as I wanted to wallow in self-pity, I could not afford to do so just then. I had a broken-hearted best friend to care for, a business to set up, a job to return to and a date to go on. Jesus, with all the drama I completely forgot about Robin. I shook my head.

Note to self—schedule a mental breakdown for later.

Chapter Seventeen

The choice here is mine,
Your problem, not mine,
This emotion, it's mine,
What I do here—mine,
Call it initiative—fine.
—MONDEZ, "Together Apart"

Poor Grace, she was an absolute mess. As soon as she stepped out of the elevator and shuffled toward me, with dark circles under her eyes and the most defeated expression I had ever seen plastered across her face, I dropped my bags and ran toward her. Throwing my arms around her stooped frame, I hugged her as hard as I could. "I'm so glad I changed my flight."

And I was. By the looks of it, apocalyptic zombies slowly being eaten alive by a flesh-eating virus had more life left in them than her. So I let go, grabbed our stuff and whisked her outside into a waiting taxi.

Apart from the intermittent sobbing coming from G's direction, the flight and drive back home was fairly uneventful. Dominic must have infiltrated my phone at some point last night because as I scrolled through my playlist for something to listen to, I noticed Mondez's EP was front and center. I shook my head, trying to fight the smile that threatened to overtake my face before realization hit—we were never going to see each other again—and I suddenly lost all reason for happiness after that. As though sensing my somber turn of thoughts, Grace sniffed loudly beside me.

I know exactly how you feel, G.

But I straightened my shoulders and put on a brave face for both our sakes because blubbering about something I had no control over was not going to help me one iota. Doctor Powell was going to be thrilled at this new and improved mindset when I told her about it on Monday. Not that the temptation to channel my inner drama queen was not strong. Oh, boy, all I felt like doing was crawling into bed and refusing to leave it until the knot in my stomach eased up enough to let me breathe again.

Fucking Dominic.

Once we arrived back at our apartment, it was late afternoon. I ordered Grace into the shower. While she was bawling her eyes out under the spray, I quickly unpacked both our belongings. I even managed to scrape together a remotely healthy meal from the leftovers in the fridge, which was a definite win.

Thankfully, I had gotten rid of Robin's roses before leaving for the airport. So being able to navigate the kitchen without the cruel reminder of how Dominic and I christened the countertop was not the agonizing experience it might otherwise have been. Not to say I didn't stare at the laminated surface for a solid six minutes before catching myself and internally slapping my own face, there was definitely that. Well, before I sanitized the heck out of it, twice.

After feeding Grace, confiscating any and all whiskey bottles, and sending her off early to bed, I at last allowed myself to get ready for the date with Robin. To say I was hesitant would not be an exaggeration, and it was strange because logically I knew he was an awesome guy. He was intelligent, kind, attractive—heck, he built a business around women wanting to have children for Christ's sake, what could be more perfect than that? But despite it all, I just wasn't feeling it, something still held me back. I sighed.

Who was I kidding? It wasn't something, it was

someone.

Dominic.

Bloody hell.

I knew I was being ridiculous—believe me, I was well aware of the new heights my deluded fantasies had reached—but a small part of my brain still held out hope he would jump on the next plane home. My overactive imagination pictured him storming through the front door, sweeping me off my feet before declaring his undying love and lifelong commitment.

I know, I know.

I shook my head, slipping on a red summer dress. "Never gonna happen, Riley." After tidying my hair and dabbing my lips with some gloss, I muttered, "It's time to focus on yourself, for real this time."

So that's what I did.

Well, until I received a text message a minute later.

Bootycall: **Miss me yet?**

Me: **No.**

Lie.

Bootycall: **Bet ur pussy does.**

I groaned and flopped back onto my bed. Great, now I was flushed and throbbing before a date with someone who did not go by the name of Dominic. Damn that man and his sweet, filthy mind.

Bootycall: **My cock misses you … so does my tongue & hands.**

Me: **Dominic…**

Bootycall: **Angel…**

Me: **I've gotta go.**

Bootycall: **Why? Got a hot date or something?**

I did not reply.

Bootycall: **Are you fuckin' shitting me, right now?**

Me: **I'll call you later.**

I turned my phone off after that, refusing to feel bad about my date. After all, it was Dominic's decision to leave, not mine. I would not punish myself any longer. Truly. See? This was me completely nailing the whole strong, independent woman thing.

Maybe I needed some more practice.

****

"You're quiet tonight, everything okay?"

I glanced up from the half-empty wine glass in my hand to Robin's concerned gaze. His eyes were so beautiful, so expressive.

"Of course," I fibbed. "Just tired, I guess. It's been a crazy few days."

He nodded as though in understanding. "I get it."

You really don't.

Then, gently bumping my shoulder, Robin asked, "How was the band?"

"Amazing," I breathed, before catching myself and blushing. Luckily, the sun had already set over the horizon and where we sat on the sandy shoreline, eating antipasto and drinking wine, was becoming darker by the minute. So with any luck, he did not notice my flushed cheeks or obvious embarrassment.

Robin laughed, proving me wrong. "Sounds like you're a huge fan of theirs."

I took a healthy swallow of the white wine before answering. "You could say that." Clearing my throat, I continued. "I mean, they're insanely talented and when they play it's like…" I shrugged, shifting my eyes to the flickering light of a small fishing boat as it bobbed up and down to the rhythm of the ocean's current. "It's like the whole world disappears and it's just him, I mean *them*, and me, you know?"

Robin chuckled again. "Not really." I caught his

gaze, and he gave an apologetic grin. "I'm not really into music, I just listen to whatever's playing. It all becomes white noise after a while."

I tried to look away before my disappointment showed too strongly but the breeze chose that moment to pick up and Robin tucked a stray strand of hair behind my ear. "I'm glad you enjoy it though."

Not gonna lie, the heat in his stare and the contact of his fingers felt nice, really nice, so I leaned into his hand for a moment. Robin moved forward, his eyes on my lips, and a second later his mouth brushed against mine. Before long, the contact grew firmer, more insistent, and I opened my mouth to admit his seeking tongue. He tasted of crisp white wine and I surrendered to his sensual exploration, willing myself to empty my mind and stay in the moment. Robin's hand slipped into my hair. The gesture immediately transported me back to last night when Dominic tugged my head back in an abandoned passion just before thrusting inside me.

I pulled away, shocked at the direction my thoughts had turned.

What. The. Actual. Fuck?

Robin blinked a few times as though trying to regain focus, his confusion and concern obvious. "Riley?"

"Sorry, I—" I shook my head, trying desperately to clear the mental images that bombarded me the minute I let my guard down. "I just think it's best if we take it slow, that's all." My weak smile was pathetic by any standards.

"Oh, sure thing. Sorry, I didn't mean to push." He cupped the side of my face again, his thumb skimming over my cheek. "I'm not going anywhere."

Inwardly, I half-swooned, half-groaned.

Of course you're not.

Robin dropped his hand and refilled my wine glass. "Here." He raised his eyebrows in surprise as I took a huge mouthful, choked, and then spent the next few minutes trying to clear my blocked airways.

"You okay?"

I nodded.

Smooth, Riley. Real smooth.

After a lengthy pause during which time I managed to take markedly smaller sips without asphyxiating myself, I made a decision. It was time. I needed to let go of the fantasy that was Dominic Mondez. I mean, Robin was here and Dominic, clearly, was not. Surely, a man who resided in the same state was the better choice in a potential long-term relationship than a man who had moved across the country? And I wanted a relationship, one that was based on trust, honesty and mutual respect. I craved a connection which did not solely exist on the heady fumes of sexual attraction—no matter how potent.

So, if I was really going to make it work between Robin and me, I had to open up and tell him things, important things, like my new career pathway. I cleared my throat. "I've, ah, I've got something to tell you."

"Yeah?"

"It's a big deal, well, to me anyway." Those gorgeous hazel eyes begged me to confide in him so I took a deep breath and blurted, "I'm going to start my own business."

Robin's face lit up like I just offered him an evening filled with endless blowjobs. "Seriously? That's fantastic."

I nodded, grinning, thrilled at his reaction.

"Good on you, Riley. You'll make a fantastic obstetrician."

"Oh, um, I actually meant—"

"Don't get me wrong, the study is going to be brutal, especially with work. But I'm sure your parents can help you out financially so you can cut back on your shifts at the hospital."

"Whoa." I held up my hand, essentially halting that train wreck of an idea before it could build up any steam. I mean, rely on my parents when all I craved was to escape them? Hell to the no. Was he out of his mind?

"Robin, I'm not going to set up my own obstetrics practice."

He looked so confused it was sweet. "You aren't?"

"No. I'm going to start my own personal training business."

"Oh." His face fell and so did something in the pit of my stomach. "Really? But why? There's plenty of personal trainers out there and I know for a fact it's almost impossible to make a career out of it." I'm sure his smile was an attempt at softening the blow. "My cousin tried it once."

"Hang on, so if one person couldn't make a go of it then I can't either? Is that what you're saying?" I put down my wine glass, wiped residual sand off my fingers and stood. Glaring at him I continued, "You know what, Robin? I'd really appreciate some support here. This is a huge step for me and the fact you just discounted it as hopeless from the very beginning is—" I turned away, blinking back tears of frustration.

Robin quickly stood and took hold of one of my hands, turning me back to face him. It was a good thing too because then it meant I could not do something stupid with it, like punch him. For the record, I was not a violent person by nature but the way he immediately dismissed my idea hurt, a lot.

"Riley, wait." Robin took a deep breath and

slowly exhaled, his face contrite. "Look, I'm really sorry, okay? I didn't mean to be a jerk about your idea, it's just that—" He looked toward the black water, appearing to gather his thoughts before gazing at me again. His eyes were so sincere I decided to shelve all unhelpful thoughts that consisted of my fist connecting with his face. Big of me, I know.

"I don't want to freak you out by saying this but you've kinda forced my hand here." Robin grimaced at my glare. "Okay, so my dick-like behavior forced my hand." His grip on my fingers tightened, and he took another deep breath before continuing. "I think I'm falling for you, Riley." My face must have revealed my obvious shock because he started talking faster. "I know it's early and we've only just started seeing each other, but there's something about you..." He gave a sheepish smile and half-shrug that had my anger dissipating at a ridiculous rate.

"You're the kind of woman who doesn't come along very often. You're smart, beautiful, empathetic—I could go on, but you might panic even more and I really don't want you running away from me right now." Robin stepped in close until I could smell the citrus undertones of his aftershave. "Which is why I acted like an ass before. I care about you, I don't want to see you hurt or disappointed. I want to see you ... flourish."

"Flourish?"

"I know, total douche thing to say. I swear, I'm one hundred percent male and not secretly an eighty-five-year-old woman in disguise."

Moving forward until my breasts brushed his hard chest, I murmured, "I believe you."

Robin's pupils dilated at the contact.

"Thank you for apologizing, it means a lot."

Letting go of his hands, I trailed my fingers up the corded

muscles of his arms. They were not as ridiculously strong as the others I felt recently but they were still nice, solid, dependable. He wrapped them around my waist.

"And I've found a gap in the market I'm pretty sure I can capitalize on." My hands wound their way around the back of his neck and I felt him harden against me. "But you interrupted before I could tell you."

Robin rested his forehead against mine. "I'm sorry." His face grew concerned as he asked, "You sure this enterprise is what you want to do?"

"Yes. It'll work, it has to."

He nodded once, murmuring, "If you say so," before kissing me.

****

"What?"

"And hello to you too," I teased.

"Not in the mood, Riley." The sound of footsteps thudding on what I assumed were the wooden floorboards of Sunset Recording Studios, echoed down the phone line. I could picture Dominic pacing back and forth in my mind and for some strange reason the image made me smile.

"I miss you." The words left my mouth before I could gaffer-tape my lips shut.

He snorted. "You've got a fucked up way of showing it."

Okay, then.

"What's that supposed to mean?"

"My cock was inside you last night and you've already gone on a motherfucking date with someone else," he growled. "That shit's just low, and the fact the guy's a chino-wearing pussy makes it goddamn worse."

"Hey, Robin's a nice guy."

"So you're defending him now?"

I took three calming breaths. "This was your

decision, remember? You're the one who decided to stay in Melbourne, not me."

"To play in a kickass band has been my dream ever since I was a kid, Riley, I did what I had to do. Besides, I've got three other guys to consider, I couldn't back out of the contract even if I wanted to." He paused. "Anyway, you left too."

That got my attention. "Huh?"

"You left me too. Only, you don't see me shacking up with some bitch on the same day we fucked." He continued, muttering, "Though blowing my load in some easy pussy would be a fuckin' relief after the day I've had."

Now it was my turn to grow annoyed, really annoyed. "Firstly, you've never offered anything more than a one-night stand, so why on earth would I stay? Secondly, we didn't *fuck* in the shower, Dominic, and you know it."

"We fucked."

"Whatever. And thirdly, I'm not shacking up with anyone. Robin and I are dating. In fact, he's pretty serious about me."

"If I hear that fucktard's name coming out of your mouth one more time, swear to God, Riley, I'm really gonna lose my shit."

I threw up my free hand in the air, beyond frustrated. "Why are you so upset about him? Huh?"

Silence.

"This is ridiculous and you know it. You wouldn't be acting like this if you weren't jealous, so for God's sake, admit it already. Admit you have feelings for me."

Silence.

I gave the deep breathing thing another go, though this time in an attempt to stay the moisture suddenly blurring my vision. It did not work, tears trickled down my cheeks until I swiped them away. In all honesty, I wasn't sure why I wanted Dominic to admit he cared about me now. Maybe it was the fact we weren't face to face, so I was no longer distracted by his hypnotic eyes and absurdly muscular pecs. Maybe he honestly did not care about me as much as I was trying so damn hard not to care about him. Or maybe, I had no idea what the heck I was thinking—a straightjacket was looking more and more welcome by the minute.

Sigh.

When Dominic next spoke, his voice rough. "What's the point? It's not gonna change anything, is it? We're two different people living on opposite sides of the country, we were fucked before we even started."

So on that note, I hung up the phone.

****

"So Riley, how have you been?"

I glanced up from the tissue I had been systematically folding and refolding into neat little squares to look across at Doctor Powell. She waited patiently for an answer, her horn-rimmed glasses edging their way down her nose. Both myself and those glasses had been doing exactly the same thing during each session for the past year. Old habits died hard.

"Good, great. I've been—" Doctor Powell raised her eyebrows, not for one second buying my preppy facade. "Great," I finished lamely.

"Shall we try that again?"

I nod, silent.

"So Riley, how have you been?"

"Not good."

Doctor Powell offered a warm smile. "That's better. Now, talk to me, what's been going on?"

After taking a deep breath, I blurted, "Well, I had the mother of all panic attacks on Friday night, I'm trying to stop Grace from drinking herself into an early grave, I want to start a new business but am terrified, my parents still hate me and, I ah, I met someone. A guy. I met a guy."

She opened her brown leather notebook and frantically started writing. I have no idea what. I've learned it's best to ignore the scratching sound of her pen scrawling across the lined paper, it gives me a headache otherwise. "Okay."

"Actually, if I'm being honest, I met two guys."

"Two?"

"Yeah, two."

More writing. "Well, let's start with these men, shall we? Tell me about them."

I exhale. "The first guy is called Dominic." My heart started to pound at the mere thought of him, stupid heart. "He's…" I stared at the ceiling. "The most amazing man I've ever met." My gaze met hers. "But complex, so unbelievably complex."

Doctor Powell nodded her head, her pen poised in mid-air as she gazed at me. After a brief pause, she asked, "When you're with him, what does he make you feel?"

"Everything. He makes me feel absolutely everything, even stuff I don't want to feel."

"Such as?"

"Anger, fear, confusion, excitement, desire." I swallow before whispering, "Love."

"Interesting."

"What is?"

But she ignored my question, posing another instead. "And the other man?"

"Robin?"

"Yes, Robin. How does he make you feel?"

I paused for a moment. "Safe, like I'm a priority and not an afterthought."

"I see." Closing her notebook, Doctor Powell leaned forward, her arms resting on the worn leather. "Are you seeing both of these men at the same time, Riley?"

I shook my head vehemently. "No. God, no." But then I stopped. "I mean, Robin and I weren't serious when I was … connecting with Dominic."

"An interesting word choice."

"What is?"

"Connecting."

"Is it?" Shrugging one shoulder, I continued. "Anyway, Dominic has moved to Melbourne so whatever we had is now over." I bent my head and resumed folding the tissue, refusing to look Doctor Powell in the eyes.

"Why can't you continue connecting with Dominic in other ways?"

My gaze darted back to her. "How do you mean?"

"Like on the phone, for instance?"

"Why would I? The man's toxic. Besides, I called him on Saturday night and it didn't end well."

"How so?"

"We got into an argument after he found out I was dating Robin. It was horrible. I ended up hanging up on him and haven't contacted him since." Lowering my voice, I then mumbled, "No matter how much I want to."

"Well, you certainly hate confrontational situations, don't you?" Doctor Powell smiled, and I grimaced because like always, she was right.

"From what I understand," she continued, "you're avoiding Dominic because he makes you *feel*. He forces you to experience emotions—both the pleasurable and the uncomfortable—which you often shy away from. I can't stress enough how important accepting emotions is in creating resilience." She sat up straight, tapping her pen against the notebook in her lap. "I'm going to set you some homework. Before our next session, you need to phone Dominic and have another conversation with him. I don't want you to run from this experience even though fear is telling you to. You need to embrace this, you need to lean in and feel it all."

We sat in silence for a long time while I processed all she had said. I really did not want to call Dominic again. The thought of apologizing to him and then hearing about his day-to-day life—the life I was no longer a part of—hurt, a lot. What if he was happier without me? What if Mondez became a rock sensation and everything we shared was forgotten? What if he answered the phone while in bed with yet another random blonde?

Mental note—no FaceTime.

Sure, resilience was important and all, but at this point it seemed completely overrated.

"I don't think I'm strong enough."

Doctor Powell took her time before speaking— she was making me sit with my insecurity and I kinda hated her for it. "You mentioned you and Robin weren't serious while you were connecting with Dominic." I nodded in agreement. "Are you serious about him now?"

"I guess."

"You guess?"

The tissue finally disintegrated between my fingers. "Yeah, I guess."

She reopened her notebook, scribbling frantically. "Interesting."

Chapter Eighteen

I'm done waiting,
For your say,
It's time to decide,
It's my life my time.
—MONDEZ, "My Time"

It took me almost a week to pull up my big girl panties and phone Dominic. Not surprisingly, there was always something more pressing to do, but when I found myself seriously contemplating cleaning the air vents in the bathroom rather than dialing his number, I decided enough was enough.

Doctor Powell was spot on about my avoidance issues, but in my defense, I blamed my parents. Since Toby's disappearance, my family and I never spoke about important issues. Mum had the emotional capacity of a Madame Tussaud's exhibit, while I swear my father thought I had leprosy. Whenever I visited, it was like a titanium wall with a state of the art security system had been built between us and I was the only one who hadn't been briefed on the new password. Needless to say, instead of open dialogue between the three of us, there festered a simmering undertone of blame, disappointment, and dare I say it, hatred. Sometimes I wished Mum would lose her ice-maiden tendencies and scream at me, cry with me, hell do anything provided her poisonous emotions surfaced and could finally be processed. But she never did.

Thus, my preference for avoidance.

Anyway, I refused to turn into my mother. So, after packing away the unused duster, I made myself comfortable on the floor at the foot of my bed, took out my phone and dialed Dominic's number.

Waiting for him to pick up was like waiting for a biopsy result. My stomach tied itself in no less than three sailor's knots, my mouth decided to reenact the Outback during a sandstorm, and I swear my heart had taken up salsa classes.

Eventually, he answered. "Riley?"

There was a cacophony of noise in the background, people laughed, electric guitars strummed and I distinctly heard the metallic crash of Finn's high hats.

"Dominic, hey. How are you?" I was so nervous I didn't even wait for an answer before continuing. "Look, I wanted to call you because—"

"Hang on a sec, I can't hear a word you're saying." As the sound of his heavy footsteps strode through what I assumed was a hallway, the racket gradually faded. Eventually, a heavy door slammed and the noise stopped altogether. "That's better. What's up?"

"You seem pretty busy, do you want me to call back later? Or, you know, not at all?"

"Why would you say that?"

My voice was soft. "Because it might be true."

"Angel." Dominic exhaled, and rather than be grossed out, the sound of his breath in my ear sent a shiver down my spine. "I was a jackass the other night, so if anyone's got a right to be pissed, it's you."

My head flopped back onto the mattress as relief flooded me. God, I missed the sound of his voice, I didn't realize how much until that moment.

"Look," he paused, "if Robin is giving you what you need then that's … good. I'm happy for you." Ironically, he sounded anything but happy. "But for the record, his taste in clothes sucks balls."

I laughed. "You've really got an issue with him

wearing chinos, don't you?"

"Fuckin' yeah, I do."

I chuckled again and so did Dominic, it felt amazing. It was like we were finally back to where we started, sharing an easy friendship with only the sprinkling of sexual tension to keep life interesting.

"I'm sorry for being a dick."

"I'm sorry I wanted you to admit something you didn't feel."

"It's not…" Dominic sighed. "I'm so fuckin' sorry I can't give you what you deserve. I wish I could, you've no idea."

Squeezing my eyes shut, I whispered, "I wish you could too."

Neither of us spoke for a moment, each of us lost in thought. I don't know how we did it but our conversation had transformed from rainbows and butterflies to flash flooding and newts quicker than a prostitute changed her bed sheets. It was weird. Eventually, Dominic broke the silence by declaring, "Right, enough of this emotional shit, I get enough of it from Levi. Tell me about your day."

So I did, and suddenly my day wasn't nearly as horrible as I first thought.

****

I'd like to say the next five weeks flew past as though I were starring in a film montage. You know, with shots of me running along the beach, assisting in a natural birth, yelling at Mae for more squats, typing rapidly on my laptop, walking hand-in-hand with Robin and hiding yet another whiskey bottle from Grace. But I'd be lying. Each day consisted of the full twenty-four hours and each hour contained the appropriately appointed minutes and seconds. Yeah, trying to get my life back together was a long and exhausting process.

I tried to embrace the new and exciting opportunities that presented themselves, truly I did. I mean, my business was taking off and Grace even cracked a smile not that long ago. So for the most part, life was fine, good even. But something was missing. It was like I spent my days on autopilot and it was only in the evenings when Dominic called that I realized what it was—him.

You see, I didn't need to pretend with Dominic. I could openly say parts of my life were shit, that I was struggling with a marketing issue, or was disappointed when Grace drank spirits for breakfast on weekends. I could finally drop all pretense of perfection and be myself. It was a relief, let me tell you, because maintaining the illusion of composure for everyone else's benefit was beyond draining. In fact, for the first time ever, we spoke openly about everything. Well, everything except our love lives. Thankfully, that topic was off the table because the mere thought of him with another woman made me want a stiff drink with my cereal too.

Anyway, Dominic never judged me during our nightly phone conversations. In fact, he encouraged me to see situations from an alternate perspective, provided super-helpful ideas, and best of all, reminded me that I, Riley Jayne Sears, was important. Needless to say, I coveted my time with him like an addict savored a fix. So when his name flashed across my phone's screen as I entered my bedroom early one evening after a shower, I dived for it—literally. My towel may or may not have dropped to the floor in my haste.

"*Dominic.*"

"Hey, angel."

His low, gravelly voice spoke straight to parts of me I emphatically tried to ignore, I really needed to throw some clothes on ASAP. "Can you wait a minute? I need to get dressed."

"You answered the phone naked?" Dominic swore. "You're killing me, woman."

Laughing, I returned, "I was in the shower. Besides, it serves you right for calling ten minutes early. Hmm, now what lingerie should I wear? My lacey black G-string or—"

"Get. Dressed."

Stifling more laughter, I quickly threw on a pair of underwear—sadly, not the ones described—some grey yoga pants and a sky blue tank top, telling myself the color in no way reminded me of Dominic's eyes because, you know, that would be silly.

After plonking myself down on the bed and picking up the phone again, I said, "Okay, I'm back."

"Thank fucking Christ. Being left alone with the mental image of you wet and naked is enough to drive a man insane."

"Oh. In a good way or in a *Silence of the Lambs* way?"

"Definitely in a good way."

I flushed.

"You're blushing, aren't you?"

"Maybe."

Dominic groaned. "I can't deal with this shit, Riley, it's fuckin' messing with my brain. I'm almost as bad as Levi and he's a goddamn joke at the moment."

"What do you mean? Is your brother okay?"

"Only you would care about my loser bro when I'm seriously hurting here."

"You'll be fine. I'm sure there are plenty of blonde women with generous C-cups in Melbourne more than ready to help ease your hurt."

Dominic muttered something under his breath but it was too quiet to make out. So, ignoring him, I asked,

"What's wrong with Levi?"

"He's pussy-whipped, that's what."

"How is that even possible? He and Grace aren't even living in the same state."

"No idea but he's as miserable as fuck and that's not even the worst of it."

"Really?" I frowned. "Because it sounds pretty horrible so far."

Dominic snorted. "Save your pity for the rest of us, angel. His vocals are off, he's as forgetful as fuck and I haven't seen him play his Gibson this bad since he first learned how to hold the damn thing. Glaciers move faster than our recording."

"Wow, poor Levi. If it's any consolation, Grace isn't faring much better."

"Did she lose her shit at the mailman again?"

"No, I think they've reached an uneasy truce after he 'accidentally' dropped her bills in Mrs. Jenkinson's bird bath."

"Then what's her deal?"

"She misses him," I said simply. "She's in love with the guy and he's not here."

We were both silent. I laid back on my bed, closed my eyes and hated fate with the passion of a gazillion flaming suns because that last statement wasn't really about Grace at all.

Truth be told, the more time I spent talking to Dominic, the more I realized I'd stupidly fallen in love with the man. I know, right? I mean, what kind of self-respecting woman let her guard down around the likes of him? One who was dating someone else, of course.

Fuck my life.

"Serves her right for falling for the douche."

See what I mean?

Rolling my eyes, I muttered, "Can you be a little

more cynical, please? I'm not sure my faith in love has been crushed quite enough."

"Just sayin' how it is."

"No, you're being a rude jerk who's clearly never been in love before."

"I've been in love."

I sat bolt upright and the room swam as my equilibrium played chase with my brain. "Hang on, what? You've been in love?"

"Yep."

"When?"

"Do you really wanna know?"

Not really.

"Well, yeah. I wouldn't have asked otherwise."

Don't do it, Riley.

Dominic took a deep breath, it seemed like he was bracing himself for a punch to the gut and to be honest, I was too. I mean, him in love? As much as I wanted it to, the idea just did not compute. For some strange reason, my free hand clenched the bedcover, tightly.

"Mac hired me to custom fit cars straight after I finished my apprenticeship. I thought I hit the jackpot the day I walked into his garage because apart from playing music, working on classic cars was a dream job for me."

"You're very good at it."

"Thanks." I could hear the smile in his voice, it warmed my insides and my grip on the coverlet loosened.

"One afternoon, his daughter, Allie, walked into the workshop."

"Allie?" I interrupted. Okay, so my fingernails might have accidentally torn a hole in the quilt at the mention of her name. I let go and smoothed the fabric flat. "Wait up, wasn't she the woman you spoke about in Melbourne the night we, um…" There was no way I could finish my sentence, doing so brought back way too many blissful/painful memories—I was still undecided which.

Dominic sighed. "Yeah." He paused for a moment and I found myself once again clenching the bejesus out of my coverlet. I'd have to iron it later. "Anyway, the moment I laid eyes on her I was a goner. She was fuckin' stunning, with long black hair, dark eyes, legs which went on forever and her tits—" He groaned.

"Enough, I get the visual."

He chuckled. "Jealous?"

"No," I lied.

"Trust me, you've got nothing to be jealous of. That woman might have looked like a supermodel but underneath she was a cold-hearted bitch."

"Ouch."

Dominic continued. "At the time, I thought Allie was the holy grail of pussy. We started seeing each other, one thing led to another and soon enough we became inseparable. Or so I thought. You see, Mac had me working on this 1956 canary yellow Chevrolet for a priority customer so we needed it done on a tight turnaround. I started pulling extra hours at the garage—" He swore. "Levi warned me, said she was nothing but trouble, that she flirted with men all the time behind my back but like a fuckin' idiot, I ignored him."

My heart ached at the anger-laced regret in his voice and for the billionth time, wished I was in Melbourne with him. "Don't talk about yourself that way, Dominic. You weren't an idiot, you were in love."

"It's the same goddamn thing."

I sighed.

"A month after we restored the Chevy, Allie tells me she's pregnant." There was a high-pitched choking sound which I think came from me. "We hadn't been together long, but I stupidly thought I was in love with the woman so was gonna make it work. My own flesh and blood didn't deserve the title, dad, so unlike him, I was determined to do right by Allie and our kid."

Closing my eyes, I took several deep breaths, only it did very little to ease the anxiety slowly unfurling in my stomach.

"Anyway, Allie and I moved in together not long after she dropped that mother of all fuckin' bombshells. It seemed to work out great for a while, I took her to all of her medical appointments, cooked her weird-ass meals whenever she had a craving. Christ, I even massaged her swollen feet at the end of each day."

Accept these emotions, Riley. They're uncomfortable but necessary, you need to make room for them.

"The day Charlotte was born… I … I can't even describe it, Riley."

Amidst the hazy fog swirling around me, I somehow murmured, "You don't need to. I've seen enough men break down at the sight of their newborn child to understand how life-changing it must be."

Dominic took a deep breath. "It was like my world suddenly made sense, you know? I finally knew what my purpose was, what I was put on this earth for— to stand by my woman and raise my baby girl."

He paused, and I took the time to identify the emotions coursing through my body just as Doctor Powell instructed.

Hmm, sadness, yep, you're definitely there. Envy, yeah, wish you'd piss the hell off. What else? Oh, there you are, heartbreak. Damn, you really hurt.

"Allie changed completely after Charlotte was born. She cried all the time, refused to get out of bed, and wouldn't even look her own kid in the eye. I thought she had postnatal depression or some shit, so did a heap of research about what would help and who she could get support from, but she wasn't interested. She just locked herself in our bedroom wanting to be left alone."

"I ended up raising Charlotte by myself for the first few months. Not that I minded, the kid was as cute as anything despite chucking-up on every clean shirt I owned and hardly ever sleeping." He paused and sensing something big was about to unfold, I trained my mind to focus solely on rhythmic breathing.

In and out. In and out. In—

"One Saturday, a knock at the front door changed everything." Dominic's voice turned hard. "Some asshole named Chad stood on my goddamn doorstep, claiming to be Charlotte's father."

I gasped.

"As soon as she heard his voice, Allie raced to where I had the motherfucker by the throat. She screamed at me to let him go," his laugh was bitter, "because she loved him. Apparently, they had been screwing the entire time we were together but when he learned she was pregnant, freaked out and left. Not wanting to raise a kid by herself, Allie then led me to believe Charlotte was mine." His voice turned soft, the pain in it momentarily robbing me of speech. "She felt like mine."

I sat with the agonizing grief streaming its way through my limbs for a full minute before collecting myself. "Dominic, I'm so sorry."

He coughed. "I took a paternity test and the asshole was right, Charlotte was his biological daughter. Since he decided to have a crack at father of the year, he took both my baby girl and pathetic excuse of a girlfriend back with him to Perth." I could hear the hurt and frustration in his voice as he continued. "Legally, I didn't have a leg to stand on so I had to let them go, even though it felt like he took a part of me with him."

Dominic paused, cleared his throat and said, "So, I've learned two powerful lessons, Riley. Never fall in love, it's not fuckin' worth it, and always suit up before bagging a chick."

"You didn't use a condom with me."

"No." I heard him swallow. "I didn't."

Finally, the last pieces of the puzzle that made up the man, Dominic Mondez, fell into place. And it was strange because the picture I saw staring back at me wasn't at all what I expected.

****

I'd had a terrible day. Now, when I say terrible, I mean, being stabbed in the eye from a razorblade-wielding bandicoot would have been a welcome alternative. It was always like this. Doctor Powell told me that with time the hurt would heal, it would eventually fade, and in some respects it did, but in others… I groaned, curling myself into a tight ball on the couch.

Thankfully, I took the day off work so no one witnessed my emotional demise. Even Grace did not get a front row seat since she stumbled her way to bed after drinking three-quarters of a bottle of whiskey with lunch. That girl had way too much emotional baggage to deal with already, I simply refused to off-load on her. Reckon she'd wind up in hospital needing her stomach pumped if I did. With that in mind, I pretended to keep my shit together—for the morning at least—and acted as though it was not the anniversary of my brother's disappearance.

It was so. Fucking. Hard.

Everything reminded me of him. I burned my toast and remembered how he once jammed the toaster and we had to call the fire department when the thing caught fire. I went for a jog and saw an elderly woman walking a Beagle almost identical to the stuffed animal he nicknamed Sergeant. Heck, I even made the mistake of turning on the TV only to be taunted with an episode of his favorite cartoon, *Spiderman*. And nothing helped, not cleaning the kitchen, organizing the linen closet or even rearranging my wardrobe. Needless to say, by the time evening rolled around, I refused to do anything but sit on the couch in the hopes the painful memories would somehow disappear.

They didn't.

By the time the sky darkened and I found myself staring past the shadows which played on my living room wall from the streetlamp below, I gave up and dialed Dominic's number. It wasn't yet time for our daily phone call but I needed him, badly.

"Hey, angel, what's up?" He paused, and I imagined him checking the time on his watch. "It's a bit early, isn't it?"

"I, ah—"

There was a rustling in the background and what sounded like him putting on some clothes. My head must have been seriously messed up since I didn't even attempt to picture him naked.

I know, right?

"You okay to talk? I can call back later if you want?"

Despite his voice sounding slightly off, he replied, "Nah, it's all good. What's going on?" I could have sworn I heard the faint murmur of someone else speaking to him, but quickly disregarded it when Dominic suddenly grew angry. "Did that fucker hurt you? Is that why you're calling? Swear to God, Riley, if he so much as—"

"No, it's nothing like that," I interrupted. "Things between Robin and I are … fine, don't stress." Yeah, even to my own ears our relationship sounded as exciting as moldy crackers.

Don't go there, girl. Focus on one mess at a time.

He swore but other than that, my words seemed to calm him down. "Okay, if everything's so fuckin' spectacular with lover-boy, what's wrong?"

I took a deep breath and counted to five before exhaling.

This is it, Riley. It was time he learned the truth. "Did you know I had a brother?"

"A *brother?*" The shock in his voice was obvious, and I wasn't at all surprised. I mean, apart from Grace, Doctor Powell, and my parents, no one else knew anything about my sibling. The friends Toby used to play with were all grown-up now and many had moved away from Geographe Bay, while I purposefully avoided contact with anyone who reminded me of what I lost, my own childhood friends included—except Grace.

"His name was Toby." My voice trembled, so I cleared my throat before continuing. "He was one of those kids who was always full of energy, you know? From the moment he woke up in the morning to the second he fell asleep at night, Toby operated solely on one speed—full throttle." I gave the ghost of a smile. "And he could be a total shit too. He used to put sand in my bed sheets, bugs in my socks." I paused. "He even swapped my glass of water with apple cider vinegar once." Shaking my head, I muttered, "Man, I let him have it that day."

I fell silent for a moment, collecting my thoughts. "But I loved him. God, how I loved that boy. His laughter, you don't understand, it was the most beautiful—" The pain in my chest grew unbearable so I hugged my knees, curling myself into an even smaller ball.

My voice broke. "And now he's gone. He's gone, Dominic, and it's all my fault."

"What happened?" Dominic asked softly.

Squeezing my eyes shut, I told him everything. I mentioned how I begged my parents to let Toby and I go to the annual Beachside Summer Carnival unchaperoned thirteen years ago, how we spent the day going on ride after ride until we felt so queasy we collapsed together on the grass, how my little brother disappeared from my side when my back was turned, how the police detectives found no trace of him despite a nationwide search and finally, after body-wracking sobs, I even recounted how awful it was living at home because of my perceived ineptitude. I also explained how after moving out, I stopped eating and Grace forced me to seek the professional help of Doctor Powell who diagnosed me with anxiety.

By the end of my forty-minute monologue, Dominic knew every secret I had. He was the one man I trusted explicitly and, though ridiculously painful, speaking to him also helped ease some of the hurt. Not all of it, but enough to breathe again. Afterward, I felt lighter somehow, less hollow. It was such a bittersweet feeling, I uncurled myself and lay back on the couch, sighing.

"I wish I was holding you, right now."

"Yeah." I wiped away what was left of my tears with the back of my hand. "Me too."

"I hate how you have to go through this alone."

"I'm not alone, Dominic. I've got you, remember?"

He chuckled. "Yeah, you've got me, all right." There was some movement in the background followed by frantic whispering. It was a female voice. A dynamite-filled balloon suddenly dropped and exploded in the pit of my stomach.

"You're not alone."

"Ah, no, I'm not. Hang on a second, Riley."

There was an increasingly heated exchange between Dominic and whoever the hell was with him. I didn't catch everything being said, only Dominic's side of the conversation but it was enough, believe me.

My blood simmered to an angry boil.

"Give it a rest, Candi." Murmuring echoed in my ear. "I told you I would, and I will." More murmuring. "No, it's nothing." A high-pitched whine. "For fuck's sake, she's no one, okay? *No one*. Now give it a goddamn rest."

My gasp must have alerted him to the fact that I wasn't hearing impaired "Fuck. Riley, I didn't mean—"

I was beyond livid. "You didn't mean what, Dominic? That I'm nothing to you? That I'm *no one?*"

"That's not what I meant and you know it. Now, can you just—"

"No, I can't. How dare you discount me like that. I just poured my heart out to you, you selfish prick, and you have the audacity to say I'm worthless?" I was panting. "Who the fuck is Candi, anyway? What kind of parents name their kid after a confection? Oh my God, she's a stripper, isn't she? I just revealed my deepest, darkest secret and you're lying in bed next to a fucking stripper. Is this all some kind of joke to you?" I was mortified, so yeah, there was a lot of yelling. "You know what? Fuck you, Dominic. Fuck you hard." And I hung up.

Another wave of tears burst forth, crippling me as I lay curled on the couch, only this time I wasn't sure they would ever stop.

Chapter Nineteen

Only a truth can set you free,
Here is my truth now set me free.
—MONDEZ, "Finally"

Mae didn't hesitate when I called to ask for a lift to work the next day. After opening the front door, I wasn't surprised either when she scanned me up and down, bluntly stating, "You look like shit."

I didn't bother correcting her as she moved past me into the living room because she was right, I did look awful. My long hair impersonated a bird's nest, my eyes were red and puffy, heck, I was still wearing the same clothes from yesterday since my tears somehow formed an adhesive glue which stuck me to the couch all night long.

"Come on, get dressed."

I paused. "Mae, I don't think I can face work today after all. I thought I could when I phoned you but…"

She snorted and gestured to my disheveled state. "Girl, there's no way I'm letting you go into work today." She gave a wicked smile. "Hurry up and get ready. Annabelle is in child care until five and I haven't had a kid-free day in forever, so let's make the most of it."

"So, we're both going to pretend to be sick? A bit obvious, don't you think?"

Her eyes lit up. "See, that's where you're wrong. You're taking a sick day, I'm taking carer's leave— Annabelle suddenly came down with a fever or … something. I'll figure it out before I phone work."

"Oh, Mae." My eyes watered. Not again, I was so over crying.

My friend gave me a hug and the pain in my chest eased slightly. "Riley, you never take time off work so whatever was going on with you yesterday must have been pretty bad and judging by the looks of you now, it was even worse than that." She released me and turned my shoulders until I faced the bathroom, nudging me forward. "Scoot, you're not to leave that room until you've showered and put on an outfit that doesn't stink of depression."

I threw a smile over my shoulder, murmuring, "Thank you."

She winked.

"Where are we heading exactly?" We were driving south along the freeway in Mae's beat-up Corolla. The engine smoked whenever she accelerated and an ominous clunking sounded from the rear end every time she braked, but Mae simply turned the stereo up and ignored it so I did the same.

She lowered the volume from ear-splitting levels to something more conversation-friendly. "We're spending the morning at Serenity Day Spa."

I blinked. Now, don't get me wrong, I enjoyed a good pampering just as much as the next person but Serenity Day Spa was exclusive with a capital E. A-list celebrities flew in from all over the country for their elite treatment packages that promised privacy, exceptional service, and locally sourced organic products. Last time I checked they had a waiting list until February. "How did you manage that?"

Mae shrugged. "I know a person who knows a person, no big deal."

"Impressive."

She smiled.

Our day together was exactly what I needed. We received the deluxe pamper package at Serenity. Two hours, a mud bath, and a honey-soaked body wrap later, I started to feel reborn. So much so, I dragged Mae to a hairdresser after deciding I wanted a completely new style. Gazing in the mirror at my new wavy, shoulder-length bob with super cute fringe, I realized I liked the woman slowly unraveling before me. In fact, the sparkle in her eye lead me straight to a destination I never thought I would have the guts to go.

"Oh, hell no," Mae declared as I stood outside the front of Wicked Ink, Geographe Bay's notorious body piercing and tattoo studio. "I hear it's run by bikers. I've got a daughter to consider, Riley, I can't go in there."

Looking behind me as I strode through the entrance, I replied, "Okay."

Yeah, I was loving the real me, she was confident, courageous and a total badass.

With a groan, Mae followed.

An hour and a half later, I was sore but ridiculously proud of myself. Not only did I get a super cute diamond nose stud—even Mae agreed it looked hot—but I also got a tattoo.

Fuck yeah, a tattoo.

It was absolutely perfect. Lovingly placed on my right shoulder blade was a vintage birdcage, the door flung wide-open with a blue, black, and white fairy-wren soaring mid-air above. This tattoo spoke of everything I felt, of the person I was becoming. And I liked her, a hell of a lot.

You see, I changed that day, I truly did. Dominic's insensitivity the night before, though brutal in its delivery, forced me to realize something glorious…

I am someone.

I am worthy.

I. Am. Enough.

I did not need to seek forgiveness from my

parents, I did not need the affection of a man to feel whole, I did not need a job that no longer fulfilled me. I did not need any of it. All that mattered was being true to myself, loyal to my friends and fearless of the future. And once I ignored the dull ache taking up most of my hollow insides, I was excited for the future, which probably accounted for my momentous decision. I was going to quit midwifery and focus solely on my online business. For real. It was strange, what started off as the day from Satan's anus suddenly became the first day of the rest of my life—I was going to make the most of it.

Once tattoo artist, Frankie—one of the nicest guys around, thank you very much—finished and dressed my latest addition, I slowly spun in a full circle before Mae.

"Holy shit," she murmured. "Now that's a makeover."

I smiled. "It's not a makeover, Mae, it's a revelation."

My newfound positivity took a serious nosedive when I arrived back at the apartment. Grace wasn't in any of the main living areas and wanting to assure myself she was still breathing, I headed to her bedroom.

The scene before me didn't look good.

Now, to the casual observer, Grace looked perfectly normal. She was propped against the headboard of her dilapidated bed, reading a Sir Arthur Conan Doyle novel, but don't forget I'd known her for most of my life so I knew in an instant she wasn't okay.

Grace glanced up and her eyes widened. "Wow. Girl, you look sensational."

Yeah, something was definitely wrong. That woman loved me just as much, if not more so than whiskey; however, she rarely complimented anyone— myself included. Grace was overcompensating, for what, I had no idea.

So, I patted my hair, pretending to play along in the hopes she would tell me what the heck was going on. "Really? You're not just saying that?"

"Hell no." She squinted and moved closer. I honestly thought she was about to admit defeat by declaring all but I was wrong. "Hang on, Riley Sears, is that a nose ring?"

I flushed, completely forgetting my altered appearance. "I've always wanted one."

"Love it."

My head whipped up. "You do?"

She smiled. "Yeah."

What the hell? Two compliments in the space of as many minutes? I had officially entered an alternate universe, one where fairies and leprechauns frolicked hand in hand sprinkling magic dust about them like confetti.

Shit just got real, I need to sort it out.

However, before I could demand answers, Grace continued, "Not sure your mum will though."

I stuck my chin out, refusing to give a rat's ass about my mother's opinion. "Fuck her."

Grace appeared beyond impressed and clapping both hands, cried, "Bravo, it's about time you took ownership of that sexy body."

I couldn't take it anymore, I wanted my best friend back. Softening my voice, I asked, "G, what's wrong?" She turned away from me. "You're doing that thing where you're upset but trying to hide it. I don't understand. For the last month and a half, you haven't bothered hiding your emotions at all."

Grace moved back to the bed and collapsed on it. Staring at her hands, she mumbled, "I broke it off with Levi."

To say I was shocked was putting it mildly, and I

suddenly felt the need to sit down myself. "What? Why?"

"It was never going to work. Had to admit it sooner or later." I remained silent, and she continued, "Levi told me their recording wasn't going well. They're running behind schedule and still have more tracks to lay down. Which means…" She sighed. "I won't be able to see him before he goes on tour."

I remembered Dominic mentioning the boys were going to return home for a few days before jetting off to begin their tour along the east coast. My heart broke for her, the only thing keeping Grace from needing an AA meeting was the promise of Levi's return and now he wasn't going to make it … I shook my head.

She stood, pacing. "I mean, for a relationship to work you actually have to catch up at some point, right?" She faced me, hands on hips. "Six weeks has felt like a lifetime and now he's leaving for another three months." The girl was building up steam, she threw her hands in the air, exclaiming, "Christ, and after that he's moving to goddamn Melbourne." Pausing, Grace dropped her head, defeated. "I was kidding myself. We were never going to work. I just wish it didn't hurt so much."

Right. I needed to fix this.

Tapping newly manicured fingernails against my leg, I considered the best way forward. Now, the old Riley would probably organize a movie marathon night, interspersed with feeble attempts at force-feeding Grace some peppermint tea, but the new badass Riley—I smiled.

Just as I was about to execute phase one of my super awesome plan, my phone rang.

Grace rolled her eyes. "Seriously, Riley? They're your ringtone now?"

Stupid Dominic. Never should have let him anywhere near my phone.

I hustled from the room before answering it.

"Guess where you're going tonight?"

"And hello to you too, Brea." I grinned, not at all insulted by her lack of obligatory pleasantries.

"No time for that, I'm too excited." She barely took a breath before launching into the reason for her call. "I was supposed to work a late shift at The Hole tonight but Corey offered to take over after nine o'clock since I did the same for him when he got sick a while back." She stopped.

"Okay."

"So, back to my earlier question. Guess where you're going tonight?"

"The Hole?"

"Damn straight."

I laughed, loving my friend's enthusiasm; it was contagious. "This is perfect timing actually because I was just about to call you. Mind if Grace comes with us? She's pretty bummed at the moment and I think getting her out of the apartment is a good idea."

"This is easier than I thought," Brea mumbled.

"Huh?"

"Oh, nothing. Sure thing, bring Grace but make sure you're both here by nine."

"Why?"

"I already told you, that's when I get off work."

"Oh, okay then." I checked my watch, it had just gone past eight. "Shit. Gotta go, see you soon."

"*Ciao, bella.*"

Shaking my head, I grinned. That girl was nuts.

Grace was once again pretending to read when I reentered her room. Figuring it would be more effective if I was honest about the situation, I bowled right on in, giving her little choice. "Well, you can either stay in your bedroom and wallow in self-pity or you can take charge of your life and go live it."

Truer words had never been spoken.

"You've been reading motivational books again," she countered.

I narrowed my eyes, ignoring her. "What'll it be?"

"Self-pity." I narrowed them further and Grace sighed. "We're going to The Hole, aren't we?"

"Yes, we are." I rummaged through a pile of clean laundry at the foot of her bed, refusing to give in to the compulsive need to tidy her room. In all honesty, it was a mess. After some searching, I found a short summer dress and threw it on her lap. "Now get dressed."

As I strode toward the door, she murmured, "Love you, Riley."

My insides flooded with a warmth I hadn't felt since Dominic became a class A douche. Turning to her, I replied, "Love you too. Now hurry up, we're leaving in twenty minutes."

****

Grace scrunched up her nose as soon as we set foot inside The Hole. "God, this place stinks."

I laughed, loving the fact she wasn't pretending to be anything other than her honest, albeit socially inappropriate self. "You'll forget about the smell after a few drinks." Grabbing her hand, I led her through the large crowd milling around the raised stage which stood in the corner of the venue. A heavy, three-piece band were midway through their set and the short male vocalist was thrusting his hips, Elvis style, looking completely ridiculous. However, their sound wasn't half-bad. The drums were brutal, the guitars ballsy, and if I shut my eyes, blocking out those obscene hip gyrations, their music was really enjoyable.

We pushed our way to where Brea stood behind the bar, pouring and serving drinks at a dizzying speed.

Beside me, Grace sighed.

"Girls, so glad you made it. What can I get you?"

"Hey, Brea." I smiled. "Can I have a beer? And G here," I glanced over at my best friend who appeared beyond miserable, "needs a double whiskey, neat."

Brea took one look at Grace and poured her a triple instead, she then popped the cap off my beer and slid both drinks in front of us.

For the first time in six weeks, Grace's smile actually reached her eyes as she said to Brea, "I owe you one."

"Try to enjoy yourselves, okay?"

We both nodded.

"Will do."

Brea refused to take our money and moved on to her next alcohol-starved customer. If I'd been more observant, I would have thought she was up to something. It was the mischievous wink she gave us before turning away that should have tipped me off. However, I had too much on my mind, namely trying to get Grace drunk-happy—it was a stretch, I grant you, but one I was willing to attempt despite the insurmountable odds stacked against me. Shaking my head, I checked the time on my watch; there were still ten minutes of Brea's shift left, so I once again led Grace through the crowded bar in search of a booth.

We found one relatively close to the stage which was a definite win considering how packed the place was. I guessed, most people preferred to stand rather than sit while the band was playing. Lord only knew if it was Mondez, I'd be up there in a flash—a dull ache formed in my stomach.

Grace and I sat in silence. She stared at her whiskey, looking so despondent I felt like the most horrible creature with two legs and a pulse. It was obvious she wanted to be anywhere else but here.

And that's when the guilt kicked in.

You see, I'd been lying to my best friend. I hadn't been honest with her for a very long time. She knew nothing about Dominic, she knew nothing about Robin; heck, she didn't even know my heart, like hers, was broken. And yes, I kept all of this hidden under the guise of it never being the right moment or me trying to protect her, but that wasn't the real reason at all. The fact of the matter was, I was scared. Scared of admitting my own stupidity, scared of losing her good opinion, scared of seeing the truth in her eyes. Because Grace would tell me, she would have no hesitation in declaring me a deluded fool for falling in love with a man like Dominic while stringing along a nice guy like Robin.

Deep in thought, I picked the label off my beer bottle, haphazardly scattering its shredded remains in front of me. For once, I couldn't give two shits about the mess. Yeah, total badass.

It was time to come clean—figuratively speaking—both with myself and Grace. Squaring my shoulders, I turned to her. "G, I need to tell you something."

Grace looked like she was internally preparing herself for Armageddon as she unclasped her hands from the whiskey glass and placed both palms flat on the table. "Sounds serious."

I opened my mouth to continue but was drowned out by a new solo vocalist on stage. We must have been so caught up in our own thoughts, we didn't even notice the first band finish and the second artist setting up. However, when the first chord reverberated through the amps, Grace froze. All the color drained from her face and her mouth dropped open in shock.

"*Levi?*" Grace stumbled from the booth and

toward the stage as though being pulled by an imaginary chain. I spun in my seat. Sure enough, there he was, perched on a stool playing his acoustic guitar, singing a song about retribution.

My gaze flicked to the bar and landed on Brea. She grinned at me, shrugging her shoulders and doing a terrible job of feigning ignorance. My gaze shifted back to Levi and the ache in my stomach grew tenfold.

Damn, he looked like Dominic.

In black combat boots, ripped jeans and a faded green t-shirt, Levi looked so strikingly similar to the man who tore my heart out before throwing it in a blender, that if I'd had any more alcohol, I would have sworn it was him. But it wasn't. Even sitting down, he was slightly taller, his stature that bit leaner. I wrapped my arms around myself while trying to accept the emotions of hurt, betrayal and loss.

Impossible.

"I need to get out of here." Standing, I made my way to the toilets, before bending over the sink and dry heaving for a solid five minutes. Finally, I managed to sweet-talk my recently ingested beer into not making a repeat performance, so splashed some cold water on my face, before tidying my hair and makeup.

Levi was back. Once I recovered from my obvious shock, I was absolutely thrilled at his romantic gesture. Don't get me wrong, Grace would hate it, it wasn't her style of declaration at all, but at least afterward they would get the chance to yell at each other before having crazy make-up sex. It would be nice to see her smile again.

After returning to the bar and grabbing another drink off a very smug-looking Brea—finishing work at nine o'clock my ass, she just wanted us here in time to see Levi perform—I headed outside to the beer garden.

Grace and Levi would need some alone time and I did too, especially since I was about to end things with Robin.

I stepped through a doorway and out into the cool evening air, breathing deeply. The beer garden itself was situated at the rear of the building, it wasn't large, about half the size of a tennis court. It was surrounded on three sides by high brick walls with random objects such as sombreros and bikes hanging sporadically from them. There was a fully grown palm tree in the center of the courtyard with multiple strips of fairy lights connecting the deep green fronds to the corner of each connecting wall. Old wooden tables and rickety chairs or benches were scattered about the place and all of them, bar one, were occupied with people enjoying themselves.

I moved to the only free bench in the very back corner and perched myself on the edge of it. After taking my phone out of my pocket, I stared at the black screen for a few moments before unlocking it and quickly dialing Robin's number. I needed to get this over with, for both our sakes.

It rang a few times and despite my resolve, a dark part of me was disappointed when he answered. "Hey, Riley."

"Robin, ah, hi."

"What's up?"

Squeezing my eyes shut, I replied, "Look, I… I haven't been entirely honest with you, and it's cruel of me since you've been nothing but a gentleman but I, I don't think… I mean, I think it's best if we—"

His long sigh interrupted my horrendous breakup attempt, for which I was eternally grateful. "It's okay, I know where this conversation is heading. You don't have to say anything."

"I'm sorry," I whispered.

"Yeah, me too." He was quiet for a while. "I don't think I can be friends with you, Riley." I bit back the tears that threatened. "Seeing you… It'll hurt too much. I don't mean to be a dick about it but—"

"I understand." Sniffing, I continued, "Robin, you're a truly amazing guy and one day I hope—"

"Don't, please don't. You're only making it worse." He cleared his throat. "I'd better go. Bye, Riley."

"Bye."

After putting the phone away, I wiped my eyes with the back of my hand, hating how I would need to tidy my makeup for a third time unless I wanted to be mistaken for a character from *The Walking Dead.*

Vanity would have to wait. I needed a moment.

Glancing up at the night sky, I looked past the lights and counted the stars above until my tears dried. It took longer than expected, but once I was all cried out, it felt like a twelve-ton weight had lifted and I could finally breathe again.

I'd done it. As painful as it was, I made the important decision to walk alone rather than by the side of a man I did not have feelings for. Strangely, it felt both cathartic and alarming, I guess it would take time.

"Is this seat taken?"

Turning, I met the laughing gaze of dark-haired man. He was cute, in a preppy kind of way, with tan leather shoes, slim-fit navy pants and a white polo shirt. His black-rimmed glasses completed the look which, don't get me wrong was damn fine, but I could only stare at him, confused. There was a serious lack of ripped clothing, tattoos and piercings.

Maybe he's lost?

"Sure, take a seat." I went to shift over, only realized there was nowhere else to go unless I wanted to fall flat on my ass, so remained still.

"Thanks." He sat, his thigh inadvertently pressing against my leg. Holding out a hand, he said, "I'm Sebastian."

Of course you are.

However, I took it because, despite the close proximity with this complete stranger, I immediately felt at ease. "Riley, nice to meet you."

"Likewise." His face was open and kind, just what I needed after my horrendous phone conversation with Robin. "So, do you come here often?" Sebastian winked, nudging me with his shoulder and I laughed, immediately relaxing into friendly banter about the unlikely success rate of his chosen pickup line.

Suddenly, the skin on the back of my neck prickled. I stilled.

He was watching me, I could feel it. My body sensed him long before my head did and started tingling. Everywhere.

Oh, holy mother.

Just the thought of him made my heart pound. Traitorous thing. It merrily rammed against my ribcage as soon as I pictured his tall, muscular body and disheveled russet hair. My fingers itched to reach out and delve through the soft strands as I remembered what it felt like to tug on them as he groaned into my open mouth—but I shifted in my seat and sat on them instead. I wasn't going down that road again, hell no. I was done.

Done.

A low chuckle cut through the muted sounds of heavy rock music emanating from inside, its gravelly sound resonating with my downstairs department, causing a deep blush to stain my cheeks.

Clearly, I wasn't fooling anyone.

What in the name of sweet baby Jesus was he even

doing here?

I tried so hard to focus on what Sebastian was saying. Thankfully, he held up his end of the conversation despite my unexpected inability to formulate any words. We'd been sitting together for a while without a single awkward pause so I nodded, smiled, and even laughed when required. To be fair, it was a pretty decent pickup attempt. Well, until *he* showed up.

Blue eyes burned my skin.

You don't own me, you don't own me, you don't—

I swallowed, steeled myself and then glanced across the beer garden.

Own me.

Fuck.

Dominic was leaning against the wall, his black button-down shirt almost bursting at the seams. I blamed those insanely strong pecs and biceps. Honestly, they were huge. And the way his dark blue jeans hung enticingly low off narrow hips… It should be illegal. He was going to give someone—AKA *me*—a cardiac arrest if he wasn't careful.

I shook my head. With a bottle of beer in one hand and a buxom blonde in the other—this one looked nastier than most—the guy was the physical embodiment of everything I despised. Truly.

If only my body would listen.

Raising the drink to full, kissable lips, he tipped his head back, piercing gaze still locked on me. He then wiped his mouth with the back of his hand, a flicker of emotions I couldn't identify crossing his face when he noticed my breath catch.

The girl must have registered his distraction too because she started rubbing herself up against him like an overly aroused limpet. Gross. He broke contact with me and looked down at her, a dark smile tugging his lips. After murmuring something in her ear and slapping her on the ass, she giggled. I looked away, that familiar painful knot forming in my stomach once more.

Damn you, Dominic Mondez. Damn you to hell.

Chapter Twenty

I'm done waiting,
For fate to decide,
I'm done waiting,
Out from the inside.
—MONDEZ, "Fate"

"What is it with you and guys wearing chinos?"

I spun to glare at the obscenely ripped manwhore towering over me. His beer, like the blonde whose dress rivaled the size of a postage stamp ripped in half, had disappeared. Instead, he glowered down at me, his hands clenching and unclenching, testosterone practically seeping from his pores. Not that I cared.

Standing slowly, I shot him a look so disdainful even Mum would have been proud. The closeness of our bodies and the wall of heat radiating from his broad chest had no effect on me. Honest. This man couldn't hurt me anymore, there was nothing left inside to break.

"I've got nothing to say to you, Dominic. Leave me alone."

"Do you know this guy?" Sebastian's incredulous gaze darted between me and the seething pile of muscle standing before us. The poor guy looked like he needed to breathe into a brown paper bag.

"Yes—"

"No—"

I gritted my teeth. "We used to know each other." My words were directed at Sebastian but I didn't once break eye contact with Dominic. "But it's over."

"The hell it is."

Sebastian stood, attempting to skirt around us. "Sounds like you two have a lot of … stuff to sort out, so

I'll just—" I put my hand on his shoulder, preventing him from moving any farther.

"No, stay."

"Get your fuckin' hand off him, Riley," Dominic growled.

Sebastian's face looked pained when I refused to listen. "Ignore him, he's got nothing to say to me that I want to hear."

Dominic growled.

"Ah—" Sebastian looked like he would rather have root canal surgery than remain standing where he was and I shot daggers at Dominic for making him feel so uncomfortable.

Dominic scowled at Sebastian. "Fuck off."

The man did not need to be told twice, he shot out of there like a clown from a cannon and I rounded on Dominic, furious. "Why are you such an asshole?"

"We're not done here."

"I'm not a fucking burger. You can't pick me up and put me back down again whenever the hell you want. I'm a person, Dominic, with feelings and you've screwed with them one too many times. It's over, leave me alone," I panted with rage and made to move past him.

His hand shot out and gripped my upper arm, spinning me around to face him. "No."

"*No?*"

"No, you're not walking away. No, I'm not screwing with you. And no, it's not over between us."

I blinked at the ferocity in his gaze, the brutal honesty leveled at me froze my feet in place—I couldn't move if I tried. My mouth opened, closed and then opened again in a vain attempt to say something equal parts witty and cutting, only nothing came out.

Dominic stepped in close, his body flush with mine. I swear, I could feel his heartbeat, its erratic thumps pummeled against my chest. "Tell me you don't want me." My breath caught in my throat. "Tell me your body doesn't burst into fuckin' flames whenever we touch, that seeing me again isn't a dream you never want to wake from."

I shook my head, mute.

Dominic's grip tightened, his fingers branding my skin. "Go on, tell me." He leaned forward, his lips brushing against my ear as he whispered, "I dare you."

"I don't want you," I breathed.

He shifted back, his gaze searching my face. "You're lying."

A lone tear escaped from the corner of my eye and trickled its way down my cheek, I refused to wipe it away.

"And I know you're lying because it's the same goddamn lie I tell myself every single day."

I gasped.

Dominic's gaze turned earnest. "I don't deserve you, Riley, I know that. I'm a jerk, a fuckup, and I've hurt you more times than I can count." He cradled my face in his hands like I was made of precious china. "But when I'm with you it's like…" He paused. "It's like you see the man I want to be."

Closing my eyes, I attempted to quash the waves of emotion rolling through me. "Don't do this to me, Dominic, *please.*"

"Too late. It's too late, angel. From the moment you knocked me flat on my ass it was a done deal. And I tried, I really fuckin' tried to keep my distance but you were so damn determined to see the best in me." He leaned in, his breath caressing my skin as he continued, "I can't stay away." Dominic kissed me, his lips soft and worshipful. Stupidly, I let him. "You're mine."

"No, I—"

"And I'm yours."

My eyes snapped open. "*What?*"

"I love you, Riley. Took me ages to admit it to myself but now I have, I'm never letting you go."

I took a step back. This couldn't be happening, it just… It couldn't. I refused to get my hopes up only to have them pulverized into an ash-like dust once again. "But, the other women—"

"They were you. They were all you."

Shaking my head, I exclaimed, "You're not even making any sense."

"As soon as you exploded into my life every woman I touched reminded me of you. One had your eyes, another had the color of your hair, one even had your tits."

I glared at him. "You're seriously not helping matters."

"But since making love to you in Melbourne—"

"Now you admit it," I muttered.

"I couldn't do it anymore, it felt wrong."

"What about Candi?"

Dominic sighed. "Candi tried to make a move on me. She rocked up unannounced at my apartment, wanting to fuck. So, yeah, it was her voice you heard while we were talking on the phone but I swear to you, Riley, nothing happened." Dominic's gaze gentled. "Angel, don't you understand? You're it for me, there's no one else."

I turned my face away, blinking hard, hating the fact I was still standing in front of him.

"Look, I know I'm a fuckup. I've made some piss-poor decisions in the past that I'm not proud of." He trailed one hand down my arm, entwining his fingers with mine. "But I'm gonna make it up to you, I promise you that."

I really wished I had the lady balls to pull myself away. Clearly, they had shriveled up and died along with my dignity.

Thankfully, the ever-helpful image of Postage Stamp Girl popped into my head, almost singeing the back of my retinas. "How can you say this to me when only fifteen minutes ago you were groping a life-size Bratz doll? I'm not a fucking idiot, I have eyes, you know."

He at least had the decency to appear sheepish. "That was Nicole, she's Evan's other half."

"Who the hell is Evan?"

"The lead singer of Dead Man Walking, the band whose set was before Levi's."

"You mean the short guy?" He nodded, and I gaped at him, stunned. "Huh."

"She owed me a favor from a while back, so I mentioned what happened between us and she agreed to help."

"By dry humping your leg?"

Dominic shrugged. "I just wanted to test the waters, see if you'd react. Figured if you did, then you still had feelings for me." His pupils dilated as his free hand traced along my jawline, stopping briefly to hover above my lips before dropping away again. "When you looked at me, I knew."

I was almost too afraid to ask. "Knew what?"

"You loved me too."

I remained quiet, attempting to process everything that had been said. Finally, I whispered, "I do love you." Drawing on a strength I never knew I had, I continued. "But I love myself more." Dominic looked panicked and his grip on my hand intensified. "As much as I want to, I can't switch off my hurt and forget everything you've put me through."

"Tell me what I have to do." He was desperate. "I'll do anything."

"Quit Mondez and move back to Geographe Bay."

Dominic didn't even blink. "Done."

"Are you crazy?" I smacked one of his bulging pecs, wincing when the impact stung like a bitch. "You can't give up your music just because I ask you to."

"Yeah, I can. You're all that matters to me."

I scowled. "Stop being so damn nice, it's making it really difficult to hate you right now."

Dominic smiled at my petulance. He reached out and threaded his fingers through my shortened hair, tucking it behind my ear. "Angel, if you want me to move back here, I'll move. If you want me to quit music, I'll quit. I don't give a shit where I am or what I'm doing as long as we're together."

The man literally took my breath away.

And then it hit me.

"I forgive you," I murmured. "I do."

Relief washed over Dominic's features as he wrapped his arms around my waist, pulling me close. "Thank fuck." He pressed his forehead against mine.

I looked up into his face, the face of a man I wanted to spend the rest of my life with. "If you were willing to give up your childhood dream just to be with me…" I kissed him then, with everything I had, all the hope for our future, pain from our past, and confusion in between. It was all there in its messy, chaotic glory—we reveled in it.

When we finally came up for air, I whispered, "You're already the man you wanted to be, Dominic."

Love, *true love*, did not get any more selfless than that.

329

Epilogue

Love, don't hold me back now,
Love, won't hold me back now,
Love, you're all we've got now,
Love.
—MONDEZ, "Finally"

"Christ, woman, how much shit have you got in these boxes?" Grace's emerald green eyes flashed in astonishment. With a laptop in one hand and a notebook in the other, she looked ready to chair a board meeting rather than unpack the rest of my things.

I grimaced when she dumped my belongings on the floor before once again reaching into the cardboard box. "What the hell is this?"

Grace held up a black folder, its color-coded index tabs perfectly matched the copious amounts of scribbled on post-it notes attached to the front.

"My organizer."

"Isn't that what your laptop is for? And your phone? And your notebook?"

Huffing, I placed my hands on my hips. "So I like to be organized, sue me."

Grace snorted and beside me, Katrina stifled a giggle.

The three of us had spent the better part of the day moving me into my new apartment—correction, into *Dominic's* and my new apartment. There was no way I was letting him forego his childhood dream of making a living out of playing music, so I decided to make the move to Melbourne to be with him. It worked out well, considering my online business was easily transferable, and Grace and Levi lived right next door. Though I had some serious concerns about the thickness of the walls and was planning on raising the issue with Dominic's Auntie Val when I saw her next.

Turned out, not only was she a retired music teacher but a kickass real estate mogul as well. Val owned properties all over Australia, not just in the beachside suburb of St. Kilda where we now lived. Don't get me wrong, the beaches here were tame compared to the natural, untamed beauty of Geographe Bay, however, I was still able to start each day with a run along the shoreline, so I kept those unhelpful comments to myself.

Not gonna lie, when Katrina and Grace both arrived on my doorstep this morning, there was some serious tension between the two. I have no idea why, since Katrina has been nothing but welcoming since I first got here. Anyway, Grace suggested a drinking game, whereby if any of us unpacked an object starting with the first letter of our first name, we had to take a shot of whiskey—yuck—and since then everything has been peachy.

Saying goodbye to Mae and Annabelle was hard. There were tears, lots and lots of tears, but she promised to sign up to my online portal, Angel Fitness—Dominic's suggestion—and now we're in touch daily. It's fun too because I get to yell at her in shouty capital letters whenever she slacks off on her training.

It wasn't nearly as difficult to walk away from my parents. Dad was lecturing at Yale and hasn't yet replied to my email, while Mom merely nodded when I told her the news. I kinda wished she'd at least pretend to be heartbroken since her only remaining child was leaving for good, but no, she remained as stoic as always.

Thankfully, Doctor Powell also consulted over Skype, so I blubbered my way through that painful experience under her professional guidance. Since then, not only have we been working through my anxiety—

which for the most part has improved—but we have also begun focusing on forgiveness. It's been way more difficult than I expected.

Like Dad, Robin was also absent when I said goodbye, though this time at the hospital. I felt terrible about the hurt I caused, so wrote him a letter wishing him nothing but a passionate, caring woman to fall madly in love with, and left it with his receptionist. I didn't expect a reply.

While I felt beyond guilty at messing with Robin's heart, I can't deny mine is full to the point of bursting. Dominic has proven himself committed to me and our relationship time and time again. I mean, he remained silent when I purchased matching his and her bath towels, he only rolled his eyes after I reorganized his wardrobe according to season, and didn't even lose the plot when my emergency stash of chocolate took up most of the pantry space. If that's not love, I don't know what is.

I was immediately brought back from my reverie when Grace pulled out a small, rectangular book from the packing box. It had been lovingly decorated with love hearts, flowers, and rainbow stickers. I froze.

"Now what do we have here?" Grace's smile was wicked and Katrina's eyes grew wide. "Is this your *diary*?"

"Don't you dare," I warned.

"I've got one just like it." Katrina paused, her cheeks turning bright pink. "Oops, didn't mean to say that out loud."

Grace turned to Katrina, her face alight with mischief. "And does your childhood diary mention a certain Tommy Harris too?"

"I didn't crush on Tommy, G, and you know it."

The bitch opened my diary to a random page.

"Dear diary," she read. "Today, Tommy Harris looked at me from across the corridor. I think he likes me."

I lunged, tackling Grace to the ground. We rolled around a few times, squealing like pigs in mud until I managed to yank the offending book from her grasp.

"What is it with you and guitarists, anyway?" she panted.

I lay back on the carpet, exhausted. "What can I say, he was hot." I grinned. "And even hotter when he played guitar." We both burst out laughing.

Grace looked over at Katrina who was smiling at us in amusement. "Let me guess, the pages of your diary are covered in love notes about guitarists too?"

Katrina's face turned an ever-darker shade of red. She shook her head. "Drummers, actually."

"No shit?"

She shrugged, clearly uncomfortable.

"Right, then." I stood, pulling Grace up by the hand. "This office isn't going to unpack itself. Back to it, ladies."

Grace groaned and I could have sworn I heard a sigh of relief coming from Katrina's direction. Reaching into the box, I grabbed the first thing I could find.

"*Ruler,*" Grace shouted, jumping up and down with unabashed glee when she spied what was in my hand. "Take a shot, *Riley.*"

Groaning, I dropped the cursed object and traipsed after my best friend as she skipped down the hallway toward the kitchen. This wasn't my first rodeo. In fact, both girls joined forces earlier and somehow had me unpacking my *running* shoes, *running* shorts and *running* tops within the first hour of the game being played. Definitely needed some water and carbs after that experience.

"Angel, I'm home."

"*Dominic.*" I sprinted past Grace and launched myself into the arms of the love of my life. His hands grabbed my ass, lifting me up, and I wrapped my legs around his waist, burying my hands in his hair. "I missed you."

"Missed you more," he growled back.

Our kiss started out innocent enough, with soft lips and the tiniest hint of tongue, however, before long it deepened and we were once again lost in a passion-fueled mauling fest. Dominic spun around and slammed me up against the wall. I groaned, biting down on his lip, daring him to lose control.

"Damn," he muttered, rubbing his already hard cock against me.

"Gross."

I pulled back, horrified about forgetting poor Grace and Katrina who probably needed psychological counseling themselves after witnessing Dominic and I getting all hot and heavy. I tried to wiggle my way out of Dominic's hold but he was having none of it. Instead, he faced my friends, nodding in greeting. "Gracie." She scowled. "Kat." A half-hearted wave.

Dominic turned back to me, his eyes dark with need. "Now, where were we?" His lips claimed mine once again and as rude as it was ignoring the girls like this, so help me, I couldn't stop.

Somewhere in the background Grace muttered she was blinded for life, somewhere in the background the front door slammed closed, people in the street below went about their daily lives, waves crashed and gulls soared. But I did not notice any of it, not a thing. Dominic and I were too busy making love.

Again.

The End

ABOUT THE AUTHOR

Lee Piper is a lover of books. She often juggles reading seven novels at a time for the sheer joy of it. At the grand old age of five, Lee Piper decided to become an author, however found a limited market for her unicorn stories. So, high school English teacher it was.

At thirty-two, and grieving the loss of her second miscarriage, Lee Piper turned to novels—Kylie Scott, to be precise—to escape the pain. This then inspired her to write Rock My World, the first in a four-part contemporary romance series. Her debut novel became an Evernight Publishing bestseller within the first two weeks of publication.

Lee Piper lives in Adelaide, South Australia with her drummer husband, cheeky daughters, and one very crazy dog.

www.leepiperauthor.com

LEE PIPER

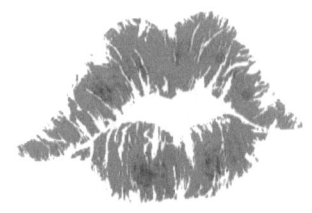

EVERNIGHT PUBLISHING ®

www.evernightpublishing.com